Garrett Haines

About the Author

KATHRYN MILLER HAINES is an actor, mystery writer, award-winning playwright, and the artistic director of a Pittsburgh-based theater company. She is the author of *The War Against Miss Winter* and *The Winter of Her Discontent.*

WINTER IN
June

Also by Kathryn Miller Haines

The Winter of Her Discontent
The War Against Miss Winter

WINTER IN
June

KATHRYN MILLER HAINES

HARPER

NEW YORK • LONDON • TORONTO • SYDNEY

HARPER

WINTER IN JUNE. Copyright © 2009 by Kathryn Miller Haines. All rights reserved. Printed in the United States of America. No part of this book may be used or reproduced in any manner whatsoever without written permission except in the case of brief quotations embodied in critical articles and reviews. For information address HarperCollins Publishers, 10 East 53rd Street, New York, NY 10022.

HarperCollins books may be purchased for educational, business, or sales promotional use. For information please write: Special Markets Department, HarperCollins Publishers, 10 East 53rd Street, New York, NY 10022.

FIRST EDITION

Library of Congress Cataloging-in-Publication Data

Haines, Kathryn Miller.
   Winter in June / Kathryn Miller Haines. 1st ed.
      p.   cm.
   ISBN 978-0-06-157956-1
   1. Winter, Rosie (Fictitious character)—Fiction.   2. Actresses—Fiction.   3. United Service Organizations (U.S.)—Fiction.   4. World War, 1939–1945—War work—Fiction.   5. Americans—Solomon Islands—Fiction. I. Title.

PS3608.A5449W55   2009
813'.6—dc22   2008043336

09 10 11 12 13   RRD   10 9 8 7 6 5 4 3 2 1

For my sister Pam,
who's never been afraid to go halfway across
the world to find what she was looking for

And for Garrett,
who gives me a good reason to stay home

Acknowledgments

Unending gratitude to my agent, Paul Fedorko, and the marvelous people at HarperCollins past, present, and future, especially Sarah Durand, Wendy Lee, and Emily Krump. Thanks as always to Gregg Kulick for making the books pretty enough that even *I* want to pick them up.

Uncomfortable hugs to my wonderful critique partners whose wisdom and advice are always appreciated: Lucy Turner, Joseph Plummer, Ralph Scherder, Paula Martinac, Jeff Protzman, Beverly Pollock, David Doorley, Judy Meiksin, Sloan Macrae, Carol Mullen, and F. J. Hartland. And heartfelt embraces to The Six for always giving me a lift just when I need it.

Sloppy kisses to the gang at Mystery's Most Wanted for supporting me in everything I do, especially Randy Oliva, Barbara Williams, Chris and Laura Bondi, Heather Gray, Steven Werber, and Scot Rutledge.

Promises of free drinks for going above and beyond the call of duty to Geoffrey Orton, Morgan Kelly, David White, and Alison Trimarco.

For the books they've foisted on strangers, the events they've helped plan, the costumes they've donned, the parties they've attended, the plane tickets they've bought, and the number of miles they've driven to get me from one bookstore to another, thanks to Stephen and Nancy Miller, Loretta Miller, and Barb von der Haar. Words can't tell you how grateful I am.

I am awed by the support of the independent mystery book world. Special thanks to the wonderful staff at Mystery Lovers Bookshop (Oakmont, PA), Aunt Agatha's (Ann Arbor, MI), and Murder by the Book (Houston, TX).

And of course, mad props to my canine crew: Rizzo, Chonka, Sadie, and the *real* Violet. We miss you, Pickleface.

WINTER IN
June

CHAPTER 1

A Little Journey

May 1943

I was hoping we'd get champagne for our bon voyage. Instead, we got a corpse.

It wasn't the first hiccup our trip encountered. So far I'd been badgered by the government, humiliated by the passport office, and innoculated so many times I was afraid to drink water just in case I sprang a leak.

"Step to the side, please."

And now my best pal Jayne and I were at the port of San Francisco waiting in a line that stretched at least half a mile so that we could board the *Queen of the Ocean*, a former cruise ship repurposed by the navy to carry us to the Pacific theater.

"Step to the side, miss." A shore patrolman bumped into me as he tried to make his way up the dock and toward the ship.

"What's the rumble?" My dogs were barking, and I was crabby

and already tired of the way the stars and bars dictated who got treated well and who didn't. The SP didn't bother to answer me. He was the third one I'd seen breeze by, each of their pusses set in unyielding stone. The sun beat down on us, but the air was cool and breezy. We'd foolishly changed into summer dresses on the train, and I found myself longing for my wool cardigan.

"How long have we been standing here?" asked Jayne. No one had budged in almost an hour. I was starting to wonder if this whole thing wasn't some sort of military exercise designed to test our ability to stand for hours on end. I'm sure it would be a useful skill if the enemy decided to bombard our troops with bank lines. "I swear I'm going to pass out if I don't get to sit down soon," she said.

More soldiers and sailors joined the line behind us. I can't say that I liked what I saw. These boys were so young that I would bet my right arm that at least half of them couldn't shave yet. As they waited in line, they smacked gum, told jokes, and read comic books bent over one hand so they could carry their bags with the other. I wondered if they were trying to catch inspiration from the wartime exploits of Mandrake the Magician and Joe Palooka, both of whom had been written into plots that had them enlisting so they could fight the Nazis fair and square. Or did that hit a little too close to home? Maybe they preferred Superman, who would never get a chance to wear a U.S. military uniform. Thanks to his vision he was classified as 4-F, probably because National Allied Publications knew it wouldn't be fair to show the Man of Steel in combat when the boys who revered him didn't possess the same superpowers.

Someone tapped me on the shoulder. I turned around to find a handsome boy looking down at me expectantly. His white Dixie cup cap was perched on the back of his head, forcing him to squint against the sun. "Is it true they found a body?"

"What?" If that was how he pitched woo, he had a lot to learn.

"We're hearing they found a woman dead in the water."

"It's true," said another fellow who wasn't with their group. He had a navy uniform and a baby face. "She's still down there. They're trying to fish her out from under the pier."

"Yeah," said his friend, a guy whose pale blond crew cut made him look bald in the sun. "I heard she'd been shot. The shore patrol's combing the boat looking for the culprit."

I stepped out of line and scanned the port for a sign that what they said was true. People were everywhere—perhaps twenty thousand total—each one with a look on their face that said they had a job to do. It wasn't just the thousands of men and women who would be leaving from here to go to parts unknown loitering about the docks, but tons of food, supplies, and ammunition—all made in America to serve the troops overseas. Immense pallets of powdered eggs and milk awaited loading. Impromptu stands were set up to provide soldiers with last-minute inoculations. Information kiosks directed those without orders to local hotels and other forms of entertainment to help them pass the time.

And then I saw her, facedown in the water. Her clothes billowed around her, deflated and looking for a way to take flight. If I hadn't known what I was looking for, I might have thought she was a doll lying discarded in the bay. A motorboat idled beside her, kicking up a current that made it seem—for a moment—that she still had life. The men in the boat used what looked like an enormous hook to catch hold of her skirt and pull her toward them.

"Oh, God," said Jayne. "How awful."

As the body was pulled toward the boat, the dead woman flipped over. Long tendrils of blond hair radiated from her head like a child's drawing of the sun. Even from our distance above her I could see that her eyes were open, still witnessing her terrifying last moments.

Jayne grabbed my arm and tried to pull me back into the line. "Don't watch," she said. "Don't think about it."

I tried to obey her, but the woman in the water held me under her spell. She looked familiar, or perhaps she wore the face of death so well that I just thought I knew her. After all, I'd seen it before. Death had a way of sticking with you.

The boy with the blond crew cut joined us and let out a low whistle as he took in the view. "Come on now—this ain't something ladies should see." He grabbed our hands and pulled us back into line. As he released us, he took us in top to tail, no doubt trying to figure out why we were in line boarding a military ship when we weren't wearing uniforms. "You're not Wacs, are you?"

"Nope," said Jayne. "We're actresses."

His brow furrowed. Apparently claiming to be actresses didn't immediately make our wartime role clear.

"We're in the USO camp shows," said Jayne.

"Where you headed?"

"The Solomon Islands," I said. "Foxhole circuit."

He turned back to his friends. "Wow, fellows. These girls are in the USO."

One of them pushed his trunk toward us and flipped it on its side to give us a bench to sit on. Our own luggage—only fifty-three pounds as the United Service Organization had directed—was with a porter who'd promised to get it on the ship before we left the harbor.

The men bombarded Jayne with questions, asking her who we knew, where we'd been, and what they might've seen us in. She answered them, listing a string of insignificant plays, minor stars, and New York boroughs most of them had never heard of. I didn't join in. My mind was in the water, doing the dog paddle to keep pace with the body.

Why did she look so familiar? I left the line and again went to the railing to observe the girl floating below. She was gone. Although I could no longer see it, I could hear the hum of the motorboat as it returned to shore. In the distance, the meat wagon wailed its warning. It rapidly encroached on us, pulling up to the dock in a cacophony of noise and flashing lights. The attendants left the cab and pulled a stretcher from the back of the truck. They were moving too quickly. Maybe they didn't know she was dead. Or maybe they'd been told to retrieve the body before it caused even more of a scene. After all, we didn't want soldiers thinking about death.

Eventually the boys ran out of things to jaw about and Jayne replaced idle chitchat with the slicks she'd brought along to entertain us on the trip. As I watched for signs of the returning stretcher, Jayne flipped through a copy of *Photoplay*.

"Unbelievable!" Her voice wrenched me out of my thoughts. I returned to the line and found her frowning at a magazine photo of a woman who wore a black velvet dress that was so tight part of her spilled onto a second page.

"What's the matter?" I asked.

"Did you know MGM dropped Gilda DeVane?"

I sat beside her and divided my attention between her and the wailing siren. "No. And I'm willing to bet that she doesn't know there's a dead girl floating in the bay." Gilda DeVane was the very definition of Hollywood star. She'd gotten her start in musical comedies, but somebody somewhere realized she was dreadfully miscast in them and helped her carve out a reputation as the ultimate femme fatale. She had icy good looks—green eyes, blond hair, perfect figure—and a way of making you feel like you were doing something wrong every time she appeared onscreen. Her characters were hard women who did bad things, but at the end of the last reel they realized the error of their ways. In real life, if the slicks were to be believed, Gilda was like her onscreen persona, only without the rehabilitation. She skated around; she'd been married twice, engaged at least half a dozen times, and was the answer to almost every blind item that ran in the fan magazines. Her latest love was Van Lauer, a new face whom everyone thought would be the next Tyrone Power. He was a pretty boy with acting chops. And a wife.

"Well she's been dropped from her contract, though apparently Van Lauer's still got his," said Jayne.

"Why wouldn't he?"

She sighed, not hiding her exasperation at my ignorance. Clearly I wasn't spending my time reading the right things. "Both of them were turning up late on set. It's been in all the papers."

"Not the ones I've seen." I read the article over her shoulder. Sure enough, the month before Metro Goldwyn Mayer had let one of their biggest female contract players go. The writer alluded to the relationship between DeVane and Lauer as the reason for her being dropped, although if the rumor mill was to be believed, their relationship was kaput too. "Why didn't they fire Lauer?" I asked. "After all, he's the one with the wife and the scandal. They have to expect this kind of stuff from Gilda by now."

Jayne shrugged. "Beats me." The most likely answer was that he was the bigger breadwinner, or at least someone at MGM thought that he was. Gilda was on the way down, so rather than kowtowing to her, they gave in to his demands to show her the gate when the relationship hit the papers. Hollywood hypocrisy was one of the many reasons why I was firmly committed to staying in New York. Well, that and because Hollywood wasn't interested in me. "I hope she gets a bigger and better deal at Twentieth Century Fox," said Jayne. She turned the page, where the dapper Van Lauer was pictured in an army air force uniform.

I pushed the magazine away. "Isn't that typical? He gets to be a hero, and she walks away a whore. It was certainly a better move than focusing on his acting career. I'd heard recently that the Oscar statue was undergoing a facelift due to wartime quotas. Instead of being made out of metal, it was now being produced out of plaster. It was an interesting metaphor for the way the war was reshaping Hollywood. It was no longer enough to be talented on film. The American public had finally realized that actors themselves were little more than painted plaster. What they wanted were real heroes fighting for our freedom, not people like Errol Flynn–who was allegedly 4-F–playing them on the big screen. And that meant that pretend heroes better shape up and ship out if they wanted to continue to be viewed as important to our lives.

Enlisting was a brilliant move on Lauer's part. The war had caused a lot of terrible things, but it had also become the publicity opportunity that rehabilitated a thousand careers. No matter how bad a person was, all they had to do was join up, buy bonds, or pay a visit to a hospital full of vets, and the public instantly forgot whatever awful thing they'd been associated with. And it wasn't limited to Hollywood stars. After all, the American public was quick to forget that Charles Lindbergh had supported the Nazi party as soon as he donned a uniform and went to fight for the Allies. The war could absolve anyone of their sins. Maybe even a murderer.

The ambulance attendants returned from the dock. The body had been strapped in and covered by a white sheet that fluttered in the breeze. One hand had worked itself free and hung limply, swaying back and forth as the men bobbed across the uneven boards. The woman's fingernails had been varnished Victory Red, and the color against the pallor of her skin made it look—for a moment—like her hands were dripping with blood.

The meat wagon pulled away, and the shore patrol began to exit the ship. If they'd found the culprit, they didn't bother to bring him back with them. "Move along," someone shouted at the front of the line, and suddenly the crowd began to inch forward. Jayne and I rose to our feet, eager to get out of the sun and onto the boat. We quickly left the pavement and walked onto the gangplank.

"This is it," said Jayne.

"This is it," I echoed. I slipped my hand into my pocket and palmed a photo I'd placed there just before we left New York. It was a picture of my ex-boyfriend Jack, the reason for this whole crazy trip. He wasn't wearing his navy uniform; this was Jack before the war, wearing an actor's smile to promote some play he was in. When he'd given me a copy of it, I'd stored it away in a drawer, thinking it strange that someone you saw everyday would provide you with something to remember him by. Perhaps he was more on the ball than I'd given him credit for.

My gaze wandered behind me to where soldiers and sailors were bidding farewell to family members who'd come to see them off. Each good-bye broke my heart a little, as mothers memorized their son's faces, wives begged for a kiss that lasted just a little longer, and children shed the tears everyone else was fighting to keep inside.

"No turning back," said Jayne.

I wasn't sure if she was talking about us or them, though I suspected it was the former.

"Nope. No turning back." I hadn't been able to sleep for the past day, and I could tell that the adrenaline that had kept me going was about to take the run out. I knew what would happen then. The manic energy I'd used to get us here would dry up and in its place would be the well of emotions I'd fought for days to suppress. We were leaving America. We were leaving behind careers that were beginning to take off and housing that no one could guarantee would be held for us. We were leaving close friends, closer enemies, and a cat who had my number. We were leaving everything that was familiar and going to a strange land on a mission that was ill advised at best.

"Do you think we're making a mistake?" I asked.

I hadn't bothered to pose the question until then. Jayne was the kind of friend who, when you suggested going to the South Pacific in search of your missing ex-boyfriend, responded by asking what she should pack. It never occurred to her to say you were off the rails. I liked to think that if the tables were turned and this were her scheme we were pursuing, I would've been a stand-up gal, too, but the limits of my friendship hadn't been tested. Yet.

Jayne put her hand on mine and squeezed. "It's not a mistake. It's an adventure."

On the pier behind us a sailor picked up his girl and swung her around. He wasn't getting on a boat to go somewhere. He'd just arrived home for leave, safe and sound, from whatever hell on earth he'd been stationed at. Both of their faces were broken apart with joy. It wasn't a pretty kind of happiness. Rather they seemed to be clawing at each other, as if the very ground they stood on was nothing more than quicksand.

"We'll find him," said Jayne.

"Promise?" I asked.

"Cross my heart and hope to die, stick a pickle in my eye."

It wasn't much of a guarantee, but it made me smile all the same.

CHAPTER 2

Among Those Sailing

An hour later we were being led through the ship by an eager-beaver sailor named Carson Dodger. He'd fished us out of the line right before we stepped onboard and said they'd been worried that something had happened to us. We were the last of our touring group to arrive, and didn't we know that we didn't have to wait with all the other poor schlubs?

"Must've slipped our minds," I said.

Carson was my height and pudgy, his body showing the results of being too long at sea with too little to do. He had the kind of face that always looked jolly, though on closer inspection I realized it wasn't because he was happy so much as fat and sunburned.

"Is it true there was a woman's body in the water?" Jayne asked him. She was a master at playing dumb.

"Yes, ma'am," he said. "It looks like she was shot and pushed off the pier."

"Did they finger the culprit?" I asked.

"Not yet, but they will. They think he might've climbed onto one of the ships, which is why we had to shut things down for a while."

"How do you know it was a he?" I asked.

"Just a guess, ma'am, but this sure doesn't seem like the kind of thing a dame would do."

Boy did he have a lot to learn about skirts.

"Rest assured," said Carson, "you'll be perfectly safe aboard the *Queen of the Ocean*."

I wasn't sure I found that very comforting. After all, the *Queen of the Ocean* was the size of two football fields. Surely they couldn't have made a very thorough inspection in two hours' time.

I didn't press the issue. As Carson continued to flap his gums about how safe the ship was, I took in the lay. Before the war, the *Queen of the Ocean* had been a luxury cruise liner that took muckety-mucks from California to Hawaii while plying them with top-drawer food, top-notch entertainment, and lavish surroundings. After Pearl Harbor, the Navy coopted it, replacing the food with army grub, the entertainment with an out-of-tune piano, and painting the bulk head olive drab so that the remaining chandeliers reflected dull, regimental surroundings.

Carson led us into what had once been a ballroom and was now one of several mess areas set aside to feed the people we'd be traveling with. The only remnants of the ship's previous purpose were the gilded wood paneling, marble floors, and a smattering of padded leather chairs. There was no chow awaiting us. Instead, two other women sat in the huge, empty space batting the breeze.

As we arrived, they stopped talking and took us in as if we were ponies up for auction.

"Hiya," I said. "I'm Rosie Winter, and this is Jayne Hamilton."

The woman on the left rose and offered us her hand. "I'm Violet Lancaster." She had a rectangular face and blue eyes that were so tiny it looked like she was squinting. Her blond hair was piled on top of her head and turned into fat sausage curls that were an ill-advised attempt to emulate Betty Hutton's hairstyle. She'd applied makeup with a heavy hand that left a clear division between her face and her neck. I suspected that if you let down her hair and chiseled off the lacquer, she'd be quite a looker, but left as she was, she could've gotten a job with the circus.

"I'm Kay Thorpe," said the other woman, offering us her hand. She had a regrettably equine appearance. At the top of her long, strong body was a face dominated by a schnozzle that would've given Cyrano a run for his money and teeth so large we could've projected a movie on them. When she spoke, she looked at everything but us. At first I thought she was rude, but it became increasingly clear that she was just shy. Great: a shy performer. That would be about as helpful as a blind bus driver.

"Did you hear they found a body?" asked Jayne.

"Hear about it? Why, I was here when the gun was fired," said Violet. She had a southern accent that I could tell she normally buried, rolling it out whenever she thought it might be useful to assert her gentility and otherness.

"You saw the killer?" I asked.

"No, I only heard the gun go off. It practically scared the pants right off me."

That was quite an accomplishment, since she was wearing a skirt. "Is that all you heard?" I asked.

"No, there was a scream too. And a splash."

"Did you tell the coppers?"

Violet lifted her head as though the question was an affront to her. "Of course."

"Who was the girl?" asked Jayne.

"I don't think they know yet," said Kay, her eyes glancing at the ceiling. If I was ever caught committing a crime, this was the witness I wanted to try to pick me out of a lineup.

"I hope it wasn't someone going on tour with us," said Jayne. "Could you imagine how awful that would be?"

And typical. In the last year two people I knew had been zotzed. If I were a prominent member of the underworld, I could understand those odds, but I was an actress for crying out loud.

The worst thing my people were supposed to face was rejection. And waitressing.

"Oh, don't worry," said Violet. "She's not one of us. Number five is safely locked away in the captain's quarters."

"What did she do to deserve that?" I asked.

Violet returned to her seat and crossed her legs. "You mean you haven't heard?" I shook my head. "Oh, this is too rich. Hold onto your hats, girls. We're not just five anonymous actresses going to the South Pacific—we've got a star among us. Gilda DeVane has joined our little troupe."

"Gilda DeVane?" said Jayne. "Really?"

Violet leaned forward and lowered her voice, as though Louella Parsons and Hedda Hopper were lurking in the shadows with their pens at the ready. "It's all hush-hush, but I've got a friend who's got a friend who put the whole tour together, and he said Gilda signed on at the last minute to go with us. Kay saw her board the ship earlier. Didn't you, Kay?"

Kay nodded. "They whisked her up to the captain's quarters right before they started searching the boat."

"Apparently, the rest of us are expendable," said Violet.

"Why would she go to the South Pacific?" I asked. "I thought the big names went to Europe."

Violet grinned, which made her squint seem twice as bad. "The ones who have nothing to lose like to go where the fighting's the worst. It makes for the best headlines."

I got what she was saying. Gilda was trying to do what Van Lauer did, but instead of enlisting and getting some plush, privileged assignment, she'd opted to go into the danger zone so the public would see her risking her life to help out the troops.

"She's more clever than I thought," said Violet. "She needs to find a way to get people interested in her again. Flash and sex are on their way out. And of course, I'm sure MGM will be mad to get her back when this is all done. If she's smart, she'll have all the fellows she meets write the studio on her behalf. No one can say no to a hero." *If* that's what Gilda set out to do. It was inevitable that whatever she did after MGM fired her would be read as an attempt to re-ignite her career. No matter what her intentions, some people would insist that she was only doing what she was doing to get a contract. "Anyway," said Violet, "the bad news is, we'll be taking a backseat to Gilda, but the good news is the weather should be nice."

When I wasn't thinking about how to find out what had happened to Jack, I romanticized my role in the USO shows. I pictured myself becoming a star attraction, the kind of gal men lined up to see hours in advance. I'd end up on newsreel footage, find my puss on posters, and directors back home would be clambering to talk to me even before I returned Stateside. I'd be doing something good, of course, but I'd also be securing my future career.

I didn't like the idea that someone had already determined that we were supporting players in the tour. I could take being demoted by virtue of everyone around me being more talented, but being forced into the backseat because someone was more famous than me? I'd been down that path before and it still didn't sit well.

Before I could share my discontent, the ballroom doors opened, and our fifth member joined us in a rush of fabric and perfume.

We all gawked at her as she arrived. Gilda DeVane didn't just command a room when she entered it. She convinced you that she had the power to make the walls disappear with a snap of her fingers. She was smaller than I would've thought, even while wearing a pair of impressively high heels. Despite her tiny size, her body curved into an ample hourglass shape that made Jayne look like Shirley Temple by comparison. Her honey-blond hair was long and wavy, framing her face in such a way that she seemed to be perpetually in silhouette. And her big, sleepy green eyes hinted that she'd just done something that she knew was naughty but that she just couldn't resist participating in.

From the moment I saw her, I couldn't take my eyes off her. Like the body in the water, she held me under some kind of spell.

She took a few steps toward us and paused, with one leg slightly in front of the other. It was the trick of a film star. She knew her best angles and exploited them whenever she could.

"I take it this is the group?" Her voice was low and musical, urging you to lean forward so that you didn't miss anything important.

We clumsily rose to introduce ourselves. She walked the remaining distance and shook hands with each of us. Her hand was soft and left my mitt smelling like lavender.

"It's just so lovely to meet all of you." She deposited a brown leather pocketbook on the table. It didn't match her shoes or bear anything in common with her outfit, but that didn't matter. Just by virtue of being Gilda's, it seemed like the perfect accessory. "After the way today started, I thought the whole trip might be canceled. When I first heard there was a woman in the water, I was afraid it was one of my girls. Could you imagine how awful that would've been?"

We all murmured that it would've been dreadful. That was the power that Gilda wielded. She could convince you that every thought she had was completely original, even if you'd just uttered the same idea moments before.

She pulled out a chair and sat across from the rest of us. "I heard she didn't have any identification with her. I hope they'll be able to figure out who she is. Poor thing." Her expression shifted from pensive to something much more cheerful. "Anyway, we've got to put this behind us now. I'm dying to get to know everything about you. Tell me: where do you come from? What do you do?"

We took turns listing our hometowns and what we'd accomplished in our careers so far. She seemed impressed by Jayne's and my theater background, though it's possible she was only being kind.

"I live in Hollywood now," said Kay. "I've only been there a few months, trying to make it as a singer. I haven't had the nerve to set foot on a studio lot." She directed her comments to her lap and the floor.

Rather than calling her on it, Gilda gently tapped her on the knee. "I can tell you have a great voice just from listening to you speak."

"Really?" Kay looked up at her and smiled. She wasn't a girl who was used to compliments.

"And what beautiful eyes you have," said Gilda. "The men are going to be in trouble when they set their sights on you."

Kay blushed, but she didn't look down again.

"And you, Violet?" asked Gilda. "How did you end up here?"

"This is actually my second tour with the USO." I might've been mistaken, but Violet didn't seem nearly as taken with Gilda as the rest of us. Something in her tiny eyes tattled that she wasn't about to be bowled over by the other woman's attempts to disarm us.

"Really? Why, I'm sure you're going to have tons to teach us. Are you a singer like Kay?"

"Nope. I'm a comedienne, though I started as an actress. I was being developed at MGM for a while. Until the war broke out. When the work dried up, I decided to join the tour." Her short, staccato sentences were begging for an interruption that never seemed to come.

Gilda's hand gracefully framed her face. "What were you in at MGM?"

"Gosh, nothing important. Only bit parts. I never had a chance to become a star like you, though a lot of folks have compared us. In fact, one director I worked with called me Baby Gilda. Isn't that a scream?'"

Gilda nodded, her face frozen in a grin. Before she had a chance to disguise her surprise, the doors opened and a man and a woman entered the room.

"Welcome, Ladies," said the man. "I'm Reg Bancroft, Captain of the *Queen of the Ocean*, and this is Molly Dubois of the USO." Reg removed a clipboard from his armpit and quickly verified that we were all present and accounted for. "Please accept our apologies for the excitement that's delayed us. I've been informed that the ship is secure, and we'll be able to get on our way shortly." My lip curled at his use of the word "excitement." A women had been murdered. Surely there was a more appropriate way to describe it. "First, a few formalities: your luggage will be taken to your rooms. Regrettably, housing quarters are quite tight onboard, so there will only be two rooms for the five of you. I can assure you that the arrangement is much more generous than what our enlisted men and women are subjected to." Kay tittered at that. Since the remark wasn't particularly funny, I wondered if she made a habit of laughing at inappropriate times. "The room you are in now is the primary dining hall while onboard the ship. Over there—" he pointed toward a cordoned-off area. While the tables we were at were bare of anything but scratches, the ones he was directing us toward were set with linens, silverware, and glasses. "That is where you will dine, along with any officers onboard. Your food will be brought to you and will be of a different caliber than what is being served to the general population." I translated what he was saying: we were the high pillows on this bathtub and that meant better chow and more privileges than everyone else. "When you are not rehearsing, you are welcome to enjoy the amenities, including our sundeck, which is also reserved for the officers, and our canteen, where we will attempt to feature nightly entertainment including, I hope, performances by you."

He cleared his throat and flipped the page on his clipboard. "From this moment forward, you are under the rules and regulations of the U.S. Navy. You will obey every order you are given without question. At no time will you be told where you are or where you're going, nor should you request that any such information be shared with you. While onboard this ship, there is no smoking on deck at night, though you are welcome to smoke when there is no chance of anyone from an enemy ship being able to see the flame. Also, we do not permit books, papers, playing cards, or anything else on deck that could be inadvertently knocked overboard, leaving a trail of debris for the enemy to sight. Once we leave U.S. waters, we will be under strict blackout conditions." My mouth went dry. I didn't think we'd be in danger until we got to our destination. It never occurred to me that we were at risk the moment we left California and headed into the open sea. "You will each be assigned a Mae West that you are to keep with you at all times. Please do not use it as a seat cushion."

We looked at one another for an explanation as to why the navy was handing out buxom blondes. Reg clapped his hands, and a sailor appeared with a stack of five life preservers teetering from his arms.

"Maybe my eyes are deceiving me, but those look like life jackets," said Violet.

"I forgot you don't know the lingo. They are indeed life vests. We call them Mae Wests." Reg demonstrated how to don the vest, and it became clear how they'd gotten their nickname. In profile, those of us who weren't already blessed would look like we had the impressive bosom of W. C. Fields's favorite leading lady.

"It is essential," said Reg, "that you listen to all intercom announcements and respond immediately to any instructions to ensure your safety. In the event of an emergency, you are to convene here in this mess hall. Finally, prior to landing, each of you will be asked to complete a medical physical with the ship's doctor." Again he cleared his throat, and I realized that the entire time he'd been speaking, he'd been directing his attention to Gilda. This man, who'd probably fought an endless number of navy battles, turned into a nervous schoolboy in the presence of Hollywood royalty. He wet his finger with his tongue, then used his fingers to smooth his eyebrows. "Any questions?"

"What time does the bar open?" Violet muttered under her breath.

"And now, ladies, I will leave you in the capable hands of Molly Dubois." He saluted us—or, rather, Gilda—and hurriedly left the room. Molly Dubois took his place and smiled in everyone's direction.

Her spiel was much shorter. Molly was simply there to advise us on the types of material we would be performing and how frequently those performances would be taking place once we reached our destination. We would be assigned a base camp and would travel throughout the islands to perform for as many soldiers as possible, including those who were currently in makeshift military hospitals. We wouldn't be provided much in the way of costumes, props and set pieces, since the extensive traveling would make it difficult to carry much with us. It would be a tough schedule, she warned, involving lots of travel by Jeep, boat, and plane, but she guaranteed that it would be an unforgettable experience for all of us.

"I must remind you that from this moment forward, you are ambassadors of the USO. Everything you do—both positive and negative—reflects on the United Service Organizations. We are providing an essential service to our enlisted brothers and sisters, and I would hate for that to be jeopardized because the U.S. military was unhappy with the way one of our girls was behaving. I ask that you remember at all times whom you are representing and maintain a high standard of moral and ethical behavior.

"Miss DeVane will be serving as your troupe's leader, and, ultimately, your performances will be at her discretion. We have provided her with collections of songs and skits that other USO troupes have used to great success. This is a chance, however, for all of you to expand your talents by creating work that best shows off your individual abilities, and I hope that you will make this a collaborative experience. As well, we encourage you to seek out other performers in camp. Many of your enlisted men are musicians and actors who would love the opportunity to get onstage and join you in your performances. Take advantage of their unique skills, and give them a chance to shine. And now, if you don't mind, I'd like to speak to Miss DeVane alone."

With that, Molly and Gilda left the room.

For the first time since we'd left New York, I hummed with excitement.

"Collaborative, my ass," said Violet. "This is going to be the Gilda DeVane show from start to finish."

"What?" asked Kay.

"Nothing," said Violet. She pulled a flask from her bag and opened and closed the attached silver lid in rapid succession. The noise got my dander up.

"I can't get over how pretty she is," said Jayne. "Don't get me wrong—I knew she was easy on the eyes from her movies, but I just figured half of that was lights and makeup. It's nice to know that a woman can look that way for real." It was funny hearing Jayne assess another woman's beauty. My pal was a platinum bombshell who thought catcalls and compliments were as common as candy, but in Gilda's world she was average at best. I hated to think what that made me.

"I expected her to be . . . well . . . mean or something," said Kay. "She always plays those kinds of characters. And with everything the slicks say about her, I assumed—"

"Don't worry," said Violet. "Your instincts were right."

"What the deuce does that mean?" I asked.

Violet's mouth opened and closed as quickly as her flask had. Gilda returned with her arms outstretched, as though she were going to embrace us in one enormous hug. "I'm so glad all those formalities are finally over and done with. I don't know about you, but hearing all those rules and regulations made my head spin. I forgot this wasn't just a show we were doing but a show for the military." We murmured our agreement. I looked for a sign that Gilda was planning on making this whole venture about herself or that she was the sort of self-centered Sally that Violet was determined to mark her as. "I want you all to know how much I'm looking forward to these shows. From here on out, we're in this together, and not one of us is more important than the other." She glanced at a wristwatch that seemed to question the idea that we were equals. It was a dazzling confection of platinum and diamonds that made the ship's chandeliers look shoddy by comparison. "We'll be pushing off in the next hour, so why don't we take a look around before the launch? And then maybe we can spend tonight getting to know one another."

CHAPTER 3

The Charity Nurse

The ship was set up like a miniature city. In addition to the mess hall, there was a commissary stocked with any number of things soldiers might want to take with them for their next destination. There was a gedunk—which I figured out was another word for canteen—where you could get ice cream, soda, and candy. At the onboard barbershop, two sailors, whose own hair was in desperate need of cutting, were employed to do for you what they hadn't done for themselves. The ship's tailor could lengthen or shorten your army-issue pants so they were no longer the standard too short or too long. You took your mail to the post office, where the ship's newsletter awaited distribution. Inside of the newsletter were fun little tidbits about the men and women aboard the *Queen of the Ocean* (seen last night: Captain Malloy cutting a rug with a pretty little lass in a WAAC uniform. We sure hope Captain Malloy is more deft in the battlefield than he is on the dance floor), and less entertaining stories about what was occurring in one of the many countries we were headed toward, brought to us courtesy of the ship's wireless (that day the rag was all aflutter about the Germans crushing the Jewish uprising and the RAF smashing German dams). For entertainment, there was a movie theater that offered three films a day—we could watch *Shadow of a Doubt*, *Girl Crazy*, and *Action in the Atlantic*. You could borrow books from the ship's library, visit the game room and play billiards, Ping-Pong, shuffleboard, checkers, and chess or attend religious services with one of three onboard chaplains.

On the sundeck where the officers milled about if the weather was nice, there were golf clubs and balls for the officers to practice their swing—a net put into place to prevent the balls from landing in the water—and a swimming pool in case anyone needed to cool off. Nobody ever did. I don't know if it's because the officers felt that it would be undignified to strip down to their skivvies, or if the thought of swimming made this whole enterprise feel too much like a vacation.

After we toured the ship, we all went up on deck to see the launch. Side by side, we stood at the rail and alternated our views between the land we were leaving and the open sea we were headed toward. As the boat pulled away from the dock, we waved at passing strangers who paused in their day to watch the magnificent *Queen of the Ocean* set sail. Among them was a cluster of newshounds with their cameras trained on us. Gilda turned her left cheek their way, and as the wind caught her dress and the sun reflected off her hair, she started singing "God Bless America." We all joined in, repeating the simple chorus until we could no longer distinguish the features of the people standing onshore.

Almost unconsciously, my peepers kept dropping to the spot near the dock where the woman had been floating in the water. Even though she was no longer there, I swore I could see her dark silhouette rippling with the force of our takeoff. Did they know who she was yet? Was she supposed to be on this boat? Had someone realized she was missing?

We stayed ondeck for a while, trading stories about other voyages we had taken. Jayne and I had only our tales of ferry rides and train trips, but the other women had been out of the country before, and they regaled us with stories of other lands and other people. I wanted to pipe in with questions and comments, but I was feeling less and less like standing on deck as the sea bounced the boat to and fro. My normally steel gut churned at the motion, and I found myself feeling increasingly dizzy. It was probably just the sun, which seemed twice as powerful now that we were away from the shore. Or perhaps the eggs we'd had on the train that morning weren't quite as farm fresh as the menu claimed. Or maybe it was the memory of the woman whose blood-red nails had been varnished in anticipation of a very different ending.

"Rosie?" asked Jayne. "You all right? You look a little green."

Just as she described the color I'd turned, I leaned over the railing and threw up what little I had in my stomach.

"Seasick," the other three women announced with the pride of a doctor making a swift diagnosis.

"Oh God," I said, as my breakfast dispersed across the miles of ocean. "Do you think the Japanese can see that?"

"If they can spot puke from that far away," said Violet, "they deserve to win the war."

Jayne helped me find our quarters. While we may have been given two rooms, it was clear that four of us were intended to sleep in one of them while our fifth, more important, member got digs to herself. Our cabin was crammed with two sets of bunk beds, a built-in bureau, and a bathroom designed to accommodate those who enjoyed peeing and showering simultaneously. I didn't have the energy to comment on the arrangements. I claimed one of the bottom bunks out of necessity and stretched out on my back.

"How do you feel?" asked Jayne.

"Jingle-brained. How come you're not affected?"

"Gilda said it might be a dancer thing. I know what to focus on to keep my balance."

I was many things, but a skilled dancer wasn't among them.

"Great. Another thing that my rotten hoofing skills have robbed from me." I closed my eyes only to realize that made things much, much worse. "Do you think it's an omen?"

"Lots of people get seasick." She wet a washcloth in the ersatz bathroom.

"I meant the woman in the water."

She wrung the excess water out of the cloth. "And what would she be an omen of?"

"That death is going to follow us to the South Pacific?"

She returned to my side and put the wet washcloth on my forehead. As soothing as it was, it did nothing to settle my stomach. "She has nothing to do with us," said Jayne.

"When did you turn so hard?"

"You know what I mean. Don't look for signs that things are going to go badly. That won't help anyone." She was right, of course. Jayne had a knack for being much more rational than me. "Can I get you anything?"

"No. I think this is one of those things I have to wait out." I tried to find what I could safely set my eyes on. The whole room seemed to be echoing the choppy motions of the ship. "On second thought—can you get me a trash can or a bucket or something?"

She brought one from the tiny bathroom and set it on the floor beside me." What do you think about Gilda?"

"She's not what I expected. I really thought I'd resent her being here, what with the special treatment, but I like her so far." In all fairness, I wasn't exactly known for my ability to read people. After all, I'd inadvertently befriended two murderers in six months.

Jayne was kind enough not to point this out to me. "I like her too. And the others?"

"Remains to be seen. I don't have a wire on Kay yet, though she seems like a good egg. Violet's a stitch. And a lush. And I'm betting the source of all our sorrows."

"What do you mean?"

I stared at the bunk above me. Calcified chewing gun clung to the bedsprings. "Haven't you noticed? Violet's got more faces than

Mount Rushmore. She's sweet as pie to Gilda one moment, and the next it seems like she's trying to get a rise out of her."

"It sounds like garden-variety jealousy to me."

I flipped the wet washcloth over. "Yeah, but we have every reason to be jealous of her, too, and somehow we keep a lid on it."

"They were at MGM together. It must be hard to watch someone come up when you're going nowhere."

Didn't I know it? It was the story of my career.

"It'll pass," said Jayne. "She's just got to get used to the idea that Gilda's not the enemy." That was the nice thing about war: when we weren't clear about who the enemy was our government made posters to point them out to us.

As though she'd been summoned by our talking about her, Violet entered the room and flung her pocketbook onto the other bottom bunk. "So this is it? I thought we had two rooms."

"There's only one bed in the other one," said Jayne.

"And let me guess who gets that one."

Jayne stood up. "I don't think the decision was hers."

Violet kicked off her heels and massaged her dogs. The stink of sweaty feet filled the small space. "That's what she wants you to think. She's playing a role right now to make sure everyone likes her. Just you wait—the real Gilda will come out soon enough. If she wanted to be down to earth, she'd share our room, use her real name, her real hair color, and her real nose."

The room lurched to the left, my stomach to the right. "She had a nose job?" I asked.

"Years ago, when they were first developing her," said Violet. "It was about the same time that they changed her hairline, gave her a bigger bosom, and capped her teeth. A big nose, flat chest and small forehead might be fine for homely Maria Elizondo of Laredo, but it's unacceptable for a glamour girl like Gilda DeVane."

As much as Violet was starting to annoy me, I have to admit I was fascinated by what she knew. I understood that Hollywood was a star machine manufacturing people with new names and new pasts, but I was strangely naïve when it came to someone completely mak-

ing themselves over for their career. The very notion seemed . . .
well, it seemed like an idea out of a movie. Had Gilda really reinvented herself so thoroughly, or was Violet creating this history to
match the scorn she felt for the woman?

"Give me a break," I said. "There's no way you could possibly
know any of that's true."

"She and I arrived at MGM at the same time. She may not remember me, but I definitely remember her. The *real* her."

"Actually," said Jayne, "I did see a picture of her once in *Movie
Story*. It was one of those sidebars where they ask you to guess who
the young woman in the picture grew up to be, and given how different Gilda looked at eighteen, it's clear she had something done."

Violet smirked at me, but I wasn't going to bite. The only bile
I wanted to deal with was churning in my gullet. "All right—fair
enough," I said. "But what's the matter with that?"

"It's deceptive." Violet fumbled inside her purse until she located
a silver cigarette case and lighter. Just the thought of smoke made
me queasy. "She's making everyone think that she got where she got
by talent."

"And who's to say she didn't?" I asked.

She checked out her reflection in the cigarette case and seemed
pleased by what she saw. "Anyone who's seen her movies."

"Come on now. If she was a lousy actress, she wouldn't be where
she is."

She lit the gasper and took a pull. "And to think they believe
the girls in New York are smarter and more sophisticated." She underlined her scorn with a long exhale of smoke. "You know those
musicals she used to do? They dubbed her voice. And the dance
sequences? If you really paid attention, you might've noticed that
they never showed her face and her feet in the same shot. All that
work was someone else's—someone who could really sing and really dance but lacked whatever was needed to make up the whole
package. Gilda got where she got because she was willing to let the
bigwigs turn her into whoever they wanted her to be and because
she didn't care how many other people's careers it took to make

that possible. And now every Tom, Dick, and Harry in Hollywood believes that's what makes a star. No matter how talented we are the rest of us don't stand a chance."

Jayne stirred beside me. "Couldn't we, though, if we did what she did?"

"Assuming you could afford it," said Violet. "Would you really be willing for someone to completely change you like that?"

Of course, I wouldn't. But I was bothered enough by Violet's attitude that I wanted to be disagreeable. "If it got me where it got her, sure," I said.

"Then I feel sorry for you."

I let her know how I felt about her sympathy by vomiting in the trash can.

Apparently, being trapped in a small room with a trash can full of upchuck was unappealing. Jayne and Violet left, leaving me in the bottom bunk cursing the irregular rhythm of wartime sea voyage. I'd always imagined Pacific passage to be relaxing and leisurely, with gentle waves rocking the boat into a comfortable lull. While that may have been the case back when the *Queen of the Ocean* was a luxury liner, during wartime the path we took was about as relaxing as a horse cart racing through rocky terrain. To avoid potential torpedoes, the ship made a zigzag course, changing directions every five minutes to ensure that an enemy vessel didn't have its sights on us. Conveniently, five minutes was precisely the amount of time it took to convince me that my stomach was better before the ship's rolling would summon the next wave of green goo.

I couldn't sleep. For a while I focused on the photo of Jack, hoping that his black and white image possessed the ability to heal the infirm. It didn't, so I tried to read, tearing through the copy of the ship's newsletter I'd snagged during our tour. Our troops had invaded Attu in the Aleutian Islands. With help from the Brits, we'd forced the Nazis to surrender in North Africa, and the Germans and the Italians had surrendered in the North.

Things weren't going quite so well for all of our Allies. The Japanese had sunk an Australian hospital ship called *The Centaurian*, and the newsletter said officials were predicting several hundred dead, including the wounded who were being transported on the vessel. It was hard to wrap my head around the scope of the tragedy, not just because of the numbers lost in a single submarine attack but because many of the dead had probably believed that after suffering whatever injuries they'd endured, they had finally won their ticket home. What had their final moments been like? Were they hopped up on morphine to ease their transport, or were they alert and helpless as they met their end?

You were never safe when there was a war on. Not on a ship headed for home. Not even within your barracks.

That was what Jack had learned. He and his CO were the only survivors of a capsized boat that had claimed ten lives. The CO said it was an accident, but Jack apparently knew otherwise. Word was his own CO had shot him to try to keep him quiet. Faced with the possibility that he was the guy's next victim, Jack had done the only reasonable thing: he'd run.

I traded the newsletter for Jayne's slicks.

A pretty blonde smiled at me from inside *Screen Idol*. Above her face were the words: THE NEXT BIG THING. Her details were included beside her picture.

Name: Joan Wright

Age: 22

Where you can see her: this fall in MGM's film *Mr. Hogan's Daughter*

Who she might remind you of: a young Gilda DeVane

I cringed on her behalf. Sure the girl looked like Gilda, but who had decided that Gilda was old?

I traded one magazine for another. There was a time when Gilda DeVane was on every other page of the fan magazines, handing out advice, showing off the finished product for a knitting pattern, hawking Max Factor, and being snapped at some fabulous event in a four-page spread. Either Jayne's slicks were the exception, or Gilda was no longer as popular as she used to be. Perhaps that wasn't it.

Once a star reached a certain level, maybe they no longer needed puff press. It had to be a relief not to have to constantly engage in self-promotion.

The only photo I could find of Gilda was the one accompanying the article about MGM dropping her. I stared at her carefully lit face, her body sprawled across a divan we were supposed to believe was in her bedroom. Her expression was solemn. This was a woman wronged, and unlike the characters she played on film, she wasn't seeking revenge for what had been done to her. She was grieving the two terrible losses she had experienced—the man who'd left her and the studio that abandoned her—and she wanted the public to know how much both of them wounded her.

"How are you feeling?"

I jumped at the sound of the voice, and my hand automatically went to my mouth lest my surprise should manifest itself in any way other than sound. Gilda was at the door, holding a small tray in her hand.

"As long as I don't close my eyes or focus on any part of the ship that's moving, I'm great."

"I thought this might help." She entered the room and set the tray on my bed. On it was a glass of what appeared to be ginger ale and some soda crackers.

"Thanks. That's swell of you."

"I got terribly sick the first time I ever stepped on one of these things. Of course, I wasn't smart enough to take to bed like you. Instead, I insisted I was fine and ended up humiliating myself in front of a hundred strangers, two of whom were European royalty."

"Ouch."

Her eyes fell on the photo of Jack lying at my side. "He's handsome. Boyfriend?"

"Ex."

She picked it up and smiled down at Jack's static face. "But apparently, if you're toting his photo across the Pacific, you don't want him to stay that way."

"He's missing in action."

Her breath caught in her throat. She returned the photo to my side. "I'm so sorry, Rosie."

"He's in the Solomon Islands, or at least he was."

"This trip must be awfully hard for you then."

"Actually, he's the reason I agreed to it." I didn't want to explain the rest. How our well connected friend Harriet had arranged for us to travel with the USO to the South Pacific. How I was hoping not to say good-bye to Jack but to find him despite the military's repeated—unsuccessful—attempts to do the same. After all, I didn't want to make myself feel sicker.

Gilda sat on the edge of the bed, pushing the slicks to the side so that they wouldn't crinkle and tear beneath her weight. I wished I'd had the smarts to cheese them under my pillow when she'd first arrived. "I hate those things," she said.

"Me too. I mean, I was short of reading material. A gal back home gave them to us so we'd have something for the trip."

She picked one up and idly flipped through it. What was it like when the photos in a magazine weren't just pictures of famous people but famous people you *knew*? "I wish someone had warned me about what it would be like. I probably never would've gone to Hollywood if I'd known."

"It can't be all bad."

She smiled at her lap. "Of course not. But there are some days when it just doesn't seem worth it anymore."

"Is that why you decided to tour?"

"After MGM dropped me, I had a meeting with Jack Warner." He was the head of Warner Brothers. It must've been nice to have those kinds of connections. "While I was there, he was telling me about the talent he was losing to the war—who had enlisted and who had been unlucky enough to have their numbers come up in the draft. He was living in terror that the Japanese might try to bomb the studio."

"Sounds like someone's a little paranoid."

She shook her head. I could see the barely visible line where her makeup ended and her skin began. Violet could learn a lot from her. "It wasn't entirely paranoia. Warner Brothers has a big building not far from the Lockheed plant. Jack was so worried about it that he decided to have a big arrow painted on his roof that said LOCKHEED THATAWAY."

I tipped a swallow of ginger ale. "You're kidding me."

"Nope. I think he expected me to find the story reassuring, but the whole thing really chafed. Didn't he realize that he was helping out the enemy by doing that? Was his studio really so important that he'd put the entire country in danger? The more I thought about it, the more I realized that maybe I should be going 'thataway,' too, out of Hollywood where I might be able to use my fame for good, if you can do such a thing."

I put the cold glass against my cheek. Oh, that was better. "I'm sure Mr. Warner didn't take that very well."

"I didn't phrase it quite that way. And truth be told, it wasn't all about helping out my fellowman. I wanted to escape for a while. I thought if I did, everyone might forget about me."

"I think it will take more than six months for that to happen. You saw those photographers today. You're pretty unforgettable."

"Tell that to MGM." She traded the magazine for the issue that discussed her firing and flipped through the pages. When she landed on the picture of Van Lauer, she paused.

"What was he like?" I asked.

"I can't say that I ever really knew. "

"I heard a rumor that he was the reason you were fired."

She raised a penciled eyebrow and ran her hand over his photo. Her fingers brushed his cheek as gently as they would if he were standing right before her. "I've made a lot of mistakes, Rosie. I've rushed into relationships thinking that if I just found the right man all of my problems would be solved. Only by doing that I created a new problem. Suddenly every fellow I smiled at was rumored to be husband number three. My love life became a punch line."

"So you and Van weren't involved?"

She was silent for a breath too long. "He's married."

"And?"

Tears filled her large green eyes and threatened to engulf her fake eyelashes. "And I'm not the kind of woman to steal another woman's man."

"But what about him? Was he the kind of guy who would step out on his wife?"

She didn't respond for a long time. Her chest shuddered as she attempted to keep her emotions under wraps. "He was under development, and MGM thought it would help raise his profile if he was seen in the company of a star. I didn't expect to . . . we tried to keep it quiet."

"So what happened?"

"The studio got wind that he was planning to divorce his wife. That wasn't the image they wanted for their new leading man."

"Wow. So how come you got fired but he didn't?"

She pushed her hair back, and for a moment she wasn't the glamour girl who fueled a thousand fantasies but just another woman who'd had her heart broken and dreaded having to face the world alone. "I was unredeemable. I was more expensive. I was the one always getting bad press for my behavior off set. I didn't have nearly the money-making potential that Van had anymore. Or so they assumed."

"Did you fight to stay?"

"I didn't think I should have to. I thought my career spoke for itself. I didn't realize they already had a woman in development to fill my shoes."

"And what about Van?"

"When he chose to stay with MGM, he made it clear that he wasn't choosing to stay with me."

"You must've been so angry."

She closed the magazine, hiding Van's picture from her view. "If I'm really honest with myself, I suppose he's the reason I left. I needed to forget him and I knew that wasn't going to happen if I stayed in Hollywood. That's the thing about being a star. There are copies of you everywhere—magazines, billboards, posters. Wherever I looked, there was a reminder of him. I needed to be someplace that had never heard of Van Lauer."

I hated to tell her, but as the slick just proved, distance wasn't an effective way of forgetting someone. When you've fallen in love, there wasn't a place you could run to that could help you escape those memories.

"It all seems so unfair," I said.

She fluttered the edge of the slick, turning the pages so rapidly that the images seemed animated. "Hollywood's not about fair. Believe me." She put her index fingers to the corners of her eyes to stop the tears from flowing. "We're a pair, aren't we? Here." She reached into her pocket and pulled out a white capsule. "It'll put you to sleep. You'll lose a night, but the nausea won't bother you."

"Thanks."

She patted my leg. "Feel better."

In fact, after I took the pill, I felt nothing at all, which was almost the same thing.

CHAPTER 4

What's in a Name?

By morning I was on the mend. Not well enough to eat but at least capable of remaining vertical for more than ten minutes. The other girls left me to sleep while they grabbed chow, so I took my time waking up and went for a walk on the deck, trying to get my sea legs. We were in the middle of nowhere without a sign of land to be found. We weren't alone though. There was another ship in front of us and one behind, both of which were U.S. Navy vessels.

The briny salt air was strange and refreshing, counteracting the bounce of the ship and setting my stomach at ease. I leaned over the rail and watched dolphins bob out of the water. They seemed to be attempting to keep pace with the boat, as though they were our guides on this long passage. Every once in a while a bird flew overhead, and I marveled at how seagulls could be in the middle of nowhere without any place to land. Weren't they tired? Didn't they need to rest? Or were they like warplanes, loaded with enough fuel to take them from one destination to another? From my vantage point, I could see guns that had been retrofitted on the sides of the ship. While we may not have been prepared for battle, our mode of transportation was.

Despite the roar of the ship's engines and the tinkle of music playing through the loudspeakers, the ocean seemed quiet and peaceful. I was moved by the sheer size of it, by how no matter how far I looked in any direction, we appeared to be alone. As amazed as I was to discover that there were still places in this world where people didn't knock elbow to elbow, it was intimidating too. We were completely vulnerable out here. If catastrophe struck, there was no one to fish us out of the bay with a hook.

With no land to shield us and no clouds to protect us, the sun beat down on the deck until I could feel my skin prickling from the heat. If I stayed out there too long, I was going to look like a tomato. I left the deck and went below, where the offices we'd seen the day before were stowed. A few men who weren't at breakfast greeted me with wide grins that made it clear they weren't used to seeing women. I returned their smiles and tried to keep out of their way as they gave in to the rhythm of their tasks. To pass the time, I grabbed that day's edition of the ship's newsletter and positioned myself on a lounge chair outside the mess hall. A group of soldiers marched past, their eyes set forward, as they practiced some drill that could be essential to their survival on land but seemed pretty useless on a ship in the middle of the Pacific.

The newsletter was abuzz about the body from the day before. More information had come down the wireless, and the writer had done a fine job putting together as many pieces of the story as he had access to.

Body Found at Port of San Francisco
Identified as Former WAAC

The body found yesterday at 1300 hours floating in the water off the Port of San Francisco has been identified as former WAAC Captain Irene Zinn, originally from Gary,

Indiana. Identification was possible because of dog tags
found around Miss Zinn's neck.

Miss Zinn, who had been stationed in the Solomon Islands for the past year, resigned from her post in January
and returned to civilian life in Los Angeles. Thus far there
is no indication as to why she was in San Francisco nor her
reason for being in the vicinity of navy ships.

Military police searched all ships at port following the
discovery of Miss Zinn's body and were unable to appre-
hend a suspect. Although the port was crowded during
the time of the murder and several individuals reported
hearing a gunshot, shore patrol were unable to determine
if anyone had witnessed the crime. If you believe you may
have observed something or someone associated with
Miss Zinn's murder, you are asked to report to the captain's office.

"There you are." Jayne appeared at my side as I closed the newsletter. "I've been looking for you everywhere."

"Sorry. I had to get out of that cabin. How was breakfast?"

"Delish. Real eggs, bacon, toast. Real coffee, too, strong enough
to take the rust off the ship. I'm sure we can grab you something if
you want it."

My stomach churned a warning. "Thanks but no thanks. My goal
is to keep my insides inside. Tomorrow I'll worry about food."

I tucked the paper beneath my arm and followed Jayne back to
the vacated mess hall, where we were scheduled to have our first
rehearsal. Violet was on her feet, trying to demonstrate a series of
dance steps. As we arrived, she paused, and Gilda greeted me with
a warm smile. "Good morning. Feel any better?"

"I'm on my way. That pill of yours sure did the trick." I set the
newsletter on one of the tables. "Where's Kay?"

"She went in search of a pianist. Rumor has it there's a fellow in
the dental corps who did two semesters at Julliard," said Gilda.

"A musical dentist?" I asked.

"Yeah, he plays everything in the key of pain." Violet snagged the newsletter and started tearing through it as if she was searching for a review of a play she was in the day after opening night. "The corpse has a name," she said. "Irene Zinn. She was a Wac."

"A former Wac," I said. "She left the military a few months ago."

"What's a Wac?" asked Gilda.

"The Women's Auxiliary Army Corps," I said. "It's the women's division of the U.S. Army." The WAAC, the WAVES, and SPAR were the female divisions of the different armed forces (army, navy, and army air force, respectively). Recruitment posters were all over the home front, urging us to join the WAVES and "free up a man to fight" or "speed them back, be a Wac." Only the Wacs got to travel abroad—the other divisions were strictly stateside for the time being—though rumor had it the WAVES might get to see the other side of the ocean before the war was over.

That was an unsettling thought: the war had gone on long enough that the rules made at its beginning were now being changed out of necessity. What would happen next? Would we run out of men and send our women to fight?

Gilda smiled at me with such appreciation you would've thought I had just pushed her out of the way of a runaway streetcar. "Thank goodness they were able to identify her," she said. "I wonder if she came to see someone off."

I'd been wondering the same thing. Why else would Irene have been in San Francisco that day? It's not like Los Angeles was a hop, skip, and a jump away. "I'll bet we were the only ship headed for the Solomons yesterday. If that's where she was stationed before, it was probably someone on this boat she came to say good-bye to."

"Of course, if that's the case, why didn't she have any personal belongings with her?" asked Violet.

It was a good point. If it weren't for the dog tags, it was very likely Irene would still be an unidentified body.

"Who are you talking about?" asked Kay. Behind her was a short, sturdy man loaded down with sheet music. Even from a distance I could see that he had perfectly straight chompers.

"The dead girl in the water," said Violet. "They identified her. Her name's Irene Zinn."

Kay faltered. In slow motion she began to lean backward, forcing the pianist to drop what he was carrying so that he could catch her.

"Are you all right?" asked Jayne.

The dentist slid Kay the remaining distance to the floor, keeping her torso propped up on his. Her upper body teetered from right to left, before settling in the middle.

"I'm just feeling a little faint," said Kay. "I think I'm. . . . I'm . . ." She clasped her hand over her mouth and scrambled to her feet. With the grace of a stilt walker cursed with uneven legs, she stumbled out of the ballroom.

My stomach lurched and the soda crackers I'd had the night before threatened to evacuate. I took a deep breath, hoping it would pass, but the ship chose that moment to switch from a zig to a zag.

I ran after Kay with my own hand plastered across my mouth.

I heard her before I saw her. She was kneeling in front of one of the toilets in the ladies' room. I entered the stall next to her and completed my own foul business. Stomach emptied, I did my best to clean myself up before turning my attention to her.

"You all right?" I asked.

"Oh, you know." She lurched again. When she came up for air, her face was a mess of smeared makeup, tear stains, and blotchy skin.

"I would've thought that after twenty-four hours at sea you were safe."

"Guess I'm just lucky," she said. If there was more to this story, she wasn't sharing it.

"The good news is it will pass eventually." I handed her a wad of toilet paper and helped her mop up her face. "I'll bet by tomorrow you'll be good as new."

She rested her forehead in her hand, and a shiver passed through her body. "I hope you're right, but I doubt it."

I helped Kay back to the cabin and arranged for her to get some ginger ale and crackers. By the time I returned to the mess hall, the pianist—Dr. McDaniels—was playing some fast paced instrumental piece that the others were whirling around to, their faces red from effort and laughter. Even though Jayne and Violet both performed the steps with much more skill, it was Gilda that my eyes were drawn to. She was radiant as she twirled, acknowledging her mistakes with a grin and a roll of her eyes. Eventually she conceded that she couldn't keep up with the two of them, and she left them to their energetic jig while she joined me to catch her breath.

"How's Kay?" she asked me.

"I'm not sure. I get the feeling that it wasn't just motion sickness that hit her. She's an odd one."

"And a talented one," said Gilda. "You should've heard her sing earlier. It gave me shivers."

Rehearsal lasted for two hours. Practicing dance moves on a ship at sea was a terrible idea, even when the routines that Gilda choreographed were so simple that . . . well . . . under normal circumstances, even I could do them. Gilda was a patient teacher, though, who never demanded perfection out of any of us but rather praised us for simply putting in the effort to be there.

In other words, she was the exact opposite of every director I'd worked with in the past.

I should have found it cloying, but it was clear Gilda wasn't paring things back because she didn't think we were capable of doing any better. She understood that spending our days putting polish on footwork and all those other little niceties that turned a show into a Show was silly. The people we would be performing for wanted to be entertained. They didn't care if we had perfect extension, timing, or pitch.

Violet was wrong in her prediction that Gilda would make herself the focus of the show. Gilda insisted that, in addition to the group numbers, we would each share the spotlight based on whatever particular skill we excelled at. I wasn't sure the audience would be so thrilled if our star periodically receded into the background; nor did I think it possible that they wouldn't be staring at her no matter where she was onstage, but it was nice of her to at least try to give us each our moment in the sun.

The question was: what was I good at? My most prominent skill was acting, but I had a feeling the men weren't going to want to suffer through a Shakespearean monologue done by yours truly. They'd been through enough unpleasantness.

After lunch I mused with Jayne about what my skill should be.

"We could dance together," she suggested.

"I think I've already exhausted my limitations in that arena." In our last show I'd been grossly miscast in a corps de ballet, where my limited hoofing skills made the other incompetent dancers look like Pavlova by comparison.

"Not ballet, you dumdora. We could tap."

While I wasn't a good dancer when set side by side with Jayne and just about anyone else with legitimate training, I was a reasonably good tapper. Not Eleanor Powell or Fred Astaire good, but I'd had some classes, and with a little rehearsal I'd be passable. And if we combined the not-so-fancy footwork with some verbal hijinks, the soldiers would never be the wiser. "We could do a Burns and Allen thing," I told Jayne. "You know—jokes between the steps just in case the dancing loses their attention. You mind playing dumb to my straight man?"

"What do you think I've been doing for the last five years?"

Fortunately, we were in the land of improvisation, where adding taps to shoes involved nothing more than stopping by the inventive onboard cobbler. Within a half hour our shoes were done. By late afternoon we had the skeleton of a routine and a few nasty bruises on our shins.

Rather than spending our free time before dinner up on the sundeck, the four of us decided to go back to the cabin and check on Kay. She was lying on her bunk when we arrived, a wad of tissues clutched in her hand. The ginger ale I'd brought her was gone, although she hadn't touched the crackers.

"How are you?" Gilda asked.

Kay looked at her as though she didn't understand the question.

"Kay?" I said.

"What?"

"Gilda asked how you were."

"Better. I'm better."

Violet, Gilda, Jayne, and I shared a look of concern. Jayne climbed the ladder to Kay's bunk and started to gab at her as if there was nothing unusual going on. She described our efforts to choreograph our dance and the difficulty we had coming up with jokes for an audience we didn't know. As Jayne spoke, Kay stayed in her daze. Her reactions were delayed, as though she were listening to us from a great distance away and had to account for the time that lapsed between when we spoke and when she heard us.

"The pianist is great," I said. "You're going to love working with him."

"I'm not so sure about that," said Violet. "He had the nerve to say I had summer teeth."

"What are summer teeth?" asked Jayne.

"You know: some are there and some ain't." She grinned and pointed out a missing molar.

Kay smiled for the first time. We took that as a sign that she was coming back to herself and started suggesting songs she could sing. She got excited about the repertoire, and the color came back into her skin. With Jayne's help, she left the upper bunk, and the five of us ended up sprawled on Violet's bed, talking through the show.

"This is going to be fantastic, girls," said Gilda. "I can't wait to get onstage with you."

"It's going to be a far cry from Hollywood," said Violet. "No sets, no costumes, no money."

"What's it like in Hollywood?" asked Jayne.

"Efficient," said Gilda. "Very, very efficient."

I think I got what she meant. While Hollywood's depiction of itself often contained caricatures of bumbling studio heads and inept directors, the reality was one studio could churn out a hundred movies a year. Movie-making was a well-oiled machine that knew from the get-go that while you needed the right script, star, and timing, only having two of those three elements would still allow you to succeed.

Gilda told us about the studio that used to be her home, where she not only went each day to work but also did her banking, signed for a house loan, had her hair done, got her insurance papers notarized, had her annual dental exam, and took her dry cleaning. The studios were mini-cities that understood it was much more cost-effective to bring everything to the talent rather than to waste time by making the talent leave the lot to take care of the their daily drudgeries.

"The department stores even come to us," said Gilda. "Last year I did my Christmas shopping on the lot by picking out what I wanted to buy from an array of things the Saks Fifth Avenue gal brought us."

"It sounds like they own you and they want to make sure they get their money's worth," I said.

Gilda tilted her head to the left, showing her good side to full advantage. "I suppose they do in some ways. I worked six days a week, fourteen hours a day, and when I got home at night, I spent another hour or two memorizing scripts before making sure I got enough sleep to look decent on the set the next day. I couldn't turn down any part because I'm contractually obligated to do whatever they tell me to do, which explains some of the duds I've been in. I had to go where they said when they said, wearing the clothes they picked out and in the company of whomever they wanted me to be seen with. I wasn't even supposed to get married without their permission."

"But apparently you had no problem bending that rule," I said.

She winked at me. "In retrospect, I probably should've listened to them."

"If you think it's so awful, why do you stay?" asked Violet. I looked for hidden venom in the question, but I didn't see any. She really wanted an answer.

"Because deep down I love it. And because, honestly, given who I am and where I've come from, this is the best possible life I could achieve on my own. I'm just a small-town Texas girl raised by a single mother who took in washing to pay for my dance lessons. I'm never going to be a doctor or a lawyer, but a movie star—that I can be. And people will remember me."

It was an honest answer, but it made me terribly sad. I was an actress because I loved to act. Sure I took lousy jobs sometimes so I could keep acting, but I made those sacrifices because I couldn't imagine doing anything else with my life. Gilda didn't do what she did for the love of performing, even though, despite what Violet said, she was remarkably good at it. She did it because she wanted the fame and recognition that came with stardom, and all the little perks like department stores bringing her presents to the set.

Maybe that was the difference between Hollywood and Broadway. On Broadway you could still convince yourself that you were doing it for the art.

"I'll never forget the first article I read about you," said Kay. "They included pictures of you on a sweet little farm, and in one of them, you were milking a cow. Where was that?"

"Probably *Movie Scene*," said Gilda.

"No I mean the place," said Kay.

"Your guess is as good as mine."

"Is it true you were discovered at a malt shop?" asked Jayne.

Violet snorted. Gilda threw her head back and laughed. She was sitting next to me, and I found myself scrutinizing her roots. Was Violet right? Was even her honey-colored hair and high forehead something the studio had ordered? "No. No. Absolutely no. I was a contract player for years before I got a good role."

"So why do all the magazines say otherwise?" asked Kay.

"Because it's more interesting, I would imagine," said Gilda. "Nobody wants to hear about a girl from Texas who worked her way through the system until the bigwigs thought she was ready for a break." I did. At least it let the rest of us know what it would realistically take to get where she was. "The whole myth started when I was in *Moon over Madrid*. I remember giving my first interview, and instead of printing anything I said, the press made it sound like I had just appeared out of nowhere and become this big star. But the thing was, I'd been in development for three years at that point. I'd probably been in a dozen films."

"What's 'development'?" asked Jayne.

"It's a trial by fire," said Violet. "They're making a product, so they test you out in small parts, track the audience response, and try to figure out where you'll fit in the studio. Sometimes they decide you don't, and they drop your option."

"And sometimes they decide you do," said Gilda. "And the parts get bigger and your name gets higher until eventually it's directly above the title."

"Why do you think they decided you were ready to become a star after all those years?" I asked.

"I don't know. Maybe it was just the luck of the draw. Someone somewhere realized they needed fresh blood, and they decided I was a serviceable performer and that I'd paid my dues long enough to be it. They do that, you know, hiring on girls who might one day be able to fill a void they have because a star leaves or public taste changes. Everyone is replaceable."

"But why you?" asked Violet. There was something sad in her question. What she was really asking was, Why you instead of me?

Gilda shrugged. "I think because I did everything they asked me to. Every time I was criticized, I took it to heart. If I was too fat, I lost weight. Too ethnic, I changed my name."

"So why didn't you ever tell the press that story?" asked Jayne.

Gilda laughed again, flashing that brilliant grin of capped white teeth toward Jayne. What had her smile been like before Holly-wood? "Because it's an old story that a thousand other girls had already been through. Nobody wants to hear about that. They want to hear how you're just like them and that everyone has an equal shot at fame. And so that's what I gave them. Hollywood is about manufac-turing legends and myths. No one's that lucky or beautiful or witty in real life. Believe me. I've spent time with these people, and there's not one of them who's accurately depicted on screen. Clark Gable is dull, Norma Shearer is short, and Olivia DeHavilland would cut her own mother's throat to get ahead." While her words initially seemed directed at all of us, her focus seemed to shift to Violet. She knew, I think, the grudge Violet carried, and she wanted her to understand that she wasn't the one who made the choice about who succeeded and who failed. "I understand that the decisions I've made aren't for everyone. We shouldn't have to make them, but here's the thing: they're not going to change the system for us. And I honestly don't think it's MGM or Twentieth Century Fox, or any other studio's fault that an actress has to change herself to fit the mold. That's what the people want, and so the suits are smart enough to know that that's what they need to give them. And frankly, if you want to be part of this business, you have to be part of the system."

CHAPTER 5

Soldiers and Women

Over the course of our week and a half on the ship, our schedule went like this: wake up at seven and enjoy a leisurely breakfast with the officers. Once the mess was cleared, we rehearsed until one. The enlisted men were given only two meals a day—breakfast and dinner—so rather than staying in the mess hall for our midday meal, we joined the officers in a smaller room in another part of the ship. After lunch, we had two hours to ourselves, which, weather permitting, we spent on the sundeck. Then we had another two hours of rehearsal. We usually retreated to our cabins after that to relax, nap, write letters, and take showers. We would start the evening off with another dinner with the officers, and then we spent the remainder of the night in the canteen. There we'd dance and chat with the men while a ragtag group of enlisted musicians serenaded us with whatever popular song they'd figured out how to play.

The nights at the canteen, by necessity, ran late. As much as we wanted to go to bed, we knew that there was an unspoken rule that we be there until the bitter end. If the captain was obligated to go down with the ship, the five of us were expected to leave with the band.

During my first night in the club, the evening's activities were interrupted by a burgeoning chant. By the time it reached us, I crabbed what the men were saying, "Gilda, Gilda, Gilda!" When they had her attention, the chant changed to a song sung in four-part harmony that I later learned was called "I Want a Girl Like Gilda DeVane." It was a silly little ditty, with a catchy chorus that went:

Her hair is gold, her eyes pale blue,
Her gams they stretch for miles
She has a way of looking at me
I'm weak whenever she smiles
I want a girl like Gilda DeVane

When they finished singing, Gilda rewarded them with enthusiastic applause, and they plied her with requests for an impromptu performance.

"Oh no," she said. "There's no way I could follow that. Besides, the band is doing a fabulous job."

The men wouldn't listen to her excuses. When it became clear that the only way she was moving was by force, two sailors took her by the arms and playfully pulled her onto the stage.

Clad in a simple dress she had brought from the States, her honey hair pinned back with a barette on one side and falling in a cascade of waves on the other, she slinked up to the microphone and, with a wink at the band, started a song in a low luscious voice that certainly seemed like it wouldn't need to be dubbed for the movies. Nobody danced; we were all too far under her spell for movement. Her pipes may not have been as good as Kay's, or her hoofing as polished as Jayne's and Violet's, but she was an expert performer, directing that song to each and every man in the room until they all had to feel as if they were alone with her in that marvelous moment.

I knew much of what Gilda did was manufactured. She wasn't

so humble that she didn't want to sing. She didn't care for each of the men who stood wide-eyed as she performed. But I still found everything about her magical, even after spending untold hours rehearsing at her side.

Jayne fell under her sway too. As we sat on barstools at the back of the room, we whispered our praise of Gilda back and forth like two small children who were amazed to see their normally plain-clothed mother dolled up for a night on the town. Her song reached its conclusion, and the men yelled for a repeat performance. Rather than giving in to their demands, she announced, "I want my girls up here with me." The crowd parted and the four of us made our way onto the stage.

Gilda gestured for us to huddle around her. "How about 'Boogie Woogie Bugle Boy'?" she asked. It was a song we'd practiced in rehearsal, a sure crowd pleaser that relied on all of our voices. We agreed it was a good choice, and she asked us to put our hands in the middle of the circle we made. With a squeeze that managed to encompass us all, she instructed us to enjoy ourselves. The pianist plucked out a note, and my body instantly snapped to attention. As we invoked the harmonies we'd practiced that morning and the steps none of us had mastered, the crowd stood rapt. I'm sure we missed notes and forgot moves, but for three and half minutes I felt like we were channeling the Andrews Sisters.

Never had I felt that kind of energy onstage before. As I'd witnessed when I volunteered at the Stage Door Canteen back in New York, we could've read the phone book and the men would've been grateful for the time and diversion. But as their eagerness for our performance pulsed across the room, I found myself wanting to give them everything I had. I sold the song like I didn't have a dime to my name and my rent was due the next day. As my commitment to the performance grew, strangely, so did my skill, causing me to hit notes and execute moves I was certain I didn't have the stuff for. When Kay finished up the song with her solo, "He's the boogie woogie bugle boy of Company B" the crowd went wild with hooting and hollering. We sang two more songs, to even greater response, before turning it back over to the band and dispersing into the crowd. After that night, Gilda wasn't the only star in the room. We had all arrived.

The remaining time on the ship passed quickly and quietly. My stomach grew used to the sea, I focused on rehearsal, and I enjoyed the amenities that were being offered to us. I was starting to think I could stay on the *Queen of the Ocean* forever when, the day before we were scheduled to land at our destination, we were awakened by the eerie call of "Now hear this. All men to general quarters," on the loudspeaker. As we lay in our beds trying to make sense of the message assaulting us, it became clear that the ship—and everyone on it—was in danger. A submarine had been spotted in the distance, and we were all to take our posts with our Mae Wests in hand. For the five of us, that meant heading to the mess hall to await further instruction.

There we sat at our dinner table drinking coffee and taking in the scene around us. The room was filled with enlisted men who had no direct role on the ship, though you could tell it was killing them that they didn't have something to do. They sat in clusters conversing in low, tense tones that made the air crackle with excitement. The anticipation made my stomach burn. Our ship was a target, and that meant that at any moment it could be ripped apart by enemy fire. And what would we do if it were? At least the other men and women had training. The five of us were as impotent as the bed-bound injured men aboard *The Centurian.*

Did people who were about to die know what was going to occur? I liked to think you were in the dark until the moment it happened, if only because that meant my even contemplating that we could be killed assured us that we wouldn't be. But I knew that wasn't likely. After all, men standing before a firing squad had to know what was about to pass.

"It's going to be fine," whispered Jayne. She put her hand on my leg, attempting to calm me. It might have worked if her arm wasn't vibrating with fear.

I scanned the hundreds of other people in the room. "Why aren't they scared?"

"I think they're just grateful for the change," said Kay. "You spend so much time waiting for something to happen that when it finally does you're just excited for the activity, never mind the danger. Being in the armed forces is a whole lot of waiting."

It seemed like a rotten way to live.

"Now hear this," came the mysterious voice over the loudspeaker again. "All nonessential personnel are ordered back to their cabins, where they shall remain for the duration of the trip. From this point forward, no one is permitted on deck without orders from the captain. All nonessential activities are canceled."

I didn't need Kay to explain that message to me. We were headed into enemy waters . Our days of performing late into the night and sunning on the deck were over.

We were permitted one final excursion out of our cabin before arriving on land: we each had to have a physical or, as the sailor taking us to the infirmary described it, we were going to the "pecker checker."

"Come again?" we said in unison.

He flashed us a wide grin peppered with missing teeth. He was probably a victim of biscuit blast: the unfortunate side effect of eating the stale crackers that came in K rations. "You know—'the penis machinist.'" Our soundless gawks made it clear we still didn't know what we were in for. "They're going to check you for VD," he said at last. "Every time you go somewhere new they make you drop your pants first."

We didn't bother to explain that we lacked the required equipment to make such an examination useful. Our physician was a hundred and eighty years old. He took us one at a time, examining our eyes for scurvy, our hair for bugs, and our skin for any number of rashes that would signal our imminent demise. It seemed to me that if we'd just spent a week on ship with these maladies, the entire population was at risk.

Rather than asking us to strip down to our unmentionables, he instead trusted us to be honest about what we'd been doing and what we might've caught in the process. It was clear he was as uncomfortable asking us the questions as we were answering them.

"Have you recently engaged in intercourse?"

I had to bite my tongue to keep from laughing. "No."

"Have you ever been pregnant?"

"Not that I know of."

He squeezed the skin on my right hand. It turned red before sinking back into its usual flesh color. "Do you have an itching or burning sensation in your private parts?"

Another bite. My poor tongue wasn't long for this world. "Um, no."

On his wall was a hand-drawn cartoon depicting a physician with his finger paternally raised. "Flies breed disease," he instructed in his cartoon air bubble. "So keep yours zipped!"

"Have you noticed any sores or discolored skin on your privates?" the doctor asked.

"No, sir." Who were these women who had enough time to look for this sort of thing? And how the hell did they have that kind of flexibility?

He attempted to hit my knee with his hammer, but the tremors in his hand caused him to miss. He swung a second time, landing on his target. My leg kicked into the air, narrowly missing his groin. "Have you experienced any sort of discharge, especially one that could be described as emitting an unpleasant odor?"

"Definitely not."

Satisfied that I was as healthy as could be expected, he handed me a bottle of Atabrine tablets, the military's cheap, synthetic version of quinine, which we were supposed to take to ward off malaria.

"It'll turn you yellow," Violet told us back in the cabin. Gilda was with us as we exchanged our tales of the grilling we'd each been subjected to. "Trust me: I've had to take it before, and it turns almost everyone yellow."

Jayne examined the smooth, pale skin of her arm. "Almost everyone?"

"There are a lucky few who don't change color at all. I'm not one of them." Violet chucked the unopened vial into her purse.

Jayne fished out a lemon-colored pill and stared at it as though she hoped she could figure out a way to separate its pigmentation properties from its medicinal benefits. "We'll change back, right?"

"If we're lucky."

Gilda slid her own pills into her pocket, clearly debating whether or not prevention was worth a blazing new skintone.

"We're going to a tropical region," said Kay. "Malaria is every-where."

"And so are men," said Violet. "I don't know about you, but I'd rather be sick than lonely."

CHAPTER 6

All the Comforts of Home

The ship made three stops over the course of the next twenty-four hours. Two of them were under the cover of night, and although we didn't know who left the ship at that time, it was obvious it was the majority of our population. As we arrived at our third and final stop, Carson Dodger knocked on our doors and let us know we would be leaving shortly.

We didn't know where we were, and given the orders we'd received about questioning our destination, we knew we weren't supposed to ask. But when I looked out a porthole and saw nothing but water, it was impossible not to demand an explanation.

"You are going to put us on land, right?" I asked.

Carson led us to the lower deck, where a small gangplank had been lowered into the ocean. Beside it was a motorboat being driven by a sailor with a deep island-tan set off by his summer whites. "The coral reefs won't let us get close to land. Shore patrol's going to take you to the island."

"And that's where exactly?" asked Violet.

He pointed toward the other side of the *Queen of the Ocean.* "Don't worry—the ship's blocking the view. You're not but a ten minute ride from your new home."

One by one, he helped us into the boat. Our luggage soon followed, landing with a boom as each bag was dropped overboard.

"There goes my grandmother's antique punch bowl," said Violet.

As the boat pulled away, we leaned over the edge and took in blue water that was so clean and clear I had no doubt we could see the bottom of the ocean if we looked hard enough. Fingers of coral reef danced beneath the surface, beckoning us to lean a little closer. Colorful fish, traveling so fast their movements seemed choreographed, disappeared beneath the white waves kicked up by the boat.

"Are there sharks?" asked Violet.

"You betcha," said our suntanned escort. "I think we have them to thank for half the Jap casualties. They've developed a taste for the slant-eyes."

Within seconds the island came into view, a lush green paradise that looked much more inhabited than I would've thought. For some reason I assumed the South Pacific had been untouched by civilization until the war broke out.

A pulse of electricity passed through me. I wasn't one for intuition, but in that moment I was positive Jack had been here. I knew it as sure as I knew my own name.

"This is it," said Jayne.

"This is it," I repeated.

Buildings on stilts faced the water, their roofs made of thatched grasses, their windows empty eyes observing our arrival. As we approached increasingly shallow water, crocodiles disguised as driftwood eyed us suspiciously.

"This is Blue Beach,' said our escort. I tried to figure out why it was given that name, but there was no obvious reason for it. The sand was stark white and peppered with seashells.

We reached the shore, and another man, this time in shorts with a brilliant tattoo of a Polynesian dancer on his right bicep, appeared to help us out of the boat and onto the utilitarian dock that seemed out of place in this jungle paradise. The air was moist and heavy, so full of rich and foreign scents that I felt as if my head was going to explode from too much stimulation. It was early afternoon, and the sun was still at its highest point, baking us in its oppressive heat. A third man greeted us with a wide smile, his eyes hidden behind the reflective lenses of his cheaters. His skin was tan, his shoulders broad, his legs bare beneath the shorts he'd cannibalized from his khaki pants, showing off an angry scar that covered most of one knee. Instead of dog tags, a camera hung around his neck.

He lifted the viewfinder to his eye and stared at us through the lens. Before we could react, he fired the camera once, capturing our disheveled arrival for all eternity.

"Welcome to Tulagi, ladies. I'll be riding along with you to camp. I'm Ernie Dwyer, but you can call me—"

"Dotty," said Kay.

He removed his glasses and took her in. "Kay?"

A smile trembled across her lips. "The one and only."

"Oh my God. Aren't you a sight for sore eyes?" They took a tentative step toward each other. Their heads bobbed with uncertainty.

"Well, hug him already," said Violet.

Kay blushed before extending her arms. Dotty grabbed her and swung her around.

"I had no idea you'd be here," he said.

"You? I didn't even know you were still in the army."

"I'm not. I'm a war correspondent now."

"You always were a hell of a writer."

He flexed his scarred knee. "I'm lucky I had that to fall back on. After what happened to my leg, they decided my soldiering days were over."

"But you couldn't stay away, could you?" said Kay.

"You know me. But what about you? Did you change your mind and decide to re-up?"

Kay forced a smile. "No. I'm with the USO now."

"No, sir! You're doing the tour?"

Kay's arm swept behind her to acknowledge the rest of us. "We all are. So I take it you're writing about the Pacific campaign."

"Partly, sure. But when we got wind Gilda DeVane was coming here, we decided to make a feature of it."

"That's great," said Kay. "Just great."

We all stared at the two of them, trying to make what we could of this reunion. With the forced smiles and reluctant hug, it was clear that Kay wasn't overjoyed to see Dotty. One couldn't say the same for him. I had a feeling that he'd like nothing more than for us to scram so that they could be alone together.

Dotty fiddled with his camera. Kay made a show of rolling up her sleeves. It was getting to be too much for me. Someone had to save them.

"I'm Rosie Winter." I thrust my hand toward Dotty. He took it in his giant mitt and shook it like he'd been promised a five spot if he could wrestle my arm to the table.

The other girls followed my lead. "Jayne Hamilton."

"Violet Lancaster."

Gilda put out her hand to make her own introduction, but before she could get her name out, he said it for her.

"Gilda DeVane," he said. "I'm a huge fan. I can't tell you how excited I was when I got word you were coming here. The fellows are going to flip when I tell them I got to meet you first. I think you're on half the bulkheads in the Pacific." Apparently, Gilda's decision to tour wasn't as last-minute as Violet claimed. She had done a pinup poster that was distributed in advance of her arrival. Dotty clapped his hands together. "Well, ladies, your Jeeps await."

While he led the pack with Violet and Gilda, Jayne and I hung back to talk to Kay.

"You all right?" I asked.

"Fine." She could no longer sustain the grin. Her lips quivered and she dashed her fingers beneath her eyes. "I just never thought I'd see him again."

I hoped I got the chance to experience that kind of surprise. "How do you know him?" I asked.

"He dated a friend of mine for a long time."

I knew there was more to it than that, but I wasn't going to pry. Not until Kay was ready.

She fixed another smile on her face and immediately submerged the despair that had been bubbling to the surface. That was the nice thing about being a performer: you could fake whatever emotion you needed on a moment's notice, even when the real feelings were struggling to be heard.

As we reached the shore, natives wearing army-issue pants and shirts decorated with necklaces of woven grass watched us. Their skin was almost black, their hair frizzy, their features wide and friendly. On closer inspection, I realized they were all men. They welcomed us in surprisingly good English, saying "Hello, Jane. You have cigarettes?"

"How do they know my name?" asked Jayne.

Dotty laughed and turned to look at my pal. "They call anyone in a skirt Jane. And all the fellows are Joe."

I was relieved that they didn't call them Jack.

"Where are the women?" asked Violet.

"Most of them were taken to another island by the French."

"Why?"

He winked at her. "For their protection. Apparently the U.S. military's reputation with the ladies precedes it."

We passed the natives, offering them waves, smiles, and a few cigarettes. In return, they carried our luggage, balancing the smaller bags atop their heads.

"They seem happy to have us here," said Gilda.

"They are. The marines got the Japanese off their island. The Allies can do no wrong in their eyes."

It seemed impossible that the military had set up camp here. Vegetation was everywhere: eucalyptus, mahogany, and a strange tree I was told was called a flamboya, which was twice as wide as it was tall and was covered in reddish orange flowers. Instead of Manhattan's skyscrapers, we had banyan trees with their thick, knotty roots and palm trees dropping their yield everywhere for the picking. Fruit could be had with the mere extension of your arm: bananas, limes, oranges, pineapples, and something called the paw-paw. Where the path hadn't been cleared, there were tall grasses that waved gently in the breeze.

Despite its beauty, it all felt incredibly foreboding, as though nature herself were trying to warn man off. Who could blame her when we could take a place even this beautiful and turn it into a war zone?

Dotty took us down a ragged jungle path. All of us folded into ourselves, trying to keep our arms as close to our bodies as possible. Vines threatened to grab at us, their sharp teeth glinting in the afternoon light. Enormous webs warned of the existence of frightfully large spiders. Bees and blue flies buzzed around us and the thick jungle foliage was alive with the sounds of creatures that buzzed, clicked, slithered, and sighed. Birds with eerie voices that sounded more like men imitating them than the real thing called out their welcomes. At last we reached a clearing, where two vehicles were at our disposal. After the luggage was loaded, we were forced to divide into two groups. Jayne and I ended up with Dotty and a driver named Ace in the first Jeep, while Violet, Kay, and Gilda rode in the second.

"I guess she doesn't want to ride with me," said Dotty as we claimed our seats.

"I'm sure it's nothing personal," I told him.

Over a bumpy road outlined by a mishmash of rocks, Ace took us toward the military village that would be our home base over the next few months. As we moved away from the shore, the landscape changed into rocky terrain bordered by craggy hills. A sign made of weathered boards cheekily pointed out the distance to New York, Los Angeles, and Chicago. For a moment, we rode in silence, Jayne and I being too awestricken by our surroundings to bat the breeze. It wasn't just the beauty of the place that stunned me. After months of worrying, praying, and suffering, I was going to finally have all the answers to my questions. I wanted desperately to ask Dotty if he knew Jack, but given what had just transpired with Kay, I figured he had enough on his mind. Besides, I wanted one last moment when I could believe that everything was going to turn out all right.

"It's not as bad as it looks," said Dotty.

"Excuse me?" Had he read my mind?

"Things seem primitive, but the military's done a fine job making sure we have all the comforts of home."

"How long have you been here?"

He let out a puff of air that ruffled the fringe around his face. "I've been on Tulagi for about a month now, though I island-hop quite a bit. Got to go where the news is happening."

"And where exactly is Tulagi?" I asked.

He turned around in his seat. "You ladies have landed yourself in the former capital of the Solomon Islands."

"Are there Japanese around?" asked Jayne.

"No worries. We took this place over last August and flushed out the Japs at the same time."

"So if the Japanese aren't in Tulagi anymore, why are we?" I asked.

"Because we want to make sure they don't come back. This is one of our base camps here in the Solomons. We use it as a staging place for the rest of the South Pacific. We got boys from every division working here."

"Not just navy?" asked Jayne.

"No, ma'am. We got army, marines, air force, navy seabees—we even got some Australian and British troops camping here."

That was a lot of men in one place. It would be easy for someone like Jack to get lost.

"And what do they do here?" asked Jayne.

"Outfit the ships with supplies. Enjoy some R & R. Survey the island. Code break. Repair the damage the Japs left behind. You name it, they do it."

"How big is the island?" I asked.

Dotty let out another gust of air as he thought about the question. "Not quite four miles long. You landed in the laguna." He pointed off in the distance. "Over there is the harbor where the ships come in for refueling and to take on more ammunition. We'll pass through the village as we head toward camp. To the right of it is the cricket field."

"That's a cute name," said Jayne. "Are there a lot of crickets there?"

His face crinkled as he laughed. "Probably, but they call it that because that's were the Brits used to play cricket. The island was under British control before the war. In fact, there's even an Anglican church in town."

On cue, the tiny village appeared, still bearing the scars of recent battle. The remnants of a private girls' school awaited clearing. Buildings had caved in and pieces of mortar bombs lay scattered on the edge of the street like refuse. People clearly were still living here though. Hand-scrawled signs let us know that we could buy grass skirts for two dollars, beaded necklaces for a quarter more. British-made bicycles leaned before homes. As we kicked up dust on the dirt road, children came to open doorways and waved at the passing vehicle. Dotty waved back, greeting some of them by name. "Hello, Thomas," he called out to one little boy. "Hello, William," he said to another.

I stared at these small dark-skinned people, many of whom bore their own physical scars from battle. "I kind of figured their names would be more exotic," I said.

"More British influence," he said. We passed a mission hospital where we saw a native woman sweeping the porch. This wasn't Dorothy Lamour primped for film with her flower-dotted hair and brightly colored sarong. This woman was naked from the waist up, her massive brown breasts swaying as she worked.

We drove and he continued narrating what we were about to see. "There's the governor general's house. And the British high commissioner's. Up there are the caves—that's where the Japs had their headquarters when they were here. And those are the Suicide Cliffs."

"The what?" asked Jayne.

"The Suicide Cliffs. When the Japs had the island, they threatened the natives, telling them that if they were friendly toward us Yanks, they'd skin them alive and rape their wives. When we invaded, rather than face what they thought was certain Japanese wrath, some of the natives opted to dive to their deaths instead."

Jayne put a hand to her mouth. "How awful. Why didn't anyone stop them?"

"Some of them tried to. But they were so scared of the Japanese they wouldn't listen. Eventually the hysteria died down, the Americans got control of the island, and the natives realized they had nothing more to fear." No wonder they were so nice to us when we arrived.

"What's up on that cliff?" I pointed toward what looked like a roadside billboard faced away from us. "Don't tell me Burma Shave is advertising all the way down here."

He shook his head and stifled a laugh. "Nope, that's a sign Admiral Halsey put up."

"What does it say?"

"You really want to know?"

I nodded.

He took a deep breath. "Kill Japs, kill Japs, kill more Japs. You will help kill the yellow bastards if you do your job well."

My stomach churned. We were used to anti-Japanese sentiment at home—lord knows they'd earned it—but it didn't seem so . . . overt. We dealt with them by sending them away to work camps and making them villains in our movies (played by Chinese actors, since we didn't want to reward our enemy by employing them). Sure we called them nasty names and encouraged kids to join in the effort by distributing official Jap hunter cards, but I couldn't recall ever saying anything quite so pointed. If I couldn't handle the language of war, how was I going to deal with the violence of it? "That's subtle."

"The military's not known for subtlety. The admiral did it to boost morale at a time when his men really needed it."

"And apparently it did the trick." Did the opposition have similar signs encouraging our deaths? What nicknames had they reduced the Allies to?

Dotty pointed in the opposite direction, at a number of buildings with curved rooftops that rose above the trees. The sun reflected off the steel structures, making them seem even more out of place against the rest of the environment. "You can see the enlisted mess and PX through there. Just past them is the commissary, the infirmary, and the supply huts."

"I was expecting everything to be made out of twigs and leaves," said Jayne. I shared her surprise. There was something disturbing about seeing these permanent-looking structures. If it was necessary to build buildings and make roads, then our government expected this war to go on for a very long time.

"Some things are made the native way, but when the military wants to put up something fast and sturdy, they do it by Quonset hut," said Dotty. Ace followed the curve of the road, where canvas living quarters were lined up in clusters. The roof of each dwelling peaked at the center the way a circus big top did; only instead of inviting us with brilliant colors, these tents were made of army green canvas bleached by the sun. Wires strung from poles made it clear that while the living conditions were simple, there was, at least, electricity to be had. "And here we are."

The Jeep in front of us stopped, and we followed suit. Jayne scanned the sight before her, her mouth so wide I was worried one of the myriad bugs flying about might go inside and set up camp. "This is it?" she said.

"What were you expecting?" asked Dotty.

She stepped out of the Jeep and examined tents that were little more than olive drab sheets tied to poles. "Walls."

"Trust me," said Ace. "These are A+ accommodations. You guys have a floor. Not many people can claim that."

The others climbed out of their Jeep, and they led us into a large tent outfitted with five cots that hadn't yet been made up. Stacks of rough blankets and linens awaited our attention on each bed. There was another object there, which I think was a pillow, though from the condition of the fabric covering, I wouldn't have been surprised to learn that they were filled with coconut husks rather than goose down. Two-by-fours forming crossbeams were mounted to the tent poles, and at our eye level nails stuck out every which way. Ace hadn't lied; the tent had a concrete floor that immediately reignited every knee injury I'd ever done to myself. Someone had recently swept the floor, leaving a broom and dustpan full of island detritus leaning against one of the walls. The driver who'd brought Gilda and the other girls pulled a string dangling from the ceiling and illuminated a twenty-watt bulb that didn't do much more than tease us into remembering what real light looked like.

On the bright side, Violet had to be pleased to see that Gilda wasn't getting special treatment.

"Where are the closets?" asked Gilda.

"Where are the bathrooms?" asked Jayne.

"Where's the bar?" asked Violet.

Their driver made a sound that was something between a chuckle and a guffaw. Whatever it was, he spit when he made it. "Those nails there are your closets. The latrine is out that flap and to the right. As for the bar—the U.S. Navy's been dry since 1914."

"Then it sounds like I'll be hanging out with the army, air force, and marines," said Violet.

Dotty tipped his cap at her and smiled. "Don't you worry. You'll never go thirsty here. The men who get a ration are always happy to share. And rumor has it that the men who don't have figured out how to make their own brew, though I wouldn't recommend drinking it."

Jayne nudged me with her elbow. "What's a latrine?"

"The bathroom," I said.

"A shared bathroom," said Violet.

I wanted to kick her. Jayne could take only so much bad news at once.

In the corner of our tent was a barrel turned on its side with a faucet sticking out of it. The top of it had been cut open, and this exposed portion reached beyond the tent, where it could catch the water whenever it rained.

"What's that?" asked Gilda.

"That's your sink," said Dotty. "And you're one of the only tents that has one. The men rigged it up for you special." He gestured for her to move close to it and took a picture of her posing, unenthusiastically, beside it.

We looked at the barrel warily. It was like no sink I'd ever seen before, but now that we knew it was an honor to have access to it, we felt obligated to use it.

Dotty disappeared to help the drivers with our luggage, while the five of us slowly took in what we'd gotten ourselves into. I won't lie—when I'd thought about what awaited me in the South Pacific, I hadn't pictured anything quite so . . . bleak. In my imagination, there was a veranda, palm fronds, ample booze, and a hammock that swayed gently in the island breezes. The word *latrine* hadn't entered my vocabulary.

But then I'd also kidded myself into believing that I would be able to find Jack. Clearly, I was batting a thousand when it came to realistic fantasies.

Gilda clapped her hands together. "Well, girls, I know it doesn't look like much, but we're not going to be here very often anyway. And I think that between the five of us, we can make this place quite homey."

A siren sounded somewhere on the island. A loudspeaker crackled, but my ears couldn't discern what was being said.

"Gilda's right," I said. "We just need to use our imaginations."

"Well, my imagination just saw a rat duck under one of the cots," said Violet.

The four women screamed and climbed onto the furniture. I decided to be more proactive and grabbed the broom. I poked it beneath the bed, flushing out something that was at least two feet long and one foot wide. If that was a rat, I was a monkey's uncle.

The men returned with our trunks and hurriedly piled them on the floor. "Sorry, ladies, but you're on your own for a while," said Dotty. Ace passed out what looked like large green steel bowls to each of us. Some sort of cloth had been wadded up and shoved inside them.

"What's this?" asked Jayne.

"Helmets and nose bags," he said. "And I suggest you put them on. We're at condition red. That alarm means there's enemy aircraft in the area. "

"But I thought you said the Japanese weren't here anymore," said Jayne.

"I said they're not on the island," said Dotty. "I can't account for the sea and the air."

CHAPTER 7

Neighbors

The good news was that we had a roof over our heads. The bad news was ... well, we were in the middle of nowhere with bombs dropping out of the sky. All in all I'd had better days.

For a long time we sat on the cots each of us had claimed for our own and waited for the world to blow up. When it didn't, one by one we found the courage to put on our M1 helmets and stick our heads out of the tent flap to eyeball what was going on.

There wasn't much to see. Our part of camp was a ghost town, though we could hear men shouting and planes flying somewhere in our vicinity. Nevertheless, we kept the steel helmets on, grateful not only that they protected our noggins but that their rain visors obscured our view of any destruction that might come within our line of sight.

"Comfy, aren't they?" said Violet.

"Not the word I was thinking of," I said.

She removed her helmet and showed us the plastic liner inside it. "The beauty is not only will it protect you from shrapnel, but you can use it to cook, wash yourself, even sleep on if the mood suits you. They had something in *Stars & Stripes* once about a nurse who came up with over twenty ways to use her M1."

I wondered if one of those uses was clobbering your tent mate to get her to close her head.

Jayne tried to fasten the chin-strap on her own helmet, but her fingers couldn't quite close the clasp.

"Don't bother," said Violet. "You're never supposed to fasten the strap. It makes it much worse if you do get hit with something." She flopped her head to the right, illustrating the fatal neck injury we were headed for.

While she rattled on about the wonders of military ingenuity, Jayne and I once again wandered outside the tent. "I didn't think it would be so close," she whispered. Her hand was in mine, squeezing my fingers to the rhythm of her clanging heart. I didn't know what to say to her. Usually, when one of us was scared, the other one would reassure her that everything was going to be just fine. But I didn't know that it would. In fact, I didn't know anything. This whole trip was unexplored territory. "Tell me we're going to survive this."

"Of course we are," I said. I was an actress after all. If I couldn't fake confidence, I didn't deserve to be on the stage.

"Do you know what today is?" she asked. "It's Dedication Day. You'd think it would be the one day the men wouldn't have to fight."

She had that wrong. More likely, it was the one day when the men would be driven to fight their hardest.

Gilda joined us outside, and for a moment the three of us stood in silence, straining to hear the sounds of battle taking place perilously close to us. Why couldn't we see anything? Why did it sound like the noise was coming from all around us?

"Let's unpack," said Gilda. "Worrying about what's going on isn't going to accomplish anything."

She was right. We each set to hanging up our clothes on the crooked nails that dotted the tent frame. As we worked, Kay began to sing "When the Lights Go on Again," and soon all of us were belting out the words with her to drown out the sound of the planes.

"You know if the bombs don't work," said Violet, "our singing might be enough to disable the enemy."

While most of what we hung consisted of cotton shirts and light-weight dresses, Jayne's clothes looked oddly out of place.

"I don't mean to be judgmental, but what did you pack?" I asked her.

The remaining contents of her luggage spilled across the bed. Along with the few summer things she'd worn for the trip, she'd brought sweaters, wool skirts, scarves, and gloves.

"Winter clothes of course. You said it was winter here."

Why hadn't I caught her error back home? Because I was too full of Jack, I suppose. She could've put the cat in her suitcase, and I probably wouldn't have thought twice about it. "We're on a tropical island, Jayne. We'll be lucky if it gets cool enough at night to need a sheet."

"Oh." Her face fell. Poor Jayne didn't realize that we'd entered a topsy-turvy world where summer was winter, men were plentiful, and murder was just another act of war.

Gilda hooked her arm in Jayne's and pulled the tiny woman to her side. "Don't worry, Jayne: I almost made the same mistake myself. Luckily, I always overpack. You're welcome to borrow anything you need."

Gilda pulled out a number of items she thought would fit Jayne, and soon we were all admiring the clothes she'd crammed into two trunks. Rather than shooing us away, she handed out items like she was distributing for Bundles for Britain, encouraging us to try on her couture shoes, jackets, and gloves.

"Where did you think you were going?" asked Violet as she wrapped a mink stole around her neck.

Gilda laughed. "I know, I know. You just never know what you might need."

If Jayne thought it was winter in the South Pacific, Gilda apparently thought it was award season. I rifled through her trunk and found a dazzling array of hats, hosiery, and pocketbooks to match each pair of shoes she'd brought along. There were satin handbags with sequins, beaded ones that must've taken months to make, and the everyday bag in brown leather that she'd carried the day we met her.

I put one of her hats atop my head and caught my reflection in the mirror affixed to the trunk lid. It was a strange little jumble of fur, ribbons, and what looked like Christmas ornaments. It did nothing for me.

Gilda removed the hat and turned it around so that the front was no longer facing the back. "Like I told Jayne: you're welcome to use whatever you like."

I planned to take her up on that.

Soon the clothes hanging around the tent had transformed the place. It may not have been the prettiest joint I'd ever lived in, but the colors of our dresses and the combination of fabrics did a fine job gussying up the humble army surroundings. By the time we were done, the all-clear signal sounded and we were once again serenaded by the sounds of Jeeps and convoys heading back from wherever the men scurried to when their services were needed.

Violet produced a bottle that had miraculously made the Pacific journey unscathed and passed it to me so I could take a swig. "Congratulations, ladies—we've survived our first brush with the enemy." We each took a pull until the liquid reached the halfway mark. Then, like a generous uncle who realizes that if he gives out too much cash he won't have a dime left for rent, Violet returned the bottle to her bag and pushed it out of sight.

Outside, passing men made shadow plays on our canvas walls. Kay began to sing again, and the silhouettes paused near our tent debating whether or not it was an actual woman they were hearing. Finally, one of the men decided the only way to find out for sure, was to poke his head inside our living quarters.

"Knock, knock," he said, to warn us of his imminent intrusion. "Anyone here?" He was a towheaded boy with large blue eyes and skin so tanned by the island sun that his flesh was darker than his

khakis. As he gave us the up and down, his peepers expanded in
shock. He disappeared and we watched as his shadow excitedly
joined the other silhouettes and announced, "Real girls. Five of
them. And one of them is a dead ringer for Gilda DeVane."

Soon, each of them was popping his head in, after uttering the
requisite "knock knock" to verify that the initial scout hadn't gone
goofy from heat and stress. They stayed long enough to take us all
in, before the next man was encouraged to verify the news on his
own. At first, the sight of those heads popping in and out was a riot,
but we quickly tired of being a zoo exhibit. Besides, if we had hope
of maintaining any sort of privacy during the tour, we had to set
some ground rules.

Violet took the lead and stepped outside the tent. She was greeted
by a chorus of wolf whistles, further elevating her good mood. "All
right, boys," she said. "There are real live girls in here who need real
live privacy. If you want to see us in the flesh, let us know where a
girl can get a stiff drink and a little conversation. Now scoot, so we
can get our beauty rest."

Her approach seemed to work. Violet and Kay headed for the latrine to clean up. Gilda lay down on her cot and put on a black satin
eye mask to block out the sun streaming through the thin walls.
Jayne searched the floor to see if there was an electrical outlet at
our disposal, and I unpacked the pulps I'd brought and hunted out
a story to distract me from reality.

I was just starting a tale called "Give Me Murder" that wasn't giving me anything but a headache when another male voice sounded
his warning before sticking his head through the tent flap. Given
the distance and the angle, I was pretty sure I could throw my shoe
and nail him in the forehead.

"Out," I said. "No visitors allowed."

"I've got the mail, ma'am."

"Mail? For us?" said Jayne.

"Probably not all of you, but I do have a few pieces for Jayne
Hamilton and Rosie Winter."

Jayne and I leaped from our spots and approached him at the

flap like hungry dogs awaiting dinner. He was so taken aback by our speed that he shoved all of the mail into my hands before fleeing.

I divvied up the letters and was thrilled to see that I had three of my own. One was from my ma who, while not much for writing, wanted me to know she was thinking about me and hoped I was safe. It was a funny change from our usual correspondence. She'd never been thrilled with my chosen line of work, but when she learned that I was joining the USO it was as if she'd decided that acting was a perfectly noble profession as long as I was doing it for the military.

The second letter was an official bit of correspondence from the USO. Or so it appeared. Inside the envelope was a note from Harriet Rosenfeld, our former roomie who'd pulled strings not just to get us into the camp shows, but to see to it that we ended up with the newest crew headed for the Solomon Islands.

Rosie,

I hope you and Jayne arrived safely to your destination. It might be wise for the moment if you keep our relationship on the QT for both of our sakes (after the USO story hits, I think I'll be persona non grata). Also, keep your eyes and ears peeled for anything weird going on in camp. I'm hearing rumors about problems with supplies and I'd loved to know what's what.

Be a pal would you and destroy this letter after you read it. And remember: while I don't have to worry about the censor, you do.

Harriet

I grinned as I tore the letter into tiny pieces. Harriet and her fiancé had been working for months on an expose on USO spending, and it sounded like it would be hitting the press soon. Most people would've waited until the war was over before biting the hand that feeds them. Harriet knew that wasn't wise. After all, what if the war never ended?

The last letter was from Zelda DeMarcos, our newest roommate at our rooming house in New York:

Hiya, Rosie (and Jayne).

The place has been quiet as kittens since you two left. Belle rented out your room to a magician's assistant who we're pretty certain is making our valuables disappear. Ruby's up for a lead (of course) and seems to be quite taken with that feline you left her in charge of. I'm killing time doing an American Theatre Wing tour of the local schools, showing all the boys and girls out there what they can do to help out the red, white, and blue. The stuff's pure schlock, but the kids seem to like it, probably because they get to miss class to be with yours truly. Tell Jayne that Tony finally stopped calling. Belle let it slip that you two were West Coast–bound and I think he finally caught the hint that that meant Jayne wouldn't be calling him back any time soon.

Drop me a line and let me know how tricks are.

Zelda

"I got a letter from Zelda," I told Jayne. She hummed a response that I took to mean *Please go on.* "Belle rented our room."

"That was fast."

"And Zelda says Tony stopped calling."

She waved one of her letters at me. "That's 'cause he started writing."

"How'd he get the address?"

She shrugged. "How does he get anything?" Jayne's ex-boyfriend, Tony B., was a well-connected mobster. When she'd given Tony his walking papers, he'd had a hard time taking no for an answer. I was thrilled the two were finally kaput. Right before we left New York I'd heard from a reliable source that Tony wasn't just a criminal—he was a murderer.

Jayne sifted through her other pieces of mail. They all looked as if they were written in the same hand. If Tony had any positive qualities, he was persistent. And had excellent penmanship.

"Are you all right?" I asked.

"I thought I would've heard from Billy by now. It's been almost a month." Billy DeMille was a sailor Jayne had met at the Stage Door Canteen and developed quite a correspondence with. After all of the drama between her and Tony, I'd been thrilled to see her focusing on a man whose only record involved 78 revolutions per minute. Jayne didn't talk much about him, other than to report when he wrote and when she replied, but it was obvious the two were becoming more than mere pen pals. She was sweet on the guy, and it was impossible to believe that he wasn't feeling the same for her.

"Did you tell him we were leaving?" I asked.

"Of course."

"Maybe he forgot and wrote to the Shaw House. I'm sure his letters will show up soon."

"You're probably right," she said, though I knew she didn't really believe that. If a man in the military stopped writing you, it was usually because he no longer could.

Kay and Violet returned, their faces much paler than when they departed.

"How was the latrine?" I asked.

Violet fanned herself as though she needed to push away the scented memory that orbited her. "It's basically a glorified outhouse. Only a paper-thin shower curtain separates you from the rest of the camp."

Knowing Violet's propensity for drama, I turned to Kay to verify that it was as bad as she claimed. "It's fine," she said. "I've dealt with worse."

Her face didn't look right. I may have known Kay only a week, but it was clear that she wore her emotions like a stripper wore her brassiere—outside where everyone could see it. "Why the glum puss?" I asked.

"The bathroom isn't ours alone. We have to share it," said Violet. "Apparently, there's a large contingency of G.I. Janes that just moved in over the hill."

"Wacs? That's cozy," I said.

"Turns out Kay knows some of them. Don't you, Kay?" said Violet.

Kay nodded slowly, as though her head weighed two tons.

"Isn't that a coincidence? Are they old friends from home?" I asked.

"Not exactly," said Kay. "I was a Wac myself until a few months ago."

CHAPTER 8

The Captain of the Watch

Before we could give Kay the third, Dotty returned with another sailor in tow, a stout man with a bald head that had been burned red by the tropical sun.

"This is Spanky," he said to us. It was obvious how he'd gotten the name; he was a dead ringer for the kid from *Our Gang*. "When Spanky's not breaking hearts here on the islands, he's the radar operator on an attack transport called *The McCawley*."

"Nice to meet you, ladies. We thought you might enjoy a tour of camp." Spanky had a brash midwestern accent and the kind of body that was made for tilling soil and herding cattle. When he spoke, he didn't immediately gravitate toward Gilda. Rather his eyes landed on Violet and lingered there. She blushed beneath the weight of his attention, although I could tell that she was thrilled that, for once, she was the one being stared at.

"You have such pretty eyes," he said. The minute the words left his mouth he snapped to attention as though he'd just remembered

that they weren't the only two people there. "Er . . . this way, ladies."

We followed him out of the tent and onto the road. Kay and
Violet kept pace with Spanky, while Gilda, Jayne, and I walked with
Dotty.

"Why does everyone have a nickname?" asked Jayne.

"When you're around as many people are we are, it helps to have
shorthand to remember who everyone is and where they're from. It's
less confusing too," said Dotty.

I suspected there was more to it than that. The nicknames were
a way to distance the men from the lives they'd left behind and
help them slip into their new roles as warriors. It was a bit like giving them stage names, I suppose. The soldier on the battlefield was
a very different character from the man he'd been at home, just
as Gilda DeVane was probably a very different woman from Maria
Elizondo.

"So what was all the commotion before?" asked Gilda.

"Just a normal Tuesday afternoon in the South Pacific." His mood
was dour compared to when we'd first met him. I couldn't tell if it
was because of the events of that afternoon or if Kay's attempt to
avoid him was what was affecting him.

"I couldn't figure out where the noise was coming from," I said.
"Were they bombing Tulagi?"

"Guadalcanal, but Tulagi was in their flight path. What you heard
were some of the depth charges going off in the ocean. Water's got
a way of amplifying things."

"Was anyone hurt?" asked Gilda.

"Probably. Someone's always hurt. This is war."

Sensing his mood, Gilda looped her arm in his and pointed toward a tree in the distance. "What on earth is that brilliantly colored bird?" she asked. "I've never seen anything like it."

The two men took us to each of the major structures on the island and introduced us to the men responsible for running things
behind the scenes. We went into the commissary, the PX, the infirmary and the rec hall. Just like the ship, the island felt like a

miniature city, set up to provide the men with everything they could possibly need, save the people they'd left at home. I wondered if the department stores even sent girls around in December so the men could pick out their gifts without ever resting from their work.

Our last stop was the enlisted men's mess, where preparations for dinner were already underway. In enormous vats that seemed more appropriate for baths than food, huge quantities of potatoes were being mashed by electric implements that looked like they could also be used to break up asphalt in a pinch. While the men waited for kettles to boil and for the mixers to finish churning, they threw dice and played cards.

Most of the people working in the mess were black, Mexican, or Italian. From what Dotty and Spanky said they'd gotten their jobs not because of their skill in the kitchen but because of the color of their skin or what they'd done before the war. "That's where they put the men with records," said Spanky, his voice making it clear this information was on the QT. The men had lean, hard bodies that reminded me of the tough guys who worked for Tony B. In fact, I could swear I saw the bulge of a revolver peeking out from one of their waistbands.

"Dotty," said one fellow, whose gut professed that the food he prepared met with his own approval. A cigar dangled from his mouth, leaving a trail of ashes on the kitchen floor. I wondered how much of the cigar was going to end up in the potatoes that night. "Who're your friends?"

"These are the USO girls I was telling you about. Spanky and I are giving them the VIP tour. Ladies, this is Deacon."

He made a great show of wiping his mitts on his apron before offering one of his hands to us.

"That's an unusual name," I said.

"It ain't a name—it's my job. I'm a man of the church."

"Is the food really so bad that it requires divine intervention?"

He laughed and turned off the vat of potatoes.

"What's for dinner?" asked Jayne.

"SOS."

She cocked her head to the right. "We're having an emergency signal for dinner?"

"It stands for stuff on a shingle," he announced. Only he didn't say "stuff." As the profanity left his mouth, his black face took on a red cast. "Pardon my French, ma'am. Chipped beef on toast, potatoes, and green beans. Don't you worry though; if you're VIPs, you're not eating anything that passed through this kitchen. What's your name?"

"Jayne Hamilton," she said.

"Hey, fellows!" he called out. "Come meet Jayne Hamilton and her friends!"

In a portion of the kitchen unseen to us, but which must've housed the sinks, a tremendous clatter warned that some catastrophe had just taken place. Deacon left us to bump gums with the gamblers while he went to investigate the source of the sound. The card players had colorful nicknames like Lefty, Gris, and King that I was dying to learn the history behind. As with everyone we'd met, the men were gracious and welcoming despite the fact that I was pretty certain none of them had a cement floor or an ersatz sink in their tent.

Deacon returned with a grim look on his face. "Gris, you got a problem back there."

"Again?" Gris dropped his cards facedown. "I swear it's sabotage."

"Sabotage or not, you better mop up that floor. If the SP catches a whiff, you're cooked for good."

Gris started toward the back of the kitchen.

"Hey, wait up," said Spanky. "I'll give you a hand." He crawled under the pass-through and together they disappeared into the back.

Spanky, a cardboard box in hand, returned just as we were getting ready to leave. The contents rattled all the way back to our tent.

After the tour, we got our first week's performance schedule. Or, rather, Gilda did. She gave it a cursory look before hanging it on one of the spare nails in the tent. "The bad news is we start tomorrow. The good news is our first show isn't until ten."

We all approached the schedule and tried to figure out what the typed abbreviations meant. I thought they might be locations, but since no key was provided to help us decipher them, we decided the information wasn't important. What was crucial was the number of shows we'd be doing: three a day.

"What the deuce?" I said. "What is this—boot camp?"

"There's hours between them," said Violet. "And believe me: three shows will feel like a vacation when you see what they throw at you later on. Toward the end of my last tour we were doing seven a day."

I groaned at the news. Singing a few songs a half dozen times a day was one thing, but tap dancing? I'd be lucky if I ever walked again. More important, having a schedule of constant performances was going to make it awfully difficult to accomplish what I'd come to the islands for in the first place.

By the time 1800 hours arrived, we were starving. No one had told us what the arrangements were for dinner, so we assumed that the officers would be in the same mess area as the enlisted men, just as they'd been on the boat. We high-tailed it to the mess and paused in the doorway, too stunned by what we saw to enter. It seemed impossible that so many men were on that little island, much less inside that one Quonset hut. The room was an overwhelming hodgepodge of noise, as steel trays were put onto metal tables, bodies settled heavily onto benches, and men communicated with one another through grunts, smacks, and four-letter words. As word of our arrival spread about the room, the words the men chose to speak underwent a cleansing so drastic that many of them shut their yaps entirely. New skirts were here, and that meant they had to be on their best behavior.

Of course we weren't the only women there. The Wacs were already in the room, dining on their SOS. They were an interesting-looking crew of women. At head of the table was a blonde who wore her hair in a chignon that was pulled so tight that the skin around her hairline turned red with strain. Her uniform was pin-neat, the chicken on her hat declaring that she was the leader of the pack. And what a motley pack it was. Unlike their CO, most of the Wacs had shed their formality and adapted to their new home as best they could. Their skin was tan, hiding the yellow tint of their Atabrine, their clothing altered to better fit the island climate. Some of them had cut through their thick, black army-issue Abner shoes and removed the toe portion to create a kind of sandal to better weather the heat. Many of them wore necklaces made of beads or seeds around their necks. Still others had silver rings and bracelets fashioned, I was to learn later, from hammered Australian coins, most likely presented to them by whatever men they were currently seeing. The bizarre outfits were topped with bandanas and the hobby hats that were their signature, though even those had been adapted with swaths of mosquito netting.

It was disconcerting observing the men, comfortable in surroundings they had grown to consider their own and afraid to curse like the sailors they were. I felt like we had walked into a private club we didn't hold a membership for.

"Excuse me," said Gilda to a woman with an upturned piglike nose. "Can you tell us where the officers sit?"

The woman turned to the Wacs sitting around her, and they shared a private giggle. "No," she said, her tone a caricature of Gilda's careful enunciation. "I cannot."

We backed away from their table. As we scanned the room, the Wac CO's cold eyes watched our every move. I'm not sure I could blame her for her attitude. In a matter of seconds we had deposed them by doing little more than wearing civvies and counting a certain famous actress among us. It had to chafe her but good.

"You're the USO girls, right?" A man appeared at our side as we struggled to figure out if we should just grab the first empty table we saw.

"That's us," said Violet.

"Then you ladies are in the wrong place. You're supposed to be eating at the high commissioner's house."

We followed him as quickly as we could out of the mess and into an awaiting Jeep. He sped down a dusty road that made no concession to our freshly styled hair and painted faces. Within minutes we were at the high commissioner's mansion, a beautiful home on a hill that seemed as out of place as diapers on a monkey. Hyacinths and rosebushes hugged the building and filled the air with their rich, sweet scent. Inside, ornate English furnishings tried to pretend the building was on a very different island in the same way that a carefully rendered set could convince an audience that they were in eighteenth-century France rather than a dingy little theater in Greenwich Village. After seeing our own living conditions and the sparse accommodations shared by the natives, it was impossible not to view this joint without a little resentment.

We were ushered into a lavish dining room where the men already assembled stood to greet us.

"Sorry we're late," said Gilda.

The tables were set with linen and china, imprinted with military insignia. Chairs were pushed aside to accommodate the five of us, each scattered among the officers to make sure we bumped gums with as many of them as possible. I sat between a captain in the Royal Air Force and an American with hair so blond it appeared white. As soon as my bottom met the seat, a native man appeared and deposited a plate on the table in front of me.

Just like on the ship, the food was much better than I could've imagined. After hearing about what the enlisted men were eating, and having been subjected to such military favorites as SPAM, it was disorienting to eat better than I ever had at home. Each of us was given a steak, baked potatoes, and a variety of fresh vegetables drowning in butter. Real coffee circulated the table in silver urns, along with what looked to be some sort of fruit punch.

"Pardon me, but what is this?" I asked the Brit as the serving man poured some into my glass.

"Flavored water. The local supply has bacteria in it. And the men don't like the taste or the color of the stuff the Yanks bring in, so they add colored tablets to disguise both."

What would the military think of next? "Are all the officers' meals like this?"

He cut into his steak and stabbed a cube onto his fork. "Usually it's a sight better, but the air raid cut preparation time in half." He looked at my plate. "Don't you eat meat?"

I'd pushed the steak to the side. A few months before I'd found out exactly what was in the black-market beef so many New York restaurants were buying, and the knowledge had killed my once-voracious appetite for flesh. Even though the USDA had put new regulations in place to make sure the meat we ate had once mooed, I knew better than to trust them. "Nope," I told the Brit. "You want it?"

"You're getting me on." I assured him I wasn't. He took my meat and paid for it with a hefty portion of his potato. While I devoured the food, the other officers kept up the conversation. They may not have had as colorful language as the enlisted men, but the topics they chose to discuss in front of us were anything but sanitized. They told us tales about the kidney-wrecking PT boats, missions gone awry, and the weapons employed by the Axis and Allies, which had amusing names like hedgehog, bazooka, and bouncing betties. Based on the monikers, they sounded quaint and charming until you remembered that this was stuff designed to kill people.

As one course made way for another, they debated the ongoing problems with submarine torpedoes and what it would take to improve the Mark 14. The first problem was its magnetic exploder, an issue I couldn't exactly follow, but merited spirited yapping. The second issue was that the device involved some sort of drinkable alcohol to power it. The men onboard the submarines had fallen into the nasty habit of drinking the stuff, leaving the torpedoes with so little fuel that they fizzled and died upon ignition.

"Wait a second," I said. "They're drinking their weapons?"

"They call it torpedo juice," said one of the naval officers. He was from Chicago, which morphed his *th*'s into *d*'s and did a number on most of his vowel sounds. "You mix it with a little grapefruit juice to make a cocktail they call a pink lady."

"But why would they do that?" asked Kay.

"They're stuck on a submarine in the middle of a war," said Violet. "Why wouldn't they?"

The conclusion drawn by the men assembled was that they would have to replace the drinkable alcohol with something toxic to discourage pilfering. Personally, I thought a better tactic might be to end the days of the navy being dry. At least, that way, nobody ran the risk of dying for a drink.

The atmosphere in this officer mess was drastically different from what we'd faced on the boat. There I'd felt a camaraderie with the men, but here there seemed to be a constant, quiet reminder that they were the ones in charge and we were there only at their pleasure. In fact despite the coy looks and careful use of manners, I had a strong impression that they would rather we weren't there at all.

There was something else though. After being in New York during two years of war, I had grown used to being part of a world where being a broad meant something very different than it had for my mother and grandmother. The war had brought a change to the States. Women were finding themselves in more and more important roles that had previously been open only to men. We were traveling the streets alone, working in munitions factories, running corporations, and taking jobs, even when there were children at home that we also needed to tend to. Being among the military made it clear that what we had experienced was a civilian phenomenon only. In the world of the armed forces, women were still second-class citizens.

Gilda sat on the other side of the American I was seated next to. She feigned polite interest as he changed the subject from torpedoes to tales of naval espionage. There was something about him that I didn't like, aside from his mature Aryan good looks, and I spent much of the meal eavesdropping on him, trying to figure out what it was that was bothering me. He was arrogant, that was flat, but then you could say the same about half the actors I knew.

I caught the Brit's eye and gestured him over to me. "Who is he?" I asked.

He leaned in close enough that his voice tickled my ear. "Rear Admiral Nathanial Blake. The men call him Late Nate. As the senior-most American officer, he's the king of Tulagi."

I tried to make sense of the fruit salad on Blake's shoulder, but it was just a bunch of pretty ribbons to my eyes. He launched into a tale about an enemy capture that occurred days before our arrival. They had ambushed three Japanese on foot near the Quonset huts where the supplies were kept.

The other women were hanging on his every word.

"What do you do with them after you capture them?" asked Jayne. "Do you torture them to get their secrets?"

Blake turned toward her and smiled a warm, reassuring grin that I wouldn't have believed if it had been on my own face. "After they are captured, they are interrogated, and then as prisoners of war they're detained at a facility at the other end of the island. We certainly don't torture anyone, and it's not necessary. Trust me: to them a warm bed and a nice meal is worse than any torture."

That caught my attention. "How so?"

His lips were freakishly thin. In fact, it almost looked like he didn't have any at all. "The Japs believe that being captured is the greatest dishonor they can suffer. They would much rather be killed in the line of battle and suffer a heroic death. Their people won't exactly hail their homecoming when they learn they were held by us, and they certainly won't be impressed when they hear how well we treated them."

"So you're being nice to them to get them in worse trouble later on," I said.

He turned his attention to me, his eyes never blinking. "The Japs are savages, plain and simple. They're raised that way. They have no regard for human life. If they wish to punish their own, I say let them."

The American papers were lousy with stories about the savagery of the Japanese. We were told tales of how they would eat any Allied airman who landed on Japanese soil, and there were whispers of the terrible atrocities they'd done to the Chinese prior to the outbreak

of the war. Just a few weeks before, the *Times* had run a piece trying to dissect just how hard the Japanese were compared to soldiers
from other nations. While they dismissed the theory that the Japanese were less afraid of death than other cultures, they described
the Japanese as being well trained, uniquely suited to the South
Pacific terrain, and free of cowardice. Lest it seem that the writer felt
impartial to this one particular Axis nation, in the end he concluded
that the Japanese weren't any tougher than other soldiers but that
they were less intelligent, which made them much more susceptible
to their training, and possessed an egotism, rudeness, and brutality
that was unique to their culture.

The piece had been illustrated by a cartoon depicting a Japanese
soldier as King Kong. I wanted to believe it was propaganda on our
part, trying to indict the enemy by showing how they weren't even
capable of playing fair. And perhaps some of it was. But when you
read about the things they did, it was hard to dismiss claims that
this particular enemy was worse than most.

Still, despite my own moments of war-induced racism, and I'd
had plenty of them, I didn't like the way Late Nate—and the press—
painted all the Japanese with the same brush. If I knew there were
Americans who were capable of evil—and I'd certainly learned that
there were—didn't it follow that there were good Germans and good
Japanese? Besides, we were hearing just as many awful things about
the Russians, who'd also held out on agreeing to the terms decided at
the Geneva Convention. And we considered the Ruskies our *friends.*

I wanted to express my confusion to him, but before I could, he
relaxed his smile. His eyes seemed to change color as his expression
altered. No longer were they blue; they were as gray as the sky right
before a heavy rain. "Don't tell me you're a Jap lover." It wasn't a
joke. He really wanted to diagnose what ailed me, and I was certain
that if I so much as hinted at empathizing with the Japanese, something very bad would happen.

"I'm not anything," I said.

He folded his hands and placed them on the table before him.
"Have you ever heard of the Rape of Nanking?"

"No. Who was she?"

"She wasn't a who, she was a they. The Japanese slaughtered hundreds of thousands of Chinese in the city of Nanking. They raped women no matter what their age and littered the city with grotesque souvenirs of their crimes."

"Why?" I asked.

"Because they could. And what about the Bataan Death March? Have you heard of that?"

"Yes." I felt incredibly small. I longed to climb under the table and remain there until the end of the meal.

"That time it was our men they killed, forcing many of them to walk until they died of hunger and exhaustion. They were the lucky ones." He smiled, keeping his voice at such an even keel that I had to wonder if I wasn't imagining his menace. "And yet you still wonder if it's all right if we let the Japanese suffer at their own hands?"

"That's not what I meant."

"Have you captured a lot of them?" asked Jayne. I looked her way, but she was careful to keep her eyes on the rear admiral.

"Not on Tulagi. Ever since we took the island, I don't think there's been more than a handful found here."

"Why do you think the ones you captured were here?" asked Gilda.

"They claimed they were deserters. They had satchels with them, though, so I'm pretty certain they were doing supply recon."

"What's the matter? Did they run out of toilet paper?" asked Violet.

"Actually, that's not too far off," said another man. This one had a pencil-thin reddish mustache that made him look like a nineteenth-century rake. "There's an embargo on Japanese cargo ships. Their ships can't get here, so they can't get what they need. We think they're sneaking onto the island and taking it."

"Think?" asked Kay.

"Well, there's no proof, other than the missing supplies. And the quantity has sharply decreased in recent months, which you wouldn't think would be the case if the enemy was plundering. The only other explanation is that someone internally is taking them. In fact, the Wac CO thought—"

"I certainly hope you're not suggesting that woman's theory was accurate," said Blake. "There was no evidence that our men had anything to do with the missing supplies. And, frankly, given that she chose to leave here, it's clear even she realized her opinion didn't have merit."

An uncomfortable silence fell over the room. Red Mustache swallowed hard and then took a long drink of colored water. Across the table, Kay stiffened. Did she know the Wac they were talking about?

"What sort of stuff is missing?" asked Jayne.

Red Mustache looked at Blake for permission to answer the question. Blake gave him a subtle nod. "Some food, but most of it is medical supplies. Morphine. Bandages. Antibiotics."

"And that," said Blake, "is exactly the sort of stuff that would be of most value to the Japanese."

Yeah, I thought. Or a dope addict.

CHAPTER 9

Soldiers and Women

"What was that all about?" asked Jayne. We opted to ankle back to camp from the high commissioner's house, whereas the others waited for the Jeep to return.

"I don't know. Rear Admiral Fancypants has it in for me, that's for sure."

"He's dangerous, Rosie. You don't need to be making enemies."

"I know. Believe me, I know. I'm keeping my trap shut from here on out." We hooked arms and took the road toward camp. We passed groves of cacao plants that were dotted with the brightly colored pods that would eventually be harvested. All around us the skinny trunks of palm trees jutted out of the soil at odd angles, forming triangles with the ground. It seemed so strange to see the botanical symbol for Hollywood here in its natural habitat. Shouldn't there be a movie premiere happening around here somewhere? "Pipe this," I said. "What if the Wac he was talking about was Irene Zinn?"

"The dead girl?"

The sun was setting, turning the sky a brilliant medley of orange, pink, and red, the colors blending as gently as the brushstrokes on a watercolor. "According to the *Queen of the Ocean*'s newsletter, she was a captain stationed in the Solomon Islands."

"But surely there are other Wacs who were stationed here who resigned?"

"Probably, but I just can't get her out of my head. It can't be a coincidence that she's dead and we're here, right? I feel like I'm supposed to find out what happened to her."

We made it off the hill and onto the main road. Even from a distance away, we could hear the activity taking place at camp: men laughing, music playing, Jeep engines purring as they drove over uneven surfaces.

"What about Kay?" asked Jayne. "If she knows the Wacs who are stationed here, she was probably stationed here too."

"Blake doesn't strike me as a subtle guy. If Kay was the squeaky wheel, he would've pointed his finger at her and said so."

Jayne struggled to keep pace with me. I sometimes forgot that her gams were only two-thirds the length of my own. "She could've known Irene."

"Maybe." That would certainly explain her behavior when she found out Irene was dead.

"It's strange she didn't say anything before now," said Jayne.

"About being a Wac? She's pretty shy," I said. "We're lucky she's started making eye contact."

Jayne hummed a response that I couldn't quite read.

"What's got your goat?" I asked.

She took a deep breath and set her shoulders back. "I heard something. Back on the boat." I raised an eyebrow, urging her to go on. "Kay had her physical before me, and they left the door open. I didn't mean to eavesdrop."

"Stop with the justification and give me the dirt."

Jayne stopped walking. "When the doctor asked her if she'd ever been pregnant, she said yes. Five months ago."

"Did she say if she had the baby?"

"No, but her tone pretty much implied she hadn't."

"Wow. So I guess we know why she isn't a Wac anymore."

We arrived at camp. As we headed homeward, we peeked inside each tent we passed. It was amazing the ways the men occupied themselves. Some played poker. Some napped. Some listened to baseball games being broadcast all the way from the States. Some made primitive furniture from scrap wood, working the piece as if it was an antique constructed of the finest mahogany. Many of them wrote letters that never really told what was going on, since they knew the censor would delete it anyway.

All of them left their tents open, encouraging one another to drop by to kill time. Inside were chess sets awaiting a new game, posters of Hollywood stunners like Gilda, and photos of wives and children propped up in frames that had long before had the glass broken out of them.

Had one of these tents been Jack's? Probably, though I imagine he spent most of his time at sea.

Jayne squeezed my arm. "Have you thought about how you want to start looking for him?"

"Jack? I suppose I should just start asking people." Somewhere a tinny radio broadcast a woman speaking English tinged with a strong Asian accent. "I have a feeling he was here."

"On Tulagi?"

"Yeah. I don't know why, but the moment I stepped off the boat I just got the sense that we were in the right place."

Jayne swatted a fly away from her face. "What's with you and the feelings? First Irene, now Jack?"

"I don't know. Maybe it's this place. It's like I'm finally in touch with my instincts here. At home everything was static, but here I can finally hear the radio." A wolflike dog trotted past us, his fur caked with mud. He gave us the once-over and, deciding we were friends not foes, continued on his way. A whistle rang out and he stopped in his tracks. With a look that I assumed was canine reluctance, he turned around and headed back the way he came.

"Where are you ladies headed?" A voice stopped us in our path, and I immediately feared we'd broken a rule nobody had bothered to share with us yet.

"Nowhere in particular," I said. "We're just walking." I couldn't quite make out our companion in the setting sun, though our four-legged usurper had joined him.

"It's me. Spanky," he said. Our tour guide from that afternoon stepped out of the shadows. His bald head reflected the setting sun the way a crystal ball reflected the future.

"Hiya," I said. "Who's your friend?"

"This here is Mac." He winked at us. "Short for Macarthur." I had a feeling the general wouldn't be flattered to find that this scrawny little beast had been named in his honor. At the sound of his name, Mac wagged his pitiful excuse for a tail, a set of military dog tags tinkling around his neck. He was a mishmash of German shepherd and a dozen other breeds that all added up to generic dog. His tongue was too long for his mouth, and the scruff around his snoot was in desperate need of a trim. He smelled like the grave, but there was something about him that said he was a good egg.

"We have a cat named Churchill," said Jayne.

"Had," I corrected her. "He's Ruby's problem now."

"No sir," said Spanky. "Macarthur and Churchill? I'd love to see what would happen if we got the two of them together."

I hated to tell him that Mac wouldn't stand a chance. Our Churchill had the fire but lacked the diplomacy of his namesake.

"Rumor has it you girls are looking for a cocktail and some conversation."

Jayne and I looked at each other. "Twist our arms," she said.

Spanky offered us his wings, and we each took one. He led us down a winding path that grew closer and closer to the ocean, as Mac followed on our heels. At the end of it, practically teetering off the edge of a cliff, was a wooden deck shaded by a roof made of palm fronds. Torches mounted on poles framed the space and illuminated the edges with flickering flames. At one end was a stage outfitted, remarkably, with a piano. At the other were mismatched tables and chairs, where enlisted men were already gathered, saluting one another with beer bottles in their hands. A phonograph played a tune whose volume varied depending on which way the wind blew. It took a couple of sea changes before I figured out that we were listening to Kate Smith singing "I Blew a Kiss in the Ocean."

"Wow," said Jayne. "How the heck did all of this get here?"

"Navy ingenuity," said Spanky. "If it needs to be done, we find a way to do it."

Strangely, more than anything else, the makeshift dance hall made it clear how complex the logistics of war really were. It was a matter not only of moving men to a remote island nation but also all the things those bodies needed to survive. For some reason, even after seeing all the activity at the port of San Francisco, I hadn't pictured the enormity of it all. In my mind, a ship arrived, boys with guns hopped off, did what they needed to do, and sailed away. There was none of this need for toilets, mess halls, cantinas, and pianos.

Of course I knew otherwise. The newspapers were terribly fond of reporting statistics of how much stuff it took to supply the troops. Because of the news articles we knew it took seven hundred thousand different items to outfit the forces, from darning needles to tanks. A single soldier needed a ton of supplies a month to adequately do his job. No wonder the Japanese were sneaking on the island and taking our stuff. We were better supplied than the local A & P.

There was something terribly sad about seeing this little bit of America plopped down in the middle of the jungle. These men had to eke out their own little world, and rather than adapting to the environment and customs of wherever they landed, they tried to make the place they were trapped in like the home they were missing. Even I could tell what a poor substitute it was.

Spanky released us from his grip and pointed out a table that was currently unoccupied. As we made our way toward it, the other men hollered out greetings, hailing Spanky as a savior for showing up with two dames in tow.

"How did Spanky lure you here?" one of them asked.

"Spanky had nothing to do with it," I said. "I only agreed to come at Mac's urging." We told the other men where three more women could be found, and a group of them took off to try to fetch them. We were offered a variety of libations: from plain Coca-Colas in bottles to beer donated by other branches of the armed forces, including those from other countries, and Japanese lagers and sake that were considered spoils of war. As we mulled over our choices, Spanky took me by the elbow and brought me to the cardboard box he'd retrieved in the mess tent. He lifted the lid just enough to show me jars full of clear liquid.

"If none of that's to your liking, we've also got jungle juice, kava, night fighter, and plonk." Given what we'd heard about the navy's tendency to drink liquids intended as fuel, we opted for something delivered in a sealed and labeled bottle. In a matter of moments Jayne and I each had a lukewarm bottle of beer in our hands and a cluster of men at our side.

I tossed back the first beer and eagerly liberated a second. For one dizzying moment I kept up five conversations at once, but the complexities of figuring out which person had asked which question was making my head spin.

Word of our arrival spread fast, and soon a wolf line formed of men clamoring to jaw, dance, or just exist with us. Violet, Kay, and Gilda arrived, and the attention momentarily shifted to the fresh meat.

I wasn't a beer drinker—I limited my booze to the truly potent kind—but the combination of heat, exhaustion, and a long week of teetotaling was giving that libation a curious power over me. I soon found myself dancing cheek to cheek with one sailor after another, so lightheaded and relaxed that I didn't even patrol their hands as we moved across the floor. Eventually I begged for a breather and gratefully slumped into a chair. Before I'd been there ten seconds, Violet joined me.

"Hiya," I said. "Having fun?"

"How couldn't I?" She bit her lip and her wide grin disintegrated. "That was some scene at dinner."

"Yeah. Sorry about that. I promised Jayne I'd close my head from now on." I mimed locking my mouth and throwing away the key.

"Now don't go overreacting. It was kind of nice to have someone else be the center of attention for once."

The beer was begging me to talk, even though I knew it would be better not to. "Do you still have a bee in your bonnet about her? I thought you'd made your peace."

"I tried. Believe me, I tried." She took a drink from her flask and chased it with a gulp of Coca-Cola. What would she do when she ran out of booze? Start drinking people's blood? "But then she makes little remarks like how you and Kay faked being sick to get out of rehearsal and I can't help but get my dander up."

"She didn't say that."

She fished a gasper out of her cigarette case. "Right, and she didn't say that she's known dogs who were smarter than Jayne either."

My hands involuntary contracted into fists. "Watch yourself, Violet. I'm three sheets to the wind."

She raised her hands. "Don't shoot the messenger. I just want you to know what's going on when you're not in the room. That's all. Like it or not, she's not all sweetness and sunshine."

"Thanks for the tip." I left her alone and headed for the dance floor. Spanky had just left Jayne. Before he could exchange my pal for a beer, I grabbed his hand and pulled him back onto the floor.

"Dance with me, Spanky."

He sighed dramatically and tipped his head back. "I love a woman who takes control."

"Easy, sport, I'm just using you to get out of an awkward conversation."

He spun me to the left before rolling me back toward him. As the room passed in a blur I could see Mac sitting on the edge of the dance floor, wagging his tail to the rhythm of the music.

"So how'd you meet Mac?'

"Found him on the beach in Guadalcanal. He was a scrawny little guy, destined to become a meal if someone didn't take charge. We made him *The McCawley*'s mascot and we've been inseparable ever since."

"Then how come he didn't join us on our tour today?"

He leaned into me. His breath had a sharp antiseptic smell that I suspected came from drinking ample amounts of plonk. "He was in training."

"Let me guess: he's a code breaker."

"Close: we're training him to be a Wag. You know, sniff out bombs and booby traps and the like. If he's going to bunk with us, he's got to earn his keep like everyone else. I won't tolerate feather merchants in my crew." The music picked up and he swung me around with much more grace than I would've thought possible. "So what's Uncle Sugar like these days?"

"The same I suppose, but with less stuff. The things you want they don't make anymore, and the stuff they have they expect everyone to ration."

"What don't we have anymore?"

I fought a yawn. Spanky was a hell of a nice guy, but sleep was starting to sound a lot nicer. "Chewing gum, Scotch tape, marshmallows."

"That's okay. I didn't care for any of that anyway."

I lifted my hand to silence him. "Hold on: I'm not done yet. They've limited our canned goods, meat, shoes, and dairy."

"No meat?"

"No good meat." I thought of my last ill-fated attempt to eat what I thought was roast beef and shuddered. "And don't even think about getting an omelet."

"Yikes."

"Now can I ask you a question?"

"Shoot."

"Do you know a man named Jack Castlegate?"

He spun me again. Mac let out a bark of approval. "Is he navy?"

"Yeah. A lieutenant."

"What crew?"

"Not a clue."

"You do know we don't all know each other, right?"

I could feel myself blush. I really was naïve, wasn't I? "Still, I figured it was worth a shot. I heard he was out here in the islands. He's MIA and I thought maybe that would've gotten him a little attention."

Spanky's brow furrowed. It wasn't hard to imagine what he'd look like as an old man. Assuming he survived that long. "So who is he to you?"

"He was my boyfriend. Now he's my ex."

He shook his head. "Boy, that's a snafu."

My words were slurring when I talked, and I didn't think it completely irrational to worry that my thoughts were doing the same. "Huh?"

"Snafu," he repeated.

I raised an eyebrow. "Here's how it works when I don't know something: I still don't know it, even though you've said it twice."

He gave me an "Aw shucks" grin. "Sorry. I forget that some of the stuff we know because we're in the military. It's getting harder and harder for me to remember what I came here with and what I'll leave here with."

"So what's it mean?" I asked.

He blushed. "I can't tell you. You're a lady."

"So now I'm a lady?" I leaned into him and lowered my voice. "Don't worry, you won't shock my virgin ears."

He tilted his head to the left. "All right. It means 'situation normal all fouled up.'" Only he didn't say fouled.

The profanity caught me off guard. "I can see why you prefer to use the acronym." It was a good one too. Snafu was the best description of war—and relationships—I'd heard yet.

"I did you a favor—now will you do me one?" he said.

"Shoot."

"Tell me about your friend."

"Gilda? She's sweet. Not at all like you'd think she'd be."

"Not Gilda." His eyes danced sharply to the left. "The other one."

I scanned the crowd trying to figure out who he was talking about. "Violet? You're asking about Violet?"

"Absolutely. She's one of the prettiest women I've ever seen. What's she like?"

It depends on the day of the week. "Funny. A real cutup."

"Does she have a fellow?"

Heaven help us if she did. "Not that's she's mentioned. In fact, I get the distinct impression she's hoping to meet someone here."

He looked at her with such longing you would've thought he was the dog instead of Mac.

"Here." I dragged Spanky over to where she was sitting and held out his hand. "Violet, you remember our tour guide, Spanky? He'd liked to dance with you."

I didn't stick around to see what happened. I was thinking about sneaking out when I saw Dotty arrive. His eyes landed on Kay, who was dancing with another man. When he saw her with someone else, his face fell, and he looked ready to turn tail and leave.

"Hey, Dotty!" I got his attention and he moved my way. "Got time for a dance?"

Again he looked toward Kay, who showed no sign of leaving her partner. "Sure," he told me, "that'd be swell."

Despite the bum knee, he did a fine job on the slow song. He held me at a distance, like we were at a school dance being monitored by habit-wearing proctors.

"So why do they call you Dotty?" I asked.

He rolled his eyes. "Before the war I was dead set on being a writer. Had some short stories and poems published here and there, and the fellows started calling me Dorothy Parker. That evolved into Dotty and the nickname stuck."

"And now you're a journalist?"

"I wanted some way to help out after I was discharged. This seemed like a good way to use my skills." His eyes left me and once again made their way over to Kay.

"You keep that up and I'm going to get my feelings hurt."

His attention snapped back to me. "Sorry."

"You can make it up to me by answering a question. Since you've been here, have you heard anything about a navy lieutenant named Jack Castlegate?"

"The name's familiar, but I don't know why."

"He's MIA," I said. "And prior to that, there was some sort of falling out with his CO. There was another guy in his unit—a Corporal M. Harrington. Everyone called him Charlie. He supposedly committed suicide a few months ago."

"You sure about that?"

"Absolutely. My source is good."

"No, I mean about Charlie being in his unit. Corporal's not a navy rank."

Could I have gotten it wrong? The military was an elusive world of colors, titles, and insignia to me. But it didn't seem likely that I would misremember the rank of the man who'd told me Jack was missing.

"Well, if he wasn't navy, what would he be?"

"Army or marine. Assuming he was American."

"He was. He definitely was. He was from Charleston, South Carolina."

His eyes gravitated away from me. I followed his gaze. Kay was gone. "I can ask around if you like."

"That would be swell."

We finished out the song and went our separate ways. Between the beer, the heat, and my aching feet, I wanted nothing more than a little time out. I found a table at the back of the platform and eased my way into a chair.

How could I have screwed up Charlie Harrington's rank? I had so few details about Jack's life in the navy. I hated to think I wasn't keeping the meager things I knew straight.

A sound like a drumroll begged for my attention. Mac was sitting at my side. He nuzzled my hand with his cold nose, and I patted his filthy head out of gratitude. Together, we watched as Spanky and Violet continued to dance, their laughter rising above the music.

They weren't the only ones on the dance floor. At some point while I was dancing, the Wacs had arrived, and now the room was alive with couples talking and hoofing. Despite the fact that we were all there to do the same thing, there was a curious divide between them and us. They were the girls who'd been here for dozens of nights before. We were the new blood who hadn't yet tired of the boy's jokes, battled their clumsy feet, or fought off their well-intentioned advances. And yet, even if we were more interesting by virtue of the fact that we were new, I could tell that the boys viewed the Wacs as a more comfortable alternative to the five actresses in civvies. They were familiar to them.

"Having fun?" Jayne arrived at my side with a beer for me in hand.

"It's a kick. How 'bout you?"

She told me about her various dance partners while I watched the blonde with the tight chignon take a seat a few feet from us. She must've sensed me watching her because she turned around and glared at me. I decided to return the favor.

"What are you doing?" asked Jayne.

"Giving her a taste of what she's serving."

"What if she has a gun?"

"She's a Wac, Jayne. She's lucky she has a uniform."

"Still . . ."she said. "It wouldn't kill us to be nice."

"Speak for yourself."

Jayne raised an eyebrow to let me know she was planning on doing exactly that. She grabbed my arm, pulled me to my feet, and dragged me toward the woman's table. "Hiya," she said. "I'm Jayne and this is my friend Rosie. You're in the Women's Auxiliary Army Corps, right?"

"It's just the Women's Army Corps now," she said with the tone of someone who had grown tired of correcting the pronunciation of her long and unwieldy foreign name.

"I didn't think they'd changed it yet," I said. Before we left the States, there was a rumble that the name change would be effective that summer.

"They haven't, but they will, and the sooner everyone gets used to it, the better."

As much as I hated her attitude, I could empathize with the reason behind it. It wasn't just about losing a vowel; when the WAACs lost their A, they'd be gaining full rank, pay, and status.

"So where are you from?" asked Jayne.

"Gary, Indiana."

A memory bounced about my noggin. "So was that girl they found in the water in San Francisco," I said. "Her name was Irene Zinn. Did you know her?"

"No."

"Are you sure? She was a former Wac captain stationed out here."

"I'm positive."

Despite the woman's short, clipped answers and lack of interest in anything we were saying, Jayne rambled on. "We're from New York. We're in the USO camp shows."

That caught the gal's interest. She had assumed we were just garden-variety patriotutes.

"We're primarily actresses," said Jayne. "Although Rosie and I are going to be tap dancing in the show."

A strange sound left the woman. Part exhale, part laugh, it was subtle enough that to someone not hunting out signs of her obvious disdain, it might have looked like a suppressed sneeze.

"So what do you do here?" I asked. My knowledge of WAC activity was pretty unimpressive. I assumed they performed those womanly jobs that men didn't want to do—secretarial work and the like—to free up soldiers to fight. In fact the organization seemed like nothing more than a way to give skirts something to do to delude them into thinking they were helping out the war.

"We're code breakers," she said.

I raised an eyebrow. "Really?"

"Really."

I was intrigued. She may have been rude, but this woman was vastly more interesting than I'd given her credit for. "So you get to intercept enemy correspondence and figure out what it says?"

She nodded.

"Rosie wrote a code once," said Jayne. "It made it past the war censors and everything." I cringed at Jayne's proud announcement of my accomplishment. My code had been nothing more than a simplistic attempt to write to Charlie Harrington to find out what had happened to Jack. It was hardly going to change the course of the war.

"Well, aren't you clever?" said blond chignon.

"It was nothing. Really," I said.

Her mouth became a perfect horizontal line. If we'd had a ruler, we could've used her face to map out right angles. "Then I guess you're lucky that I didn't have to break it."

I pulled Jayne back to our table. "That was rude," said Jayne.

"You shouldn't have told her about the code," I said.

"Why not?"

"Because . . . you just shouldn't have." I was embarrassed but not because of the way the woman had treated us. She had a role—an important one that might well help determine how the war was going to turn out. She had to think that the two of us were nothing but a silly bit of fluff.

A man approached the blond commander and extended his hand in an invitation to dance. "Did you ever think about enlisting?" I asked Jayne.

"No. Why?"

"I was just thinking about the posters that are everywhere back home. You know the ones that say things like food or free labor will win the war. Notice how there aren't any that say 'tap dancing is the key to victory'?"

"Hollywood and Broadway have done a lot of good things."

"But will any of it really matter in the end?"

Jayne sighed and crossed her arms. "Food and labor are just as likely to fail."

The blonde headed toward the dance floor. Her voice rose in imitation of Jayne's high-pitched squeak. "It got past the war censors and everything."

I made it two steps before Jayne grabbed my arm. I spun back and looked at her in disbelief. How could she possibly keep me from giving that broad a piece of my mind? "She deserves to be put right and you know it."

"It doesn't matter," said Jayne.

"She was aping you."

"So? Maybe I deserved to be aped."

"You were trying to be nice."

She shrugged. "Maybe she didn't see it that way."

The party ended around two a.m. By then we were all so ossified that the only hope we had of finding our tent was if someone took us by the arm and walked us to it. Fortunately, there were plenty of offers to do just that.

"Where's Gilda?" I asked as our entourage started down the hill, following the small globe of light provided by a military torch. Never had I been anywhere so dark. Even during the dim-out, Manhattan had a faint glow about it that made it possible for you to navigate the streets.

"I haven't seen her for hours," said Violet. "Last time I saw her she was with that reporter."

"Dotty?" asked Kay.

"That's the one," said Violet.

Even in the darkness I could tell that Kay wasn't happy with that answer. "What was she doing with him?"

"Hell if I know," said Violet. "But they sure looked friendly together."

CHAPTER 10

The Life of an Actress

It was a good thing I was drunk that first night. Had I been sober, I doubt I would've been able to fall asleep. It was so hot in the tent it was hard to breathe. But the temperature wasn't the worst of it. Unlike the city where I could depend on the noise diminishing to a dull roar once the sun went down, the jungle came alive at night, screeching at increasingly louder volumes. It wouldn't have been so bad if I knew what was making the noise, but the unknown factor lifted the sounds from annoying to terrifying. For a while the four of us lay in the dark trying to match each cry with its maker,. Although we could easily identify the more commonplace animals, there were many we city folk hadn't heard before. I pictured cheetahs, snakes, and magical, mythical creatures surrounding our tent waiting for just the right opportunity to launch their attack.

If nature could make my heart pitter-patter with fear, I could only imagine what seeing the enemy would do.

Of course the noise wasn't restricted to the outdoors. Inside, we heard shuffling that suggested our rodent friend had returned for a visit. Despite our canvas walls and the mosquito netting we'd been provided, insects buzzed around our heads, fighting for the right to feed. Some even made their way under the netting, forcing us to jolt ourselves out of near sleep with painful slaps as we smacked mosquitoes, blue flies, and God knows what else.

Eventually, exhaustion won out, and I came to accept that the jungle wasn't trying to scare us. It was singing its lullaby.

Gilda was there when the loudspeaker got us up the next morning, playing the bugle calls that were instructions for the entire camp to get up and grab chow. I struggled to find my wristwatch in the glow of not-quite-morning, but my efforts were for naught.

"What time is it?" I moaned.

"O'dark thirty," said Kay. The other women were still passed out. Violet had her M1 helmet over her head to block out the coming day. Jayne wore an eye mask and the earmuffs she thought she'd need to weather the South Pacific winter. I envied her wisdom in bringing them.

Since no one else was making a move to get up, I buried my own noggin beneath my pillow and tried to sleep through the sounds of the rest of the camp rising. I was doing a pretty good job nodding off when a second horn blast sounded right outside our tent entrance.

"Show yourself, bugler!" said Violet.

"Time to get up, ladies," said a young man who had no idea how close to death he was.

"Our first show isn't until ten," moaned the lump that used to be Gilda.

"But the plane to get you there is leaving at oh-eight-hundred."

"The what to what?" asked Gilda.

"The plane," repeated the voice. I was fairly certain its owner possessed horns and a forked tale. "Unless you ladies would prefer to swim."

"All right already. We're getting up," I said.

"The Jeep will be outside the enlisted mess in an hour to take you to the airstrip."

The voice and its horn left us to the ugly business of waking up. Jayne was still blissfully unaware of what was going on around her, so I poked her leg until she finally roused.

"How could you sleep through all that?" asked Violet.

Jayne removed an earmuff. "What?"

"I said how can you sleep through all that?"

"I'm from New York," said Jayne. "I've slept through worse."

We showered, got dressed, and packed up our costumes in record time. With our bags in tow, we headed out in search of java at the enlisted men's mess, all of us too exhausted to make conversation. Breakfast was finished and the camp was alive with inspections and roll calls. I saw some of the boys we'd danced with the night before standing stone-faced before their commanding officers, their bodies showing no sign of the wear and tear that was making us moan. I wanted someone to pay for my aching head and tortured feet, but so far it looked like I only had myself to blame.

Inside the tents, we passed were men making up their beds, polishing their shoes, and doing all the other busywork that gave shape to their day. The Wacs marched in formation before us, led by the girl with the blond chignon. As she shouted orders to her weary unit, her bun bounced along like the ball you were supposed to follow while singing along to the lyrics in cartoon shorts. I closed an eye to see how easy it would be to get my sights on her. Then, with a gun made of my hand, I fired a shot.

We barely had any time to grab a cup of joe before the Jeep arrived to take us to the airstrip. It turned out it was a good thing we had empty stomachs. As the plane that served as our transport danced over the water before swooping through the air, my stomach mimicked our motions a moment too late: rising when it should've been falling, banking when it should've been horizontal. I'd never been on a plane before, and the excitement was quickly replaced by fear. How on earth were we supposed to stay airborne? I spent most of

the journey digging my fingers into the seat in front of me, pretending that Jayne's reports of what she could see out of the window
weren't making everything much, much worse. I did my darndest
to keep my agony to myself. If Violet was right and Gilda had made
comments about my digestive discomfort, I didn't want to add any
more fuel to her fire.

At last we arrived on an island that Jayne described as having a
real live volcano on it. From the small landing strip, we took a Jeep
into camp, where the troops were already convening in preparation
for our performance.

"So how was your night?" Kay asked Gilda as we drove into camp.
It may have seemed like nothing more than friendly conversation,
but I thought I knew Kay better than that. She wanted to confirm
that what Violet had said about seeing Gilda with Dotty was true.
Who could blame her when it was clear Violet was doing everything
she could to set us against Gilda?

"It was fun," said Gilda. "Though I'm worried the show's going to
suffer for it. I hate to sound like a mother hen, but we can't be doing
that every night if we want to give these men good shows."

Violet seemed to catch wind of what Kay was really talking about,
and rather than letting the subject die, she decided to needle. "Meet
anyone special?"

"No. Though I met a ton of nice fellows," said Gilda.

"The war's full of them," I said. I was too tired for this game of
cat and mouse. "Where did you disappear to last night, Gilda? We
were worried when we couldn't find you."

"Sorry about that, girls. I got dragged off for an interview."

"With Dotty?" asked Kay.

"Yes. He figured last night was the only chance he'd have to get
me alone before the touring started."

Kay visibly relaxed. An interview was very different from Violet's
description of Gilda and Dotty going off for a private rendezvous.

"And then after the interview, I was invited to Rear Admiral
Blake's tent for the officers' poker game."

"That must've been a gas," I said.

Gilda lifted an eyebrow. "It wasn't as bad as you think. He's actually an interesting man when you strip away the pomp and circumstance. His brother's a producer, and it turns out we know some of the same people. In fact, he said when he heard I was interested in touring, he tried to get his brother to pull some strings to get me here."

Blake's connections hardly endeared him to me. It was bad enough that he could affect my life on the island; I hated to think he had any pull off it as well.

"How did the interview with Dotty go?" asked Violet.

"All right, I guess. I mean, Dotty seems very sincere, but I'm always so scared about what the press will make of what I say. He didn't seem interested in Hollywood gossip though. He just wanted to know why I decided to commit to a six-month tour and what I hoped to get out of it."

"And what do you hope to get out of it?" asked Violet. It was amazing how she could ask the most cutting questions and with a bat of her eyelashes make it seem so innocent.

"The same thing we all do," said Gilda. "I'm hoping to lift the men's days and do what I can to make their lives a little more pleasant here."

"What about you, Violet?" I asked. "You meet anyone special?"

Jayne caught my swerve and helped me make the turn. "Spanky seems sweet on you."

"He's a swell guy," she said. "Although I don't know if I could ever love a man without hair. And that dog has got to go."

"Mac's sweet," said Jayne.

"So's honey-baked ham, but that doesn't mean I want to cuddle with it," said Violet. "What about you two? Did you meet anyone last night?"

"Not really. I just danced until my feet bled," said Jayne.

"Oh, come on now," I said. "We did meet that lovely Wac."

"Uh," moaned Jayne. "I forgot about her."

"You talked to one of the dovetails?" asked Violet.

"Their queen," I said. "A real charmer. In less than two minutes she found a way to insult both of us. I've known vipers that are more pleasant to be around."

"The Wacs don't like USO performers," said Kay.

"Why?" asked Gilda

Kay tried to tuck her hair beneath a scarf to keep it from flying around. "We're not enlisted, we take attention away from them, and they think what we do has no value."

"So I gathered," I said.

"And I'm probably not helping things," she added.

"Why'd you resign?" asked Jayne.

Kay played with a silver bracelet dangling from her wrist. Two charms tinkled together. On closer inspection I realized they weren't charms; they were dog tags. "I missed performing. And, quite frankly, I couldn't handle military life. All those rules and regulations. I can memorize a song like that." She snapped her fingers. "But ask me to remember who to salute when, and it all drops out of my head. I just don't think I was made for the military."

I could see that. From the little interaction I'd had with soldiers and sailors, it seemed clear you needed more confidence than Kay possessed, if not for yourself, then for the safety of those around you. "Good for you for realizing it. How'd the Wacs react?"

"About like you'd think. They were so angry when I left. Everyone was, including my family. My pop's military, and so were my brothers."

That *were* spoke volumes. You didn't use the past tense unless the people you were talking about were past tense.

"We lost them both last year at Bataan," said Kay.

"I'm sorry," I said.

"I thought my parents would be relieved that I didn't want to put myself at risk, but I think they think I'm a coward."

I knocked her knee with my own. "Going to the South Pacific hardly makes you a coward."

She smiled, a rare sight from Kay, and I realized that her horse features were much prettier than I'd given her credit for. "But as your new Wac friend will probably tell you, it's a lot different going to war when you're wearing an evening gown instead of a uniform."

According to the schedule, we'd be doing three shows that day. As we walked to the performance venue, we rapidly talked through song lyrics, sketches, and performance order. I had a horrible feeling that everything we'd rehearsed on the ship had leaked out of my brain while I was sleeping and been replaced by lukewarm Australian beer.

As we were to discover about many of the camps, there was an actual amphitheater set up on this island, with a stage that had already accommodated a number of traveling performers and musicians. The army had chosen the spot because of the way the rocky outcroppings that surrounded the performance area isolated it from noise. It was funny how a cluster of islands that had become the heart of the Pacific theater was so conducive to performances of real theater, as though even the land recognized the necessity of engaging in all types of human drama. In addition to the stage, there was a small dressing area where we stored our few costumes and props and prepared ourselves for the first of the shows.

We were lent a pianist for the day, who was happy to get out of his normal job repairing Jeeps in the army's motor pool. Despite his grease-stained fingers, he was a fast study, ripping through our sheet music with the confidence of a man who'd played hundreds of performances before. He taught us a number of sly hand signals to use if we wanted him to speed up, slow down, or vamp during the show. After a quick rehearsal, we were confident we were in good hands.

My nerves took the run out and made way for excitement. This was a kind of theater I hadn't done in a long time. There were no fancy lights, expensive sound system, or carefully crafted sets to distract our audience from our talents and limitations. The only thing the men would be paying attention to was us.

Backstage we all put on our first costume and fixed our faces. The camp had supplied us with a platter of sandwiches made fitting for feminine enjoyment by having their crusts removed. Between soft, fresh bread nestled egg salad, tuna, and what they called GI turkey, which Violet discovered was another term for corned beef. While the rest of us eagerly dug into the chow, a silent Gilda continued to get ready, her hand shaking as she patted a powder puff across the bridge of her nose.

"You okay?" I asked her.

She looked down at her trembling arm and lowered it to her side. "I'm nervous."

"How on earth can you be nervous?" asked Violet.

"I can't remember the last time I was in front of a live audience."

Jayne put an arm around her waist and squeezed. "They'll love you."

"But what if they don't?"

I could hear something in her voice that I wasn't sure the other girls recognized. This wasn't just a movie star scared to see her fans in person but someone who desperately needed their love if she wanted her career to survive its most recent blow.

"If they don't," I said, "I'll eat every hat on every head in that room."

The pianist played several minutes of music while we peeked out at the audience from the wings. I wasn't sure how many men were there, but if I had to guess, I would say at least five hundred. Many of them had brought their own camp chairs, others were on blankets, and still others sat on the rock ledge that surrounded the performance space. For a moment I thought about climbing on the stage and asking if any of them had heard of Jack, but I couldn't stand the thought that a crowd of so many men might respond to my question with silence.

We set up the show to delay Gilda's entrance until the last possible moment. Her thinking had been that this way the men would focus on us rather than the big-name star sharing our stage. First, Kay would sing a solo; then Violet would tell some jokes, then Jayne

and I would do our tap and chat bit. The four of us would do another song, in the middle of which, Gilda would appear. As soon
as the song ended, she'd do a solo and interact with the audience.
When that was over, we'd join her again for a ridiculous patriotic
pageant Violet had thrown together to finish out the show.

The problem was, Gilda's appearance was being billed far in advance of our arrival and all the men knew she was supposed to be
there. So rather than patiently awaiting her arrival onstage, they
spent the first part of the performance calling out her name, asking where she was, and telling us to move on already and get to the
star.

Kay didn't cope with it very well. She struggled to belt out her
lyrics in what should've been a showstopper. From the wings we
could see her hands shaking and her face turning pink with embar-
rassment. She rushed through her song, forcing the pianist to double his pace to catch up with her, and ended it a verse too soon. The
men noticed her agitation, but they didn't try to quell it; they only
screamed louder for her to get off the stage and send out Gilda.

It was terrifically rude, and if it had happened to me in New York,
I probably would've wanted someone's head for it. But I was able to
hold my tongue when I thought about who was doing it. After all,
these men had been in the middle of nowhere for God knows how
long. Of course they wanted to see a star. Who were we to deny them
that chance?

Violet fared much better. It didn't hurt that she was a born performer, commanding a stage the way Patton commanded the army.
Effortlessly, she adjusted the jokes she'd rehearsed and worked
Gilda into each one, providing the men with a little appetizer of
what was to come.

"When we first arrived on the island, we headed into the enlisted
men's canteen for dinner. A sailor pulled Gilda aside and said, 'Excuse me, Miss DeVane, but you mess with the officers.' Gilda smiled
and replied, 'I know I mess with the officers, but where do I eat?'"

The men howled appreciatively. Violet took it as a sign that she
should continue along the same path.

"Before we came to the South Pacific, Gilda was in England. There she met a very friendly member of the RAF, who asked her to dance. He was admiring her outfit and asked her what kind of dress it was. Gilda said it was a V-neck. The soldier replied, 'Right, like V for victory.' His eyes fell below her neckline until Gilda clapped her hands to get his attention. 'The V may be for victory,' she said, 'but those bundles aren't for Britain.'"

The men laughed again, but it was clear that their patience was waning. Another chant for Gilda started in the back of audience. Violet held up her hands in surrender and said, "Easy, boys, like the monkey said after he got his tail caught in the lawn mower, it won't be long now."

Jayne and I decided to follow Violet's lead and throw out our original routine. First, we took off the modest dance skirts that reached to our knees. Then we pulled our necklines down until we were able to create—in my case—the illusion of cleavage. We both tapped our way onto the stage, our bodies clad in nothing but bowties, top hats, leotards, and tights. The sight was enough to earn us a few seconds of silence followed by a chorus of "hubba, hubba."

We started off doing the shim sham shimmy, a tap routine that's made up of the shim-sham, the pushbeat and crossover, the tack Annie, and the half break. Or as I liked to think of it: the two steps I can do, the one where I always trip myself, and the one that inevitably leaves me with an angry bruise on my leg. It's hard to do and looks impressive, even when you manage to screw it up. And when you're wearing nothing but a leotard and shaking what your mother gave you, it can be more tantalizing than a burlesque. We ended with a big finish—hands out to the side, fingers splayed. We hadn't stopped moving for ten seconds when the men started their call for Gilda again.

Clearly if we wanted to maintain their attention, we were going to have to be naked.

"Gosh, I can't get used to the military," said Jayne once we wrestled back their focus. "The men are so different here. So brave and strong. Why, just yesterday I saw a bunch of them playing football on the beach at Tulagi. One of the fellows tripped when he went to catch the ball and landed right on a pile of sharp rocks, one of which went right up his . . . well, you know."

"Rectum?"

"Damn near killed him, but he got up and kept playing. I guess ignoring pain is one of those army things."

"You mean like snafu?" I asked.

"Snaf-what?"

"Come on, now," I told her. "Haven't you heard the soldiers use that before? It's an acronym."

Jayne thumped herself on the head. "That's right. Someone explained that one to me last night."

"And what did they say it meant?" I asked.

"Rosie? Do you really need me to tell you?"

I nodded.

She sighed. "It's a word that's made up of the first letters of other words."

It was all terribly corny, but we got some laughs out of the crowd, even if it meant that everything we rehearsed went by the wayside. As soon as Gilda took the stage, the men went nuts, drowning out the rest of our group song with proposals of marriage and offers of other sorts that involved less commitment and more pleasure. When it was time for Gilda to go it alone, the four of us took to the backstage area to get some air and water.

"Unbelievable," said Violet.

"What's the matter?" I asked.

"What do you mean, what's the matter? Did you see what they did to poor Kay? They practically booed her off the stage."

"They're excited," said Jayne. "You can't blame them."

"It's not them I blame. She planned it this way, you know."

"Who planned what now?" I asked.

"Gilda. All that talk about sharing the stage with us and not wanting to steal the limelight was a lot of bunk. She knew they'd act like this."

Kay was off to the side as we talked, and as the subject of the conversation became clear, she moved closer to us. "She didn't know the men would know she was here," she said.

"The hell she didn't. It's in all the star's contracts that they're promoted first."

"So we'll change things around," I said. "Next time, we lead with Gilda and let the men get it out of their systems so that by the time the rest of us go on, they're ready to listen."

Violet removed her flask from where it was secured in her garter and took a swig. "Like that'll work. They'll just clamor for her to come back onstage."

Gilda's song ended and the four of us rejoined her for the remainder of the show. The crowd had settled considerably since the start of the performance, their appetite for Miss DeVane finally quenched. But despite the fact that we had their attention, I couldn't help but notice Violet staring daggers at Gilda every time she opened her mouth.

CHAPTER 11

The Three of Us

Over the next few days we altered the show so that Gilda was the first person onstage. While it eliminated some of the problems, it was clear that what the men wanted was Gilda, regardless of when they'd first been given her. Our only hope was that someday the novelty of having a movie star around would wear off. In the meantime, we would have to be patient. Or concede that a one-woman show would be more successful.

While we were halfway to solving that dilemma, a new one was popping up. Having reluctantly accepted that the show was all about Gilda, Violet sought her revenge by drinking before each performance. She could be a jovial drunk, but when her tippling was fueled by anything other than her desire to relax, she turned meaner than Bette Davis. I don't think sober Violet would've dared to say half the things her sloshed counterpart covered, but that didn't take the sting out of the words. Especially when she said them onstage.

"I have to admit," she told the crowd one night, "I was a little nervous about meeting Gilda DeVane. I mean, you've seen her films, right? So I was expecting this smart, sophisticated woman who wouldn't give me the time of day. Turns out I didn't need to be worried. The first night we were together I offered her a penny for her thoughts, and she gave me change. I'm not saying she's dumb, but just like a beer bottle, she's empty from the neck up. I kid, of course. She's a bright girl, though you wouldn't know it from her love life. I don't want to say Gilda's popular with the men around here, but I couldn't help but notice that even the generals are starting to salute her. They used to let her hang around the strategy sessions, but one day one of the colonels ordered the men to take those hills and half of them looked at Gilda and announced they already had. I don't even want to tell you about the confusion that arose at the pinning ceremony."

The men liked the jokes. They weren't so enamored of Gilda that they couldn't laugh at her image. Being told she was dumb or a floozy made her real to them. And accessible.

It was clear, though, that the jokes were wearing on Gilda. At first she smiled at each bit delivered at her expense, but I could see the muscles working in her jaw as she struggled to hold her tongue. And Violet fueled the fire, asking all of us what we thought of her act after each show. Gilda would lie and claim she hadn't heard it, though we all knew she had. Anyone else would've let Violet have it good, but Gilda wasn't about to pull the curtain on something the men were enjoying. That is, until the end of our first week, when Violet's material became a tad too personal.

"Did you hear Gilda was dating Van Lauer? All was going great until she started hinting that she wanted to get married. Gilda has always believed marriage was grand. Or if you ask her ex-husbands, twenty-five grand. Don't worry—Van doesn't have anything against marriage. Just ask his wife. But obviously the poor guy didn't want to be accused of bigamy. We all know what the sentence for that is: two mother-in-laws."

At the end of the show, all of us went onstage to sing "You're a Grand Old Flag." As we sang, we swung flags with great ferocity while mimicking the fabric's motions with our bodies. Normally the routine was perfectly safe, but Violet had drunk enough that night that she seemed unaware of how far off her mark she was. Rather than compensating for Violet's spatial issues, as the rest of us were, Gilda edged closer and closer to her so that when we lowered our flags and swept the floors with the poles, the wood tripped Violet and sent her flat on her stomach.

There are only two things to do when another performer has fallen: stop everything or keep dancing. Professionals do the latter. Professionals out for revenge insist on it.

"Keep going!" hissed Gilda. And so we did, stepping over Violet's body and making it impossible for her to sit upright and rejoin us. The men howled with laughter at the sight of her sprawled on the floor, her underwear momentarily on display. Gradually her horror became comical, and she tried to pass off the whole unfortunate situation as a planned bit. The audience may have bought it, but the rest of us knew better.

At end of the show, we examined Violet's injuries and helped her patch up her scraped knees.

"I just don't know what happened," she said. She was searching for her flask to self-medicate, but it wasn't where she expected to find it.

"I think I do," said Gilda. She produced Violet's flask from where she had hidden it and held it out. Before Violet's mitt met metal, Gilda lifted it out of her reach. "Not so fast."

"Give me that! It's mine."

"Not any longer. It's mine until you learn a little self-control."

"So what? Now we're a bunch of teetotalers?"

"If that's what it takes, then that's what we'll be."

I didn't like the way she was throwing that "we" out there. While I was happy to stand behind Gilda's efforts to get Violet to sober up, I would consider withdrawing my support if my own cocktail hour was being rationed.

Violet's mouth became a half moon. "Is this about the jokes?"

"This is about you being too ripped to safely do anything onstage. You're lucky you weren't hurt worse out there. You could've taken one of us down with you."

"It wasn't that bad."

It was clear what was going to happen. Violet was too stubborn to accept that Gilda was angry for any reason other than her jokes. We would be at a stalemate if someone didn't back up what Gilda was saying. I caught Jayne's eye and dropped my own gaze to her ankle. She followed my line of sight, not getting my point until I widened my peepers. With a roll of her own, she kicked herself in the shin with her tap shoe and, wincing against the pain, shifted her weight.

"Actually it kind of was that bad, Violet," she said. All eyes turned to Jayne. She lifted her leg to show off the cherry red mark marring her skin. "When you fell, your pole whacked me in the leg. I almost took a spill myself."

"Is that why you grabbed onto me?" I said.

"Of course," said Jayne. "Did you think I tripped myself?"

"I'd hoped not. Thanks to you, I almost poked my eye out."

"It was a disaster," said Kay, following our lead. "I thought all of us were going to topple over like dominoes. I've never been so embarrassed in my life."

"Geez, I didn't mean for it to happen," said Violet.

"Of course you didn't," said Gilda. She shook the flask. "But this is a problem. Here's how it is, Violet—either you're clean and sober for these shows or you're out of the cast."

"You can't do that!"

"I can and I will. I don't want to. You're brilliant at what you do and the men adore you, but I have to put everyone's safety first."

Violet surveyed the scene through red-veined eyes. She'd provided Gilda with the perfect excuse to can her—no questions asked—and no matter how great the thrill may have been to tear down Gilda in front of thousands of men, the privilege of performing was too great for her to continue to risk it.

"All right," said Violet. "No more drinking. Now may I have my flask back?"

"Of course," said Gilda. She took the flask from me, unscrewed the lid and poured the contents onto the ground.

For the first two weeks, we did a minimum of three shows a day, island-hopping throughout the Solomons, dining in a dozen different officer messes, and hearing enough tales of bragging and bravery to last a lifetime. At least once a day I managed to ask someone if they'd heard of Jack. I was so used to being told no that I think I would've collapsed from shock had someone owned up to knowing him.

That was the greatest mystery of all: How could we have seen so many men and traveled to so many places without encountering one person who'd met him?

Somehow we managed to evade the war everywhere we went. We landed in towns that had faced the Japanese days before or left islands as the first bombers entered their airspace. In fact, it seemed to me that you could time enemy activity based solely on our schedule. If we performed for you, odds were you'd be under attack in the next twenty-four hours.

We often heard the distant sound of mortar shells, but without actually seeing the damage they wrought, we were able to convince ourselves that it wasn't destruction we were hearing, but a Fourth of July celebration come early.

Each evening we returned to Tulagi. Most nights we immediately hit the sack, but on those rare occasions when we still had energy, we hung out with Spanky and his friends, drinking at the canteen or sitting in one of the swimming holes under the light of the rising moon. At least most of us did. More and more often Gilda pleaded exhaustion, and while the four of us gave in to an hour or two of cocktails and conversation, she disappeared. Usually she was in the tent when we returned. Usually.

The Wacs continued to join us at the canteen, though I was smart enough to keep my distance. I was doing a pretty good job avoiding them when one night, my dogs barking from too much activity during the day and way too much activity at night, I sought refuge at a table hidden in the shadows and propped up my aching feet on a chair.

"Mind if I have a seat?"

I looked up and found one of the Wacs looking down at me. Even though it was the last thing I wanted to do, I freed the chair and with a gentle kick pushed it her way. "Be my guest."

"Thanks." My companion had curly dirty-blond hair and a heart-shaped face. She didn't wear any makeup, but she didn't need to. Hers was a natural kind of beauty that required very little intervention.

I hated her on sight.

"Doesn't anyone want to dance with you?" she asked.

"I'm taking a break. What's your excuse?" I followed her gaze to the dance floor, where Jayne was being tossed about by a sailor who seemed to have learned most of his swing moves from King Kong.

The Wac had a beer in her hand, and with a swift knock of the cap against the table, she opened it. "My partner of choice isn't here. So how's the island treating you so far?"

Was she really being nice? I couldn't tell if this was sincerity or a setup. "Swell as far as I can tell. You been here long?"

"Too long. I've been in the islands since last July. Did you hear about Leslie Howard?"

The actor had been killed two weeks before at the Bay of Biscayne, though the news had just reached us. In some ways it hit me harder than when Carole Lombard had died. Howard had been a crush of mine, even if I'd found his Ashley Wilkes passive and annoying. "Yeah, it's still hard to believe. Gilda said he was a really nice man. Very personable."

She sat down, and for a moment we shared a tense, uncomfortable silence trying to think of what to say next. As far as I saw it, I had two options: leave and find my way back to my tent, or figure out what it was that made the Wacs dislike us.

Bolstered by the beer, I decided to explore the latter.

"So what did we do?" I asked.

"Excuse me?"

"I can't help but notice that most of the Wacs want nothing to do with us, and I'm trying to figure out why."

"We have nothing against you."

"Could've fooled me. So, is it actresses in general?"

She tossed back a swig of beer while she considered the question. "Most of us have been here a long time doing a lot of hard work. It's not easy when someone else shows up and gets the attention, you know?"

I nodded. So Kay was right. "You can hardly blame that on us."

She smiled wryly. "And yet we do."

"So what can we do to make it right?"

"Give up a chair. Share a beer. Remind the fellows that there's a thing called loyalty."

"I'll try, but you can lead a horse to water . . ."

"Too true. I'm Candy Abbott, by the way." She offered her hand. Her grip was strong and confident.

"Rosie Winter."

Across the room I spied a pair of Wacs whispering furiously while bouncing their attention between each other and an energetic fellow in army air force duds dancing with Kay. As Kay tripped over one of the pilot's unusually large feet, the two women broke into laughter loud enough to be heard above the music.

"It goes both ways, you know," I said. "If we're going to play nice, it would be nice if your friends would too."

"She's a special case. I don't think I can call my dogs off her."

I worked at peeling the label off my beer bottle. "What's the wire on Kay?"

"She's a traitor to the armed forces. She convinced our CO to go home, promised us she'd stick around, and then decided she wanted to leave too. The way we see it, she's got some nerve coming back here after all of that."

"Come on now—don't mince words. Tell me how you really feel."

She threw her head back and laughed. Despite all the reasons I shouldn't, I liked Candy Abbott. "Truth be told, there was a time when I was friends with Kay, though I could be shot for admitting it," she said. "The three of us were pretty close before she decided to desert."

"Three of you?"

"Yes, you're looking at one of the original Tulagi Musketeers—Kay Thorpe, Irene Zinn, and yours truly."

The name made my breath catch in my throat. Kay was friends with Irene? Why hadn't she said something?

"What's the matter?" Candy asked me.

Did Candy know she was dead? I didn't think so. And I didn't want to be the one to tell her. "Too much beer. So why did they leave?"

"Irene had better opportunities Stateside."

"How so?"

Candy set down her beer and worked on rolling the cuff of her camp shirt. "Before she signed up, she was an actress. That's how she and Kay first met. I think she always regretted coming here instead of staying home and seeing where Hollywood might've taken her. Don't get me wrong—Irene was a great soldier and a brilliant code breaker, but you could tell that she was always asking herself 'What if.' She felt like being here was her moral duty though. It was really important to her to feel like she was doing whatever she could to help the war effort."

I knew the feeling. "If she felt that way, what made her change her mind and go home?"

"Kay, for one. When she found out Irene had a studio contract waiting for her, she told her she'd be a fool to pass it up."

"And what else?"

Candy leaned toward me and lowered her voice. "There was some stealing going on in camp."

So I was right—Blake had been talking about Irene. "Missing supplies?"

"You've heard about it?"

I nodded.

"The higher-ups said it was the Japs, but Irene was sure it was someone here at camp who was behind it. She tried to get the brass to hear her out, but they wouldn't listen. I think that was the last straw for her. She said she expected that sort of messed-up logic in Hollywood, but she never thought people would behave that way in the military."

"And why did Kay leave?"

Candy shrugged. "I don't know. She was a good Wac and I thought she was happy here. Everyone knew she wanted to be a singer, but she seemed content putting that on hold until after the war. She got sick, and then the next thing we knew, she'd arranged for a discharge."

"Seems a little unfair to hold a grudge against a girl for getting sick."

Her eyes drifted to where Kay was still struggling on the dance floor. "If I'd thought it was for real, I would've given her sympathy and more. She was pretty tight with one of the Red Cross nurses, and I'm sure the girl helped her trump up a good reason to go Stateside."

I drained the rest of my beer and caught a sailor's eye to ask for another. "Where's the rest of your unit tonight?" I asked.

She looked around the room. "I think we're all here."

"No, you're missing one. Blond bun, couldn't smile if her life depended on it."

She removed a pack of cigarettes from her camp shirt pocket and tapped out a gasper. "Oh, you mean Amelia Lambert. She's our new commanding officer. She replaced Irene. Cig?"

"No thanks. When did she replace her?"

Candy tweaked her mouth to the left and blew the smoke away from me. "About the same time you five showed up. We were without a CO for months, and we thought it was going to stay that way, but a few weeks ago we got word that they were bringing in someone new."

"You don't seem too happy about that."

She rolled her eyes to confirm that I spoke the truth. "She doesn't exactly fit in with the rest of the group. We were a pretty casual unit, and she's a little obsessed with rules and protocol. We got an hourlong lecture on the way we dress." She wiggled her toes through the cannibalized Abners. "She's also instituted a weekday curfew. We're all supposed to be in bed at eleven."

"She can do that?"

"She's our CO. She can do whatever she wants."

I limped through one more dance before I saw an opportunity to corner Kay.

"Hello, stranger," I said.

She smiled through a mouth of Coca-Cola and joined me at a table. "Hi, yourself. I'm exhausted. I was thinking about trying to sneak out of here. Are you game?"

"Absolutely." I signaled to Jayne that we were heading out. She was trapped in a foxtrot and mouthed that she'd be on her way as soon as she could free herself from the wandering hands of her marine partner.

Kay and I walked the dark path together, concentrating on making sure we stayed on the makeshift road.

"So I met a friend of yours tonight," I told her once we were far enough from the canteen for conversation.

"Who's that?"

"Candy Abbott." Kay didn't say anything. It was too dark to catch her expression, though I had to imagine she wasn't too pleased. "How come you never told us you knew Irene?"

For a moment, the jungle held its breath. The only sound was the scuffle of our feet moving across the dirt and gravel road. "I don't know. I was so shocked when Violet said her name, . . . I wasn't sure what to say. I kept hoping I'd misheard her, and then later I read the article for myself and realized it was true."

"I take it that's why you took sick on the boat."

Kay nodded. "I knew I should tell someone, but I just wanted to forget about it. The longer I waited, the more I worried about how odd it would seem that I hadn't said something." In some strange way, I understood that urge she'd had to stick her head in the sand. There had been plenty of times since Jack disappeared that I wanted to pretend that all was fine because it was easier than contemplating what might've happened to him. "I'm the one who convinced her to leave the WAACs. I keep thinking that if she stayed, she would still be alive." She played with the dog tags dangling from her bracelet. She noticed my gaze and flipped the charms. I could just make out the name, rank, and serial number engraved on the aluminum. "We both wore them. It was kind of a tribute to what we'd been through. I never imagined they would be used to identify her body once she was discharged."

Who could imagine a thing like that? "Candy doesn't know Irene's dead," I said.

"You didn't tell her?"

"I didn't think it was my place."

"She's not the only one I didn't tell." She stopped walking and turned to face me. Moonlight glinted off the tears sliding down her cheeks. "Dotty was her boyfriend."

"Really?"

"They broke up when she went home, but he was still crazy about her. It's going to kill him when he finds out. I keep hoping that he'll get a letter or something, so I don't have to be the one to break it to him. Pretty cowardly, huh?"

So that explained her odd behavior around him. "I can't say I wouldn't want the same thing in your shoes. Is that why you've been avoiding him?"

"It's impossible to be around him without thinking of her. And right now, that's just too hard."

I bit off the urge to offer to tell him for her. That wouldn't help anyone, least of all her. "You need to though. You know that, right? There's nothing worse than getting bad news in a letter from someone you don't know. I've been there, believe me, and I would've much rather heard it from someone who was prepared to grieve with me."

She wrapped her arms around herself. "I'm just so scared that when I say the words out loud, it will mean she's really dead."

"She is, Kay."

She turned away from me and looked toward the ocean, where a second moon rippled on the water. "I know, but I keep thinking I can undo it."

CHAPTER 12

Face the Music

Kay talked to Dotty that night. I didn't ask how the conversation went. I didn't have to. The red-rimmed, swollen peepers she greeted us with the next morning were clear evidence that it had been hard on both of them. As we traveled by Jeep to the airstrip, Kay sat in silence, hugging her costume bag to her chest as though it was the only thing that could possibly give her comfort. Sensing that something was awry with our little group, our driver did his best to entertain us by catching us up on the latest news. There was heavy fighting going on in someplace called Kahill in the western Solomon Islands. The army air forces were doing most of the work, though the navy had sunk at least twelve Japanese submarines.

He paused in his recitation of our latest conquests and pointed into the distance. "And over there are the graves," he said.

"Graves?" asked Jayne.

"Mass graves, really. Can't let bodies sit topside too long, or the smell will drive you nuts. And it destroys the water supply. 'Course, a lot of the bodies end up in the ocean. It's just easier that way."

For the first time Tulagi didn't seem like a paradise. This wasn't just a tiny British-held island we'd won back from the Japanese. Death was everywhere, poisoning its land and its waters.

That day we flew to Guadalcanal, landing at Henderson Field. Our first show was scheduled for the main military hospital, where many of the injured from neighboring islands had been sent.

I had seen pictures of military hospitals before, and tons of movies and newsreels that featured them, but it still didn't prepare me for what we were about to encounter. Oh I knew to expect the size (enormous) and the number of injured men (incomprehensible), but one thing the movies hadn't been able to capture was the smell of the place. Like most Stateside hospitals I'd been in, the first scent you identified was the odor of antiseptic cleanser. But hovering above that was the stench of infected wounds that never got the airing they needed in the close, humid air. I wish I could equate the stink in some way, but it was like nothing I'd ever smelled before.

"Wow," we said in unison as we surveyed the ward we'd been directed to. Some men sat alert in their beds, their injuries undetectable to our untrained eyes. Others played checkers and chess or read magazines. But the majority of them were too ill for idle entertainments. They lay asleep, courtesy of the morphine coursing through their veins, hopefully making them forget—momentarily— the limbs that were no longer there, the eyes that could no longer see, or the face so badly disfigured that their own mothers wouldn't recognize them when they finally came home. Still others were conscious in the loosest sense of the word, moaning in rhythm to the pain that emerged in waves that were constant but unpredictable. These were the ones who cared the least about our arrival. They were too focused on surviving whatever agony their bodies unleashed on them next.

I took it all in, hoping I might discover a familiar face. And fearing that very same possibility.

"Welcome, ladies." A nurse in a crisp white uniform greeted us at the door. She was taller than me with a voice so deep that, for a moment, I wondered if it wasn't a man wearing the carefully pressed skirt. The gender issue was further confused by several hairs poking out of her chin. "You're a little early. We were just about to serve the men lunch. Would you be interested in joining them?"

"No thanks," said Violet, speaking for all of us. "We're just fine." The truth was we were starving, but Violet wisely recognized that none of us were up to eating food in a room full of seeping wounds.

"Then you're welcome to make yourselves comfortable until we're ready for you to start. There's a latrine out that door and to the left."

"Would it be all right if we visited with the men while they ate?" asked Gilda.

The matron's face burst into a wide smile. Her teeth were so crooked and overlapped that I feared that if a dentist removed one, the rest would come tumbling out. "Of course. That would be lovely. Just lovely."

She bustled away to see to the final preparations for lunch, leaving the five of us staring, slack-jawed, at Gilda. "Well, go on," she said. "This is what we're really here for."

While Violet and Gilda moved forward to greet the men, Jayne, Kay, and I hung back. I know it sounds awful, but the idea of talking to them terrified me. What would I say? How could I avoid staring at their wounds? Would some of them even know I was there?

"Come on, Rosie," said Jayne. "It won't be so bad." The men who still had the capacity to do so, greeted Gilda with a gasp of surprise. Soon the majority of the room was murmuring her name as word of who was there spread about the ward.

Jayne gently pushed me forward, and I headed toward the first bed I saw. The man there was awake and alert, playing a game of solitaire to pass the time. His feet were wrapped in a thick layer of bandages. Something pink stained the outermost layer of his left foot. The blob of color looked like a Rorschach test. It was an empty vase. No, it was a face in profile.

"Hiya," I said. "I'm Rosie Winter. What's your name?"

"The boys call me Whitey." He barely looked up from the cards. "You with the USO?"

"That I am."

"When's Gilda coming over here?"

"She's got a whole ward to visit with. Give her time."

He laid a ten of clubs on top of a queen of spades.

"I don't think that's how you play," I said.

"My game. My rules."

"Suit yourself." He didn't laugh at the pun. I sat in a chair beside his bed and waited for him to initiate further conversation. It was going to be a very long wait. "So what are you in for?"

"Jungle rot."

I didn't know what that was, though I could hazard a guess. "You getting out of here soon?" He hummed an answer that may have been a yes, a no, or a *mind your own bee's wax*. "Any chance you know a sailor named Jack Castlegate?"

He didn't pause in his card slapping. "Who wants to know?"

Me, you dumdora. That's why I asked. "Do you know him or not?"

"Nope," he said. "Never heard of him."

It was obvious this guy couldn't have cared less about me. I left him and moved on to the next bed. This fellow was in considerably worse shape than mister personality. One of his legs had been reduced to a stump that ended above the knee. The other one was elevated at a forty-five degree angle, his pale, bare toes wiggling like they were seedlings struggling to find the light.

He didn't look like he was up for conversation, so I started to pass him by.

"Miss! Miss!"

I turned and found that he was more alert than I'd given him credit for. "Hiya," I said. "I didn't think you were awake."

"Is it true Gilda DeVane's here?" It never ended, did it? Even the wounded wanted to see her first.

"It's true." I started to leave again.

"Aren't you going to stay and talk?"

"Do you want me to?"

"Sure. It's not every day that a fellow gets to chat with someone who knows Gilda DeVane." It wasn't quite a compliment, but I decided to cut him a little slack. Somebody had to.

"I'm Rosie Winter. What's your name, soldier?"

"Leo Thistlewaite. But folks call me Gumball."

"Looks like you've had a hell of a time, Gumball."

The toes wiggled again. "Better than some. How's your handwriting?"

"Worse than most."

He grinned. "It can't be that bad. Mind writing a letter for me? My hands aren't working so good these days."

"I'd be happy to."

He told me where to find pen and paper, and I dug both out from the kit bag hanging over the end of his bed. The pen was an army-issue ballpoint. We couldn't get ballpoints back home, but the army made a habit of passing them out to its men as one of the spoils of war. It seemed terribly cruel that a boy like this would end up with a fancy pen to remember the war by and no functioning hands with which to use it. Together, we cobbled a letter to his ma, assuring her that he was okay and that he'd be coming home soon. There was no mention of the missing leg. That, he'd rightly decided, wasn't the kind of news you put in a letter. He then had me write a similar note to the Hershey bar he had at home, assuring her that as soon as he was Stateside, they'd finally get hitched.

I prayed for his sake that the girl still wanted to.

As though he read my mind, Gumball asked. "Would it bother you?"

"What?"

"The leg. If you were her, would it make things different for you?"

I couldn't help but transfer the question to Jack. Would it bother me? There was a time when it might've given me pause but not anymore. I would've been so grateful to know that Jack was alive that he could've been missing both legs and I don't think I would've batted an eye.

The question was: How would Jack feel about it?

"Things would be different, sure," I said. "But that doesn't mean I wouldn't be thrilled to have you home safe."

"Thanks." He closed his eyes. "That helps."

I asked him about Jack before I moved on. He'd never heard of him.

The next man needed help spooning his broth into his mouth, his bandaged hands making it impossible to maneuver the utensil. He wasn't much for talking; in fact I wasn't sure if he could. But when I got up to leave, he grabbed onto my arm with one of his white swathed lobster claws and insisted that I stay sitting beside him until he fell asleep. I remained in his grip, too afraid that if I detached myself from him he'd awaken again. And I didn't want him to because for the first time since I'd sat with him he was smiling.

Across the ward, Gilda signed a man's cast. Violet chatted animatedly with two men lying side by side. Kay wrote a letter, a pair of glasses perched atop her nose. And Jayne . . . Jayne—

"Billy!" she shouted. The entire ward turned to look at the tiny blonde as she raced across the room and joined a man at the end of the ward. I was afraid she was hallucinating for a moment, but it became clear that he knew her just as she knew him. I watched their reunion with an odd mix of elation and jealousy. Why did Jayne get to see her missing sailor when I didn't? How was that fair?

"Rosie!" Jayne stage-whispered from across the room. She frantically waved for me to join her, so I carefully pulled the sleeping soldier's paw from my arm and lay it across his chest. When I arrived at Billy's bedside, Jayne was perched on his bed and holding on to both of his hands. "Rosie, this is Billy DeMille," she said. "The sailor I met at the Stage Door Canteen."

"So I figured."

"Billy, this is Rosie, my best friend in the entire world."

Jayne released one of his mitts long enough for me to shake it. He was small, like Jayne, with the largest brown eyes I'd ever seen. "We were wondering what happened to you," I said.

"He was in Attu and got a bad concussion when his plane got hit," said Jayne.

"I didn't realize you were a navy pilot," I said.

"It was his first time on an air mission." She was so slap-happy I expected her to bounce like a rubber ball. "He's been flat on his back for two weeks now. But he's going to be out soon."

"Does he talk?" I asked.

"I do now." He put his second hand back in Jayne's. "I thought I was dreaming when I saw you all walk in. Never in a million years did I think Jayne would show up here."

"Are you going Stateside after this?" I asked.

"Hell no. As soon as the doc gives me clearance, I'm back in the air. I think Peaches would have my head if I didn't return."

I froze, certain I must've heard him incorrectly. "Peaches?" I said.

"My CO. His real name is—"

"Paul Ascott," I said.

Jayne stopped glowing at Billy long enough to realize what was going on. "I didn't know you knew Peaches," said Jayne.

"I was about to say the same thing," said Billy.

"So he's here?" I asked. Peaches was the man who told me Jack was lost forever. But that wasn't all he was.

"Sure as shooting. In fact, he'll probably be by later tonight. We have a standing chess game." His brow creased. "Say, how do you know him, Rosie?"

I tried to respond, but the words wouldn't come. Billy knew Peaches. Peaches was on Guadalcanal. If they were in the same unit, that meant Billy knew Jack.

I didn't get to ask Billy anything. Before I'd found the strength to form the question, the matron clapped her hands together and announced that we would be going on in five minutes.

Jayne was buoyant as we headed to change into our costumes. "I can't believe he's here. It's kismet."

"It is pretty amazing," I said.

"He said he wrote me a few days ago. Before then, he couldn't even think about putting pen to paper, his head was hurting so much. He thinks he'll be out by the end of the week and said it's nothing to get one of the pilots to take you to another island. He said when we first walked in, he thought I was an angel." She finally noticed the look on my face and stopped her gushing. "What's the matter?"

"If he knows Peaches, isn't it possible he might know—"

She froze with her skirt half off. "Oh my goodness! I didn't even think of that! We'll ask him as soon as the show's over, that's for sure."

The performing conditions were more primitive at the hospital. Instead of a stage, we used the center aisle. Instead of a dressing room, we had two hospital drapes that served as our wings. Because there was no piano, there was no pianist, so all the songs would be performed a cappella. But despite the setup, the men were enthralled with us. We still started the show with Gilda, though it probably wouldn't have been necessary, given that this captive audience didn't have the strength to demand that she appear earlier than scheduled. Besides, after getting a chance to spend time with us before the show, we had all become stars in their eyes, more because of our compassion than any fame we'd managed to acquire. In the more intimate space, we didn't have to project as hard, and our voices soared into the building's peaked ceiling, mingling with the voices of the soldiers and sailors who felt the urge to sing along. When it was over, the men who could stand did so, and rather than dismissing their ovation as a reward well earned, we sang two more pieces.

Never had I felt so moved performing. Certainly every show during the tour had received expressions of gratitude from the audience, but for the first time I felt a sense of purpose in what we did. We may not have been breaking enemy code, but for that hour of songs, jokes, and dance, these brave wounded men were able to forget about their aches and pains—both those that were temporary and those that might never go away. We had given them peace and respite, neither of which were available to them through any other avenues. And it felt great.

No wonder Irene had enlisted in the WACs. This was the purpose she was searching for. She just didn't realize she didn't have to be in the military to get it.

When it was over, we didn't gnash our teeth over who got more attention or who missed what steps. Instead, we hugged and silently acknowledged the awesome experience we'd just shared.

"We're going to have to be leaving, ladies." Our driver popped his head into our curtained-off backstage area. "We're already running an hour behind."

"Can't we stay a little longer?" asked Jayne.

"It's not my orders, ma'am. The officers expect you for dinner at eighteen hundred hours, and I was instructed to have you back at least an hour before then."

I hadn't realized how long we'd been at the hospital. The time had flown by.

Jayne's neck strained as she tried to set her eyes on Billy.

"Can we have ten minutes to say good-bye?" I asked.

Our driver conceded that that was fine. While Kay, Violet, and Gilda dispersed to say their farewells, Jayne and I headed toward Billy.

"You were great," he said with a smile. For the first time I really took in this boy who made Jayne's heart flutter. His hair was the color of hay, his eyes as rich as coffee spiked with real cream. "I've got to say, the last thing a guy with a headache like mine wants to hear is tap dancing, but you two made it pretty darn riveting."

I couldn't tell if it was a pun or not.

"Billy," said Jayne. "Rosie has something she wants to ask you."

He raised an eyebrow. "About Peaches?"

"No. I mean, kind of." Just get it out, my head screamed. "Do you know a sailor named Jack Castlegate?"

He paused too long for me to have any hope. "Nope. It doesn't ring a bell."

"Peaches knew him," said Jayne. "So we thought you might too."

"He transferred into my squadron after we got back from Stateside. Maybe Jack was someone he knew on his old carrier?"

"Peaches transferred ships?" I asked.

Billy fidgeted with a wristband that stated his name, rank, serial number, and blood type. "Yeah. I guess there was some sort of problem. He never told us what. I'm glad he made the move though. The guy he replaced was a real son of a bitch." As soon as he said the words, he caught himself. "Sorry."

"We've heard worse," I said. I knew Jayne was dying for a moment alone with Billy, so I took my leave. "It was nice to finally meet you. I hope the head heals fast."

CHAPTER 13

Life and Death of an American

Everyone but me managed to sleep on the way back to the base camp. My head was too full of Jack for rest.

I knew I shouldn't be discouraged. After all, I couldn't have expected to find Jack after only a few weeks in the islands, but it still felt like every conversation I'd had about him was a preview of more disappointment to come. And the knowledge that Peaches was so nearby was gnawing at me, and not only because he was a potential source of information. When I'd last seen him, he'd told me about the events leading up to Jack's disappearance, and I'd confessed that I wasn't a sweet little Stage Door Canteen waitress named Delores. Up until that point I think we both thought we were headed toward a relationship, but the knowledge that I still harbored feelings for an old flame was enough to extinguish the beginnings of a new one.

I never thought he'd be back in the South Pacific. To be honest, I never thought about him at all. Not because Peaches wasn't worthy of it—if memory served, he was a handsome, witty man who any girl would be a fool not to fall for—but because my mind had been so wrapped up in getting out of the States and finding out where Jack was. I didn't like the idea that I was going to have to confront my guilt over the way I'd treated him again. I had assumed that phase of my life was over.

We arrived at the base camp, where we had landed that morning, and were mercifully shown to an area that had been set aside for our R & R. We had an entire luxurious hour until dinner, after which we'd do our last show of the day.

This time I slept. When I awoke, the others were scrambling to get themselves ready for dinner at the officers' mess. Out came lipsticks, combs, and vials of perfume they'd been wise enough to stash away with their costumes. At 1800 hours, we were taken by Jeep to a house up on a hill behind the encampment. Torches flickering like fireflies lined the drive. From inside we could hear music—not a phonograph playing the latest platters, but a pianist plucking out a tune live and in person.

"Holy smokes," said Violet as we parked in front of the building. "What is this place?"

"Welcome, ladies," said a man with a British accent. He helped us step down from the Jeep before introducing himself. "I'm Lance Upchurch of the RAF."

"Where are we?" asked Gilda.

"We call it Shangri-La. It's a plantation owned by a private French citizen who's been kind enough to invite us to join him. It's much more pleasant than eating at camp, don't you think?"

We agreed that it was and followed him into the house. Just like the high commissioner's house on Tulagi, it was the sort of big-island structure that seemed to have been lifted whole cloth from *Casablanca*. The house itself was nothing special—just four walls and a thatched roof—but the interior was immaculate, outfitted with rugs and furniture that had clearly been imported from Europe. The centerpiece of the joint was a stone fireplace that had been cobbled together out of a mismatch of rocks. Verandas ran the length of two sides of the building, both screened in to allow visitors to enjoy the great outdoors without suffering her pests. As we arrived, a group of men left one of the porches with glasses of scotch in hand and heralded our arrival.

Our host was a portly Frenchman named François Le Clerk. The rest of the men weren't the lieutenants and captains that typically dined with us. They were the elite of the armed forces, the ones who strategized but never had to worry about their own hands getting dirty. Dinner was a formal affair. Tonkinese men in white jackets delivered food from the left and cleared from the right. We ate four courses off china so fragile I could see the table through it and chased each delicious dish with copious amounts of whiskey. Conversation was lively, though I was both tired and famished enough to keep to myself for most of the meal. Instead, I watched the way the men leered at the five of us, feigning interest in our tales of performance, even though I knew the only reason we were there was because they hoped we would provide dessert.

Eventually, the conversation turned away from us, and the men began to discuss what they'd really hoped to talk about: strategies, plans, supplies, and manpower. The level of detail was overwhelming. As they tossed about figures, named countries I'd never heard of, and described the peculiarities of particular military leaders, I tried to make sense of what it all meant. What was the "fog of war"? Were the figures they quoted fatalities or injuries? Did my ears deceive me, or did one of them praise the Nazis for their ingenuity?

Through it all the pianist played a variety of classical tunes. Just when I was worried his fingers would fall off from overactivity, he took a break. In the distance I could hear other music—snippets of folksongs like "Home Sweet Home" and "Swanee River."

"Is that coming from the camp?" I asked.

Le Clerk cocked his head toward the veranda to hear what I had heard. "No, that's the Japanese."

"So what—they want our music now too?" asked Violet.

"It's a wartime maneuver. A form of propaganda, if you will," said Le Clerk. "They broadcast the music every night in hopes that it will make your men homesick."

I filled in the rest of the strategy. "And the homesick don't sleep well and don't fight as effectively."

He rewarded me with a flick of his fork. "Exactly."

"Is it working?" I asked.

He laughed, sending out an unpleasant combination of spittle and flecks of bread. "Oh no, your men are much too strong for that. I should say it succeeds in annoying them more than anything."

"If we're hearing their radio signal, then they're close by, aren't they?" I asked.

He nodded. "Close enough that we can hear them breathe. I often get radio broadcasts designed to demoralize the men by claiming that the war has turned in the enemy's favor. Sometimes you can even see flickers of the Japanese's campfires."

The idea that we were so close to the enemy killed my appetite. How could men sleep knowing that at any moment a grenade could be thrown into their tent? And what must it be like to live on a battle-front of information? How did they know they could trust what the Americans told them but not what the Japanese said? "It must be terrifying, living like this," I said.

Le Clerk shrugged. "It's just war, my dear."

After coffee and cake our driver took us to the amphitheater. We were running behind, and already the performance space was filled with thousands of anxious enlisted men awaiting our show. Men crammed themselves into every available inch of space. Even the cliffs surrounding the performance area had been taken over as seats.

We got into costume and quickly reviewed the program. The booze from dinner was making my head swim, and I forewarned Jayne that I wasn't going to be able to go off script much. I'd washed away my wit with the whiskey.

Gilda's face was flushed red. Perspiration formed droplets just below her hairline.

"Too much hooch?" I asked.

She patted her brow dry with a tissue. "Too much something."

Violet leaped to her aid and placed a maternal hand on her fore-head. "You're cold and clammy. Open your mouth." Gilda did so, revealing a bright red tongue. "You look okay to me, but if you don't feel like going on—"

Gilda closed her mouth. "No. I'm okay. Really." She lifted her foot to change her shoes and wobbled slightly. I don't think the other girls caught it, but I could tell she knew I'd noticed. She shot me a look that begged me not to say anything. I mimed zipping my lips to assure her I'd keep quiet. For now.

As the show began, the men's enthusiasm seemed muted. I couldn't tell if the crowd was more subdued or if the whiskey scrambling my thoughts merely made it seem that way. I suspect it was a combina-tion of things—after all, many of these men had been working all day and were now sitting through the show in preparation for sleep. De-spite being under the weather, Gilda gave it her all. Everything went off without a hitch until we came onstage for "Boogie Woogie Bugle Boy." As the song began, I caught a flash of light up in the cliffs to my left. One by one our attention was drawn to the spot high above the soldiers who were using the earth as their seats. Soon the men were searching out what was drawing our attention away from them. As the song came to its climax, a commotion rumbled through the crowd. Someone drew his weapon, and a wave of men rushed to the cliffs, oddly silent as they climbed the craggy rocks. We continued singing because we didn't know what else to do. The men never re-turned. We finished the show and accepted lukewarm applause from the remaining audience.

"What the deuce was that?" I asked as we went backstage.

"Beats me," said Jayne.

"Do you think we were under attack?" asked Violet.

"I didn't hear any gunfire," said Kay. "Besides, if we were under attack, they wouldn't have let us keep singing."

I hoped she was right, though part of me was convinced that in the eyes of the military we were expendable.

"Where's Gilda?" I asked.

"She went to get the scoop," said Violet. "She said she'd be back in two shakes of a lamb's tail."

We put on our street clothes and remained hidden in our dressing area as we waited for Gilda's return. At last she joined us, her face even more flushed than before.

"There were three Japanese up in the cliffs watching us," she announced breathlessly.

"Were they going to kill us?" asked Violet.

Gilda laughed. "Heavens no! The men said they'd snuck up there to watch the show. I guess they were so engrossed in what we were doing, they didn't even notice when the group of men disappeared to go after them."

"And did they capture them?" I asked.

"You bet they did. And the men are attributing all of it to us."

"Did they have guns?" asked Jayne.

Gilda shrugged. "I didn't think to ask."

"We're heroes," said Violet. "Though I've got to say—I'm kind of disappointed there were only three of them. I mean, aren't we talented enough to rate an entire platoon?"

"Maybe the other fellows went away after they heard your jokes," I said.

"Why? Were they afraid my clever repartee would slay them?"

We all groaned.

"So can we can get out of here now and go back to Tulagi?" asked Jayne. "I don't like the idea that the Japs are out there watching us. This place is giving me the heebies."

Gilda said the Jeep would be there to take us to the airstrip in ten minutes. I was eager to leave, too, though not for the same reasons as my pal. I didn't find the idea that the Japanese had been eyeballing us frightening. In fact, it was quite the opposite. I was fascinated by an enemy that would risk everything for a little entertainment. At any point they could've attacked the crowd, but that hadn't been what they were there for. What did it say about them that they were as desperate for laughter and amusement as the rest of us? I wanted to ask the other girls what they thought about it, but

I knew I was treading on dangerous territory. After all, the last thing anyone wanted to hear was that the people we were hoping to kill were just like us.

Outside the dressing area, a score of men were waiting for the chance to meet us. We shook hands, signed programs, and posed for photos with the eager beavers while they showered us with praise for how we'd handled ourselves during the disturbance.

"Ya'll were as cool as ice cream," said one guy. "For a moment I thought the whole thing might've been part of your act."

"Rosie's known for being calm in the face of danger," said a voice. I turned toward the sound and found Peaches with his hat in his hands.

"Hiya," I said, my icy exterior melting as heat rushed to my head. "I guess you saw Billy."

"I guess I did," he said. "He asked me to give you this." He passed Jayne a thick letter that refused to remain folded. "He wanted to come himself, but they wouldn't discharge him yet."

Jayne beamed and backed away from us so that she could tear through the tome. As though they sensed the amount of baggage each of us was toting, the crowd also moved away and directed their attention to the three remaining performers.

"You look good," I said. He did too. The color was back in his skin, and his face showed the peace and exhaustion that came from doing a full day's work. His eyes still possessed the wry twinkle I'd first been drawn to, and his voice was flavored with the lazy Southern drawl of his native Georgia.

"So do you," he said.

"I thought about writing," we said in unison. As we each heard the other parroting our words, we broke into a laugh.

"I didn't really," I said.

"Me neither," said Peaches.

"Gosh," I said. "I can't believe I ever thought this would be awkward."

"Should we start over?"

I delivered my permission with a wave of my hand. "Be my guest."

He took a long, deep breath and showed me his palms. "You are the last person I ever expected to see here."

"The feeling's mutual."

"I thought for sure it was the concussion talking when Billy said he'd met you."

"I guess you would've preferred it that way, huh?"

He didn't answer. In fact, I don't think he would've preferred it that way at all. If he could've changed anything, it wouldn't have been my arrival but who I was to begin with.

"Anyway," he said. "I thought I should say hello before we accidentally ran into each other. The islands are smaller than you think."

"So I'm learning." The Jeep arrived, and the driver jumped from his seat and began loading our costumes. If I was going to ask Peaches about Jack, it had to be now. "Look—"

"You have to go, right?"

I nodded.

He tapped my shoulder with his closed fist. "Be safe. Maybe if I'm lucky, I'll run into you again."

He turned to go and I grabbed his arm to stop him. His eyes dropped to where my skin touched his, and I knew he was misreading the moment. I dropped his wrist as quickly as I had grabbed it and pulled my hand to my side.

"I need to ask you something," I said.

Hope flickered in his eyes, and I hated myself more than I ever had before. This was all going so wrong. No matter what I said, it would feel like I was toying with him, and that's the last thing I intended to do.

"Ask away," he said.

Kay and Violet were climbing into the Jeep. This opportunity was going to be lost. I could keep my big mouth shut and feed into the same fantasy I'd wrongly cultivated at the Stage Door Canteen, or I could be brave for once in my life and put aside all the game playing so that I could ask him the thing that I desperately needed to know.

"What is it, Rosie?"

I licked my lips and plunged into the icy cold water. "Have you heard anything else about Jack?"

The light left his eyes, as though his face had been illuminated by nothing more than a match that my breath had extinguished. "That's what you want to know?"

I nodded. There was no point in apologizing for my lousy timing. It spoke for itself.

Peaches took a step toward me. "Are you sure you want me to tell you?" His voice was cold, and I could swear a smile lingered at the corners of his mouth.

"Yes," I breathed.

"He's dead."

CHAPTER 14

Bury the Dead

"And then what did he say?" asked Jayne.

We were back on Tulagi, huddled on my cot as I recounted my conversation with Peaches. We weren't alone. The other women were gathered around us, demanding an explanation for my bizarre silence the entire journey home.

Home. It was funny how quickly a new place took on that designation.

"They sent his body Stateside three weeks ago." I buried my head in my hands. I was hoping to cry, but so far not a single tear had fallen.

"So, I'm confused," said Violet. "Who was the guy you were talking to?"

Jayne bravely took on the task of explaining my convoluted life for the second time. "That's Peaches, the guy Rosie met at the Stage Door Canteen back in New York."

"He's the one who fell for her when he thought her name was Delores," said Kay.

"Gotcha," said Violet.

"But why was Jack's crew chasing him to begin with?" asked Gilda.

"A few months ago, Jack's boat disappeared," I said. I was shocked by the clinical tone in my voice. I could've been Edward R. Murrow recounting someone else's tragedy. "They thought the whole crew was lost, but Jack and his CO survived. Not long after they got back, Jack started making noise that what happened wasn't an accident— the men who died were murdered by their CO. There was enough to the claim that the CO decided the only way to keep Jack quiet was to kill him. Jack escaped and hid somewhere on the island for a while. A month or so ago, word got out about where he was hiding. They flushed him out, a chase ensued and he went into the water. He was attacked by sharks, but they're not sure if that happened before or after he died. The official cause of death was drowning."

Even at night the world around us was made up of vivid greens, yellows, and browns that I had forgotten had originated in nature only to be duplicated by man, not the other way around. It was such a beautiful, perfect place, and yet I couldn't believe it existed in the same world as the story Peaches told. Could that really have been Jack's end? Not at the hands of his CO, not on a battleship, but in shark-infested waters by animals that had no stake in the outcome of this war?

I closed my eyes and tried to picture the scene. It had to have been terribly dark. Traveling on foot through the dense vegetation, his leg still wounded from when the CO had shot him the first time, Jack knew he couldn't outrun his pursuers. A gun fired, igniting a jolt of fresh pain in his body and cementing how futile his hopes of escape were. And so borrowing a page out of Hollywood, he made the decision to jump into the water and remain low, only coming up for air when he was certain he was masked from observers. Perhaps it even worked and they left thinking he was gone for good. Jubilant that the plan was a success, Jack began to swim to shore only to realize the one truth the navy should have taught him: the water offered just as much danger as the land.

It seemed so ironic and sad. If he had to die, didn't he at least deserve a hero's end?

"Could he have been lying?" asked Jayne.

Though the evening was warm, I was freezing. That was something at least. "Peaches? Of course not. Why would he?"

"He obviously still cares for you," said Jayne. "Maybe he thought if he told you Jack was dead, he'd have a chance."

As if I were that irresistible. "He wouldn't be that cruel. Besides, it would be too easy to disprove."

"But we never heard anything."

"Wouldn't his folks have let you know?" asked Kay.

I shook my head. Jack's parents never cared for me. They were Upper East Side and I was the Village-dwelling actress they were worried would trap their son into marriage. Besides, as far as they knew, we were kaput. I would be the last person they would think about contacting.

"We've been touring for the past two weeks, and before then we were en route to the Pacific. Peaches said the whole thing was kept on the QT when it happened." And I hadn't been vigilant. For months I had checked the papers every day to see if Jack's name was included among the missing and dead. But after being told he was missing without seeing anything in the papers to verify it, I decided the newspapers were untrustworthy. And then we'd come up with this stupid plan to try to find him, and in the rush to leave the States, I hadn't considered the possibility that there might be nothing left to find.

"I'll bet it was quick," said Violet. "I've heard drowning is one of the easiest ways to die."

"It's peaceful," said Kay.

They were liars, the both of them, but I appreciated what they were trying to do.

"We can probably get you home," said Gilda. "I'm sure under the circumstances the USO would be willing to send you back. And if they make a stink about the money, I'll pay for it. All right?"

A shudder passed through me. It sounds terrible, but much of what I was feeling was relief. This great mystery that I'd been toting around for months was finally solved. Jack was dead. End of story. Roll credits. "I don't want to go home," I said.

"Are you sure?" asked Jayne.

"Positive."

Rather than going to sleep as I knew everyone wanted to, that night the five of us went down to the beach and downed a few warm bottles of beer while I dug a hole in the wet sand and buried Jack's photo.

"I think I want to be alone for a little while," I told the group. I assured them I could find my way back to the tent on my own, and they slowly dispersed. Jayne lingered the longest, wanting, I'm sure, to know that I was okay. She had been with me since the first night I'd met Jack, and through all the turmoil of our up-and-down relationship. But I needed to do this by myself. This was between Jack and me.

"I should've written," I said to the mound of sand once I was certain I was alone. "I should've told you I loved you. I should've understood that your enlisting had nothing to do with me. I wish you would've tried to explain it to me. But then who knows if it would've made any difference—" I stopped myself. Could it have changed things? If he'd known that I loved him and respected what he was doing, would he have been more careful? Would he have kept his mouth shut? "Just please know that I'm so, so sorry."

The words seemed terribly inadequate. I had hoped that by speaking them aloud I could force the tears I knew wanted to come, but for the time being they remained stubborn. I closed my eyes, sat cross-legged in the sand, and tried to conjure the Jack I'd known. The first time I'd met him had been at an after-party for a show he and Jayne had been in. She was already dating Tony at this point, but every night she came home with tales of the amazing actor she got to share the stage with. He was funny, he was handsome, he was talented, and, when I finally got to see him for myself, she pronounced that he was perfect for me. I didn't agree though. Based on our first conversation, I concluded he was spoiled, arrogant, and not half as witty as he thought himself to be. Later, he told me that he found me cold, my humor cruel and biting, and, frankly, I was too damn tall, even though he managed to tower above me. I'm not sure what made him change his opinion, but I know what forever altered him in my eyes. I finally saw the show he and Jayne were in, and as he moved about the stage, saying words that weren't his own, I caught a glimmer of the man he really was. I can't describe it any better than that, but on the stage he laid himself bare, and I realized that the man I'd met was the character and the man I watched was the real person.

"Why couldn't you have kept your mouth shut?" I asked the mound. "Who appointed you the savior for those men who died? They didn't need you. They're dead. And now so are you, and there's no one left to be *your* voice. You died for nothing. Do you hear me? Nothing."

"Rosie?"

Candy Abbott stood a few feet away, her flashlight drawing a full moon in the sand.

"Are you all right?" she asked.

I offered a weak smile. "Just needed a little time to myself."

"Oh." She took it that she was intruding and turned tail to walk away.

"It's okay," I said. "I mean, it's fine that you're here. What are you doing out so late?"

She adjusted a knapsack dangling from her right shoulder. It looked heavy, but perhaps what I was observing was the weight of some other burden. "I guess I needed a little time too. I wasn't tired so I thought a walk might help."

"How'd you escape the curfew?"

"Amelia waits until she thinks we're asleep, and then she high-tails it out of there. Rumor has it she's shacking up with Late Nate." She peered at me more closely. "Are you sure you're all right?"

"I got some bad news about someone who meant a lot to me."

"I'm so sorry."

I ran my hand over the sand covering his photograph. Should I make a tombstone to mark the spot, or was it better to let it disappear? "I thought if I buried a picture of him it might help say goodbye."

"Is it working?"

"Not yet."

She squatted next to me. "I know this sounds trite, but I know what it's like. I just found out that a friend of mine back home was killed."

"Irene?" I asked.

Her face showed her surprise. "How did you know?"

"Kay told me."

Her expression changed, showing a look of disappointment that was so frequently experienced that it was becoming a permanent part of her face. "I can't believe she didn't say anything to me. I've been walking around all night wondering how I was going to break the news to her."

I wasn't in the mood to deal with whatever baggage Kay and Candy were toting around. Candy seemed to sense that, and instead of continuing on this conversational path, she sat next to me in the sand. "Who did you lose?" she asked.

"A friend. Well, he was more than that. A lot more before he enlisted, and not as much since then."

She nodded knowingly. "Only you realized he was everything to you, right?"

I nodded. "I'm not sure what to feel. There's this horrible emptiness inside me right now, and it seems so disrespectful. And I'm just so angry with him. I should be crying, shouldn't I?'

"You're in shock. It's perfectly normal. When you're ready, the tears will come."

"I've had to fake grief so many times, but no matter how many tears I shed onstage, I don't think anything I manufactured ever approached what real grief feels like."

"Have you lost anyone before?"

"My pop, though I was too young to feel anything. A guy I worked for was murdered a few months ago. I didn't have any problem crying for him." I worked my finger through the wet sand, inventing cursive letters that had nothing to do with the Western alphabet.

"That's different though," said Candy. "That death was a total shock."

She was right. Anyone who knew anyone who had been drafted or enlisted had to consider the possibility that they weren't returning. In some small way they must've prepared themselves for that inevitability, biting off the emotion like a squirrel storing its nuts for the winter.

She put her hand in mine. "The last thing you should be doing is beating yourself up for not grieving properly."

But it was so much easier than feeling the grief that I knew was waiting just beneath the surface.

Candy offered to walk me back to my tent. I was grateful for the company, especially once I realized I had no idea where I was going. As we approached my home away from home, silhouettes formed against the lit canvas walls.

"Is there a man in your tent?" asked Candy.

"Wouldn't surprise me."

Sure enough, the figure of a man and woman were putting on a shadow puppet show before the dim illumination of our lone lightbulb. As I told Candy good night, the man's figure raced out of the tent opening opposite from where we stood.

I entered our encampment and found Kay alone. "Where is everyone?" I asked.

"Spanky and his crew came through and kidnapped them. He promised to have them back after one beer." She dipped a washrag into our sink and mopped her face.

"Jayne too?" I hoped it didn't show in my voice, but I was disappointed that she wasn't there waiting for me. Not that it was fair for me to expect her to sit around while I mourned, but it was so unlike her not to.

"No, she went looking for you. There were two men with her. I think one of them was your friend from today."

"Peaches?"

"The one and only."

Why had he come to Tulagi? Was he mad that he hadn't gotten a chance to witness my breakdown? "What did he want?"

"From what I could tell, he was looking for forgiveness."

I squeezed my hand closed until my nails bit into my palm. "Then he came to the wrong place."

What if Kay was wrong? Maybe he wasn't here for forgiveness. Maybe he'd come to tell me he'd gotten it wrong and Jack was still alive.

"It might help to talk to him," said Kay. "If nothing else, directing your rage at someone might help the grief come out."

Or maybe Jayne was right: Peaches could've made up the whole awful story just to hurt me.

"Any idea which way they headed?" I asked.

"To the beach, I imagine."

I dashed back into the night. I followed the path to the beach by the dim light of the moon.

"Rosie!" said Jayne.

Peaches and Billy were with her. I waited for her to jubilantly announce that a terrible mistake had been made, but the words never came.

You couldn't undo death.

"Kay said you were looking for me," I said. I couldn't meet Peaches' eyes, so I focused on everyone but him.

Jayne released her grip on Billy's hand and gently pushed Peaches toward me. "Peaches wants to talk to you." They must've spent their time searching for me gabbing about the reason for his visit since Jayne didn't seem to have a problem with leaving him alone with me. Or maybe it was Billy who convinced her. After all, she had to be dying to be alone with him.

"I'm not so sure I want to talk to him," I said.

"Please," said Peaches. "Give me five minutes. And then I'll leave you alone for good."

Jayne widened her eyes in a silent plea. I couldn't help but feel that she was betraying me in her eagerness to get away.

"All right." I splayed my fingers. "Five minutes."

"We're going back to the tent," said Jayne. "You come back there the minute you're done."

We waited until she and Billy had disappeared around the bend, and then the two of us walked toward the ocean. "How'd you get here?" I asked.

"I'm a pilot, remember."

"So you can just take off whenever you want to?"

"Not exactly, but I thought this was important enough to break a rule or two."

"Come on now—what really happened? Did you feel guilty about today, or did your pal have a hankering to see Jayne and you decided to tag along?"

He stopped walking. "Why do you have to think the worst of me?"

"Because you haven't given me any other option." I wrapped my arms around my chest and shivered in the night air. "You've got four minutes left. If you've come here to speak, speak."

His shoes dangled from his hands. His socks were tucked inside of them, and as a breeze passed through they wagged like the stubby tails of dogs. "I never should've told you about Jack like that."

"Spoonfeeding never helped anyone."

"Maybe not, but there was a right way to say it. I was hurt when you asked about him and so I wanted to hurt you too."

"So I figured."

"Doing that was unforgivable." No—dead was unforgivable. "Once you left, I couldn't stop thinking about the look on your face when you got the news. I know in light of what I told you, how I said it is probably the last thing on your mind, but I wanted you to know how sorry I was for both the way I acted and for your loss. He was a good man, Rosie."

Of all the things that had happened that day, Peaches' apology surprised me the most. "Thank you." I took a deep breath and was relieved to feel tears finally appearing in the corners of my eyes.

"I suppose I should go. You must be exhausted."

I couldn't find words. All I could find was water, so I shook my head.

"Do you want me to stay?"

I nodded. I had to keep my mouth closed. If I opened it, I was certain I would never stop sobbing.

Peaches dropped his shoes and gently pulled me into his chest. I buried my face in the crook of his arm and wailed until I was hoarse.

CHAPTER 15

The Guest of Honor

Whoever said things always look better in the morning deserved to be shot. To my eyes, the morning looked even bleaker, probably because a heavy rain was falling all over the island, turning the ground into thick, impenetrable mud. Lightning momentarily brightened the sky outside our tent, while thunder rumbled a warning that mimicked the sound of bombs so perfectly that it took my breath away. Water leaked through our roof, revealing dozens of small holes the sun had worn into the fabric. Someone had placed our helmets beneath the leaks, and the sound filled the thick jungle silence with the funereal march of horse-drawn Victorian hearses: *pling plop, pling plop, pling plop.*

I was still wearing my clothes from the night before, and my mouth made it clear that it hadn't met a toothbrush in at least twenty-four hours. I had a vague memory of Peaches leading me back to the tent and helping the girls put me to bed. I had been limp by then, so spent from crying that he'd had to carry me part of the way.

I rubbed my eyes and searched the room for my companions. I was alone. Someone had left a note pinned to the nail that held our performance schedule:

Rosie,

> *We thought you might want to sleep in. Our shows are canceled on account of the weather. If you feel up to it, we'll be rehearsing in the mess tent. I'll make sure to save some chow for you.*

Jayne

P.S. We got some rain gear for you. It's hanging near your cot.

I didn't feel up to rehearsing, but I felt even less like sitting in the rain-drenched tent entertaining myself with my thoughts. I dressed and pulled on the military-issue rain gear. It billowed like the garb of a vinyl ghost. As I stepped outside, I saw dozens of men and women dressed just like me, all of us anonymous beneath the sameness of army issue.

Did Jack have rain gear and an M1 helmet? Had he been supplied with a mess kit full of K rations? Did he have multiple pairs of navy-issue underwear and a sewing kit for mending tears with thread that was white, khaki, and blue? Where was that stuff now? Did the armed forces recycle a dead man's possessions or retire them like the Yankees retired Lou Gehrig's number? And what about the rest of his things, the stuff he'd brought from home? I wanted all of that to take with me as evidence that he'd been here and hadn't disappeared in a puff of air the minute he climbed aboard the bus headed for the Brooklyn Navy Yard. I needed that proof. Maybe if I accumulated enough remembrances of him, it would be like having him back.

"I thought that was you!" Gilda's voice reached across the downpour, and her hand extended out of her rain gear and waved me over. "I was just going back to the tent to check on you."

"Is rehearsal over?"

"We're taking a break." She looked worse than she had the day before. I wanted to ask her if she was all right, but the rain picked up its rhythm, preventing further conversation. The storms were never like this in New York. There, the concrete buffeted the downfall, turning the noise of the falling drops into something manmade and industrial. Here, for all the attempts that had been made to turn the island into a suitable home for Westerners, it felt as though nature was trying desperately to reclaim the earth. The rain actually hurt as it hit the vinyl cape, each drop a stinger desperate to get past the barrier protecting me and burrow into my skin. We had to focus our efforts on navigating through the sheet of water that seemed determined to foil us. At last, we made it into the enlisted men's mess, where the other women were drinking coffee.

"Look who I found." Gilda removed her cape and wiped her forehead dry. "*Whew*! I didn't think it could get any worse. Never in my life have I seen rain like that."

"Get used to it," said Kay. "The rainy season is upon us."

"You're kidding, right?" said Violet.

While they continued to ruminate about the weather we'd be experiencing for the next few months, Jayne helped free me from the rain gear and showed me where the others had hung theirs to dry.

"Are you hungry?" she asked.

"No. Not really."

I knew she had a thousand other questions she wanted to ask, but Jayne was keenly aware when it was better to dance around a subject than approach it directly. "I wasn't sure if I should stay with you this morning."

"And watch me sleep? That's not your job." The other girls were starting to send looks my way. They wanted to know, just as much as Jayne did, how I was really doing. "Did Peaches make it out okay?" I asked.

"I think so. He took off before the lightning started anyway." She tore at a fingernail. She'd chewed her entire left hand down to the quick. "I hope you don't think we ambushed you last night. When he told me why he wanted to see you, it seemed like it might be something you needed to hear."

I pushed my damp hair out of my face. "Don't worry about it. Talking to him was the best thing that could've happened." I felt weak and weepy, but I didn't want to give in to it. "So what are we rehearsing?"

Violet caught wind of my query, and she stopped pretending to be gabbing about the weather. "We're trying to come up with material for a new show. We've picked a few songs, and Jayne has a swell idea for a dance, but we're a little uncertain about the other stuff."

"Such as?"

It was clear that some sort of battle had started before my arrival and that Violet was currently on the losing end. Rather than conceding, she decided to use my presence as a chance to bolster her argument. "I was thinking we should put some political content into the show. You know, maybe a sketch or two making fun of the Japs and the Krauts. Spanky and I came up with a whole slew of jokes last night."

I relaxed my scowl. I kind of liked the idea. So far the content of our show had been going along with the idea that the war was one big party. Why shouldn't we acknowledge the elephant in the room and poke a little fun at the Axis nations? "Sounds fine by me. So what's the problem?"

"I think it's dangerous," said Gilda. "Jayne and I both do." Where did Kay stand in all this? I looked her way, but her face was blank. If she had a vote, she wasn't willing to share it yet.

"And why is it dangerous?" I asked.

"The men are here to forget," said Gilda. "If we start making fun of the Germans and the Japanese, it's only going to remind them of the danger they're in. Do we really want to do that?"

"Do you really think they've forgotten just because we're strutting around the stage singing songs from home?" asked Violet.

"It's not just that," said Gilda. "I'm afraid they'll think we're devaluing the danger they're in."

"I doubt anyone's going to think that," said Kay. I was shocked to hear her siding with Violet. Had the world gone topsy-turvy since the night before?

Gilda crossed her arms, and I could see a hint of her onscreen persona fighting to come out. "You don't know that. There are some things that are sacred. How would you feel about the Germans making jokes about how stupid American soldiers are?"

Violet cracked a smile. "It would be a relief to know the Krauts had a sense of humor."

"But would you still feel that way if you'd known someone who'd been killed by one of them?" asked Gilda.

Violet never got a chance to respond. Spanky and Mac had entered the mess, and they weren't alone.

"Sorry to interrupt, ladies," said Spanky. Mac shook himself from head to tail, spraying the room with rainwater. "I have a favor to ask. It's not mine really, but . . . well . . ."

The man beside him had the bars and bearing that branded him as someone important. "What RM Gallagher is trying to say is that he is making this request on my behalf. I'm Colonel Reed Hafler of the Fifty-second Airborne."

We said our "how-dos" and introduced ourselves.

"A number of us have been grounded here since last night, and we just found out that the camp is host to the five of you. I was told that you weren't traveling because of the weather, and I was hoping we might be able to persuade you to do a command performance for my men."

Spanky's face made it clear that he'd had about all of Colonel Hafler that he could take, and while the good colonel might be making a show of politely extending his request, it hadn't been anything less than an order when he'd first shared the idea with Spanky. "If you're too tired after yesterday, we understand—"

"No," said Gilda. "We're happy to perform. Of course, if we were to do so, we'd insist on doing it for the entire camp. They've been kind enough to host us, and they aren't even on our schedule yet. I'd hate to hurt their feelings by performing for a limited group."

"Of course," said Hafler. He scowled and turned to Spanky. "Will the rain let up by then?"

"I'll see what I can do, sir."

"Do, Gallagher. Do." Hafler turned on his heel and marched out of the tent.

Spanky lingered, waiting until the man was out of range before speaking. "I'd like to wring his neck."

"So they're army air force?" I asked.

"Yep. There are only twelve of them, but they've been making a stink since they arrived last night. There's some VIPs in the group, and being stranded in Tulagi wasn't exactly in their plans." Spanky pulled a handkerchief from his pocket and wiped the rain from his head. "You don't have to do the show. You're not under any obligation."

"Hogwash," said Violet. "We'd be thrilled to do our part for the red, white, and blue."

The afternoon passed in a heavy haze of grief. I think we rehearsed, but whether or not I participated in it, I can't recall. I suspect my body was there going through the motions while my mind traveled beneath the ocean, plumbing its depths for the spot where Jack spent his final moments. What was the last thing he saw? The last sound he heard? What was he thinking as he began to descend to the bottom of the sea? Knowing Jack, I figured he was angry and embarrassed that he couldn't get himself out of this fix.

If he was still alive when the shark attacked, he would've fought hard. I knew that for certain. He would've struggled to the very end. There was probably a shark out there bearing the permanent marks of his last moments. A missing eye. A lost tooth. A heel mark emblazoned on his back. Was it possible to hate an animal? Because I think I did. This unknown, unnamed creature that was only fighting for its own survival, following the instincts nature had given him, made me hungry for a taste of blood. If I had the strength, I would've dived into the ocean and hunted him out.

Was Jack scared? He had to be. No matter what Kay and Violet claimed, drowning had to be an awful, panic-stricken way to go. Add a fresh bullet wound and potential shark attack to the mix, and his last minutes must've been terrifying. Not only was death fast approaching, but he had no idea if the truth about what had happened to him would get out. Jack was a proud man, and I imagine the idea that his parents would be told that his death had been anything but honorable would seem like the cruelest blow of all.

"What are you thinking?" Jayne asked me at regular intervals.

"Nothing." My tone was short and irritated. I wasn't able to share my strange, disjointed thoughts with anyone, much less the one person who'd always been there for me.

I owed it to Jack to tell his family the truth about what had happened between him and his CO. Perhaps I could get Peaches to write them a letter outlining what he knew. They were wealthy people. They had connections. They could see to it that Jack had justice.

"We need to get ready for dinner, Rosie," said Jayne.

While I'd been lost in my own head, Gilda talked to a former pianist assigned to the motorcade and gave him the sheet music for the songs we were planning to perform. He was thrilled for the chance to do something other than repair Jeeps and convoy trucks, and we agreed to be at the amphitheater a half hour before curtain.

I went back to the tent with the others and dressed for dinner. We arrived ahead of our guests at the high commissioner's house. The men we'd already met were in place, welcoming us back after our week of travels. My mind wasn't in the room with me. I stared dully at each face, trying to figure out the name that went with it. Jayne whispered something to one of the men, and he took me by the elbow and led me to my usual seat. Rear Admiral Blake, the man with the pale eyes who'd branded me a Jap-lover, watched me with a bemused smile on his face, and I silently dared him to say something to me. I desperately wanted to take the rage I felt and direct it at someone, and Late Nate was just as good as anyone else. As though he sensed that I was already wounded, he left me alone and focused his attention on Gilda. With a smile, he patted the seat

beside him, inviting her to once again share his company. She hesitated, hoping, I'm sure, that the new guests would show up and save
her from another meal with this insufferable companion. She had no
such luck. By the time they arrived, we were already working on our
soup course, and our fates—and seat assignments—had been sealed.

I heard the men enter before I saw them. Not just the sound of
their footsteps and the murmur of new voices, but quiet gasps emit-
ted from each of the women at the table. I didn't have the strength
to turn around, so I looked toward Jayne for confirmation that
something interesting was happening. Her eyes were wide, and her
mouth was a perfect circle.

Please, God. Let Jack be alive. Let him be standing behind me
ready to apologize for the awful joke he'd decided to play. Please.

I turned to find Colonel Hafler and another man I recognized,
even though I'd never met him in person.

"Van Lauer," Jayne mouthed. Excitement rippled around the
table, and Kay, Violet, and Jayne all looked toward Gilda expectantly. I looked toward her, too, desperately hoping to see someone
suffering as much as I was. Never mind that it was Gilda, whom I
actually liked. I needed to know that I wasn't the only one whose life
was being turned upside down.

For a woman who was receiving the shock of her life, she was
amazingly calm. Her body was strangely still, as though she was
holding her breath in anticipation of what would happen next. A
hint of a smile rippled across her face, ready—in an instant—to con-
vert itself into either a full-fledged grin or a frown. She kept her eyes
glued on Van, silently daring him to say the first word.

The man who had been dubbed the heartthrob of Hollywood
had the sort of good looks that made you think he might be accessible. He was handsome and athletic, perfectly suited to a military
uniform. Maybe his eyes were a little too blue, his hair a shade too
dark for him to be just like other men, but on screen you could believe the lie that this was a boy you knew who'd grown up to be the
man you loved. As the four of us gawked, Hafler introduced his men
to the group. I felt like I was watching a film and prayed it wasn't a

Saturday afternoon serial headed toward a cliffhanger. What would the famous movie star do next? Would he acknowledge his spurned ex or pretend that she was a complete stranger?

In his place, I probably would've done the latter. And had it been a room full of men, he might have chosen to do just that. (After all, how many of those men were aware of the romantic travails of Hollywood stars?) But I'll bet seeing four women who recognized both him and the awkwardness of the situation convinced him that to do anything but greet Gilda warmly would cause him to be tarred and feathered.

"Gilda," he said, in that wonderful voice of his that had begged many a big-screen woman to be his wife. His smile ignited the dimples that always made him look younger than he really was. "It's so wonderful to see you. I'd heard you were doing a tour."

She returned his plastic smile, and I marveled at what a truly skilled actress she was. "Van, I'm so pleased to see that you're safe." She rose and he planted a kiss on each of her cheeks.

"I hear you'll be performing for us tonight," said Van.

Gilda stepped away from him and gestured to where the rest of us were sitting. "All of us will be. I'm hardly the only person in the show."

"No, but you're the star, aren't you?"

Gilda didn't answer, though the tension the comment created in her was palpable. Rear Admiral Blake rose from his chair and directed our guests to the open seats. "Please forgive us for starting without you, gentlemen. The ladies are anxious to have time to get ready for their performance."

"We should be the ones apologizing," said Van with a wink. "I certainly know better than to keep a lady waiting."

Dinner was an unpleasant affair. Those of us who were aware of the awkwardness between Gilda and Van were working overtime to distract them however we could. For a while Violet took up the banner as center of attention, bombarding Van with questions about his career that I knew she couldn't have cared less about. When she ran out of things to ask, Kay jumped in with questions for the army air force officers about where they'd been and what they'd done. While that conversation could've lasted into the new year, it wasn't sufficiently interesting to hold the attention of the men we usually dined with. Late Nate, sullen after having met Gilda's ex-boyfriend, decided to steal the focus away from the new arrivals and redirect it at me.

"Still empathizing with the Japanese, Miss Winter?"

He couldn't have diverted attention faster if he'd put a fruit bowl on his head and started to merengue.

"I think you misunderstood my remarks that night," I said. The rage that I had wanted to aim at him returned in hot, strong waves.

"So you *do* think the Japanese are vicious savages?"

I looked to the others for assistance, but there was such relief that whatever we were talking about wasn't Gilda and Van that no one seemed anxious to jump in and help me. Even Jayne seemed to have forgotten that I was on the ledge and about to tumble off. "I think they're human beings, Rear Admiral Blake. That's all."

"Really? And would you still feel that way if it were your husband or boyfriend who was dead at their hands? Not just dead but savagely ripped apart and left to suffer in the most excruciating manner possible."

I lunged at Late Nate. If he wanted to talk suffering, I would show him suffering.

"Rosie!" Jayne latched on to my arm and wrenched it backward.

I kept my eyes locked on Late Nate's, telling him without words what I wished I could say out loud. Jayne jerked my arm so hard I heard my shoulder pop. I stumbled from my place at the table to a space just beside her.

"She's not herself," she said. "She just found out that a friend was killed."

Blake said something in response, but I couldn't hear it above the roar of the blood pulsing in my ears. Jayne pulled me out of the high commissioner's house and kept walking until we were safely out of earshot of the building.

"I'm sorry," I whispered.

"Don't be. He was baiting you. In your shoes, I would've done the same thing."

But she wasn't in my shoes. Jayne had Billy and Tony, if she still wanted him, two men who were very alive and very in love. I just had memories of a man I hadn't loved enough, who'd left this earth in the worst possible way.

"You shouldn't do the show tonight," she said.

"No." The rain had stopped and been replaced by a fine mist that was turning my hair from lank to frizzy. In fact, everything about me felt like it was curling up. If the sensation continued, I'd be half the size I started at.

"I mean it, Rosie. Your heart's not in it, and your brain isn't very far behind. You need rest. And while I don't blame you a bit for how you reacted in there, I'd hate to see Blake decide to punish you for it. If you're up on that stage tonight acting like everything's fine, it's going to be awfully hard for him to excuse what happened. Gilda's going to be a nervous wreck as it is, and I just think it would be better for everyone if you took the night off."

Deep down, I knew she was right. I had threatened a commanding officer and no matter how justified I'd felt in my actions, there could be repercussions. With everything else that was happening, it was the last thing I needed.

"Can I watch the show?" I asked. I was afraid to go back to the tent by myself, afraid of spending two hours lost in my own thoughts.

Jayne took my hand. "Sure."

We headed toward the performance area. While Jayne got ready, I watched from a chair in the dressing area, as limp as an exhausted child waiting for her nap. Eventually, the other girls arrived and Jayne informed them, in a low voice, that I wouldn't be performing that night. They each cooed their regrets, agreeing that it was wise for me to sit the night out and reassuring me that Blake wouldn't do anything to punish me. "I talked to him," said Gilda. "He understands that grief makes people do strange things."

Nobody mentioned the fact that Van Lauer was going to be in the audience. His arrival seemed to have been forgotten in light of what had happened, which I'm sure Gilda was grateful for. She oc-cupied herself by talking through the changes they would make in the show to cover my absence. She seemed invigorated by having a new calamity to focus on.

Just as the four of them were getting ready to go on stage, there was a knock outside the dressing area. "I need to talk to Gilda." The voice was unmistakably Van's.

Gilda rolled her eyes. "We're getting ready to start the show," She told the door.

"Two minutes," he said. "I think you owe me that much."

She shifted her attention back to us. "I'll be right back, ladies," she said.

As soon as she was gone, Jayne, Violet, and Kay huddled to-gether to analyze what was going on.

"What a jerk," said Jayne. "I can't believe she let him treat her like that during dinner."

"What choice did she have?" said Kay. "I doubt any man in there understood the significance of his arrival. If she'd been cold toward him, she would've looked like the one who wasn't behaving appro-priately. She didn't need that."

"And talk about nerve," said Violet. "Demanding that she talk to him. She doesn't owe him anything. Look, girls, she's going to need our help tonight. Whatever he's saying is bound to rattle her good. Let's make sure we're on our toes just in case she's off hers."

"Absolutely," said Jayne. Rising voices came from outside the dressing area, but I couldn't make out what they were saying. Both were letting each other have it, though, that much was clear. A third voice unexpectedly joined them, abruptly cutting off the heated ex-change.

"Can I get you anything?" asked Jayne.

It took me a moment to realize that she was directing the ques-tion at me. "No."

"Are you sure?" She put her hand on my shoulder.

I swatted her away. "Just stop with the babying, okay? Your hov-ering over me isn't helping anything."

Jayne backed away, a scrim of hurt darkening her eyes. I didn't care. Let her hurt. Nothing I said to her could make her feel half as bad as I did.

Gilda joined us, her eyes red and her face flushed. "Colonel Hafler would like us to start now," she said. She picked up a powder puff and tried to pat the sheen out of her face.

"Is everything all right?" asked Jayne.

"Van has impeccable timing as usual. Leave it to him to upset someone the moment before they have to go onstage." The powder was doing a poor job disguising the feverish flush of her skin. She sighed heavily, and I feared that her tears might be getting ready for a second performance. Just when I thought I saw water glistening at the corners of her eyes, she forced a large smile and removed any hint of despair from her face. "Come on, girls," she said. "We have a show to do."

CHAPTER 16

The Command Performance

I angled a chair in the wings so that I had a good view of what was going on. The show started seamlessly. Beneath a star-filled sky and before an audience full of men we'd met over the course of our weeks there, and the few we'd unfortunately encountered that evening, Kay, Violet, Jayne, and Gilda sang the songs, did the steps, and told the jokes that had become second nature to them.

I was the only one aware of my absence. I had become expendable.

The small amphitheater was packed, which necessitated putting men up in the cliffs that surrounded the performance space. As though they sensed the tension in Gilda's performance, the enlisted men laughed a little louder and hooted with more enthusiasm than we were used to. The army air force officers had been seated in a special section with real chairs and a table to rest their after-dinner drinks on. While the majority of the group seemed to be enjoying the show, Van Lauer remained expressionless. Part of me wondered if he hadn't fallen asleep.

I had verification that he was still conscious halfway through the show. As Gilda sang her second solo, he got up and left the theater. Gilda must've noticed as well because her voice made a peculiar skip, faltering on a note she'd never had problems with before. Someone else in the audience got up. Dotty. He left the same way Van had and disappeared.

Gilda's song ended, and Jayne joined her for "Anchor's Aweigh." As Gilda gave the song all her gusto, Jayne shim sham shimmied before the appreciative crowd. Up in the cliffs a flash of light grabbed my attention. Could it be the Japanese again, watching us the way they'd watched at Guadalcanal? But they weren't on Tulagi, where they?

A crackle sounded across the theater. Somebody screamed. Gilda stopped singing and the piano quickly came to a halt. The *rat-a-tat* of Jayne's tap shoes could no longer be head over the sounds of the audience.

"Medic!" someone screamed.

"Sniper on the hillside. Two o'clock!"

A wave of people stormed the stage and filled the wings, pushing me back into the dressing area. Violet was in the middle of a costume change and covered her upper half with her arms while screaming for a little privacy.

"Oh it's you," she said. "What the hell is going on?"

Another crackle sounded somewhere in the distance.

"Gunshots," I said. "Someone's throwing lead." I tried to force my way onstage, but the crush of people wouldn't let me pass. Where were Jayne and Gilda? I grabbed the arm of the sailor nearest to me and tried to get an answer from him, but he shrugged me off and told me to get out of the way so the medic could get through.

I shoved him back, twice as hard, until he had no choice but to look at me. "Listen, Buster, I need to know what's going on here. Has someone been shot?"

"It looks like the two women on stage are down. You know—Gilda DeVane and that other girl."

Violet paced the brief length of the dressing area, her shoulders hunched like she was an animal waiting to pounce on its prey. "We shouldn't have to wait. We should be there with them."

"I know," I said. We'd been told to stay in the dressing area while the men searched the area for the sniper. I was starting to shake. I did this when I was scared, no matter what the temperature. Jayne had been shot. She could be dying or dead. Was I going to lose everyone who meant something to me?

"Hey you!" Violet marched over to the door and got the attention of the nearest sailor. "We want out of here."

"Sorry, ma'am, but orders are the two of you are to stay put."

"Then, at the very least, I think we deserve to know what's what. Our friends were hurt. We need to know how they are."

I admired her moxie. And I was ashamed that I hadn't made the same demand myself. But I was in shock, so shattered over the idea that Jayne was somewhere suffering that I could barely get my own mind to work.

"I'll see if I can get word for you, all right? That's the best I can do."

Violet left the doorway and sank onto an army-green folding chair. "You got to get yourself together, Rosie. They're going to be fine. Jayne . . . she's a tough cookie, like you." Or like I used to be anyway. Violet reached under her skirt and pulled out her flask. She chugged the liquid, her throat pulsing like it was a vein receiving a fresh push of blood. She pulled the bottle from the baby's mouth and offered it to me. "Want a tickle?"

"Yeah, that would be swell." I gagged at the first taste. This was Spanky's homebrew.

"It gets better the more you drink," said Violet.

I mustered up some courage and took a long swallow before returning the flask to her. As the liquid tingled its way down my gullet, it brought me back to myself. Jayne needed me. I couldn't shut down like this. The sailor may have been wrong, and even if he wasn't, she could pull through this. She was young and strong. There was still hope. "Where's Kay?" I asked.

Violet snapped to it like she'd been in her own grief-induced haze. "I don't know. She was back here with me changing and then she said she had to use the latrine before we went back on. I told her she was never going to make it, but she said she had to go *now*. I don't think she ever came back."

The same grim thought seemed to occur to both of us: Gilda and Jayne might not be the only people injured.

I rushed to the entrance. "Our friend's missing," I said to the sailor at the door.

"We know. We're trying to find out what we can."

"I'm not talking about the two onstage. There's a third girl—Kay Thorpe. She went to the latrine right before the gunshots started, and no one's seen her since."

He barked an order to the guy next to him, instructing him to check out the nearest latrine. He was off in an instant, calling out the names of other men to accompany him.

Violet and I returned to the flask, hoping we might be able to pull more commonsense from it. In the distance, men shouted out orders and directions. More shots were fired. "We got 'em!" someone shouted jubilantly, and a rush of footsteps stormed past where we were hidden, making strange sucking noises as they moved over the rain-drenched earth.

We were about to poke our heads out and ask what happened when a face appeared at the door. Kay!

"Are you all right?" asked Violet. My eyes scanned her tall body, searching for a sign of injury.

"Just shaken, that's all. Where are the others?"

"They've been shot," said Violet. I winced as she said it. Would it have killed her to wrap the news in a kind little euphemism?

"Both of them?" Kay sank into a nearby chair.

"Where were you?" I asked.

Her face was pale, or at least as pale as it could be after taking two weeks' worth of Atabrine. "I ran to the latrine. I got scared when I heard the gunshots. I couldn't tell where they were coming from. And so I decided I'd better stay put—" A tear fought to leave the corner of her eye. There was more to the story than just a frightened woman hiding from what she was certain was a scene of danger. There was something in Kay's voice that said that she hated herself for deciding to hide rather than help. As though she recognized that we sensed what she hadn't said, Kay nodded twice and lowered her voice. "It was a cowardly thing to do. I shouldn't have stayed there. I have training after all. If I'd run toward the hills when the first shot was fired, maybe I could've stopped them."

"That's silly," I said. "More likely you would've turned yourself into a moving target. Besides, the second shot came right after the first. There's no way you could've prevented it."

"But I shouldn't have run," she said. "That's not what Wacs do."

"You're not a Wac anymore," said Violet. "You're a human."

For two hours we waited for word in the cramped dressing area behind the stage. At last the door opened, and Dotty and Spanky appeared. If I didn't know any better, I would've thought Spanky was shell-shocked. His face told of horrors he never anticipated having to see. Dotty looked haggard, the skin beneath his eyes stained a sickly blue gray. I hadn't seen him since Kay had told him about Irene, so I couldn't tell if his appearance had changed with that bad news or with this fresh rush of awful. For the first time since I'd met him, I found it impossible not to notice his limp. It had become the most prominent thing about him.

"What's going on? How are they?" Kay rushed toward the door and took hold of Dotty's arm, as though she feared he would change his mind and turn around and leave.

Now it was his turn not to meet her eyes. "Jayne's in the infirmary. It looks like she was just grazed."

I smiled. I couldn't help it. Jayne was all right. I hadn't lost her. "What about Gilda?"

"I don't know. They took her into surgery."

Violet went to Spanky's side and took his hand. Instantly, both their mitts turned bright red from the strength they exerted in holding each other. When had they gotten so close? I was surprised to see it but strangely pleased by it too. Violet was capable of caring about someone other than herself. Who knew?

"It'll be fine," whispered Violet.

"They're not the only ones who got hurt," said Spanky.

Violet's face became a question mark.

"Somebody shot Mac too."

His dog? What was this—was someone on a streak, gunning down everyone who meant something to us? What did it say that Violet, Kay, and I were spared?

"Oh no," said Violet. "How bad is it?"

"Woof thinks the bullet missed the organs and arteries." His words slurred together. "He already got the slug out. You're not going to believe this, but he was shot with a revolver."

"Who's Woof?" asked Kay.

"One of the Aussies used to be a vet," said Dotty. He looked like he was about to say more when Rear Admiral Blake poked his head into the room.

"You ladies are free to go to your tent now."

"That's it?" I said. "What happened? Who do you think did this?"

"Are we safe?" asked Violet.

"What if it happens again?" asked Kay.

"Relax, ladies," said Blake. "The culprit has been caught."

We decided to go down to the swimming hole to commiserate. I couldn't help but notice how Kay stuck to Dotty's side on the walk there. In fact, with Kay clinging to Dotty and Violet to Spanky, I was starting to feel like the odd man out.

That was all right though. Jayne was alive. *Grazed* was the word Dotty had used. Never had there been a more benign word in the English language.

"Can I see her?" I asked.

"They've got sickbay locked up tight with guards at every door," said Dotty. "No one's getting in there tonight."

At least I knew she was safe.

"Where did Mac get shot?" asked Violet. She produced her flask and passed it to Spanky.

"In the chest." Spanky took a long pull from the bottle.

"No, I mean where was he?" asked Violet.

"I found him up in the cliffs when we went after the sniper. He must've followed me up there. I thought he was gone for sure, but the minute he saw me, he wagged his tail. I just can't believe someone would shoot a dog like that."

To say nothing of two humans.

We arrived at the swimming hole and spread out on the grassy ledge that surrounded it. None of us had our bathing suits on, and the subject matter demanded modesty, so we all sat with our feet dangling in the warm water, swatting at mosquitoes that seemed intent on feeding on us.

"Who did they capture?" asked Kay.

"There was a Jap up in the cliffs," said Spanky. He still had Violet's flask and I longed for him to pass it to me. It was becoming increasingly clear, though, that he was depending on it to make it through the night.

"Did you see him?" asked Violet.

"Not when they grabbed him, but I saw him when they brought him down."

"I didn't think there were any Japanese on the island," I said.

"Neither did I," said Spanky. "But I heard they caught two nips by the supply hut a few weeks ago. And word is that more supplies went missing last night. Not much, but enough to be noticed. I'm thinking they must've come back tonight to get more."

"But the supply huts are on the other side of the camp. What was the shooter doing up in the cliffs?" I asked.

Spanky shook his head. "Beats me. Maybe the sniper was put up in the hills to make sure no one left the theater until they were done with their supply raid. He had a radio with him. Once they realized that most of the men were congregating in one place, they probably posted him as a lookout."

"But why shoot Gilda and Jayne?"

"Something might've gone wrong," said Dotty. "Maybe he needed to create a distraction."

I shivered in the warm night. We were all expendable.

"God, that's terrifying," said Violet. She was putting two and two together and realizing, as I was, how lucky we were that we hadn't been onstage. "They had to know they were civilians."

Dotty shook his head. "I don't think the Japanese know how to distinguish between the two. They slaughtered thousands of natives who never had a role in this war. They do whatever they perceive they have to do to win, and that means they play by very different rules than we do. They're savages."

"Dotty." Kay's voice held a hint of warning. They were sitting thigh to thigh. What had changed between them? Was he the man Candy and I had seen in silhouette in the tent the night before? Had their grief over Irene united them?

"You know it's true," said Dotty. "They showed no mercy in Bataan."

Kay didn't respond. Space grew between them. It wasn't much, but it was clear she didn't want him touching her anymore.

"He had to know he would get caught," I said.

"That's the last thing the Japs would worry about," said Spanky. "The guy had to complete his mission, and if that meant getting caught while everyone else got away, so be it."

Violet scanned the jungle around us. "If he was creating a distraction so that someone else could steal supplies, do you think the men who were with him are still here?"

A flash of light grabbed my attention and I peered toward the Suicide Cliffs looking for its source. A flicker of light danced near the entrance to the caves, though from this distance it seemed no bigger than a firefly.

"They swept the island pretty good," said Spanky. "If there are any Japs here, they'll want to lie low until the heat's off them, which means they won't try anything else tonight. In the meantime, they're posting guards up and down the Suicide Cliffs and along the shore, just in case they try to make a run for it before dawn."

I was amazed he could be so confident about that. If they had no problem shooting Gilda and Jayne, surely we couldn't predict what they would or wouldn't do next.

"What about the supply huts?" I asked. "Is anything else missing?"

He didn't get a chance to answer me. The PA system crackled to life. We were all ordered back to our tents. Only authorized personnel were permitted to leave their quarters until first light.

It took me hours to fall asleep. The humidity seemed to grow by the minute until I swore someone was sitting directly on top of me. The jungle was no longer full of unusual animals sounding their nocturnal calls. It was riddled with Japanese soldiers toting their guns, looking for a chance to take a shot at the rest of us. My mind kept turning to Gilda and Jayne. Was Gilda out of surgery? Was Jayne in much pain? Would either of them be permanently scarred or damaged? It would be a terrible irony for Gilda to come all this way to reignite her career only to have it stolen from her when a sniper's bullet ruined her face for film.

Even though we'd all been ordered back to our tents, I could hear our men walking the road, talking in low voices about which way to direct their search. There were no loud whoops signaling that anyone else had been found. Eventually, I accepted that whatever was going to come to pass was going to happen regardless of whether or not I was awake for it.

It was only as I began to finally drift off that I realized I hadn't thought about Jack once since Gilda and Jayne were shot.

CHAPTER 17

Watch Your Neighbor

I slept through the morning bugle call and awoke shortly before 0800. I probably would've slept well after that if a young male voice hadn't told us that Rear Admiral Blake wanted to see us.

The three of us dressed in nervous anticipation of what this meeting would bring. At a quarter to nine we walked to his tent and waited for his secretary to lead us in.

Late Nate's makeshift office was impressive. While the building was nothing more than the same olive-drab canvas walls we inhabited, he made the place more permanent by adding a large oak desk, an Oriental rug, and pictures hanging from the rafters. He also had a typewriter and a phone, both of which seemed remarkably out of place on the island. But then that was the military. If they needed it, they got it.

As we entered the tent he gestured us into three camp chairs that had been lined up in front of his desk. A tower of papers was awaiting his attention. They were letters that he was supposed to help censor. "Good morning, ladies." If his demeanor had been unpleasant before, it was downright Machiavellian now. "I hope you had a good night's rest."

"We've had better," I said. "How're Gilda and Jayne?"

"Miss Hamilton is doing quite well. In fact, you're welcome to visit her in the infirmary if you wish."

I could feel my mood instantly brighten. Poor Jayne. She had to be terrified by everything that had taken place. I should've found a way to visit her last night. She would've done that for me.

"What about Gilda?" asked Kay.

"I'm afraid Miss DeVane had a very rough night." He nodded toward the secretary to dismiss him. The younger man saluted him before turning on his heel and exiting. "She made it through surgery quite well, but the doctor is concerned that infection may have set in."

"She hadn't been feeling well," I said. "She's had a fever the last few days."

He nodded. I wasn't telling him anything new. "The doctors are fairly certain that she has malaria, which is complicating her condition."

"Can we see her?" asked Kay.

"That is up to the medical staff. Given her fragile condition and the worries about worsening infection, they are restricting access to her for the time being. I can assure you she is receiving the very best of care here. Once her situation stabilizes we'll want to take her to one of the better-equipped hospital facilities. I'll make certain that you have regular updates as needed."

As needed. Did the military have a course on making vague commitments to keep you out of a tight spot?

"What about the sniper?" asked Violet.

"He has been locked up and will be doing no more harm to anyone."

"But did you find his accomplices?" asked Violet.

"What accomplices?" Late Nate's tone made it clear that the fact that there may have been accomplices wasn't a surprise, but our knowing about them was.

"We heard a rumor," said Kay. "Some of the men were theorizing that he was creating a distraction while the supply huts were being raided."

Late Nate's mouth twitched into a smile. "You shouldn't listen to scuttlebutt, Miss Thorpe. Nevertheless, I can assure you we have combed every inch of the island to make sure there is no one else here."

"Were any more supplies missing?" I asked.

"I'm afraid that information is above your pay grade."

My dislike of Late Nate came back in waves. "Look, we deserve to know why our friends were shot."

"It sounds to me like you already do. An enemy sniper saw the opportunity to injure our morale and did so. Why he chose to do that is of no import."

Tell that to Gilda and Jayne, I thought.

"The important thing is that we stopped him before anyone else was harmed."

No, the important thing was that Gilda and Jayne were still alive.

We hoofed it to the infirmary after meeting with Blake. A large red cross painted near the roofline helped differentiate it from the nearly identical Quonset huts that surrounded it. Inside, it was divided into a series of small rooms that were marked with their intended purpose. This wasn't a place you convalesced for a long time. If you were that bad off, you went to Guadalcanal or one of the hospital ships.

As we entered the building, Kay faltered. "I don't think I can go in there," she said.

"Why?" asked Violet.

"I just . . . I just don't think I can." She whirled around and walked out the way we'd entered.

"What was that all about?" I asked.

"Maybe she can't stand the sight of blood," said Violet.

"Can I help you?" The voice belonged to a nurse with a head full of tight gray curls topped by a white cap. Atop her schnozzle was a pair of rimless glasses slowly traveling the length of her nose. Her eyebrows were thick and unkempt. In fact, her whole appearance told of long days and longer nights stationed at the infirmary. She wore a sweater, cape-like, around her shoulders and a white nurse's uniform that had long since lost its crispness. She wasn't part of the bedpan commando; she was Red Cross. In her hand was a paperback book that two of her fingers were attempting to mark her page in. It was *War and Peace*. I wondered if she could clue us in to how it turned out.

"Rear Admiral Blake said we could see Jayne Hamilton. She was one of the girls brought in last night," I said.

"Of course." She glanced behind us. "I was told that Kay Thorpe was in your group. Is that correct?"

Her knowing Kay rattled something in my memory. She had a friend at the infirmary who'd helped to arrange her discharge. "Yes. She wasn't feeling well, so she went back to camp."

"Tell her Ruth said hello. And please tell her to come by sometime. I'd love to know how she's doing." The nurse showed us a smile marred by a pronounced overbite and ushered us into one of the larger rooms, where men stricken with jungle rot and heat rashes that had grown infected reclined while they waited for the antibiotics to kick in. At the end of the space, cordoned off from the opposite sex, lay Jayne. She sat upright in her bed and spooned some sort of liquid into her mouth.

"Hiya!" she said. Before she could put the spoon down, I flung my arms around her and forced her into an embrace. I would never take advantage of her again. I would never direct another cross word at her. I would make sure she was safe until the day I died.

"Ow!" she said.

I pulled back. "Am I hurting you?"

"More like suffocating me."

"Sorry."

She noted the look on my face and relaxed her own. "It's all right. It's nice to be cared about."

I scanned her body—so childlike in the hospital bed—and tried to find a sign of the injury that had felled her. She looked exactly the same.

"What's the crop?" said Violet. "We heard you'd been shot."

Jayne tucked her hair behind her left ear and showed us an angry red burn mark that marred the fleshy part at the top. "The bullet barely touched me. It was the fall that caused most of the damage." She lifted the blanket covering her feet and showed us her swollen right ankle. "It's not broken, but it sure hurts like it is."

While Violet seemed disappointed in the extent of Jayne's injuries, I was stunned by them. Just another inch and the bullet would've hit her skull. And what would my last words to her have been? Stop babying me?

My eyes welled up. I was such a selfish, awful person. First, I push Jack away and get him killed and now Jayne—

She took my hand and squeezed it so hard I almost yelped. "Stop it," she said. "This wasn't your fault. I'm fine. I'm better than fine." She fished something out of her pocket. "Look, they even gave me a souvenir. One of the men found it lodged in the upstage wall."

It was a monster. Not a revolver's slug but a combat round designed to stop a man in his tracks.

"What about Gilda?" asked Violet.

"No one will say a peep," said Jayne. "They have her in another room, and they won't let anyone see her. She must be terrified." She licked her lips as she carefully chose her next words. "There was a lot of blood. At first I thought she must be dead for sure, but then I heard her moan."

I sat on the edge of her bed, still clutching her hand in mine. "What else did you see?"

"Nothing. I mean I heard the gunshot. I felt the bullet whiz past me, and I grabbed ground, but I never saw where any of it was coming from. Have they figured out who did it?"

"They caught the guy," said Violet. "It was a Jap hiding up in the hills."

"You mean like those fellows who were watching our show on

Guadalcanal?" Jayne shook her head. "I guess we're too entertaining for our own good."

We found Kay back in our tent flipping through *Stars & Stripes*.

"What happened to you back there?" asked Violet.

She blushed and pushed the paper away. "I'm sorry. I just started feeling woozy, like if I was in there another moment, I was going to pass out."

"Ruth told us to tell you hi," I said.

Kay blinked twice. "Did she? That's nice. How's Jayne?" If she changed the subject any faster, we would've gotten whiplash.

"Good," I said. "Better than good. She'll probably be out in a day or two." A new rush of rain rapidly flooded the cement floor. I snagged Kay's copy of *Stars & Stripes* and sat on my cot. An article described the tough time Clark Gable was having in the air force. In the B Bag column (allegedly named for the synonym for female dog), soldiers groused about the delay in getting V-mail and the censor's inconsistency. There was a brief article about Irene Zinn's death. As of the Pacific theater edition's printing, there'd been no leads in her murder.

"Did you get to see Gilda?" asked Kay.

"Nobody can," said Violet. "She's in a private room and not allowed visitors."

Kay nodded at the news. Water trickled across the uneven ground looking for a place to puddle.

"She should've taken her Atabrine," said Violet.

"She probably would've if you'd kept your big mouth shut," said Kay.

I was so shocked by Kay's outburst that I bit my tongue. Had she really just said that?

"What's that supposed to mean?" said Violet.

Kay left her cot and stepped toward her, dodging puddles in the process. "You're the one who went on and on about how yellow it would turn us. It's a miracle we don't all have malaria."

Violet sat up. "You think this is my fault?!"

I left my cot and stepped between them. "Of course Kay doesn't think that."

"The hell I don't."

I took Kay's arm and tried to pull her back toward her bed. She resisted my attempts, pulling me forward with her. "Violet didn't fire the gun," I said.

"No, but she certainly didn't help matters—"

I squeezed her arm. She was going to be wearing a colorful bracelet of bruises if she didn't close her head. "And she didn't force her to ditch her pills either. If anyone's to blame it's Gilda for being vain."

Kay looked down at her arm and seemed acutely aware that I'd squeeze her until she was black and blue if I had to. "Okay, it's not your fault," she said with all the sincerity of a Bund member saluting Roosevelt. "But you have to admit you forced her hand."

"I don't have to admit anything," said Violet.

Leave it to her to help the situation. I released Kay's arm. "Break it up, you two. Gilda would hate to know we're at each other's throats like this. We know who the culprit is. There's no point in blaming anyone else."

Kay rubbed her arm and retreated to her cot.

"He'll probably commit maui maui or harem harem or whatever you call it," said Violet. "Some punishment that'll be."

"I don't think they'll let that happen," I said. "They watch them pretty closely. And it's not like he has weapons in there."

Spanky popped his head into the tent. "What's the dope, ladies? We heard Blake met with you this morning."

"Jayne's fine. Gilda's hanging on, but she has malaria," said Violet.

"That's rotten luck."

Kay shot another look Violet's way. "Tell us about it."

"He wouldn't tell us anything about the supplies," I said. "Or the accomplices."

Spanky entered the room, dodging the raindrops where he could. He surveyed our deteriorating ceiling and pulled a roll of gray tape from his pants. He tore off strips and plastered *X*s over the larger holes.

"Word is, not much is missing," said Spanky.

"Do you think they got scared and ran?" asked Kay.

"Could be. Men went to battle stations pretty fast. My theory is that they were picked up, and Blake is too embarrassed to get the word out that there wasn't just one Nip loose on his island but a whole flock of them."

"How could he keep something like that quiet?" I asked.

"When you're a rear admiral, you can make your men declare the world is square. There's power in that star."

"It makes sense to keep it quiet from us," said Violet. "But from the men? You'd think he'd want them to know the sort of threat we're under. Otherwise, who's to say that there won't be more Japs on the island tomorrow?"

"Between you and me, the men are pretty riled about what happened. I think Blake's trying to keep the lid on things to keep the peace. It's not going to work though."

"Why not?" I asked.

A drop of rain made it past Spanky's handiwork and landed on his head. "Because the men want blood. Heaven help those Japs if Gilda dies. I have a feeling if that happens, any Nips in the South Pacific are going to find themselves with a bullet in their brain pan."

The day passed achingly slowly with no further word about Gilda. Kay and I played cards to pass the time while Violet read and wrote letters home. The rain kept up its steady thumping, though thanks to Spanky the room remained much drier. None of us were up for eating with the officers, among whom Van Lauer would still be included, and so we munched on what provisions we had among us. Violet passed her flask as though it were a peace pipe and Kay accepted her offering warily.

It felt good to be tipsy. Anything would've felt better than being worried and sad.

We hit the sack early that night. At some point I awoke with a start, though I wasn't immediately aware of why. I sat upright in the cot, trying to pinpoint what it was that had roused me. There, beneath the sounds of the animals and the rustling of plants as the wind passed through, was another sound—footsteps.

It could be anyone. The island was no longer on lockdown, and it was possible there were men stumbling drunk past our tent on their way back to their own. But drunk sailors weren't known for their discretion. They sang and laughed and announced their presence, like a parade passing down Fifth Avenue. Maybe it was the WACs. Their barracks were nearby, and they were very likely to tiptoe quietly past us on their way to their destination. Especially if they were trying to get somewhere after their curfew without being seen.

I tried to soothe myself back to sleep, but the sound continued outside the tent. They weren't productive footsteps. This wasn't someone on his way to or from somewhere. They were lingering outside our thin canvas walls.

I decided it wasn't going to do me any good to lie there analyzing what might or might not be going on. I needed to look outside and see for myself.

I wrestled free of the mosquito netting and plopped my helmet on my head. I crept to the tent opening and carefully peered outside. There was a full moon, which provided some light, though not nearly enough to see more than a few feet in front of my face. The shuffling and rustling sounded again, and I pinpointed the source at a cluster of palm trees about twenty yards from our tent. I stared into the darkness, trying to make out the shape of what was hidden there. I heard the distinct sound of flesh hitting flesh followed by an "Ow!" A second voice advised the first to "*Shhhhh.*" The first voice obeyed.

"What is it?" asked Violet. "Is it the Japanese?"

I hadn't realized she was awake. I closed the tent flap and returned to my cot.

"Well?"

"Relax. I think it's our boys standing guard."

"Are you sure it's not the Japs?"

"Pretty sure. They said 'Ow' when a mosquito got them. That strikes me as a relic of the Western world." Violet seemed satisfied by my answer, but I can't say that I was. After all, if they could share our pain and our anger, there was no reason why the Japanese couldn't also borrow our exclamations of annoyance.

CHAPTER 18

Good-bye in the Night

We were summoned to Blake's office just after reveille the next morning.

He was seated behind his desk, waiting for us. I wondered what he did with the rest of his time, when he wasn't attempting to deliver bad news and destroy morale. Perhaps that's why they called him Late Nate—everything he was involved in was shrouded in a cloak of darkness.

Or maybe it was because everyone who encountered him wished he was dead.

He waited until we were seated before speaking. "Miss DeVane is gone."

"Which island did you take her to?" asked Violet.

"I'm afraid you misunderstand, Miss Lancaster. Miss DeVane passed away last night."

The three of us shared a gasp. Did he really just say that? Surely we'd misheard him.

"She's dead?" I said.

He clasped his hands and placed the tips of his index fingers beneath his chin. "Regrettably, yes."

"Why didn't someone come get us?" I asked.

"It wouldn't have helped things. She was at peace when she died, I can assure you."

"She was alone. She should've been surrounded by friends."

"It seemed foolish to wake everyone. It was quite late when she expired."

He continued talking, but I no longer heard him. I was too busy trying to wrap my head around what he claimed had come to pass. How could Gilda be dead? She was too beautiful, too talented, too famous to have been picked off so callously in the middle of a show. People like her didn't die.

But then Jack had died. If I could lose him, anyone was fair game.

This stupid, stupid war. Neither Jayne nor Gilda had ever killed anyone, nor had they ever intended to. They weren't part of this game of hurting and hatred. All they wanted was to bring a little relief to the people stationed here. Why couldn't the Japanese see that? Were they so blinded by hate that they thought every American was a potential target? Did they know they could hurt so many more people if they picked off the ones who were young, female, and famous?

"Obviously, Miss DeVane's death presents a variety of problems. Her body will be shipped home tomorrow. We are uncertain what to do with the four of you. We have notified the USO of the situation, and although they are certainly sympathetic to your plight and to the emotions you are undoubtedly going through, they agree that the best thing for all of us would be if you stayed here for the time being."

"Why?" I asked. Our leader was dead. She was the star of our show. How could they possibly expect us to continue performing?

"You have an obligation, Miss Winter. The USO has spent a great deal of money promoting your show and organizing a tour here—the first of its kind in the South Pacific. These men deserve entertainment, and I'm sure you'll agree with me that we must put their needs first. Obviously we'll give you a brief period of mourning." Gee, that was swell of him. "Though I think it would be in everyone's best interest if we didn't dwell too long on these tragic happenings. Our men are surrounded by death, and constantly being reminded of it is not useful for anyone." I wondered if he'd feel the same way if it were his friend who was lying dead in the infirmary. "Since the three of you were present during the shooting, I would like the opportunity to question each of you about what occurred."

"What for?" asked Violet. "You already caught the culprit."

"Indeed, but we want to make sure we are clear on exactly what took place."

"Fine," said Kay. "We'll do whatever we can to help."

"I figured you would. One other *small* thing. While we were happy to have Miss DeVane provide your group with leadership during your time here at the camp, now that there is a threat to the performers, we need to more closely control your movements."

"But, like Violet just said, the culprit's been caught," I said.

"One of them has, Miss Winter. If one Jap has infiltrated Tulagi, there's a very good chance others may do so as well. To ensure your collective safety, we've decided to put your unit under the control of the Wacs during the remainder of your time here. As such, you will immediately answer to your new commanding officer, Captain Amelia Lambert."

Kay was the first one Blake questioned. While she was grilled, Violet and I went to grab some joe at the enlisted men's mess and gab about the unfortunate turn things had taken. Deacon saw us arrive and with a hand to his lips, slipped us a few pieces of toast and some jam to enjoy with our watered-down java. Not that either of us felt like eating.

"I can't believe they didn't tell us she died," said Violet. It was the first time any of us had said that sentence out loud since leaving Blake's tent. Gilda was dead. She was gone. Forever. "I hate the

Japs. Our men would never shoot at civilians like that. We respect the rules."

"Maybe it was an accident," I said.

"Don't be so naïve. If it were an accident, he wouldn't have fired twice. That sniper knew the impact he'd have if he shot them. We represent everything they're against. He probably would've picked off the lot of us if he'd had the chance."

It was terrifying to think that three of us were spared because of a costume change, a small bladder, and a broken heart.

Violet's eyes grew red and rheumy. I have to admit I was surprised she was so upset. While I doubt she would've wished for Gilda's death, out of all of us she was the one I expected to be the least shaken by it. "And to shoot a dog too? You mark my words, Rosie: the person behind this was evil."

"I can't believe they're not sending us home," I said.

"Blake's right about that." Violet dispatched her tears with a flick of her fingers. "We don't want to disappoint the men. And we don't want the Japs thinking they've defeated us. If we go home now, they'll think we're nothing but a bunch of cowards."

Honestly, it wouldn't have bothered me if they did.

We picked at our toast, sipped our coffee, and felt the terrible absence left by someone who should've been with us at the table.

Eventually, Kay returned and announced that Violet was to report to Late Nate. Kay slumped into the chair beside me and buried her head in her hands. "It's all so sad," she said. "This is the last thing I ever thought would happen." She dissolved into tears. Poor Kay. First she loses Irene, then Gilda. She must've been wondering, as I was, how much more loss she'd be able to endure.

"It will be all right," I said. The words were beat up, even to my ears. I tried on another cliché for size. "She's in a better place now."

"Do you really believe that?"

Did I? I think so. After all, Gilda was with Jack, and if I had my way I'd change places with her in a minute. "Absolutely."

Kay decimated one napkin, then another, so I went in search

of fresh paper for her to mop her tears. I found what I was looking for stacked beside the steel trays the enlisted men ate off of. As I grabbed a fistful of napkins, a male voice in the kitchen announced, "I'm back in the game."

"How'd you get scratch, Lefty?" asked someone.

"Who cares how he got it?" said a third voice. "As long as he's willing to lose it."

They laughed, and their conversation was lost in the clanging of pots and pans.

What if the sniper hadn't been working with his own men but with someone here on the island who could easily get access to supplies? It would certainly be a way to make money. And if you were already disenfranchised by your own military and forced to do jobs you weren't appropriate for, maybe it wouldn't bother you to help out the enemy. Given their predilection for gambling and their criminal pasts, it wasn't a huge leap to imagine that some of the men might be willing to take a chance to make some cush.

"Here." I brought the napkins back to Kay. She looked like she was close to being cried out, which was fortunate since Violet arrived and sent me to get the third. As I walked to Late Nate's office, my mind pored over my latest theory. Was it really conceivable that someone would make a deal like that with the enemy? We'd all heard about spies trading information for money. Exchanging supplies was at least less likely to change the outcome of the war, especially in such small quantities. And if the sniper was working with someone on the island, it would explain how the shooter knew about the last-minute performance.

"Miss Winter. Have a seat."

I sat before the desk, where now there was only one chair optimally positioned so that Rear Admiral Blake could ask his questions.

"I understand this is your first tour with the USO camp shows. May I ask what made you decide to be a part of them?"

Had Violet and Kay said anything about Jack? I didn't want to run the risk of looking like I was lying, and yet the last thing I wanted to do was talk about my dead ex with this guy.

"Jayne and I were feeling like we should be doing something more meaningful with our time. We had a housemate who joined the European tour, and I guess hearing about her experiences made us want to do the same."

He nodded and scratched something on a piece of paper. A wire recorder was in motion on his desk. "You were quite upset at dinner the night of the shooting."

I cleared my throat. "Yes. I had just found out a friend of mine had been killed, and I'm afraid it made me a bit more emotional than usual."

"Was this friend here in the islands?"

This wasn't any of Blake's business. What happened to Gilda had nothing to do with Jack. And if he was aiming for a repeat of our scene at dinner, he'd be wise to remember that there was no one there to stop me this time. "I'm not sure where he was stationed. I knew he was in the Pacific theater, but I never knew where. I met one of his shipmates, who gave me the news."

He nodded. Apparently my answer was acceptable. "You opted not to perform that evening. Where were you during the performance?"

"In the dressing area. I watched the show from the wings."

"And what did you observe?"

"What do you mean?"

His pen underlined his question in the air. "What did you see immediately before Miss DeVane and Miss Hamilton were shot?"

"Nothing really. I thought I saw a flash of light up in the cliffs, but I can't be sure. It wasn't until the gun fired the second time that I think I realized what it was."

"And what about after they were shot?" he asked. "Did you observe anything or anyone unusual?"

"No. I was forced into the dressing area almost immediately. I barely had time to register what happened."

He made another note. "Thank you for your help, Miss Winter. I'm sure you'll be pleased to hear that Miss Hamilton will be released from the infirmary tomorrow."

"That's great."

"Indeed. And please accept my apologies for my behavior the other night. I had no idea you had suffered such an awful tragedy."

I felt sideswiped. Late Nate was apologizing? To me? "Um . . . don't worry about it." I waited for him to say something more, but his attention returned to the pad he was writing on. For the first time I noticed how worn his own face seemed. His schnozzle was red, the skin beneath his eyes the color of charcoal.

"That's all, Miss Winter. You're dismissed."

I started to leave, but something stopped me. "Can I see her?"

"Miss Hamilton? Of course."

"No. Gilda. Can I see Gilda?"

His brow became a series of waves. Had I a boat, I could've sailed them. "You want to see the body?"

I nodded.

"Why?"

I didn't owe him an explanation, but I gave him one anyway. "My friend who died—I'm not going to be home for his funeral. If I could see Gilda and say good-bye, maybe—" Maybe what? I could bury them both?

He returned to his notes. "Yes, I think that can be arranged."

CHAPTER 19

Shadowed by Three

Late Nate had one of the men escort me to the infirmary. Gilda was in a small, private room with a sheet pulled over her body. There was no attempt made at preservation. She would be flown home in a plain casket just like every other American life lost in the war.

Her hair was visible beneath the sheet, fanning out from her head in such a way that made it clear it was no longer attached to a living being. I stared for a long time, waiting for her body to ripple with a sign of life. The stillness was devastating. Never had I seen anything so completely without motion.

I pulled the sheet back to her waist. Her face was pale and looked bruised. The immaculate beauty we had all observed and envied was gone at death. Her roots were dark, her eyebrows craved plucking, and her face seemed hard and uneven. Perhaps it had never been her physical beauty that we found so alluring. It was Gilda herself that we marveled at.

I touched her arm and felt the unyielding flesh. The hand of her platinum wristwatch struggled to move forward from the minute it was stalled at. I took her cold hand in mine and wound the watch. Time marched on.

Kay and Violet weren't at the mess when I returned. I found them in our tent, packing up Gilda's belongings.

"Hiya," I said as I entered. "What's going on?"

"We figured we should get her things ready to send home," said Kay.

Violet put a hat on her head and checked her reflection in the trunk's mirror. "It's such a shame to send everything back."

I joined them before her trunks and helped fold the dresses that had once hung about the room on nails. Her clothes seemed different when not hanging from her body—thinner and frailer, like they were party balloons that had been deflated the day after a celebration. We each took turns holding up the fancy duds against our bodies, but rather than exciting us, it only seemed to reinforce how dreadfully out of place these garments seemed when they were on anyone other than their original owner.

"We decided not to pack the stuff she loaned to Jayne," said Kay. "I'm sure she'd want her to keep them."

"God, she never even wore half this stuff," said Violet. We searched through these things as though by seeing clothes that were unfamiliar we could spend a little more time with a woman we'd only begun to know. As fascinating as the new things were, they weren't what held our interest. We wanted things we had seen her wear, that had become part of the memories we had left of her. "Do you think it might be all right if I kept a souvenir?" asked Violet. Her fingers danced across the black satin eyemask Gilda wore to bed each night.

I wasn't in the mood to argue about the impropriety of it. "I don't suppose it would hurt," I said. "As long as it's something small."

In the end, Violet chose a small beaded evening bag, and I kept the hairclip she'd worn the night we'd sung "Boogie Woogie Bugle Boy" aboard the ship. After some agonizing, Kay went the utilitarian route and decided on Gilda's rain gear.

"Don't you want something flashier?" asked Violet.

Kay stared down at the sad, hollow, vinyl cape. "That's not how I want to remember her."

We resumed packing. Our once-careful attempts to fold grew increasingly sloppy as we all fought to get this dreaded task over and done with. "So how did your conversation with Rear Admiral Blake go?" Violet asked me.

"Oh, you know," I said. "How 'bout yours?"

"He asked me a hundred times where I was when the shots were fired. I was afraid I was going to have to reenact the whole thing for him."

"What about you, Kay?" I asked.

"Same story. He wanted to know why I was in the latrine and what I might've heard or seen while I was there."

"And did either of you see or hear anything?" I asked.

"No," they said in unison.

Why did Blake care? Did he think, as I thought, that someone at the camp could've been in cahoots with the sniper?

"Was it just me, or did he seem beat up?" I asked.

Violet frowned. "He definitely looked like he'd been crying."

"I think everyone's going to be," said Kay. "She touched a lot of people."

She was right about that. The famous had a way of making a bigger impact when they left this world—larger-than-life personalities left big holes. But Late Nate's grief still seemed odd to me. Perhaps it was just that I was amazed to learn that he felt anything at all.

The tent flaps rustled and Spanky appeared. "Is it true?" he asked.

"Is what true?" asked Violet.

"About Gilda. There's a rumor going around that she's dead."

The three of us looked at one another, none of us wishing to volunteer to be the bearer of bad news.

He cracked his knuckles. "Come on—we deserve to know."

Since no one else was willing to do it, I nodded my confirmation.

"Goddamn it," said Spanky. Violet went to him and took him in her arms.

"We just found out ourselves," I said.

For a moment he was limp in Violet's embrace. Just when I thought he might've lost consciousness, he repeated the profanity and put his hand on his head, as though he was hoping to find hair to ruffle. "There's going to be hell to pay for this."

Before he could say anything else, blond chignon walked into our room. She gave him a look that simultaneously asked him what he was doing there and ordered him to leave. Spanky cowered beneath her gaze. Without uttering another word or even tossing us a silent good-bye, he turned tail and left the tent.

"I'm Captain Amelia Lambert. Some of you I've met before." Her cold blue eyes scanned me, effortlessly asserting her superiority. "And some of you I've heard about." Her gaze landed on Kay, passing silent judgment for all of the sins that had been reported, if not confirmed, about her. "For those of you I'm not acquainted with." Violet looked behind her, trying to figure out who, other than herself, hadn't yet had the pleasure of meeting this woman. "I am the new commanding officer for the Wacs stationed here at Tulagi. And from this moment forward, I am also your commanding officer. During your remaining time on the islands, you will report to me."

"Does this mean we're Wacs now?" asked Violet.

Amelia Lambert didn't like interruptions. In fact, I was pretty sure Amelia Lambert didn't like anything at all. "Of course not. Wearing our uniform is a privilege. You have merely been placed under my control during your tenure here to ensure your safety."

"So we're prisoners of war," I said.

She didn't even turn in my direction. "From this moment forward, you must obey any command I give to you. Failure to do so will result in disciplinary action similar to what the enlisted women face. In order to keep a closer eye on you and to place you in a more secure environment, you will be leaving this tent and moving into the WAC barracks." She looked at a clipboard that was so much a part of her I hadn't even noticed it. "Miss Winter will be in bunk twenty-five.

Miss Lancaster, bunk twenty-six. And Miss Thorpe will be in bunk twenty-seven. Please gather your things and in ten minutes we will bring you to your new accommodations."

"Wait a second," said Violet. "Do you mean we don't even have our own tent any longer?"

"Of course not," said Captain Lambert. "It's impossible to supervise you when you're placed separate from the rest of the women. You will be integrated into their living quarters from here on out."

"What about Gilda's trunks?" asked Kay.

"Leave them here. I'll arrange to have them shipped home. Ten minutes, ladies." She turned to leave and stopped right before she reached the flap. "By the way, I'm sorry for your loss."

The barracks where the Wacs were staying was just a stone's throw away from our tent, though from the way our privacy was immediately stripped from us, it might as well have been on the moon. The other women were gone, performing whatever work it was they did, so we had the large crowded space to ourselves. There was no unpacking to do. Trunks were set at the ends of the narrow cots and were to remain closed at all times except when we were dressing or undressing. As for the cots themselves, every one in the joint had been prepared to Captain Lambert's specifications, meaning that the blanket was pulled and tucked so tightly you would've thought the mattress was wearing a girdle. No personal items were on display. This, we were told, encouraged thievery and other individual impulses that had no place at an army camp.

Just as in our tent, there was a concrete floor here. Apparently, that was a privilege reserved for women.

We put our things away and sat on our beds waiting for the other shoe to drop. It didn't take long to fall.

Amelia Lambert walked a line in the center of the Quonset hut. "You are expected to follow our rules while you're here. That includes no male visitors in our tent." She looked at me as she said it. Apparently she'd surmised that, in Gilda's absence, I was the one egging on immoral behavior. "Since you are sharing our quarters, it is only fair that you share our duties." Captain Lambert passed each of us a typed sheet listing the various kinds of tasks the Wacs did every day. "I have penciled in your names beside the jobs I think you would be best suited for. On the days when you're traveling for performances, I recommend that you do your job prior to departing. Now, if you'll excuse me, I must see to other things."

She left us alone to stew over the tasks we'd been given. Violet would be sweeping out the barracks once a week. Kay had to assist with hauling water. I wasn't so lucky. I'd been assigned to clean the latrine.

"This is ridiculous," I said. "We're not soldiers. We certainly didn't do anything to deserve being sent to the henhouse."

"I don't think we have any choice," said Kay. She looked even more depressed than she had that morning, if such a thing was possible. Not only had she lost Gilda and Irene, but now she was being forced to bunk with the enemy.

"On the bright side," said Violet, "we're barely here as it is." Her words echoed Gilda's that first day at camp, when our dreary new surroundings had rendered us mute. I found it strangely comforting.

"And what's this business about needing to look out for us when they've already caught the shooter?" I asked.

"Because they think their guy wasn't working alone," said Violet. "Surely you caught that from all the questions Blake asked?" She fished a jar out of her trunk and took a quick swig.

"Spanky seemed pretty upset," said Kay. "You don't think he and the other fellows will do something to the sniper, do you?"

"Who cares if they do?" said Violet. "He killed Gilda. He deserves the same or worse."

"It's against the Geneva Convention," said Kay.

"And you think those yellow fellows are upholding the letter of the law?" asked Violet.

"That's not the point," said Kay. "If we don't obey the rules of war, no one will."

It was such an absurd idea, this notion that there were rules, like this entire war was an enormous game of Monopoly. Did every man and woman who joined the military know the rules? Or did they learn it bit by bit the way Gilda figured out Hollywood?

Kay and Violet continued sniping at each other, but I couldn't bear to listen to either of them anymore. My head was pounding as I struggled to make sense of what had happened. Why did the gunman fire twice? If he'd fired once, he might've been able to get away. He lost time by sticking around to pop off a second shot. Surely he couldn't tell that he'd only grazed Jayne. After all, she'd fallen to the stage. She had to have looked like she'd been hit.

"What if it was an accident?" I asked.

Kay and Violet shut their yaps and turned my way.

"What if what was an accident?" asked Violet.

"Gilda and Jayne both being shot."

"So what—the sniper fell on his rifle and accidentally shot them?" said Violet.

I struggled not to snap at her. "What I meant was: What if one of them wasn't the intended victim but got caught in the crossfire? The sniper was shooting from pretty far away. It would've been easy for him to mess up."

"If that's the case, which was which?" asked Kay.

I punched the air with my index finger. "Jayne was fired at first. She was probably the mistake. The sniper realized he hit the wrong person and fired the second shot."

"That doesn't make any sense," said Violet. "How could the sniper know which one of them would cause a bigger reaction?"

I didn't have an answer. If the whole point of shooting at the performers was to create a distraction, two shots certainly felt like overkill. To say nothing of the dog.

Mail call broke up our afternoon. I didn't have anything, but Jayne did: one big fat letter from Tony B. I took it to the infirmary, where she was attempting to read an issue of *Doc Savage* through red tear-ravished eyes.

"I take it you heard the news," I said.

"They told me late last night. I keep thinking they made a mistake."

"Me too, but they didn't." I cleared my throat. "I saw the body."

"They let you?"

"Yeah, Rear Admiral Blake did. Isn't that a kick? Who would've thought Late Nate had a heart." I followed the shape of Tony's envelope with my finger. "You could probably see her too, if you want to."

"I don't know if I could bear to see her like that." From the cover of the pulp, a green voodoo idol snarled at me.

I sat on the edge of her bed and focused on smoothing the sheet covering her legs. Jayne was alive. Even when her legs were still, they moved. "I had to. I couldn't stand the thought of losing two people without having any evidence of it."

Jayne closed the magazine. "Oh, Rosie. I didn't even think about how awful that must be for you."

"No, it's all right. In a strange way I feel like by seeing Gilda I got to say good-bye to Jack too. Looking at her, I realized death doesn't have to be so awful. We're the ones who suffer the worst of it." Was I really okay? No, but I had come to accept the idea that death was irreversible, and neither Gilda nor Jack was going to suddenly appear at my side to brush away my tears.

"She was such a good person."

I nodded, even though I wasn't sure *good* was the right word. Generous, yes, but we didn't know her well enough to comment on her moral life. "My ma always claimed bad things come in threes."

"You mean there's more to come?"

"Not the way I'm counting. I'm assuming Irene Zinn was the first awful thing, so from where I'm sitting we're home free from here."

She traced the edge of the pulp with her thumbnail. "I forgot about her."

"I almost did too. Did you know she was an actress?"

Jayne shook her head.

"One of the Wacs told me. Isn't it weird that Irene and Gilda were both actresses and now they're both dead?"

"They weren't exactly the same caliber though, right?"

"True, but it seems like too much of a coincidence, you know?" I remembered the envelope in my hand and offered it to Jayne. "I brought you mail."

She opened the letter and read it in silence, poring over the words for longer than was necessary. After all, Tony wasn't known for his way with language. When she finished, she rolled over on her cot and turned my way.

"So what's new with Tony?" I picked up the pulp and flipped through it.

"Nothing much. He misses me. He promises things will be different if I give him another chance. The usual."

It was clear she was withholding information. Jayne's emotions were as transparent as glass.

"So what aren't you telling me?" I asked.

Her voice went up an octave. "Nothing."

I closed the pulp and pointed at the green figurine on the cover. "Come on," I said. "We know you're hiding something."

Jayne sighed, fluttering the edges of the letter with her breath. Tony didn't use V-mail. He wasn't a fan of anything created by the federal government. She folded the letter, carefully following the original creases, and attempted to cram it back in its envelope. "I just used to feel safe with Tony, and right now I'm really missing that."

"Safe? Before or after he hit you?"

She cocked her head. "That was one time, Rosie."

I showed her with my finger how enormous once could be. "One time too many."

She directed her comments at the letter. "If Tony were here, he'd make sure nothing happened to any of us."

"Or he'd hire someone else to guarantee it."

She didn't see that as a shortcoming. "Exactly. I feel so . . . I don't know . . . vulnerable here. At any moment, any one of us could die. I didn't think this place would be like that."

"No one did." And weren't we the fools for being so naïve? What did we think would happen on the battlefront? That we'd spend our days on the beach waiting for Dorothy Lamour to serve us cocktails?

"If Tony were here—" Her voice faded away, and I fought the desire to finish her sentence. If Tony were here, she wouldn't be able to relax and just be herself. She would constantly be worried that she was upsetting him. She would be a nervous wreck every time he disappeared to get involved with who knows what.

Of course, if Tony were here and supplies were missing, we could almost guarantee that he was somehow involved. At least that mystery would be solved.

"We can get through this," I told Jayne. "We will get through this. We don't need Tony to hold our hands in order to survive."

"I know." She gave up trying to put the letter in the envelope and tossed it onto her side table. "How's everyone else holding up?"

"Kay and Violet are at each other's throats. Spanky wants to take down the whole imperial army. And our new CO, Amelia Lambert, finds grief messy and inconvenient."

Jayne smiled. "Maybe she's got the right idea. Life would be so much easier if we didn't care."

I had to agree.

CHAPTER 20

A Friend Indeed

That night we held an impromptu memorial service for Gilda. We gathered in the enlisted mess where the blaring overhead lights were replaced with lanterns. There we led the men in Gilda's favorite songs and shared stories about her. As we found our material growing thin, we invited anyone in the audience to share their own memories. A quartet of sailors sang "The Gilda DeVane Blues." An Australian officer described dancing with her and how she insisted on hearing his story before she told him her own. Men from our hospital visit shared the tale of how we spent the afternoon talking with them and helping them write letters home.

And then Van Lauer volunteered to speak. We watched in trepidation as he came to the center of the room and addressed the audience.

"For those of you who don't know me, I'm Van Lauer, and I've had the great fortune to do two extraordinary things in the past year: share a screen with Gilda DeVane and become a pilot in the army air forces." He paused as though he expected to be assailed with the usual declarations of love that audiences at his appearances bombarded him with. "Gilda, of course, wasn't her real name, but one that was chosen for her in a fan poll in the back of a movie magazine five years ago. She liked to say that Gilda DeVane was created at that moment, sprung fully from the imaginations of the thousands of moviegoers who chose what to call her. And for five amazing years, she gave them everything they wanted: a woman of glamour and passion who would do anything for her career, even if it meant dying in the process. I guess, in a sense, we lost two women last night: the one she was and the one she was made to be."

He turned to leave, and I looked at Kay to make sure I hadn't hallucinated the strange, disjointed talk. He stumbled as he headed back to his seat. Violet cupped her hand and tilted her elbow to confirm what I suspected: he was lit.

The audience seemed equally confused by his remarks. Had he insulted her? Praised her? Was it possible he'd done both?

Violet leaped to her feet and returned to the center of the room. "Thank you, Van. That was . . . interesting. And it reminded me that I had a few more things to say about her myself." I braced myself. "If you've seen my act, you probably know I haven't been particularly kind to Gilda. Let's face it: it takes a better person than me not to be jealous of a movie star. But over the course of our few weeks together, she showed me what an amazing person she was. Generous, as so many of the men tonight have described her. Compassionate. And, of course, talented. Those are the things that we should be remembering her for."

I was dumbfounded that Violet felt the need to defend her. And powerfully moved. She was right. Gilda's role as a movie star was unimportant. It was Gilda as a person that we needed to recognize.

Late Nate was the last person to speak. Unlike Van, he wasn't drunk, though he made me wish I was. "This has been a most moving outpouring of emotion this evening, and I'm very pleased to see that so many of you were able to express your thoughts with heartfelt words. It would be easy to label Miss DeVane's death a tragedy and be done with it, but I think we must see it for the greater role it plays during our time in these islands. This lovely, talented woman was not taken from us for any reason other than the cruelty, greed, and inhumanity of the enemy." The crowd stirred, coming alive the way leaves rustled when the wind ran through them. "This is the same enemy that bombed Pearl Harbor. The same that raped this land and wounded its people. These are godless men who think nothing of torture and relish the smell of death, who cannot distinguish between soldier and civilian, man and woman, light and dark." The stirring evolved into something else. Whispers whipped around me as men repeated Blake's words, not Blake's exact sentences but the same basic idea pumped up with profanity and venom. The room was taut with an inaudible growl. There was a beast that had been held at bay that was getting ready to be unleashed.

Blake lowered his voice and pumped his fist triumphantly into the air. "We cannot let this treachery continue. We must punish the perpetrators of this crime. Do not let Gilda DeVane's death be in vain!"

A low rumble rushed through the crowd, like a wave pounding the beach, and morphed into a chant: "Kill the Japs! Avenge Gilda! Kill the Japs!" The men rose to the their feet and mimicked Blake's stance, striking an unseen assailant with their fists in time to their words. Kay and Violet stood, too, their voices rising to reach the volume of everyone else. Soon I was the only one sitting in silence, and the crowd seemed to direct their energy at getting me to stand. Didn't I realize how important their message was? Didn't I agree that Gilda should be avenged? She was an innocent who didn't have a stake in this war. All she wanted was to spread joy and happiness. The Japanese took advantage of her generosity and good nature, picking her off when she was at her most vulnerable, sharing her gifts with a crowd of hungry soldiers. The sniper should've shot into the audience. That would've been fair turnaround. At least those men were prepared to die.

I stood and lifted my fist with the rest of the crowd, my mouth working in time to their words, my throat growing hoarse with the power of our message. "Kill the Japs! Avenge Gilda!"

Only later did I realize what a strange spell Blake had managed to cast on all of us. It was unnerving how quickly I'd given in to it, and even more disturbing how effective his words were going to be, come the next battle. He'd made the war personal for those boys who were still grappling with the wisdom of being there or growing weary from how long the offensive dragged on. No longer were they fighting a faceless enemy. They were punishing the savages responsible for killing Gilda DeVane and all the friends and family members they'd lost—and would lose—to the war.

As the men cleared out after the show, I heard a familiar voice calling out my name. It was Peaches.

"How are you?" he asked me. We tried to find someplace away from the scurrying crowd to talk.

"How do you think?"

"I was so sorry when I heard the news."

"You and everyone here."

"Were you close to her?"

It seemed like a silly question; after all, I'd been touring with her for a month. But thinking back on Van's speech, I wondered how much of what we'd seen had been the real Gilda. Was he right to suggest there were two of her, and if so, which one had she sent to the islands? "We all were," I told Peaches. "She had a way of making friends with people. What are you doing here?"

"Billy heard about Jayne and insisted on seeing her."

"She's fine. The bullet barely kissed her. Her ankle got the worst of it."

"Still, he had to see her with his own eyes. Plus, I thought you could use the company. You've had a pretty rough week. And now with Jayne out of commission . . ."

Boy did he have that right. In fact, the whole year was looking like it was going to be a wash. "That's swell of you. Thanks."

"Are you going back to the States?"

"Nope. They won't let us. We're here for the duration. And we're now under Wac command."

He let out a low whistle. "Yikes. So it does get worse?"

"Lucky us, right?"

He looked toward the ocean. "You want to go for a walk?"

"Sure." I didn't have anything better to do. Going back to the tent would mean going back to Captain Lambert. And I didn't want to be around Spanky and the boys tonight. All that talk about getting back at the Japs didn't sit well with me. I wasn't up to hanging out with a bunch of men who were using it as their guiding philosophy.

We walked along the clean white sand watching the waves as they beat the shore smooth. The moon hung low in the sky, creating a picture postcard of paradise. The water twinkled in the night. It wasn't just the motion and the stars—the waves actually seemed to be glowing.

I commented on the strangeness of it all.

"Phosphorescence," said Peaches. "Different molds and algae make it glow like that. When we were coming over on the carrier, there were nights when you swore there were diamonds in the water."

I wasn't seeing diamonds; to me, it looked like the water was teaming with ghosts. Was Jack in there, fighting to leave the sea that had claimed him? Was Gilda part of it now, forced to haunt this island for eternity?

I shook the thought out of my head. "What's it like?"

"What?"

"War?"

We stopped walking and sat in the sand.

"Keep in mind I'm a pilot, not a hand-to-hand combat kind of guy, so what I say may not be everyone's experience."

"Duly noted," I said. "So what's it like from your perspective?"

He removed a rock from the sand and tossed it into the water. It landed with a *plonk* in the darkness. "A lot of the time? Exhilarating. You're on a constant adrenaline rush and way up in the air. Even though you know your targets are human, it becomes a kind of game. Someone on the radio is hollering for you to move a little left or right to make sure your next shot is lined up, and the two of you are cracking jokes about how many slant eyes you're about to take out or wondering if you've left enough bodies for the buzzards circling above the island to feed on."

"Wow."

"But it's not always like that. I was on one of the islands not long ago, picking up some marines who were stranded. They offered to give me a tour, and I took them up on it. I wanted to see with my own eyes what we'd been accomplishing from the air. We'd blown these huge craters into the land, which were filling with water, and that bothered me so much. It's one thing to kill the men who invaded this place, but to destroy the islands seemed just as bad as what they were doing. But even that didn't compare to the bodies. I saw things on that trip that I'll never get out of my mind. Men blown apart so they were just a foot here, an arm there. The ones who were still alive howling from the burns. And the smells—rotting bodies, cooking flesh. You can imagine what misery looks like, maybe even what it sounds like, but who knew it had a smell? A taste. And when I looked at all this, I didn't see the Japanese. Divided into pieces like that, you saw men. Just men."

I ran my hands through the sand, digging holes, then filling them back in. "Why do you think a Japanese sniper would've wanted to kill Gilda and Jayne?" I asked.

"I don't think there has to be a reason, Rosie. Maybe they weren't looking for a specific target. Maybe they were looking for any target."

"But would they do that? There was a crowd of men there that night. He could've shot at any one of them."

"Look, I don't think anyone's all bad or good, not even the Nazis, though you'd be hard pressed to find anyone around here that shares that opinion. But I have to tell you I've heard things about the Japanese that made me glad I helped kill as many as I did."

He was such a contradiction. But then all men at war were. They could mourn death and suffering in one breath and rally to kill in the other. There were so many things I wanted to ask Peaches: Did he worry that all this violence made him a bad person? Did he think the Japanese viewed us as just as cruel as we viewed them? Did he wonder if he was going to hell?

"What are you thinking?" he asked.

"Do you think it's true, all these things they tell us about the Japanese?"

He started digging his own trenches in the sand. Were we both hoping to escape here? Or were we longing to build castles that turned this place back into a paradise?

"I think they exaggerate, sure, like Rear Admiral Blake today. They want us to see them as cruel and inhuman. They need us to, otherwise we'd feel remorse every time we pulled the trigger. But I don't think they've made everything up. I've seen things with my own eyes and heard stories out of the mouths of men I trust. If anything, I don't think they're telling us all the horrible stories that they could."

I was hoping that wasn't the case. I had convinced myself that our enemies were just like us, only wearing different faces.

I was quiet for a moment, and the silence was filled with the sound of the crashing waves. How far did they come ashore at night? Based on the sand that had already been wiped clean by the water, it wasn't hard to imagine the entire island being underwater for a few hours each evening. I wasn't a religious person by any stretch, but it reminded me of a baptism. The detritus was washed away, and we were given a clean shore to taint again over the course of the next day. Perhaps Gilda believed that Tulagi could do the same thing for people.

Peaches's sand trench connected with my own. Our hands were so close that I could feel the warmth radiating from him.

"The sniper shot a dog too," I said.

His hand retreated. I could still feel his nearness though. "I'm not surprised. If you want to injure a man, you aim for his leg. If you want to kill him, you aim for his heart."

I snuck back to the WAC barracks with only the moon to light my way. As I approached the structure, rustling in nearby bushes told me I wasn't alone. I froze, waiting for whoever it was to make themselves known. The movement stopped, and I could sense that peculiar tension that arises when people attempt to mimic silence. The longer I stared into the darkness the more certain I became that there were human shapes there, crouched down low, protecting a tiny red globe that could've been the dying embers of a cigarette. It should've terrified me, but for some reason I felt comforted. Our enemies weren't subtle. They made themselves known with the report of a gun or the clamor of a bomb. They didn't watch us under the protection of foliage while trying to silence the sound of their hearts.

I lay awake for a long time in our strange new surroundings. While the jungle was never quiet, the volume was considerably louder now that we had twenty-five new bunkmates. Some women snored, some mumbled; all of them tossed and turned on the uncomfortable little cots that groaned with every movement. Although our previous mattresses had been nothing to write home about, these felt like they were twice as thin and stuffed with nails. Every time I moved, something new poked into my back. It was considerably warmer than it had been in the tent. The Quonset hut turned into a giant oven and squeaked and groaned as the heat opened up its cracks. I closed my eyes and tried to imagine that I was back at the Shaw House with Jayne an arm's reach away. The only sound would be Churchill purring his way to sleep and the sounds of the city as it wound down for the night. Outside our window the neon motel sign would pulse, illuminating my dreams with its constant light.

It was working. I was dozing off. Any second now I would be asleep and this whole awful day—the day we learned Gilda was dead—would be over.

A sound forced my eyes open. I stared into the near darkness, trying to make out the source of the noise. It wasn't the hut creaking, or a snore, or a murmur of disconcerting dreams. Somebody was walking around the tent.

I froze. Could it be Captain Lambert returning from a late-night rendezvous? Or was I wrong to assume that whoever was watching us from the jungle was there to ensure our safety?

Slowly, so the movement seemed like nothing more than the usual tossing and turning, I rolled onto my side until I faced the source of the noise. The figure was coming closer, clearly heading my way. I had no weapons at my disposal. At this point, the only thing I did have was the element of surprise.

A flashlight clicked on, and a globe of light left the floor and highlighted an empty cot beside my own. As soon as the bed had been sighted, the torch clicked off and the footsteps quickened their pace. They stopped, and the cot let out a moan as weight settled on its frame.

I breathed again and begged my heart to slow its beat. It was another good hour before I finally fell asleep.

Captain Lambert didn't need the bugle to wake us. The distant sounds of air raids did it for her.

"Rise and shine, ladies," she said in an irritatingly cheerful voice. Outside the tent, morning was still trying to free itself from night. "Inspection is in ten minutes."

The noise outside was similar to the sounds we'd heard our first day on Tulagi, only without the accompanying siren to warn us of approaching danger. There was no hope of sleeping through it, especially when Captain Lambert stopped at the end of my bed and smacked my thigh. "This means *everyone*, Miss Winter."

I sat up and gave her an appropriate glare for so early an hour. Across the room Violet struggled to make the extra-long cot with an average-sized sheet. I yawned and stretched before finally committing to swinging my feet over the side of my bed. Next to me, at the cot that had required flashlight assistance, Candy Abbott was rapidly buttoning her uniform jacket.

"Morning," I said to her.

She smiled and paused in her work. "I heard you gals were bunking with us now. How do you like the accommodations?"

"I've been in prisons with more comfortable beds."

"It gets better. The more you sleep on them, the softer they become." She sat on her own cot, not caring about the wrinkles she was making.

"Any idea what all the ruckus is about?"

"The Japs are bombing Guadalcanal. Not to worry, it's the end of the island farthest from us that they're concentrating on." She fished a shoe out from under the cot. "I was sorry to hear about Gilda."

"Thanks. We're going to miss her something awful."

"How's the other girl who got shot?"

"Jayne? Good. She should be back with us tonight." At the end of the tent, Amelia roared for someone to drop and give her ten. If it were me, I would've lifted my arm and given her one. "Is your CO as bad as she seems?"

"Worse."

"You seem to have no problem getting around her rules."

A question passed through Candy's eyes.

"I heard you come in last night," I whispered.

"Oh." She looked embarrassed. And a little afraid. She'd assumed she was better at cloak and dagger than that. "I thought it was late enough that everyone would be asleep."

"Don't worry—I'd just gotten in myself. Word to the wise: there are guards posted outside the tent."

"Seriously?" The color rapidly left her face.

"It's either that or gorillas who enjoy a cigarette. So who is he?"

She smiled and looked ready to spill when Captain Lambert's voice rang out to my right.

"You have one minute until inspection, Miss Winter. I fail to see how you're going to accomplish dressing and making your cot within that time."

"I'm not a Wac," I said.

"My house, my rules. Incidentally, while yesterday was a special circumstance, you will have to start curbing your nighttime activities. My girls are to be in their cots at twenty-three hundred hours. No exceptions."

Could she see in the dark? Because there was no way anyone could've observed me coming in the night before. More than likely she hadn't been in the barracks yet herself. "So your guards squealed," I said.

"My what?"

"The men you had posted last night."

"If there were any men around this hut, I can assure they were in violation of orders." She licked the end of her pencil and tapped the lead against the clipboard. "Who were these men?"

"Beats me. It was dark."

"What branch were they?"

"Pine? Olive? How the deuce would I know?" Surely Blake would've let her know if he was posting guards. I didn't like where this was going. Somehow we'd progressed from my being in trouble to my getting someone else in trouble. Until I knew why they were there and what they were doing, it hardly seemed fair to rat out our nighttime visitors.

"Do I look like I'm joking?" she asked. Truth be told, I couldn't picture her amused. Ever.

"I'm telling you the truth." I raised my hand. "Scout's honor. I assumed they were supposed to be there, so I barely eyeballed them. I don't even know how many there were."

"Very well. If you see them again I expect you to alert me immediately." She glanced at her watch. Fortunately, annoying us was of greater concern to her than protecting our virtue. "You now have thirty seconds to complete your task." She clapped her hands together. "Chop! Chop!"

I rose and threw my blanket over the mattress. With a speed I didn't know I possessed, I threw on fresh clothes and went to the end of my cot, standing at attention like the other women around me.

If Captain Lambert was impressed by my haste, she didn't admit it. She barely paid me notice as she walked by my cot and checked my name off her clipboard.

Violet and Kay weren't so lucky. While her bunk was made and her person seemed tidy, Captain Lambert lingered over Violet's trunk, where unmentionables hung out like the tongue of a thirsty dog. With a single finger, she lifted the trunk lid, revealing the disastrous contents to everyone in the room. Violet's folding abilities weren't what she was interested in; it was her collection of libations. Amid silky underthings, blouses, skirts, and dresses were several jars of booze nestled like eggs in their nest. In the middle of it all was a flask, waiting to be loaded so that Violet could be too.

Captain Lambert picked up a jar and, like a model at Macy's, turned so that everyone could see what she held. "Alcohol is strictly forbidden," she said. "We are a dry unit."

"You may be a dry unit, but I'm a thirsty actress." Violet made a move for the jar but found it lifted just beyond her reach.

"Where did you get this from?"

Violet raised her chin. "I brought if from home."

Captain Lambert opened the jar and took a whiff. The potency showed on her face. "Operating an amateur distillery is against military regulations."

"I'll keep that in mind if I ever decide to join the military."

"If I find liquor in your possession again, there will be disciplinary action. Understood?"

Violet's eyes didn't stray from the jar. Amelia seemed to sense that words would have little impact on her. If she wanted to make a statement, she was going to have to do it in a language Violet understood.

She walked to the tent opening and emptied the jar's contents onto the ground outside. A squeal escaped from Violet as she watched her precious booze fall onto the already wet ground. I half-expected her to hurl herself to the floor and lap up whatever hadn't been absorbed.

"You can't do that! That's my hooch!"

"And if you obey my rules, perhaps you will get the remainder back when your tour ends. There is no alcohol in my camp. And if I find it again, I'll see to it that Rear Admiral Blake starts a full investigation to uncover whoever is distilling on this island. Understood?" Captain Lambert instructed one of the Wacs to retrieve the remaining jars and take them to her office. Violet watched in near tears as her bar left the room.

Unfortunately, Captain Lambert wasn't done. Her gaze shifted from Violet to Kay, who was standing perfectly erect in front of her cot. Her trunk was latched, its contents completely concealed by the luggage. Her bed was so tightly made that we could've used it for a trampoline. And Kay herself was pin neat, her shirt tucked in, her shoes polished enough to refract the light.

None of that, however, was enough for Captain Lambert.

"Miss Thorpe, I've heard that you used to be a Wac."

Kay kept her eyes focused straight ahead. "Yes, Captain Lambert. That's correct."

"I guess you couldn't cut it, could you?"

Had I been the one undergoing the inquisition, I probably would've let her have it. Kay knew better though. The easiest way to make this end was to agree with whatever Amelia said.

"That's correct, Captain Lambert."

"Do you know what girls who quit the WACs are?"

"No, Captain Lambert."

"Cowards. Weak, pitiful cowards."

Kay swallowed. I desperately wanted to intervene on her behalf, but I wasn't certain what that would accomplish. Lambert had my number. My defending Kay would only give her another reason to dislike her.

"Private Andrews," Captain Lambert said to a Wac one bed away. "Is the manner in which Miss Thorpe made her bed acceptable?"

Private Andrews's face was a mess of freckles, and her body had a peculiar tendency to look as though she were slumping, even when I was sure she was standing perfectly straight. The Wac looked at Kay, and then at the bed. "No, it isn't."

"I agree," said Captain Lambert. She went to Kay's cot and threw back the covers with such force that all the sheets and blankets were stripped from the bed. "Do it again. Properly this time."

Kay did so while we all watched. When the bed was complete, Captain Lambert queried another Wac, this one named Lembeck. The tall brunette didn't even look at the bed before proclaiming that it was once again improperly done.

For a half hour Kay made the bed while the Wacs passed judgment on her. I was beginning to think we'd be there all day as she tucked her sheets and pulled her blankets, when Captain Lambert queried Candy Abbott on Kay's success.

"Private Abbott, has Miss Thorpe made this bed to your satisfaction?"

"Yes, Captain Lambert. The bed is fine."

Captain Lambert gave a little jolt of surprise. "What was that?"

"I said, that in my opinion the bed has now been properly made." She raised an eyebrow. "Are you certain of that?"

"Yes, Captain Lambert."

Amelia stomped over to Candy's bedside and pulled back her sheets. "Then perhaps you better demonstrate the proper way to make a bed, since you seem to believe you're an expert on the matter."

Candy did so. She only had to repeat the process twice before one of the other Wacs confirmed that it was done to her liking. That girl didn't have to face Captain Lambert's wrath. Apparently, Amelia had tired of her game.

When the inspection was complete, Captain Lambert directed the Wacs to meet her outside for their march to the mess. As they headed out the door, I grabbed hold of Candy.

"Thanks for what you did for Kay. That took a lot of guts."

She shrugged. "It was nothing. I was hungry and getting bored with it all."

"Still. Thanks."

As soon as they were out of sight, the three of us collapsed back on our cots to wait for the sun to finish rising.

"I can't take this every day," moaned Violet. "How dare she confiscate my booze. I have just as much a right to it as the men do."

I ignored her. After all, while losing her liquor was a pity, watching Kay being put through the wringer was slightly more disturbing.

"Are you all right?" I asked Kay.

"About as good as your garden-variety pariah can be."

I turned on my side. "They'll get used to you."

"Maybe, maybe not. So many of those girls used to be my friends. I wonder which one of them squealed to Captain Lambert about me."

"Does it really matter?"

"No." She rolled onto her stomach and kicked the air like she was swimming.

"At least Candy stood up for you."

The pillow muffled her voice. "For now. I bet after the girls get done razzing her for it, she'll never make that mistake again."

"Don't be so sure. I wasn't the only one who came in late last night. Candy didn't come home until after I did."

"You should've squealed," said Violet.

I grabbed a pillow and threw it at her. "What would that have accomplished? By keeping my yap shut, she knows we've got her back, and maybe she'll keep watching ours."

"Or maybe she'll decide that you're even now and all bets are off." Violet threw the pillow back at me. It landed on the floor with a thud.

"Were there really guards out there last night?" asked Kay.

"Yeah," said Violet. "I didn't see anyone."

I rescued the pillow from the floor and punched it back into shape. "They were hiding in the trees when I came in. I think it's the same men who were watching us the night Gilda died."

"Maybe Dotty put them on us," said Kay. "Or some of the other fellows. It's kind of nice to know someone's looking out for us."

"If that's what they're doing," said Violet.

"Trust me," I said. "If they intended to do us harm, they had plenty of chances when we were still in our own tent. They're either here to watch out for us or they're Peeping Toms, and frankly, after everything else that's gone on, a Peeping Tom is fine by me."

CHAPTER 21

Visit to a POW Camp

Later that morning I helped Jayne pack up her things and take them to the WAC barracks. "So how did it go with Billy?" I asked her as we started across the camp.

She grinned at her feet as a blush colored her neck and face. She'd insisted on walking even though her ankle was still bothering her and her usual quick pace was impeded by pain. "Nice. Very nice. It was sweet of them to check on us last night, wasn't it?"

"Yeah, it was pretty swell of them."

Jayne screwed up her mouth. "You don't think it was disrespectful, do you?"

"How so?"

"Billy visiting me so soon after Gilda died."

"Given how much Gilda loved men, it seems like a fair tribute to me."

She hugged her bundle to her chest. "He said he thinks he's falling in love with me."

"Thinks?"

She cocked her head to the left, and her smile went loopy. "Okay, I added the 'thinks.' Is it too soon to feel that way about someone?"

I thought about how nice it had been to see Peaches, how good it felt to have a warm body so close to mine. It was hard not to seek out company when you were surrounded by death wherever you turned. "Are you asking for his benefit or yours?"

"Both, I guess."

"No, it's not too soon," I said. "Just don't let the war rush you, okay? Those uniforms have a way of making us think that we have to do everything today."

A mosquito lingered in the air before me, and I dispatched it with a clap of my hands. Peaches weighed heavily on my mind, though I didn't want to give voice to any of the things I was thinking. While it may not have been too soon for Jayne to get serious, it was definitely too soon for me.

Jayne yawned and quickly covered her mouth with her hand.

"I know why I didn't get any sleep," I said. "What's your excuse?"

"It was a busy night at the infirmary. One of the enlisted men tried to hang himself."

"No sir!"

Jayne nodded solemnly. "He's going to be fine, but it was pretty upsetting. He was ranting and raving most of the night."

"Any idea why he wanted to do it?"

"Ruth said he was rock happy. I guess the longer the boys are here with nothing to do, the more desperate they become. The good news is he didn't try to hurt anyone else."

"That's the good news?"

Jayne squinted into the distance. "Is that Spanky?"

His bald globe of a head reflected the sun as he walked along the beach. When he saw us, he picked up his pace and trotted the remaining distance to us.

"Morning, ladies. How're you feeling, Jayne?" He took the stack of magazines from her hands like a schoolboy offering to tote her books to class.

"Swell," said Jayne. "Thanks for asking. How's Mac?"

"You can see for yourself this afternoon. Woof says he's ready to get back on his feet." He turned his attention to me. "That was some rally last night, wasn't it?"

"It was something else all right," I said. "I have a question for you: Have you or Dotty asked your friends to tail us?"

"Come again?"

"Someone was watching us from outside our tent the night Gilda was shot, and they showed up at the WAC barracks last night. I thought one of you might've put them up to it."

He turned his palms my way. "You got the wrong tree. Is someone bothering you?"

"No," I said. "It's nothing like that. We were just trying to figure out who they're getting their orders from."

"I can ask around if you like."

"If you do, keep it hush-hush," I said. "I don't think this is something the brass initiated, and I'd hate to get someone in trouble for trying to protect us."

"My lips are sealed. Speaking of secrets . . ." He leaned toward us. He was ripe with sweat and seawater, and a hint of something much more potent. Had he been drinking? Or was this last night's fun still clinging to his breath? "It's going down tonight."

Jayne and I exchanged a look that made it clear we had no idea what he was talking about.

"We're storming the prison," he said.

"Who's doing what now?" I asked.

"It's not right that that Jap is down there enjoying the lap of luxury after what he did to Jayne and Gilda. He has to pay for what he's done."

Jayne's mouth popped into an *O*. "What do you want to do that for?"

Spanky was nonplussed by her tone. I just don't think he thought it was possible that someone was opposing their actions, especially one of the people they were doing it for. "We're sending a message, and if we do it right, we just might find out who his accomplices are and when they're going to strike again."

"But haven't we already done that by putting him in prison?" she asked.

"Yeah, with pillows and hand-holding." His head snapped to the left, where a group of men congregated with a football. He returned the slicks to Jayne. "I got to blow, girls. But if you want in on the fun, we're meeting at the swimming hole at midnight."

At breakfast, the officers talked about the coming advance on New Georgia. Gilda's name wasn't mentioned once, though her presence hung in the room like the smell of bacon that clung to the walls. Van Lauer was still there, as were the rest of the men who'd accompanied him. Because of the air strikes on Guadalcanal, the army air force officers' stay had been extended for at least another day just in case they were needed. I thought we'd already won that island, but apparently these victories weren't as black and white as the press made them seem. Further complicating things was the contradictory news coming out of Guadalcanal. The Japanese claimed to have struck one of our convoys, but Secretary of the Navy Knox said no such convoy was ever in the area. The Japanese were merely lying to make their defeat a bit more palatable.

"When is it over?" I asked my RAF companion.

"When the last Jap is dead and buried," he replied.

As breakfast ended and everyone began to disperse, Violet suggested we head to the enlisted mess to rehearse. On the way there, Jayne and I filled Kay and her in on our conversation with Spanky.

"Do you think we should tell someone?" asked Kay.

"Actually, I was hoping Violet might take care of things for us," I said.

Violet put her hand to her chest. "Me?" Her squinty eyes looked bigger today. In fact, she looked better than she had since I'd first met her. The layers of makeup were gone, her hair was soft and natural, and she seemed more at ease with herself. Perhaps this was love working its magic.

"Spanky will do anything you say. If you told him you thought this was a bad idea, I'm sure he'd retreat."

She cocked her head, silently acknowledging that my description of her hold over Spanky was true. "Sure he would, *if* I thought it was a bad idea."

I stopped walking. "Come again?"

Violet turned to face me. "This man killed Gilda and tried to do the same to Jayne. I think it's noble that they want him to pay for that."

I was flabbergasted. Was she really saying this? "Well, Jayne doesn't think it's noble, do you, Jayne?"

"No," she said.

"And I seriously doubt Gilda would either. What if they kill him?"

Violet waved me off like I was an insect buzzing around her head. "They won't kill him."

Kay looked at her square on, enunciating each word with the care of a nonnative English speaker. "But what if they do?"

"Then they do," said Violet. "You're forgetting: he *killed* Gilda."

"But—but—but that was an act of war," said Kay.

Violet lifted her head ever so slightly to assert what she believed to be her superior position. "And this isn't? If they're not playing by the rules, why should we?"

We were going down a dangerous path, where no one could ever be completely right or wrong, but a whole lot of feelings were bound to be hurt in the process.

"They could end up being court-martialed," I said. "The whole lot of them could face disciplinary action if they hurt the guy, to say nothing of killing him. Do you really want that for Spanky?"

"Of course not, but that's not going to happen. You heard Blake last night—he wants us to do this. It's the right thing." Violet tossed her hands in the air. "If you want to rat them out, it's on you. I don't want any part of it. It's about time someone around here stood up for what's right."

And with that, we agreed to disagree.

By the time lights went out that evening, I was feeling beyond conflicted. Sure, I didn't like the idea that a fellow human being was about to undergo whatever torture Spanky and his pals decided to level on him. But this was the man who killed Gilda and tried to kill Jayne, and right now it looked as if he would wait out the rest of the war as a POW. When it was all said and done, he'd be sent back home no worse for wear and possibly hailed as a hero for diverting attention away from his accomplices. He would get a parade; Gilda would get a box.

But there were rules for a reason. Even if the Japanese didn't obey the same policies that we did, wasn't it our responsibility to show them that we were more moral and humane and that was why we had right on our side? If things got out of hand and the sniper was killed, how was that different from the horrible things the Allied prisoners were facing? Did we really want to provide the enemy with the rationale that they only did what they did because *we* did it first?

Besides, if what Late Nate said was true, the prisoner would be facing dishonor for being taken alive. Maybe that was the key to reasoning with our men. They could torture the guy all they wanted, but if they really wanted to punish him, keeping him alive and in impeccable shape would do more damage to him than fists and guns. Let the enemy deal with their own.

I sat up in my cot and sought out the opening in the mosquito netting. I had no idea what time it was, but judging from the snoring coming from across the hut, I was guessing it was nearing half-past twelve.

I stood up and tried to adjust to the inky night. I could do this. I would go to the POW camp and try to reason with the men. It was the right thing to do.

Bare feet padded across the floor. Jayne's hair glowed in the dark like the phosphorescence in the ocean. "What are you doing?" she whispered.

"I'm not sure yet," I whispered back.

"You're going to try to stop them, aren't you?"

"Someone has to."

"We could tell Rear Admiral Blake," said Jayne.

I let out a groan and quickly put my hand to my mouth to make sure the noise didn't wake someone. "And what would telling Late Nate do? You had the good fortune to miss his little speech last night, but trust me when I say that I wouldn't be surprised if he unlocked the prison door and handed over the sniper to the first unruly mob he saw." I fished my shoes out from under my cot and tied on a robe.

"Can I come?"

"Do you really want to?

"Yes. Gilda may not be able to tell them what she wants, but I still can."

Two voices were better than one. Besides, Jayne had a knack for being more compelling than me. "Can your ankle handle it?"

"Absolutely."

"Okay, but be quiet about it."

She snuck back to her cot and retrieved her shoes. Should we get Kay to come too? It wouldn't be a bad idea to have someone levelheaded with us. Especially someone who knew the military and could talk their talk.

I tiptoed over to her bed and gently shook her. Her eyes immediately opened, and I signaled for her to keep her yap shut. She nodded, acknowledging what I was asking and what I was proposing. Within seconds she had her shoes and had covered up her nightgown with a robe.

I gestured for the two of them to follow me. We made a beeline to the barracks door, and I peeked through a crack to see if anyone was waiting for us. It didn't look like our guards were on duty yet. Perhaps Spanky's asking about them had spooked them.

I waved for Jayne and Kay to follow me, and the three of us jogged two tents down before pausing to put on our shoes.

"Should we get Violet too?" asked Jayne.

"You heard her today. She'd be as helpful as a clubfoot right now."

Jayne struggled to tie her robe closed. "She's going to be mad as hell."

"Let her. She's not my czar."

"What's the plan?" asked Kay.

"We're going to try to reason with them. But I'm betting it will mean more coming from you than me." I told her my idea about trying to explain to them that dishonor would do more harm to the prisoner than fists could. Jayne and Kay agreed that it was a compelling reason to get them to call off the witch hunt. Assuming the men were sober. If they'd liquored up in anticipation of what they were about to do, there'd be no reasoning with them.

"What if Violet's right?" said Kay.

My jaw hit the muddy ground. "You're kidding me, right? You're the last person I'd expect to hear sticking up for her."

"I'm not saying I completely agree with her, but don't you think we owe it to Gilda to see to it this man gets more than a slap on the hand?"

I understood where Kay was coming from. She'd lost two brothers at Bataan. Who was going to see to it that the men behind that were punished? "Look, if you don't want to come, nobody's making you."

Kay gouged at a patch of rough skin on her index finger. "No, I do. I definitely do."

We made it to the swimming hole, where a cluster of beer bottles and cigarette butts made it clear that we'd missed the men by only a few minutes. In the distance ahead, twigs snapped, leaves rustled, and a low voice implored the others to "*shhhh . . .*"

"Should we call out to them?" asked Jayne.

If we did so, we might draw the attention of someone else, someone who might see to it that the boys—and the three of us—were punished for this little plot. I advised the others to remain quiet, and we followed the path toward the prison. The road made a *Y*, one side heading for the POW camp, the other one toward the village.

Kay froze at the crossroads. "Did you hear that?"

"What?" I said.

"Somebody's coming."

I strained for evidence of our intruder and picked up quiet footsteps heading toward us from the village. We ducked into a tangle of foliage and waited for whoever it was to pass.

As we crouched in the greenery, standing in puddles still left from the heavy rain, bugs and beetles attempted to make meals of us. Dangling vines quivered with the wind, tricking me into believing that any number of reptiles had just brushed past me. I yearned to swat them away, but I couldn't wince, slap, or shriek if I wanted to stay hidden. All I could do was freeze and pray.

Whoever was coming was taking their time.

"We should've just gone," I whispered. "They never would've seen us." Something furry tickled my leg.

"Too late now," whispered Jayne.

We receded further into the jungle. The air was ripe with a stench of something rotten. Above this putrid sweetness lingered the scent of new growth brought on by the recent rain. What a queer place this island was, at once repellent and attractive. Were Japanese bodies still out here? They couldn't have found all of them. Surely some of the corpses had been left behind to become a permanent part of the jungle. If this were a story in *Tales of Terror*, those bodies would reanimate and roam the island seeking revenge. In fact, maybe they had. Maybe I wasn't feeling vines brushing past my cheek but skeletal fingers marking their target.

Sometimes I hated my overactive imagination.

At last a figure appeared in the dim light, guiding their path with a flashlight. I strained to get a slant on them. It was Candy Abbott.

"This isn't good," said Kay.

"What do you mean?" I said. "It's the one Wac who likes us."

"No, it's the one Wac who did me a turn after you did her one, and who probably spent the day hearing about it from the others.

There's no telling what'll happen if she gets back to the tent before
we do and sees that we're gone. Especially if Captain Lambert ar-
rives before she does."

I got what she was saying. If Candy went back to the tent and
encountered Amelia or set off the guards, our absence would be
discovered. And rather than getting in trouble herself and risking
the rest of the Wacs' ire, it would be very easy for her to divert
everyone's attention by pointing out that we were missing.

Something rattled in the wind. It was bones. Definitely bones.
"Candy's not like that," I said.

"Maybe not where Jayne and you are concerned, but I'm not so
sure she feels any loyalty toward me."

"So then, what do we do?" asked Jayne.

I wasn't sure, but whatever it was better be happening soon, before we were gobbled whole-cloth by the undead.

"Candy," Kay stage-whispered as she disentangled herself from
the brush.

Candy jumped at the sound of Kay's voice before peering into
the darkness where we were hidden. "Who's there?"

"It's Kay. And Jayne and Rosie."

We stepped out of our hiding place. Candy took us all in.

"Hi," said Kay. Her tone was soft and hesitant, like a small child
who encounters a once-enthusiastic friend they're afraid might not
want to play with them again. "Thanks for what you did this morning."

Candy's face bent in confusion. While gratitude was nice, she
certainly didn't expect to receive it in the jungle in the middle of
the night. "You know Irene would hate them for how they're treating you."

"I like to think so," said Kay. "I'm sorry about what happened to
her. She was my best friend."

"She was mine too."

"I know," said Kay. "And I should've been the one to tell you
when she died."

Candy shrugged. "I'm not sure the news would've gone down

easy, no matter who told me." She seemed to realize that Jayne and I were hanging on their every word. "What are you doing out here anyway?"

"I was about to ask you the same thing," I said.

She had a bag slung diagonally across her body. From the way it was hanging I could tell it was empty. "Late-night rendezvous," she whispered.

"He must be pretty special to risk this much hot water," I said.

She grinned at the ground. "Oh, he is. He definitely is. Now, what are you three up to?"

"Trying to stop a lynching." I told her about Spanky and the boys' plot to punish the sniper.

"Do you honestly think talk is going to stop them?" she asked.

"No. But us staying in the tent and waiting until morning isn't going to help either. At the very least, they need to know that this isn't what Gilda would've wanted. Do you want to join us?"

She hesitated, her eyes following the trail that would lead back to camp. Her gaze returned to Kay before landing on me. "Why not?" she finally said. "I'm in the mood for an adventure."

CHAPTER 22

A Prisoner of War

Candy led the way. She knew where the POW camp was, but, more important, she knew how to approach it without being seen. We came at it from behind, hugging the hills that formed the camp's back wall and led up to the Suicide Cliffs. The entire compound was only about two thousand square feet. Barbed wire surrounded it, though I didn't think it would take much to compromise it if that's what you were set on doing. We could hear Spanky and his crew from where we stood, though we couldn't see them. Apparently, gaining entry was slightly more complicated than I anticipated, since from the sound of things, the men had to linger outside the gates for a while.

"They're probably bribing the guard," said Candy.

"There's a guard?" I said.

"Several of them. You don't think we rely on barbed wire alone to pen our POWs, do you?"

Eventually, the men's voices grew muffled, and we knew they'd entered the building. Rather than trying to climb the fence, we decided to follow their lead and walk in through the front door.

As Candy had described, there were two guards standing post at the gate. They were playing cards, and each of them had a jar of something in hand to help them pass the time. Sitting at their feet, his attention divided between us and the pen, was Mac, a wide white bandage wrapped around his torso. His tail thumped an enthusiastic greeting.

We didn't have anything to offer the guards: no booze, no cigarettes, no late-night snack. All we had was Jayne.

"Mind helping us out here?" I asked her.

"By doing what exactly?"

"Just being your charming self."

The three of us opened our robes and Candy opened a button. Jayne fluffed her hair and pinched some color into her cheeks. Her nightgown only qualified for that title because she wore it at night; there certainly wasn't enough fabric involved to call it a dress, much less a gown.

"Hiya, fellows," she cooed.

The guards snapped to attention at our arrival. One of them had a scar across his face. The skin puckered around his eye the way a ring mount clutched a diamond.

The other fellow had one of those soft bland faces that made you think of unbaked dough. My stomach growled at the sight of him.

"Evening, ladies. What brings you here?" asked doughface.

"We're looking for Spanky," said Jayne.

"Sorry," said the guy with the scar, "there's no one here by that name."

As though to verify the guy was lying, Mac let out a single bark.

"That's his dog," I said. "We know he's here."

"He and his pals were supposed to wait for us so we could come along for the fun," said Candy.

"They didn't tell us anyone else was coming," said the man with the scar.

"I can't imagine Spanky being dumb enough to leave girls like you behind," said doughboy.

"We were afraid we wouldn't be able to sneak out tonight," I said. "I think Spanky took that to mean we weren't coming at all."

"I didn't think this was the kind of thing dames would want to be part of," said the scar.

"Well, we're not just any dames," said Kay. "We were in the show with Gilda."

I pushed Jayne forward. "Jayne here was the other girl who was hurt."

Jayne lifted her hair to show off the red wound at the top of her ear. The men did a double take. Doughface jumped to his feet and offered Jayne his chair.

"I'm fine. Really I am." She took a deep breath to dramatize just how all right she was. Her chest jutted out like the prow of a ship.

"I'm sure she'll be even better once she sees the sniper get his what-for," I said.

Jayne's voice grew weak and wispy. "It doesn't seem right that someone could do something like that and end up serving time behind bars in the lap of luxury."

Even as she said it, we all recognized that this was hardly the country club Blake had described. In the States, there were tales of German and Japanese POWs being put up at resorts where they had access to whatever amenities they desired, and still some of them attempted to escape. Here on Tulagi their encampment was a prison pure and simple. It might have been slightly better than facing the danger on the warfront, but it was still a miserable way to live out your days.

"All right, ladies. Go on through. The Jap you want is in the last cell on the right."

We passed through the gate and entered the low, dark building. It was damp inside, smelling like a combination of mold, urine, and rotting food. We could hear people shifting in the darkness, but no one called out to us. Most of the prisoners were probably asleep, and the ones who weren't must've recognized that we weren't their friends and that any attempt to get our attention wasn't likely to help them.

"How many men are here?" whispered Kay.

"Not many. Probably only three or four," said Candy. "Once things get too crowded, they send them to a bigger camp on one of the other islands."

I peered into each of the small rooms to see what sort of conditions the men were living in. Each had a military-issue cot and what looked like some sort of portable toilet.

"Do they just stay in here all day?" I asked.

"No. There's an all-purpose room, where they can talk to one another, and a kitchen. I think they're allowed access to the yard during daylight hours. They would put them to work, but they're not allowed to make them do anything that would benefit our side in the war, which kind of limits any potential jobs they might give them. Of course, from what I hear, those rules are stretched at some of the other camps."

"How so?" I asked.

"I've heard rumors that they make some of the Axis prisoners clear out minefields."

If Blake considered that living in the lap of luxury, I hated to see what sort of conditions the Axis were subjecting *our* POWs to.

"This way," said Kay. We followed the sound of our men talking in the distance. We stopped just short of where they were. I didn't think it was wise to let them know we were there until we knew what they were doing.

"Put him over there!" said a man whose voice I didn't recognize. The others were egging him on, listing any number of things they hoped to do to the prisoner in question.

Someone—the prisoner?—said something in Japanese.

"He wants to know what they want," said Candy.

"You speak Japanese?" I asked.

"And German," she said. "Kay and I both do. You can't break their codes if you don't speak their language."

This was a boon I hadn't anticipated.

"You think you can get away with killing a woman like that, you slant-eyed bastard?" said one of the men. Other epithets followed, so littered with curse words that even if the prisoner knew English, he couldn't have made head or tail of what they were trying to say. We heard the sound of flesh hitting flesh and winced as a clatter of furniture followed. The prisoner yelped in pain.

"Aren't you going to fight back? Or are you too yellow?"

The prisoner responded in rapid-fire Japanese, his tone making it clear that he was both hurt and terrified.

"He's begging them to leave him alone," said Candy. "He's saying he didn't do anything."

I was itching to respond. The sniper's tone reminded me of a wounded animal. I couldn't bear to listen to that sort of agony, especially when people I used to like were the ones inflicting it.

"Kick the yellow bastard!" someone yelled. There was a sickening thud, followed by retching. That was it. I was done.

"Stop!" I yelled. We rounded the corner and found a group of five men crowded into the all-purpose room. The prisoner was on the floor on his side, vomiting as he clutched his stomach. I was shocked by what I saw: this wasn't a Japanese soldier enduring what every soldier prepared to face. This was a mere boy so terrified of what was happening to him that his eyes were filled with tears.

"What are you doing here, Rosie?" asked Spanky. His face was red, not from the sun this time but from the excitement of the fight.

"You've got to stop this," I said. "He's only a boy. It's not right."

One of the other men lectured me with his index finger. "What's not right is what he did to Gilda. He deserves to pay for that."

"Not like this," I said.

The boy spoke again in Japanese.

"He says he wants to go home," said Candy.

The men parted to let the other women through.

"Of course he does. He's a coward," said a guy they called Sheep, a name he immortalized with a tattoo of the animal on his forearm.

Candy said something to the boy in Japanese. He looked at her in shock, unable to reconcile the image of this white American woman speaking his language. She said something else to him, her tone soft and reassuring. As he replied, his eyes darted around the room, looking at the men set on doing him harm.

"He's a deserter," said Kay.

"What?" asked Sheep.

"He went AWOL a week ago."

Candy asked him something else, and he responded at greater length.

"His name's Yoshihiro," said Kay. "He's only sixteen years old. He thought he wanted to be a soldier, but after watching his friends get killed, he got scared and ran."

"So he is a yellow coward!" said a man they called Red, a nickname derived, no doubt, from his flame-colored hair.

"Why did he shoot Gilda and me?" asked Jayne.

Candy took a step toward the boy and knelt down to his level. She looked like she was about to touch him, then thought better of it. Quietly, with a gentle smile planted on her face, she continued her interrogation. His eyes widened in surprise at something she said, and he became more animated as he attempted to answer her.

"What's he saying?" asked Spanky.

Candy raised her hand to let him know that she wasn't going to tell him anything until the boy had spoken his piece. They continued this way for several minutes. As the boy's response came to an end, Candy reached into her bag and pulled out a chocolate bar. The boy eyed it suspiciously until Candy unwrapped it and demonstrated what it was. Understanding passed through his eyes as he slid it into one of his pockets.

"Well?" I asked Kay.

"He said he was trying to watch the show from up in the cliffs. He heard us singing and wanted to know what was going on. He hid in the brush up there and watched as everyone performed. He said that the women on stage were very beautiful, and he loved to hear the American music."

"If he loved it so much, why did he decide to fire on us?" asked Jayne.

"He didn't," said Kay. "He said the shooter was on a cliff below him."

"He's lying," said Spanky.

"He ran when he heard the gunshots," said Candy. "He thought they were firing at him because of his desertion."

"Ask him if he saw the shooter," I said.

This time Kay repeated the question in Japanese. The boy responded quickly and succinctly. "He says no," said Kay. "It was too dark and the sniper was too far below him."

"Ask him if he knows about the Japanese sneaking onto the island to take supplies."

Again she repeated the question. His face crinkled in confusion, and his tone indicated that he was asking her something in return. She replied, and whatever her answer was, it was sufficient to allow him to respond. "He doesn't know anything about that." The boy started talking again, his large eyes locked on Kay's face. "He said he explained all of this to the man with the white hair," said Kay. "He wants to go to America. He can't go back to his home after dishonoring his family by running away."

So Blake had known all along that this boy wasn't the sniper. Why would he imprison him and let the real culprit run loose?

"He's lying," said Spanky. "He'll say whatever he can to get us to leave him alone."

"I don't think so," I said. "If word about what he's done gets out, he'll be killed by his own men. By claiming he killed Gilda, he's much more likely to be viewed as a hero in their eyes."

"He's probably still guilty of something." Spanky's eyes were fast becoming as red as his sunburned face. "Who knows how many of our men he took out before now?" He shoved his hand in his pocket and pulled out a jackknife.

"What the deuce is that?" I asked.

He stabbed the air in front of him. "He deserves to pay. They all do."

The boy began to pray under his breath. At least, I think it was a prayer. Lord knows it's what I would've been doing in that moment. I stepped between Spanky and him.

"If you kill him, Spanky, I swear to God I'll make sure everyone knows. Got it? You either leave him alone, or I'll see to it that you're court-martialed for this."

"Then maybe I'll kill you too." He lifted the knife until it was level with my neck, the blade turned just enough to catch the light. It was so close to me that if I swallowed I would've felt the tip prick me.

This wasn't just about avenging Gilda and Jayne. Spanky had become rock happy, so long had he sat on this island with nothing to do. He needed to accomplish something that he believed would affect the outcome of this war, and he'd convinced himself that killing the sniper was that thing. With less time on his hands and more activity, he might've been able to look at the situation rationally.

And the booze I smelled on his breath probably wasn't helping things.

He held my eyes while I held my breath. Ten seconds passed. Twenty. Thirty.

He dropped the knife. Candy caught it with her foot and kicked it toward the door.

"I'm sorry," said Spanky. "I wouldn't hurt you. I swear."

"It's all right," I said. He and Violet were made for each other. My hand leaped to my neck and explored the skin to make sure no harm had been done.

His eyes filled with tears. He looked like a sleepwalker who'd just awakened to find himself teetering on a ledge. "I don't want to hurt an innocent person."

"Don't worry," I said. "You didn't."

He stumbled out of the room and headed toward the exit. Should I follow him? It would have been the right thing to do, but after having his knife at my neck, I didn't feel moved to do him any favors.

"This doesn't make any sense," said Sheep. "If the brass knew they had the wrong man, why wouldn't they own up to it?"

"Because they probably didn't believe him," said Candy.

"We have to keep this quiet," said Kay. The boys were slowly coming to accept that what we'd said was true. "I think it would be a good idea if no one knew we were here tonight."

If Blake knew he had the wrong man, he certainly didn't want to risk the chance that anyone else knew it too. And if he found out we'd been here and let the prisoner live, he might decide to discipline the men as a way of making it clear that there were consequences for not believing him.

"Kay's right," I said. "Everyone in here better keep their heads closed."

"And how exactly are we going to do that? We've got two guards in the know and a prisoner that's bruised and bleeding," said Sheep.

Candy spoke to the prisoner again. He nodded, signaling his agreement with whatever she said. "I told him if he keeps quiet about what happened here tonight, we'll do whatever we can to help him."

"We can buy off the guards," said Red. "Trust me: those fellows will say whatever we want for a couple of bottles and some cigarettes. No one's going to wonder about his bruises anyway. There's always some sort of squabble going on between the Nips."

And if what the boy said was true and he was a deserter, Blake had to know the other POWs would be just as much of a threat as the American soldiers.

"What about Spanky?" asked Jayne.

"We'll keep him quiet," said Sheep. "He's so lit he probably won't remember most of this, come morning. He needed liquid courage to come here to begin with."

"So that just leaves the rest of us," I said. "Keep whatever happened tonight on the QT. Not a word to anyone. Got it?"

We all agreed, though I for one wasn't likely to keep that promise. If someone else had killed Gilda, I wasn't going to rest until I found out who it was.

CHAPTER 23

The Wrong Man in the Right Place

As we crept back to the barracks that night, the four of us mulled over what was going on.

"None of this is making sense," I said. "Why would they deliberately imprison the wrong man?"

"What if the real killer was someone high up?" asked Candy. Her flashlight lighted a path in front us.

"You mean an officer?"

The globe of light bobbed in time to her words. "Maybe. Let's say Late Nate knows who the killer is, but he isn't about to punish him. Instead, he locks up the first Jap he can find and blames him."

"I'm not buying that," I said. "For all his flaws, I can't see Blake wanting to protect the real shooter."

"I can," said Kay. We all turned to her. "They'd much rather be able to pin this on the enemy. That way, they can dismiss Gilda as another civilian casualty."

Candy snapped her fingers. "That's a good point. Imagine the press back home if word got out that someone other than the enemy was behind the shooting."

And, more important, what sort of military scrutiny might Blake and his men be subject to if it became known that a crime happened on their watch? Problems they'd been able to cover up, like missing supplies, might come to light.

"So if it isn't just another casualty of war," asked Jayne, "what is it?"

Finally, a question I could answer. "Murder," I said.

I didn't see our surreptitious guards when we returned, though it was likely they were in the shadows watching for us. No longer did I view them as benign protectors sent to ensure our safety. If the wrong person had been blamed for Gilda's death and Blake knew it, it was just as likely that our spies were men sent by Blake to make sure we didn't have access to the true story of what occurred the night she was shot.

And if that were the case, Blake would know by morning what we'd been up to.

We made it into the hut without incident and retired to our cots. I longed to be back in our old tent or, even better, New York, mulling over what had happened while washing away the whole awful evening with a good strong martini.

Instead I reflected on the events of the past few days. Suddenly Blake's strange inquisition made sense. He didn't want to know if we'd witnessed the crime. He wanted to verify that we hadn't seen anything that would disprove what he claimed had happened.

It was all so distressing. The fact of Gilda's death was bad enough, but to know that the military had no trouble letting the wrong person take the fall for it was downright terrifying. No wonder Jack thought it would be better to flee than fight to see that the right person was punished for what his CO had done. He had to know how hopeless that tack would've been when he took off into the night and dived into the ocean. Death was probably a relief when it came. It had to be better than living in a constant state of fear that the men you lived with, the ones who you depended on to lead you into battle, would try to kill you.

I pushed Jack out of my head. Thinking about him wasn't going to help anything right now. I was toothless as far as he was concerned. At least when Gilda died, I had been there and had firsthand knowledge of who might've wanted to do her harm.

And who was that?

If Candy was right and Blake was covering up for someone high up, who could that be? Late Nate didn't strike me as being loyal to anyone but himself. Could he be the real murderer? He seemed to be enamored of Gilda, but then so was everyone else. Despite his many, many faults, he didn't strike me as the kind of guy who would kill a woman just for spurning him. Besides, if Candy was to be believed, he was involved with Amelia Lambert. No, if Blake was behind her death, it had to be for a larger purpose than that.

My mind drifted back to Irene Zinn. Candy said she'd been bothered by the Japanese being blamed for the missing supplies. It couldn't be a coincidence that two women associated with Tulagi were killed within a month of each other. Could Gilda have learned whatever it was Irene knew about the midnight requisitions? And if she had, why was that information important enough for them both to die over?

I awoke to the sound of Captain Lambert screaming in my ear. "On your feet. Now!"

I started, expecting to find the barracks on fire or the camp under siege, but what I discovered was the room in near darkness and the women around me stirring with a mixture of confusion and irritation that whatever I had done was prompting this early waking hour.

"What's the rumble?" I asked.

She looked at the floor. In the dim morning light, mud-caked footprints led from the door to Jayne's, Candy's, and my cots, like some sort of bizarre map designed to teach us the latest dance craze. Only Kay's path remained unmarked. Apparently, she'd been clever enough to remove her shoes before entering the hut.

"Oh, looky there," I said. "I guess we tracked in some mud yesterday."

"This floor was spic and span before you retired last night."

"Are you sure about that?"

Something landed with a clang on the floor beside my cot. It was a bucket. "You'll find the mop and soap in the latrine. If I find one speck of dirt on this floor, you and your friends will not be eating breakfast. Am I understood?"

"Yes," I mumbled.

"And because some of you find it impossible to remain in the barracks after curfew, the entire platoon, with the exception of Private Abbott, Miss Hamilton, and Miss Winter, will begin morning exercises now. If you don't enjoy doing physical activity before sunrise, I recommend that you keep an eye on your bunkmates and report any unauthorized absences to me before I discover them for myself."

The women groaned in reply. There wasn't a chance that we'd be able to roam the island after hours anymore. Nothing was more effective than encouraging self-policing by punishing everyone else for what we'd done.

"I'm most disappointed in you, Private Abbott. I expect this sort of behavior from the USO, but I find it very troubling that you're keeping company with these women."

I could read fear in Candy's face. It wasn't what the other girls would think of her that bothered her; she couldn't stomach the idea that from this point on she wasn't going to be able to sneak off to be with her mystery lover.

After all she'd done for us the night before, I owed her big.

"She wasn't with us," I said.

Captain Lambert raised an eyebrow. "What was that, Miss Winter?"

"Private Abbott or Costello, or whatever her name is, wasn't with us last night. Jayne and I were on our own."

Jayne's blond head bobbed its confirmation.

"Then where were you, Private Abbott?"

"Here, Captain. I left to use the latrine in the middle of the night, but otherwise I was here."

Lambert's gaze slithered toward Kay, whose cot was on the other side of Candy's. "Did you see Private Abbott in her bed last night?"

"Yes, Captain Lambert. She was definitely there when I went to sleep."

"Very well. In the future, Private Abbott, leave your shoes outside the tent if you must use the latrine. Understood?"

Candy dropped her eyes. "Yes."

"And now, ladies, you have five minutes to dress before we begin our morning exercise."

Everyone moved into action, except Violet, who remained propped up on her pillows.

"Miss Lancaster, is your hearing all right?"

"Just fine," said Violet.

"Then perhaps you can explain to me why you're not getting dressed."

"I'm not a Wac, so why should I have to exercise like one?"

"Because it's *your* friends who misbehaved. And if there's anyone who can keep them on a short leash, I have no doubt it's you."

"Gosh, I appreciate your confidence, but that doesn't mean I'm getting out of bed."

Captain Lambert's eyebrows rose an inch. "Perhaps I haven't made myself clear: not only have I been enlisted to protect you, it's also within my power to punish you. So I suggest you get dressed unless you'd like to live out the remainder of your stay here without pay."

At last she was speaking Violet's language. As the other girls began to file out of the room, Violet shot me a glare that was so hot I had to step out of the way to keep it from burning me.

"Rehearsal's at one o'clock," she muttered. "Be there."

While Violet and Kay exercised with the others, Jayne and I went to work scrubbing the floor and trying to figure out what the strange revelations of the night before meant. I shared with her my thoughts about Blake and how it might connect to Irene Zinn.

"But why would someone kill over missing supplies?" asked Jayne.

I leaned the mop against a trunk and sat beside it. "Let's say that whoever is liberating the supplies isn't just stealing. What if they were selling them to the Japanese? Remember how one of the officers was saying the Japs don't have the same protection for supply ships that we do? If they're desperate for things—even in small quantities—I'm willing to bet they'd pay a pretty penny for some sticky fingers. I can't imagine the rest of the military would look too highly on someone aiding and abetting the enemy. If Irene found out what was really going on and let the people involved know she knew, they might've decided it was easier to keep her quiet than to run the risk of her squealing."

Jayne dipped the mop into the bucket and placed the sopping wet mess on the floor. "But she was killed in California. And she'd already left the military. That doesn't make any sense."

She was right about that. "Maybe she resigned because she was scared this would happen. She goes home, thinks everything's safe; only our thief isn't satisfied that she'll keep her yap shut, so he decides to track her down to make sure she stays silent."

Jayne made a lopsided figure eight with the mop. "I'm still not buying it. California's a million miles away." She was wrong about that. If the sign at the entrance to camp was accurate it was only ten thousand miles from here. "How could someone in the South Pacific kill someone that far away?"

"With a long reach," I said.

As soon as the floor was done, we decided to track down Dotty. I hadn't seen him face to face since we'd gotten the news that Gilda had died. If anyone could answer questions about what Irene thought was going on with the missing supplies, it was her ex-boyfriend.

We found him in his tent, listening to Edward R. Murrow while he attempted to peck out a story on a typewriter. Beside him was a bottle of hooch and an ashtray half filled with spent gaspers. His hair was a series of crests and valleys, no doubt the result of his frequently running his hands through it.

He looked like hell.

"Can we come in?" I asked.

He started at the sound of my voice. Although we were several feet away, I could smell him. Dotty hadn't bathed for several days. "Be my guest."

We entered and shared the edge of his cot. "What are you working on?" asked Jayne.

"Gilda's obituary. *Stars & Stripes* wanted something to run beside my photos, but I'm having a bear of a time getting it down on the page. I usually write these Joe Blow bios on the men—you know, where you can change the name but the details remain the same. I can write those in my sleep. But this? This is hard. She was one of a kind." He pulled the page from the mill and crushed it into a ball before depositing it into an overflowing trash basket. With the typewriter empty, he seemed to notice us for the first time. "How are you two holding up?"

"We've been better," I said.

"So Kay told me. I heard a friend of yours died right before Gilda was killed."

"My ex-boyfriend," I said. When was it going to get easier to tell people about him?

"Jack Castlegate?"

That was right. I'd asked Dotty about him our first night on the island. "That's the one."

"That makes things easier."

"How so?"

"I asked around about him and just got word about his death myself. I was dreading being the one to tell you." He took a hit of a cigarette. "I never did locate a Charlie Harrington. Not in the navy, anyway. You sure you got that name right?"

Did it matter anymore? Jack was dead. "Pretty sure."

"I'll keep asking if you want me to."

"I don't think that's necessary, but thanks for the offer." He'd picked at my wound, and I found myself anxious to do the same to him. "We heard about Irene."

I had a feeling that if I were to look into a mirror, the expression he now wore was the same one I'd donned the moment before. "Guess we're in the same boat, huh? Both of us losing our exes? I tell you, it's been a weird month. If I didn't know any better, I'd swear there was a dark cloud over this entire island."

"How long ago did you break up with her?" I asked.

He leaned back in his chair, and the wooden legs groaned beneath his weight. "We were done for before she went back to the States. It's still hard though."

"Don't I know it. Jack and I didn't exactly end on the best of terms."

His face twitched into a smile. "I'm not going to win any awards for my parting words either. Wouldn't it be nice if we knew how things were going to turn out in advance? Imagine all the things we'd be smart enough not to say." The front legs of his chair dropped to the floor. "So, what can I do for you?"

I picked at a finger, working loose a broken nail that had been hanging by a thread. "This might sound crazy, but I can't help but think that Gilda and Irene's deaths are connected."

"Gilda was killed by a sniper."

"Not the one they locked up," said Jayne. She brought him up to speed on the field trip he'd missed the night before. He didn't seem surprised by the news, but he was clearly disturbed by it.

I cleared my throat. "We heard a rumor that Irene was looking into missing supplies before she left the island."

"Oh that." He exhaled a gust of air, ruffling the hair framing his face. "Late Nate was trying to pin that on the Japanese too."

"So I heard. But Irene knew it wasn't them, right?" I asked.

"I wasn't here when that was going on, but she told me she was sure it was someone internal behind it." He lowered his voice and leaned forward. "In fact, she pretty much implied that Blake was not only taking the stuff but he was selling it to the enemy. That's how he got his nickname. A number of people saw him out and about after dark, toting packages from the supply hut. He wasn't a rear admiral yet—his commission hadn't come through—and Irene debated whether to come forward with the information. If she had, he probably would've been discharged or worse."

"So why didn't she do it?" asked Jayne.

He shrugged. "It was his word against hers. She wanted out of here by then, and I think she knew that if she made waves, it would be more trouble than it was worth. And, of course, by the time she put two and two together, the stealing stopped."

I felt strangely disappointed in this woman I'd never met. I wanted to believe Irene was a crusader who fought for what was right, but to learn that she folded so easily when things got rough seemed out of sync with that image. But then that was the point, wasn't it? I didn't know her. "But I heard the stealing started back up again after she left."

"In much smaller quantities. Personally, I think someone else knew what Blake had been up to and decided to take advantage of the situation by doing a little stealing for themselves. They had to know Blake would never look into it. If he blamed it on the Japanese before, he had to blame it on them again—otherwise who knows what an investigation might turn up."

"Do you think Late Nate knew that Irene had fingered him?"

"Absolutely. She had a hard time getting out of the Wacs. He was the one who went to bat for her, helping to convince the army that discharging her was the right thing to do. Knowing Irene, she probably used what she knew as leverage to get him to help her out. She wasn't a dumb girl. She knew how to play the system."

"I'm surprised he would let her force his hand like that," I said.

He ashed his cigarette. "It all worked out for him in the end. Not only did he get rid of a potential troublemaker, but a few months later he got his mistress brought to Tulagi."

"Amelia Lambert," I said.

He punched the air with his finger. "Bingo. She got a prime post, and he got a little sugar for his coffee. Until Gilda showed up."

"What has Gilda got to do with them?" asked Jayne.

"You mean you don't know?" Dotty lowered his voice. "Late Nate and Gilda have been an item since her first night on Tulagi."

By the time we left Dotty, my head was throbbing. We headed to the beach, hoping to catch a little sun and privacy before meeting up with Violet and Kay for rehearsal. The harbor was loaded with ships and cranes. We sat on a boulder beneath the shade of a coconut grove and watched the carefully choreographed dance of supplies leaving one ship and being brought onto another. Could something as seemingly harmless as providing the troops with what they needed really be the motive behind two murders?

"How could Gilda get involved with a guy like that?" asked Jayne.

"Beats me." The whole idea made my skin crawl. Could he have forced himself on her? Was that why she hadn't told us?

"Do you think Amelia knows?" asked Jayne. Brilliantly colored lorikeets flew above her.

"Probably." A sudden thought compelled me to snap my fingers. "You know, Candy said Amelia came to Tulagi at about the same time we did. She could've been in San Francisco with us when Irene was killed."

"But what would her motive have been?" asked Jayne. "It doesn't sound like Blake was too worried about Irene squealing if he was willing to help get her discharged."

"Maybe Amelia was jealous? She was from the same hometown as Irene. What if they knew each other? Maybe there was some deep-seated rivalry between the two of them and she thought Irene was stepping out with her man. If Blake could snag Gilda, is Irene really so far-fetched?"

Jayne kicked off her shoes and pressed her toes into the sand. A few feet away a crab made its slow journey toward the shore. "I don't buy it. Besides, if Amelia got here a few days before us, she probably left long before we did. I know you think they're related, Rosie, but I think you need to consider the idea that Gilda's murder has nothing to do with Irene's. Coincidences do happen."

I didn't like that. I wanted my world to be nice and neat, where things that looked like kin were related. Happenstance screwed that up for me. Just because we hadn't found the connection between Irene and Gilda didn't mean it didn't exist.

"Okay, we'll play it your way," I said. "Let's focus on the easy one: Who would've killed Gilda?" A thump startled me. A coconut had fallen and landed on the rock beside me.

Jayne leaned back on her elbows so that she could better catch the sun. "Van Lauer, for one. He was here. He said something to upset her right before she was shot."

I cradled the coconut in the curve of my arm. "True. And he left in the middle of the show, giving him the opportunity to fire the gun. Do you want to go talk to him with me?"

"Why not?" she said. "I have nothing better to do."

CHAPTER 24

Tattle Tales

I decided that if we were going to confront an actor like Van Lauer, we better have a prop at our disposal. We stopped by the Wac barracks to get what we needed before tracking him down.

He was in his tent flipping through a copy of *Life Magazine* with marine ace Joe Foss on the cover. His duffle was packed and sitting on his cot waiting, no doubt, for someone else to lug it to the plane.

"Hiya," I said.

He acknowledged us with a flutter of the magazine. "Can I help you?"

I elbowed Jayne in the back, and she took a step into the room. "I know you're awfully busy, and you probably have a thousand other things on your mind," she cooed. "But I was wondering if there was any chance I could get your autograph."

He gave my pal the up and down. It was obvious he liked what he saw. He smiled that Hollywood grin of his that made his wedding ring magically disappear. "Of course, I'd be happy to give you an autograph, Miss—?"

"Hamilton. Jayne Hamilton. And this here is my girlfriend Rosie."

He winked my way. "And would you like an autograph too, girl-friend Rosie?"

"No thanks," I said. "I'm good."

He produced a pen, and we offered him the copy of *Movie Scene* with his photo inside. He defaced it with his moniker before return-ing it to Jayne.

"So what are you girls doing so far from home?" he asked.

Was he for real? "We're in the USO tour," I said. "You know, the one with Gilda? Jayne's the other girl who got hurt that night."

"Right." No offer to let us sit down. No inquiry about the state of her health. What a guy.

"We were so sorry about what happened to her," said Jayne.

"I thank you for your condolences, but they're hardly neces-sary."

If his words had a temperature, we would've gotten frostbite. "Still," I said, "you must be a little sad about what happened."

Something behind his eyes clicked into place, as though he realized that feigning emotion could be to his benefit. After all, it wouldn't be good for word to get out that upon Gilda DeVane's death Van Lauer didn't show a hint of remorse.

"Of course I'm upset about it." He put a hand to his heart. "Gilda was a fine actress and a wonderful friend, I just meant that it seems the four of you are suffering the greater loss."

"We weren't dating her," I said.

"And neither was I."

"Not anymore, sure, but there was a time when things were pretty hot and heavy between the two of you."

Something in his face changed. "We had a fling. That's all. I made a mistake thinking she was more discreet than she was."

"So is that why you told MGM to fire her? Because she was in-discreet?"

He picked at a lint ball on the shoulder of his uniform. "I hardly had the clout to make something like that happen. They fired her because she was too much trouble. Nobody wanted to work with her anymore."

"What did you talk to her about the night she was shot?"

He looked ready to dismiss the question as too personal, but the temptation to finally set the record straight made him plod forward. "Before she left the States, she started a ridiculous rumor that I was going to leave my wife and marry her. MGM got wind and made it clear that divorce was unacceptable. I begged Gilda to retract."

"Why would she lie about that?"

He attempted to flick the lint into the air, but it stubbornly remained stuck to his fingers. "I suppose she thought it would help her career, just like she thought having an affair with me might."

"How would that help her? She was a star long before you ever came along."

"Doors were opening for me while they were closing for her. If she could hitch herself to my wagon, she might get a second chance with the studio. And if that didn't work, perhaps public sympathy would force them to keep her."

"That must've made you angry. Seems to me the best way to fix the situation would have been to silence Gilda for good."

The lint ball flew into the air and landed on his pants. "Just what are you implying?"

"I'm not implying anything—I'm saying it outright. I think you had something to do with Gilda's death."

"That's absurd."

"Is it? How is it you ended up on the very island that served as her base camp?"

With a roll of his eyes, he removed a shoe and set to polishing it with a stained cloth. "Tulagi is the center of operations for the Pacific theater. It was inevitable that I'd end up here."

"But you knew she was here, right?"

"I knew she was in the islands, of course. But I didn't know that she was here. And I certainly had no intention of seeking her out."

"Sure. Which is why you arranged for our command performance."

He paused in his work and checked his reflection in the shiny leather. "That wasn't my idea any more than coming here was."

"Where did you go in the middle of the show?"

"What on earth are you talking about?"

"You got up and left halfway through the show. I saw you leave."

He switched one shoe for another. "I had to go to the bathroom."

"For thirty minutes?"

He waved his shoe-clad hand at me. "The length of my bowel movements is hardly any concern of yours. If I had wanted to kill Gilda, believe me there would've been ample opportunity before I ever left the States. I certainly wouldn't have come all the way out here to do it. And do you honestly think I'm stupid enough to weather a potential murder scandal as a way of getting people to forget about my affair? I enlisted to regain my credibility, not to find another way to destroy it. Gilda's death is hardly a boon for me. She'll be a martyr when word about this hits the States."

He had a point there.

"And might I remind you: Gilda's murderer has been captured. While I may be grateful to him for what he did, I certainly didn't instruct him to do it. Now I ask that you leave. Now."

We were almost a half hour late to our one o'clock rehearsal. Violet and Kay were seated in the mess waiting for us, their bodies rigid with impatience.

"Get lost?" asked Violet.

"The floor took longer than we anticipated," I said.

She lit a cigarette. If she had to wait for us, we were now going to have to wait for her. "Where did you go last night, anyhow?"

I looked to Kay to see what, if anything, she'd already told her. She shook her head so slightly that if Violet had seen her, it would've appeared that she was having a tremor.

"You tried to stop them from hurting the prisoner, didn't you?" said Violet.

"We didn't just try, we did," I said.

She spat a mouthful of smoke at me. "You really are a Jap-lover, aren't you?"

The hair at the back of my neck stood at attention. "What I am isn't up for debate. Who killed Gilda is."

"What do you mean?"

Kay slouched farther down in her chair. "They arrested the wrong man."

"Unbelievable. You went too? And how do you know he wasn't the right one?"

"Because he told us," said Jayne.

Violet raised her hands above her head, sending a flicker of ash to the floor beneath her. "Oh, he told you. Then that settles it. And did he tell you the Japs have a right to these islands too? Because maybe we should let the Allies know that we can pack up and go home."

"It wasn't like that," I said. "Trust me: they arrested the wrong hatchetman. This guy's barely out of diapers. Ask Spanky if you don't believe me."

She looked like she was contemplating doing just that when something stopped her. "Okay, fine. They caught the wrong guy. But if he didn't kill Gilda, who did?"

"That's the hundred-dollar question," I said. "Did you know Gilda was seeing Rear Admiral Blake romantically?"

"Late Nate? Sure," said Violet. "We both did—didn't we, Kay?"

Kay nodded.

I had to shake my head to make sure I'd heard her correctly. "If you knew, how come you didn't tell us?"

"We figured if she wanted people to know, she'd tell them," said Violet. "I only found out because I saw them together. And Dotty told Kay. When we realized we both knew we decided to commiserate. You have to admit she had a knack for picking the worst possible men."

"You got that right," I said. "We just paid a visit to Van Lauer."

"Why would she get involved with Blake?" asked Jayne.

"He might be repugnant, but he's powerful," said Violet. "And his brother's a big-time producer. Like him or not, he's a good man to have on your side."

Not that I ever ran the risk of experiencing that. "But why did she keep quiet about it?" I said.

"Wouldn't you?" said Kay. "We all saw the way he treated you. Who would want to associate themselves with someone like that?"

She was probably right about that, but I was starting to suspect that what we didn't know about Gilda far outweighed what we did.

It didn't seem right to reassign Gilda's songs to someone else. After all, none of us could possibly fill her shoes. Instead, we eliminated them entirely and added one act each, plus a final song that would be done as an in memoriam piece for Gilda and for all of the men who had already been lost.

With that heart-breaking process complete, Jayne and I decided to go for a walk, and Kay and Violet went back to the barracks. It was a beautiful day that was doing its darndest to show off all of the island's attributes, though I could see, to the west, what looked like storm clouds gathering. On one end of the beach a game of touch football kicked up the sand. At the other, a piece of fishing net had been strung between two poles, and the Yanks were taking on the Aussies in a game of volleyball. Everywhere you looked were shirtless men showing off their tans and tattoos, their eyes hidden beneath their reflective cheaters, none of them showing evidence they had a care in the world. They all seemed so young, healthy, and strong that I wished I had a camera to capture the moment and remember them all before they went off to the next battle.

"For the record—I believe Van," said Jayne.

"Me too. But I don't understand why Gilda would've lied." Who was she really? A scorned brokenhearted woman or an actress so desperate to stay on top that she would've done anything to stay there, including sleeping with someone as despicable as Late Nate?

"So if it wasn't Van and it wasn't the sniper, who was it?" asked Jayne.

Someone behind us cleared her throat. "Miss Winter, Miss Hamilton—Rear Admiral Blake wishes to see you." It was Amelia Lambert, her updo torn asunder by the wind.

"Thanks for the message," I said. "You can tell your pal we'll stop by a little later."

She grabbed us both by the forearms and pulled us away from the beach. "He wants to see you immediately. I assured him that I would personally escort you to his quarters."

I wrestled my arm free. "Don't bust a button—we'll go in peace. Is this about last night?"

She looked down her nose at me. "I'm not privy to what you're referring to, but I can assure you that if you've done something wrong, he knows about it."

Who was he, Santa Claus? I shuddered inwardly. If this wasn't a reprimand for our curfew violation, then it was very likely a confrontation about our visit to the POW camp. I was hoping we could depend on everyone who was there to keep their yaps shut, but apparently we were like a sinking tugboat in the middle of the ocean: full of leaks with no hope of repair.

When we arrived at Blake's tent, Amelia announced our presence. He instructed her to show us in, then he dismissed her with nary a thank you. As she turned on her heel to depart, her face made it clear that she didn't appreciate his tone. I would've felt bad for her if she hadn't just left her handprint on my upper arm.

Would a woman scorned still be so eager for a man's approval? Was it possible she didn't know about Late Nate and Gilda's relationship? Or had she resigned herself to stay with him after doing the unthinkable to get rid of her rival?

"Thank you for coming, ladies," said Blake.

"It's not like we had a choice," I said.

Jayne shot me a look, urging me to close my head. Blake gestured us into the same chairs we'd sat in when he'd told us about Gilda's death.

He folded his hands together and stared at us the way the principal did when he expected you to drop a dime on someone. "I understand you paid a visit to Van Lauer."

"We're big fans," I said. "We wanted to make sure we got his autograph before he left."

"Funny," said Blake, "but that wasn't the way he described the visit. He said that you intimated that he may have had some sort of involvement in Miss DeVane's death."

"I didn't intimate it," I said. "I outright said it."

One half of his mouth quirked into a smile. How did he do that without causing any movement in the rest of his needle-thin lips? "I'm glad there's no dispute there. Captain Lauer was very upset by your accusations, and although I must admit I'm not a fan of those men who gain rank because of who they were before they enlisted, I certainly empathize with his position. What I find most troubling about all of this, though, is that your actions imply that you don't believe we've caught the culprit. Can you tell me why?"

Jayne nudged my foot with hers, urging me to let her speak for once. I obliged. "We heard him fighting with Gilda right before the show," she said. "And he disappeared halfway through the performance. Given their history together, we thought maybe he might've hired the sniper or something."

"Is that so, Miss Hamilton? Is that why you decided to visit the POW camp last night?"

He knew. Who was the snitch?

"We wanted to see the shooter with our own eyes," said Jayne.

Blake stared at Jayne while drumming his fingers on the blotter. I expected him to lower the ax then and announce what repercussions we'd brought on ourselves. Instead, he stopped his drumming and let his smile cross the rest of his face. "I certainly am not about to discount a reasonable theory, if there's evidence to back it up."

Was he saying what I think he was saying? Was it possible Blake was willing to accept that he was wrong and hear us out?

"Whose idea was it for you and Miss Winter to tap dance?"

Talk about your awkward segues. Jayne looked toward me, obviously confused as to what to make of Blake's sudden change of subject. "Mine, I guess," she said.

"So Miss DeVane didn't put you up to it?"

What did this have to do with anything? "No," said Jayne.

I decided I'd been silent long enough. "Gilda was pretty hands-off as far as the show went. She asked us each to decide what we wanted to do onstage. Since we already had a singer and a comedi-enne, Jayne suggested that we dance."

"But why tap dance?"

I shrugged. "Why not? Jayne's a pretty good tapper. I was loads better at it than any other kind of dancing we might've taken on. And we figured the boys would get a kick out of it."

"Hmmm . . ." He scribbled something on a piece of paper sitting on his desk. "I understand there was another incident with the Japa-nese during your show on Guadalcanal. Was the show the same as the one you performed the night Miss DeVane was killed?"

Where was he going with this? "No. I didn't perform the night of the shooting, remember? Jayne danced by herself."

"And presumably the sound of one person tapping is very differ-ent from two." Since it wasn't a question, I didn't respond. "I under-stand you have some code-writing experience, Miss Winter."

I laughed. I couldn't help it. "Did your girlfriend tell you that?"

"Who told me isn't important. Is it true?"

I shrugged. "It was just a silly little code I made to write a letter."

"To circumvent the censor?"

"Sort of." The pieces were falling into place, and I didn't like the picture they made. "Sir, what is this all about?"

"I think you know exactly what it's about, Miss Winter. You and Miss Hamilton designed a tap routine that would transmit a code to enemy soldiers."

"We what?!" Jayne and I gasped in unison.

"There's no denying it. A number of us in attendance the night Miss DeVane was shot noted that Miss Hamilton was tapping out a message in Morse code. We thought it harmless at first, but with

Miss DeVane's death, the change in your routine for that particular performance, and the knowledge that you've used this system to successfully bring Japanese to your performance site twice, plus the rather odd politics you've shared with us at dinner, I think we have sufficient reason to question what you're up to."

"We're not up to anything. The dance we did—that Jayne did—it's a dance every tap dancer does. If it spells out a code, that's the first I'm hearing of it. And besides, if we were working with the Japanese, wouldn't it be stupid for us to lure them to the performance site, making it possible for you to capture them?" He didn't answer me. He didn't look at me.

"Are you going to arrest us as spies?" asked Jayne.

He smiled that magnificent sharklike grin of his and detached his index fingers from his chin. "Not yet. As I said, this is just a theory, much like the one you and Miss Winter have been cooking up. Of course, ours has a little more merit, don't you think? And more witnesses and evidence to substantiate it. If you continue to pursue your outlandish ideas, perhaps I'll choose to do the same."

"Are you blackmailing us?" I asked.

"No, I'm merely encouraging you to trust the armed forces. We're here to protect you from your worst enemy, even if it happens to be yourself."

CHAPTER 25

Sailor, Beware!

It was raining when we left his tent, though we were both so angry by that point that I half-expected the water to turn to steam the minute it made contact with our bodies.

"Can't we tell somebody?" asked Jayne.

"Who? He's top dog here. Whatever he says goes."

"Maybe we could write Harriet and ask her to get us out of here."

"No, not yet." I wasn't ready to throw in the towel. Irene may have been willing to quit when things got too difficult, but I wasn't going to. "Who could've squealed?"

"Anyone who was afraid of getting caught," said Jayne. "Who knows?"

As we passed the rec hall, a voice called out our names. It was Spanky.

"Just the girls I wanted to see."

I wasn't so sure I wanted to see him. After all, he'd held a knife to my throat the night before. I probably should've turned tail, but the possibility of an apology was too tempting to ignore.

We followed him inside, where Sheep, Red, and a host of other men were responding to the rapidly changing weather by playing Ping-Pong and poker. Spanky led us to a group of chairs clustered around a radio. Mac gave us a weak wag from a pillow on the floor that he'd claimed for his convalescence.

"What's the crop?" I asked.

Spanky's eyes were threaded with red. Even though the lighting was dim in the rec hut, he squinted against it like it was hurting him. "I wanted to apologize for last night. The fellows told me how I acted. I know words won't make up for it, but I really am sorry."

While it was nice to hear, it didn't do a very good job erasing what he'd done. "So you don't remember what happened?"

"Thanks to the plonk, not much of it." He tapped his noodle with a finger. "Though I've got a powerful headache as a souvenir."

"I guess that's a fitting punishment."

"It's not the only one. I got called in to see Blake."

So we weren't alone in that. Not that it helped lessen the sting. "Join the crowd."

"Who's the leaky lip?"

I lifted my hands. "Don't look at us. He just threatened to pin Gilda's death on Jayne and me if we don't keep our yaps shut."

"Consider yourself lucky that that's all he did. Our crew ships out for New Georgia in a few days."

"Really?" asked Jayne.

"Do you think I'd kid about that?" Excitement twinkled in Spanky's eyes. And something else.

"I'm sorry to hear that," I said.

"Don't be. It was my dumb idea to go to the POW camp to begin with. Aw, hell I knew this cook's tour was going to end eventually. And I'm glad it is—a guy can only take so many days lying around the beach. But Blake's decided to delay giving us the exam to in-

crease our rates, and Violet's not going to be happy when she finds
out I'm not getting a new pay grade."

"I didn't realize you two were so serious," said Jayne.

"Are you kidding?" He let out a low whistle, which brought Mac
to his feet. "I'd marry her tomorrow if she'd let me."

I decided I didn't want to touch that with a ten-foot pole. "What
about Mac?" I asked.

"He's not the marrying kind."

"No, I mean, is he heading out with you?"

"Not in the shape's he's in." Mac settled back on his pillow, unaware that his fate was being decided.

"Would the guards have talked?" I asked.

"No way."

"Then it was one of your friends."

He stabbed the air in front of him. "Or one of yours."

Or it wasn't either one of them. Who's to say that whoever was
watching us hadn't been the one to let the cat out of the bag?

"Anyway," he said. "I wanted to apologize and warn you about
Blake, though obviously I'm too late. You might want to give Candy
and Kay the heads up. There's nothing worse than being dragged in
there without knowing why."

"Roger, wilco," I said.

The next morning, Kay, Violet, Jayne, and I headed out before
breakfast for our day of shows. It was good to be away from camp
again, although performing without Gilda made her absence that
much more profound. We did the best we could, but I was acutely
aware during each show that we'd never get applause as loud or
laughter as overwhelming as we had when Gilda was there. The
men didn't have it in their hearts to reward us when one of our
ranks was missing. Violet wasn't helping things. She turned each
show into a mini-memorial, opening with a heartfelt speech describing Gilda's last performance and the joy she brought to the
stage every time she stepped on it. I think she hoped that by doing

so we could address the elephant in the room and move on, but rather than helping the performance, it seemed to hinder it. It was impossible to lift the solemn mood from the crowd once it had descended upon them.

That didn't stop Violet from complaining about it. As her jokes fell as flat as the hair atop newly inducted marines' heads, her body stiffened, her voice became a bark, and her jokes grew increasingly antagonistic. She wanted the men to react, damn it, and if she had to, she would arouse their ire by invoking stereotypes about the various divisions of the armed forces. The men weren't game for it, though, and instead of stating their objections at being called wimps because they lived out their days in tanks or lazy because the army air forces insignia rode their shoulder, they watched her, stone-faced or, even more humiliating, offered her a titter out of pity.

It got worse as the day went on, so much so that I feared the men would start pelting rotten tomatoes at Violet if we didn't intervene.

"She's ossified," Jayne whispered to me offstage. It was our last show of the night, and the only thing the rest of us had eaten all day was fruit and cheese.

"How can she be drunk?"

"I don't know, but she is. She almost knocked me over with her breath."

We finished the show without any major catastrophe. As soon as it was done, I took Violet aside. "Where'd you get the hooch?"

She hiccuped before answering me, which no doubt made it clear, even in her inebriated state, that lying was pointless. She pulled a flask out from under her skirt and offered it to me. I declined, though it killed me to do so. Drinking sounded like a delicious alternative to having this conversation. "I have my sources."

"Well, your sources better dry up before tomorrow." I realized how harsh I sounded and tried to soften my tone. "I heard about Spanky."

She shook her head ever so slightly. "I knew he wouldn't be here forever, but I didn't expect him to get orders so soon." She took a swig from the flask and returned it to her skirt.

"I know this is hard, but for now we just have to push through this. Sober."

She hiccuped again, and I caught wind of the smell Jayne had described. I prayed there wasn't an open flame nearby. "When is it going to get better?" she asked.

I put my arm around her and tried not to inhale. "He'll be fine. This isn't his first battle."

She brushed away a tear. "No, I mean the audience. When are they going to forget her?"

It was hard to read her tone through the layer of drunk. "Her death's pretty fresh in everyone's mind. I doubt anyone's going to forget her anytime soon."

"She would just love this," she said. "Even dead, she's the center of attention."

"I doubt she would revel in that."

A half-laugh, half-sob escaped from her. "I wonder if word has hit the States yet. I'm sure there will be all sorts of tributes, worse than what they did for Carole Lombard." She spit the words out, sending a spray of alcohol along with them.

You never know how death's going to hit you. I'd seen it again and again, where grief turned to rage not at the person who'd caused the death but at the person who'd died. I'd felt it myself the night I learned about Jack. Death seemed so selfish and inconsiderate and inconvenient. It was natural to want to strike out at the person who hurt you the most by not being there. Didn't they realize what a mess their absence made of things?

"I thought this would be easier," she said.

"Give it time," I said again. "It will be."

She began to cry for real, so I held her until her tears passed.

We were supposed to board a plane to go back to camp at 2100 hours, but we were informed by the man who'd been our escort that day that no one was going anywhere until morning.

"Sorry, ladies," he told us, "there's way too much fog in the slot. Looks like you're RON."

"R-O-what?" asked Violet.

"Remaining over night. Nobody's getting out of here until oh-eight-hundred at the earliest." I scanned the sky for this fog he was talking about, but it was too dark to see it. How was it that men were willing to fly through a hail of bombs, but a little bad weather could thwart them?

"Where are we supposed to sleep?" asked Violet.

"Oh, don't worry; we've got guest quarters for the four of you. Real nice ones too. And dinner. If you follow me, I'll take you to them right now." He walked toward a Jeep waiting in the shadows. We started to follow him when he held up his hand and directed Jayne and me to stay where we were.

"What's the matter?" I asked. "Isn't there room for all of us?"

"Not in this Jeep, ma'am. I'll be back for you two in a jiffy."

Kay flashed us a look of apology as Violet and she were whisked into the night. I was tired. And hungry. The idea of waiting God knows how long for him to return wasn't improving my mood.

"That was rude," said Jayne.

"No kidding. He could've fit all four of us easy."

In the distance, a motor purred its greeting. Headlights momentarily blinded us as another Jeep approached.

"Looking for a ride, ladies?" asked the driver.

"Billy!" squealed Jayne. He wasn't alone. Peaches was sitting in the passenger seat, grinning my way.

"What's this all about?" I asked.

"We're kidnapping you," said Peaches. "We've got grub, booze, and a great spot with an ocean view. Hop in."

Fifteen minutes later we were on a scratchy green blanket, eating a meal fit for a four-star general. The boys did their best to make us martinis out of what booze they had, and we downed them in tin navy-issue cups that somehow made them taste all the better.

As we ate, the moon rose above the water and the sky became a sheet of black velvet studded with diamonds. The booze rapidly landed a one-two punch, and I found myself wanting to see the water up close. I left our picnic and stumbled across the sand to

where the waves had pounded the beach until it looked like a cake
fresh out of the oven.

"It was all a ruse," said Peaches.

I hadn't heard him follow me to the shore. "What was?"

"The fog." He pretended to twirl an invisible mustache. "Nefari-
ous, yes?"

"You're the one who grounded us?"

He tilted his head toward where Jayne and Billy sat entwined on
the blanket. "I did it as a favor."

"You seem to do a lot of those for him."

"What can I say? I'm a sucker for a guy in love. Besides, we're
heading out in a week."

I was surprised. I had just assumed that Peaches and Billy were
both landlocked permanently. "Do you know where you're going?"

"Probably New Georgia, if the fun's not all over by then. My men
are getting rock happy."

"That seems to be going around. Does Jayne know?"

"I imagine he's telling her. I told him to, anyway." We watched
the water in silence, letting the sound of the waves do our talking
for us. "I hope you're not mad."

"Why would I be?"

"You're stranded here overnight. That can't be convenient."

"Believe me: being anywhere but Tulagi is fine by me." I caught
him up to speed on what had happened since Gilda's death and how
Rear Admiral Blake had tightened the screws.

"So what are you planning on doing?"

"I don't know. Maybe nothing. Maybe I'll wait until I get home
and then start making noise."

"Of course, if you do that, it will be even easier for Blake to claim
you're lying. Time and distance aren't very helpful in circumstances
like these."

Boy, did he have that right. "I don't want to get us in a bigger
jam than we're already in," I said. "It would be just like me to get us
locked up for a murder we didn't commit."

"He's bluffing," said Peaches. "If that theory of his were any more ridiculous, it would wear clown shoes and a big red nose. Nobody could believe you two are spies. And they certainly wouldn't buy that you were contacting the enemy while tap dancing."

"Obviously you haven't met Rear Admiral Blake. Trust me when I say he has a way of convincing people of the impossible. After all, he managed to make a whole island full of people believe a teenaged Japanese sniper cut down Gilda." There was a chill in the air. I looped my arm around Peaches, hoping for warmth. "I keep thinking this all has something to do with Irene."

"Who?"

"This Wac captain who was killed at the port of San Francisco right before we came here. Her unit's in Tulagi, and it just seems like too much of a coincidence that both Gilda and she would be murdered." Peaches smelled good. It wasn't just soap and detergent but a faint aroma of cologne. The men in the islands weren't known for their shower-fresh scent. He had taken some time getting himself ready for tonight.

"So what's the link between the two of them?"

"I don't know. Supplies are missing from Tulagi, and I know Irene was looking into it. Whatever she learned, Gilda might've learned too." Maybe Gilda had the courage to do what Irene had avoided. Rather than letting Late Nate get away with what he was doing, perhaps she'd intended to turn him in for it.

"But would Gilda have cared? There's a big difference between a Wac's sense of obligation and a movie star on tour. What else do they have in common?"

"They were both actresses. Irene left the WAACs for Hollywood. She had a contract offer and everything."

"Same studio as Gilda?"

"I'm not sure." I'd never bothered to ask. Surely Kay would know.

"Then maybe whatever is going on didn't start here but started there. In Hollywood."

I rubbed the fabric of his pocket flap. "You make a good point."

We walked as I pondered who could've been behind Gilda's and

Irene's deaths. Who was in Hollywood with both of them? We'd
already eliminated Van Lauer as a suspect. That left Kay and Violet.
The only problem was that neither of them had a reason to want *both*
Gilda and Irene dead.

We stopped walking. "Welcome back," said Peaches.

"Huh?"

"I've been talking to you for the past five minutes."

"Gosh, I'm sorry. What were you saying?"

He turned his profile toward me and looked out at the ocean.
"Nothing important."

At some point, my arm had shifted and rather than being casu-
ally looped around his, my paw was snugly clasped in his hand. It
was curious how well our two mitts fit together. In the dark of night,
it was hard to tell which fingers belonged to which person. "Seriously, what were you saying?" I asked.

"I make it a point never to repeat myself."

"Since when?"

He bumped me with his hip, sending me to the left.

"Ouch. Okay, but you were talking about me, right?"

"I had no idea your ego was this big." He looked down at our
joined hands. "I was saying it was strange to think that I might not
see you again after we ship out."

"Why?" Was he predicting his death? That was a decidedly un-
Peaches thing to do.

"You'll continue your tour and, assuming Blake doesn't arrest
you, eventually go home, and I'll do the same."

My grip on him grew tighter. "It doesn't have to be like that. We
could stay in touch."

"You mean V-mail and phone calls if I'm ever in the States?"

"Sure. Maybe you could even grab a meal the next time you're
in New York. And there's always a chance I could end up in Atlanta.
I'm in the South Pacific, after all. How much harder would Georgia
be to conquer?"

"Spoken like a woman who's never ventured south of the Mason-
Dixon line." He made a thoughtful little humming noise that seemed

to indicate that he'd never considered what I was proposing. "So you might want to see me again?"

I turned away from him, worried that if I didn't, I might start to cry. "If you don't want to see me, I certainly won't force you to."

"It would be hard," he said. "You can be awfully difficult to be around. *Trying* is the word for it. And exhausting."

Who was he to judge me? Granted, we'd had our problems since we'd first met, and I'd somehow dragged him into my drama the way Jayne used to drag Tony to plays he didn't want to see, but I had my merits, didn't I?

I released his hand and crossed my arms over my chest. "Forget it," I said. "I didn't realize I was so taxing."

He put his hands on my elbows to prevent me from turning away from him. "I'm kidding," he said.

The wind whipped my hair into my face, but I refused to lift my arms to push it away. "It wasn't very funny."

"Do you honestly think I wouldn't want to see you again, Rosie?"

"I don't know."

He released me and put a finger beneath my chin, lifting my face upward. Before I could register what I was doing, I lunged at him, meeting him with such force that our teeth clicked together.

"Ow!" he said.

We both checked to make sure that our chompers were still intact. "Sorry," I said.

"I was going to kiss you, you know."

"I know, but I wanted to beat you to it."

We tried again, this time meeting each other without causing any pain. Maybe it was the booze, or the full moon, or the fresh Pacific breezes that made everything seem more fantastic than it could possibly be, but as he kissed me, all my cares melted away and I found myself holding my breath just to make sure I didn't do anything to make this marvelous moment end. Of course, eventually it had to. After all, if I didn't start breathing, I would pass out.

"That was better than I thought it would be," he said.

"Gee thanks. By all means let me know how I can improve things."

"Next time, don't hold your breath. I was worried you might faint on me."

We kissed again, although this one was interrupted by a laugh that I couldn't seem to suppress.

"What?" he asked, pulling away.

"Have you ever murdered anyone?"

"Is this a philosophical question?"

"I don't mean warfare. I mean murder, murder."

"Of course not, why?"

"Because the last time I kissed a guy, he ended up being a murderer, and I just want to make sure I'm not repeating that same mistake."

He kissed me to confirm that his moral record was clean. Eventually, we both sank onto the sand. I sat between his legs with my back to him and we talked, not about Gilda or Jack or any theories I might have about who murdered whom, but about each other. As I answered his many questions about my life before the war, he peppered my forehead with kisses, and I entwined my fingers in each of his hands, marveling that this wasn't all some fabulous dream.

We stayed that way throughout the night until eventually we sat in silent awe watching the sun rise above the water.

CHAPTER 26

Information Please

Kay and Violet were ready to leave when we arrived at the tent. Neither was facing the other, though their faces told the same tale of a long uncomfortable night.

"Where have you two been?" asked Violet. "Did they give you better digs or something?"

"Something like that," I said. Jayne had remained out all night as well, and while the glimmer of my romantic evening was starting to wear off in the face of exhaustion, hers had branded a perpetual smile on her face that was starting to irritate even me.

"So what did you do?" she asked the other girls, with a tone that suggested what she really wanted was for them to ask her about her night.

"We slept—or tried to," said Violet. She shot Kay a look that was so full of venom I was surprised Kay didn't fall over and die.

"Why 'tried to'?" asked Jayne.

"This is a noisy place," said Kay. "That's all."

It was clear there was something else going on, but I wasn't in the mood to unravel it. I just wanted to hit the sack and dream about Peaches.

Instead, we were packed into a plane and taken to our next destination. I tried to nap during the trip, but Jayne seemed determined to keep me awake.

"You and Peaches looked awfully cozy this morning," she said.

"We had a nice night, that's all." It was becoming hard to meet her eyes. What happened with Peaches felt too private to share with her. It was silly since I knew she would be happy for me, but I wanted some time to decide how I really felt about things before the two of us started picking it apart and analyzing it. "What about you?" I asked. "I wasn't expecting to see you so cheerful this morning. Billy did tell you he's shipping out soon, right?"

"Oh, he told me all right." She stretched her left hand in front of her and examined her nails. "I was pretty upset at first, but then we decided to get married."

If I'd had liquid in my mouth, I would've done a spit take. "You what?"

She nodded, biting her lip in a way that suggested she was trying to suppress a scream. "He proposed to me last night." She wiggled her hand. On it was a ring hammered out of a silver Australian coin.

"From the looks of things, you said yes?"

She nodded again.

"Wow," was all I could manage. "It seems so . . . fast."

"We're not going to do it right away. I told him I didn't want to be a war bride. But when the war's over or when he gets his discharge . . ." Her voice trailed off. I wondered if she believed that day would ever come.

I clapped my hands together. "Well, I'm thrilled for you."

"Really?"

I threw my arms around her. "Absolutely. He seems like he's aces, and I haven't seen you this happy since . . . well . . . never."

She pulled away from me but refused to let go. "Will you stand up for me when the time comes?"

"Try and stop me."

We hugged again and shared the news with the other girls. I *was* happy for her. Sure it was fast, but there was no telling how long it would be before they could follow through with their plans. The way the war was going, there would be more than enough time for them to get to know each other beyond the superficiality of most wartime romances, and then they could decide if this was what they both really wanted.

We arrived at our next destination, and with the sort of giddiness that can only come from staying up all night doing something forbidden, we put on a hell of a show. Violet was subdued, no longer forcing the men's amusement after bringing their mood down with her tribute to Gilda. I don't know if the men reacted any differently than the day before, and I'm not sure that I cared. I was too caught up in my own head, thinking about everything that had happened the night before.

It was all so weird and wonderful. Who would think that poor Peaches, who was never any more to me than the man who repeatedly delivered bad news, would become someone capable of making my heart go pitter-patter? And who would think that after encountering nothing but tragedies on this trip, I would start to believe that I might actually fall in love again?

"Stop smiling," whispered Violet as we danced across the stage. "You look loopy. People are going to think you're simple. Or drunk."

I extinguished my grin, though it was still there, burning across the inside of my chest.

After three shows, I was ready to fall down and die. Not even thoughts of the night before could put the kick back in my step. Fortunately, we were due to fly back to camp within the hour, and it appeared unlikely the trip would be delayed by another instance of imaginary fog.

As we packed up our things and dressed again in the clothes we'd been wearing for two days straight, a contingency of men crowded the dressing area entrance to talk to us about how much they enjoyed the show. Violet glowed at the attention, offering to sign autographs for men who hadn't requested them but were too polite to turn her down. We all engaged in chit-chat, answering their praise with our gratitude for the performances they had given—and would give again—on the land and sea.

"Miss Winter?" A man at the back of the crowd tried to get my attention. I waved him forward while checking the time on my watch. Only twenty minutes until I could sit down on the plane and pass out.

"Hiya sailor, enjoy the show?"

"You don't remember me, do you?"

I looked at a face that could've belonged to any number of men I'd encountered since we'd arrived in the Pacific. It was embarrassing to think that I'd allowed all these unique people to converge into one person, stripping them of their individuality just like the enemy did. "I'm sorry—I've met a lot of men lately. I might need a reminder."

He removed his Dixie cup cap to give me a better slant. "You visited me in the hospital on Guadalcanal. The boys call me Whitey."

I studied him again. He was the fellow cheating at solitaire who'd given me the brush-off. "Sure, I remember you. How're you feeling?"

"Better. Much better. In fact, they're sending me to New Georgia next week."

How could these men be so excited about going back into battle? It didn't make any sense to me.

"I'm glad to hear it." I turned away, thinking we were done. Now that I knew who he was, I found myself still sore at the way he'd treated me. Although, to be fair, he'd never put a knife to my neck.

"Can I talk to you for a moment alone?"

Seventeen minutes until I could sleep. It certainly wasn't going to go any faster if I stood around waiting for the hands on my watch to move. "Sure."

We stepped outside, around the throng of fawning fans, and

walked back into the performance area. The space had been vacated except for the soda and beer bottles the men had left behind. I was too tired to stand, so I sat on the piano bench and looked at him expectantly.

"I wanted to apologize for the way I acted the day you came to visit us."

My fingers played over the piano keys, plucking out a tuneless melody. "That's swell of you, but it's not necessary."

"No, it is. I was awfully sore that day—my girl had sent me a Dear John."

"Ouch." I underscored how uncomfortable that had to be with a base chord.

"And, needless to say, I wasn't one for talking to the opposite sex."

I stopped fooling around on the keyboard and put my hands in my lap. Fifteen minutes until sleep. "Don't worry about it. You're forgiven. I'm not one to hold a grudge."

"Thanks. There's something else though. I've been thinking about what you asked me. That name you asked me if I knew."

My stomach churned with dread. So this was how my perfect day would end: with someone else telling me Jack was dead to remind me that maybe it wasn't right that I'd already found myself in another man's arms. "So you did know him?"

"Well, not as Jack, as you called him. The fellows called him Hamlet on account of his being an actor and his last name." Castlegate, a last name fit for a moody Danish prince. "Anyhow, once I realized I did know him, I knew I had to talk to you."

I stood up. "Let me stop you there." I put my hand out as though it possessed the power to prevent him from confirming the news I already knew. "I heard what happened."

"It was one of the most amazing things I ever saw. Here he has two bullets in his leg, and he still manages to outrun them. I never paid him much mind before, thought he was a bit of a daisy to tell you the truth, but that night he proved he was more man than the rest of us. When you find him, you tell him Whitey was honored to serve with him. The whole crew was. And if this thing comes to trial, I'm happy to speak out for him."

Dear God, this kid didn't know. And now he'd turned Jack into a hero in his head.

"Whitey, I hate to be the one to tell you this, but Jack's dead."

"What?"

"He went into the big drink that night. They think the sharks got him. Or he drowned."

"Who told you that?"

"Someone in the know. Believe me."

He returned his hat to his head. "Then they fed you a load of horse pucky. One of our men made that story up. Jack never went into the water."

I have no idea what Whitey said after that. The buzzing in my head was making it impossible to hear anything. Surely this guy was misinformed? There was a body after all. Wasn't it possible someone made up a lie to keep the men's morale up, so they wouldn't think their CO had gotten away with murder?

"You okay, Miss Winter?"

"Yes. I think so."

"Look, I didn't mean to rattle you. I'm sure whoever told you he died believed that's what happened. Gris told the CO he saw Jack go under to stop the search. The next day he produced a body and a bloody shirt. Nobody's going to look for a dead man."

No, he had to be misinformed. And even if he wasn't, there was no way Jack could survive alone in the jungle. "Whose body?"

"A Jap's, I guess. It was hard to tell after the sharks got done with him."

I swayed. The whole world had tilted off its axis.

"Maybe you should sit back down. You look a little pale." He tried to take my arm, but I stepped away from him.

"Rosie? We're heading out," Violet called to me. I snapped to attention, desperate to leave this conversation with my sanity intact.

"Thanks for coming to see me," I told Whitey. "And good luck."

Before he could say another word, I dashed back to the dressing area and grabbed my things, chasing after the others to board the plane. The combination of the fast movement, the long day, and the lack of sleep was doing a number on me. I was woozy, weak, and dying for a drink. Whitey had to be wrong. Jack couldn't be alive. Even if he survived that night, he was wounded. There was no guarantee he could keep going for two months on his own.

"Rosie?" Jayne was standing over me. Over me? I had collapsed and didn't realize it. "Rosie? Can you hear me? Are you okay?"

I'm not sure if I answered her. All I remember from that point on was being engulfed in darkness.

When I awoke, I was in the sickbay on Tulagi, in the same cordoned-off area Jayne had been in after the shooting. I tried to move and found myself pinned by an IV in my arm.

"You're awake," said the same nurse who'd tended Jayne. Ruth. Her name was Ruth.

"How long was I out?"

"About twelve hours?"

"Twelve hours?!"

"We sedated you. You were quite agitated when you arrived."

My head pounded, and I quickly probed my noggin to find the source of pain. A goose egg was on the back of my head, so tender to the touch that I moaned when I made contact.

"You have a mild concussion," said Ruth. "And you seemed to be suffering from acute exhaustion and dehydration. But, otherwise, you'll be as good as new."

"Thanks, I guess." I struggled to remember what had happened before I collapsed. Jack. I'd been talking to Whitey about Jack.

"Miss Hamilton has been waiting to see you. She's out in the lobby."

Jack was alive. That's what Whitey had said.

"Miss Winter? Do you want me to bring Miss Hamilton in?"

"Yes, please," I said.

Jayne entered the infirmary with wide eyes and arms weighed down by her collection of magazines. She put the stack of slicks on the table beside the bed and took my hand.

"We were so worried about you."

"Sorry about that."

"I'm going to give Peaches and Billy a piece of my mind, believe you me. It's a wonder we both didn't collapse from exhaustion."

"It's not their fault. How are the others?"

She released me and busied herself with pouring water into a cup. "At their wit's end. Kay and Violet aren't speaking to each other, and someone elected me as their go between. I tell you, if we could go home tomorrow, I'd do it in a second."

I took the glass she offered me. "We can't do that."

"I know. We need to know what happened to Gilda first."

"And Jack," I said.

She tenderly touched my head. "Are you sure you're all right, Rosie? That hit you took was pretty hard."

"The man I was talking to after the show was in Jack's crew. He said he's still alive."

Jayne's mouth dropped open. "But Peaches said—"

"I know what Peaches said, but maybe he didn't know the whole story. The rest of the crew wanted to keep Jack safe, so they lied when they said he went into the water. They saw him get away on foot."

"But there was a body."

"It wasn't his." I found myself starting to calmly accept the idea that Jack was still out there. Jayne struggled with the notion. It's not that she wanted him dead, but I think she couldn't stand the idea of my suffering his loss all over again.

Neither could I, for that matter. After six months of fighting to learn information about his whereabouts, I wasn't sure if I could handle another roller coaster of misinformation. As awful as it sounded, hearing Jack was dead had been a relief. Whatever had happened was done, and the only thing left to do was grieve and move forward. Uncertainty was a cruel state to live in.

Ruth returned with a book in her hand. "I'm afraid I have to ask you to leave, Miss Hamilton. Miss Winter needs her rest."

Jayne offered me a weak smile "Let's not worry about this right now. You need to get well, and then we'll decide what to do." She pushed the stack of magazines toward the bed. "I thought you might want to read while you've got the time."

"Thanks. That's swell of you."

She planted a kiss on my forehead. "Kay and Violet will probably stop by later. And I know Spanky wants to say good-bye before he ships out."

"Sure. Tell them all to come by. I could use the company."

She left, and I flipped idly through the slicks, looking for something to distract myself, but it seemed like I'd read every magazine already. I revisited the article about Gilda. I sneered at the photo of Joan Wright, her (younger) doppelgänger who was probably celebrating the news of Gilda's demise. I tried to read a poll describing how the American public was tiring of films about the war, but none of it held my attention. I gave up on the slicks and tried to fall asleep, but after talking about Whitey's news, I found myself unable to doze. Whitey said that Gris was the one who invented the ruse that Jack went into the water. I knew that name, didn't I? Hadn't we met a Gris at some point?

The face floated just out of my reach, and eventually I gave in and let sleep pull me under. When I awoke, it was late, and the only company I had was the lamp on the nurse's desk. I lay there for a while, absorbing the sounds of the infirmary at night. It wasn't a reassuring experience. The ghost of Gilda DeVane seemed to linger in the air, not Gilda luminous and alive but her pale, bruised corpse.

I sat up and was pleased to find that the pounding in my head was almost gone. My IV had been removed, and in its place was a crude bandage stained a rusty brown by my blood. I hung my feet over the side of the bed and shivered as they came in contact with the bare concrete. Gingerly I rose, pleased to discover that dizziness appeared to be the only overwhelming symptom I was still experiencing. I had to pee, so I tiptoed past the sleeping soldiers and searched out the ward for sign of a latrine. Eventually I found one and luxuriated in the sensation of relieving myself without the assistance of medical equipment.

When I returned to the ward, there was still no sign of Ruth. I couldn't stand the thought of passing the night there. I found a pen and paper at her desk and scribbled her a note indicating that I was feeling much better and was bound for the WAC barracks.

Outside, the camp was still. I started walking and found myself disoriented by my swimming head and a layer of fog that gave the night a strange rigid feel. In the distance, I could hear voices, buffered by a building. The mess hall. I had to pass the mess hall to make it back to the WAC camp.

No, I had to go to the mess hall and find Gris.

I stopped in my tracks. That was right. Gris was one of Deacon's boys, one of the gamblers who worked in the enlisted men's mess.

I pushed open the doors and found the room dark, the only light coming from the kitchen prep area in the back.

"Hello?" I called out.

A rattling noise sounded, followed by dice hitting the concrete floor.

"Is anyone back there?" I said again.

Deacon appeared in the kitchen. "Well, if it ain't Rosie Winter. What can I do for you?"

I stumbled as I walked toward him. My head seemed unnaturally heavy, and I wondered if my neck might snap from the weight.

"You okay?" asked Deacon.

"I had a nasty fall yesterday, but I'm on the mend." I made it to the kitchen pass-through, where I could hear the game of dice in full swing. "I'm looking for Gris," I said.

"Gris ain't here."

I tried to crane my neck to see beyond the kitchen wall. "You sure he's not back there brewing plonk?"

Deacon let out a hearty laugh that started some place deep in his abdomen. "Nope, Gris took off after dinner cleanup. I think he's got some girl he's seeing. He's been hightailing it out of here as soon as he can every night."

"Will he be back in the morning?"

"If he's not, I'll hunt him down and shoot him. I don't have enough help as it is."

I thanked Deacon and continued on my way to the WAC camp. At last I saw the barracks shrouded in darkness. The only light I could make out came from lit cigarettes bobbing around in the foliage.

"Hey!" I whispered at the shapes concealed by the trees. "I see you, you know. We all see you."

They didn't respond, which just made me angrier.

"Here's a tip: if you don't want anyone to know you're watching them, try not to smoke on a stakeout. It's a dead giveaway."

Still they said nothing.

I made like I was going to go into the hut, then rapidly turned and pushed my way into the jungle. There were definitely men there, their tanned skin almost lost in the darkness.

"What are you doing?" one of them asked.

"I get to ask the questions: What are you doing?" My eyes adjusted. There were only two men, both of whom I was pretty sure worked with Deacon. "I hope Blake is paying you for this."

"Hush. Someone's going to hear you," said one of the men.

"I don't care. The jig is up, fellows. You either stop snooping on us, or I'll . . ." I couldn't think of a useful threat. "Well, I'll do something."

One of them took me by the arm. He had a strong grip, and for the first time I realized that it was much more likely that he could hurt me than I could hurt him. "I suggest you close your head, turn around, and go into that hut."

"Gris, let her go," said the other man.

I helped him along by wrenching my arm free. "You're Gris?" I asked.

"What of it?"

"I've been looking for you. I'm Rosie Winter."

"I know who you are. Now scoot."

"You shared a ship with Jack Castlegate. . . . er . . . Hamlet. You were there the night he disappeared. You told everyone he went into the water."

"Who you been talking to?"

"Whitey. Don't worry, I'm not out to get you in trouble. I just need to know if it's true." He stared me down, and I could see how easy it was for people to believe his lies. This was a man made of rock who would not be swayed by threats. No, he was made of gristle. That was how he'd gotten his name. "I knew Jack back home. I just want to know if he's all right. It's important to me. Please."

He was sweating, his cigarette long reduced to glowing red ash that threatened to drop onto the jungle floor. "If you're asking if he made it out alive that night, the answer is yes."

CHAPTER 27

The Twin Sister

"Does he know I'm here?" I asked.

"What?" said Gris.

"Does Jack know I'm here?"

"I ain't seen Jack since the night he escaped. Thanks to him, I'm off the boat and on kitchen duty now. The way I see it, I don't owe him any more favors."

"Oh." So it really had been two months since anyone had seen Jack. Anything could've happened in that time, including the wrong people finding him and taking care of him once and for all. "What about Charlie Harrington? Did you know him?"

"Who?"

"He was in Jack's unit. Your CO shot him, only he made it look like a suicide."

"What was his rank?"

"Corporal."

"Ain't no corporals in the navy."

"So I've been told."

"And there wasn't no Charlie Harrington in our crew. Who told you that?"

He did. Or so I thought. "Why are you following us?" I asked. "Are you working for Blake?"

"Are you crazy? I wouldn't shine that man's shoes if he held a gun to my head."

"Then, why are you here?"

He wasn't going to answer, but his friend had no such qualms. Lefty. His name was Lefty. "Bread and lots of it."

"To do what?" I asked.

"Make sure you and the little blonde make it out of here alive."

I tried to make sense of what they were saying. "Hold on now: Someone's paying you to protect us?" Could Billy be behind this? Sure he cared for Jayne, but he didn't seem like the kind of guy who had the connections—or the cabbage—to give her nightly security. And he didn't owe any allegiance to me. Maybe it was Peaches. If he had the power to visit us whenever he wanted, he could certainly have the reach to hire guards. "Who is it?" I asked.

"That ain't none of your business," said Gris.

"Come on now—won't anything make you spill?"

They looked at each other before replying. "We ain't unreasonable." Lefty cracked his knuckles. "Our favorite color is green."

"You'll tell me if I pay you for the privilege?"

Gris nodded and finally ashed his cigarette. "One hundred dollars."

They might as well have told me they wanted the Statue of Liberty; I was just as likely to get it.

I didn't go straight to the tent. I headed out to the beach to the spot where I'd buried Jack's photograph and tried to find the miniature grave. I didn't have any luck. The rain and the waves had smoothed away any sign that the ground had been disturbed. Some day that part of the beach would erode, and the photo would be whisked into the water to suffer the same fate as all the other refuse of war.

I lay on my back and stared at the night sky, hoping it might provide an answer. Where was Jack?. He hadn't necessarily stayed on Tulagi. If the Japanese were able to sneak on the island, it made sense that he could've snuck off. And given how hard his men fought to protect him, it wasn't impossible to think that they could've arranged for his escape. He may have left the South Pacific entirely, opting to convalesce some place where he wasn't likely to be found.

"Hi, Rosie."

I snapped to attention and found Candy Abbott and her bag standing behind me.

"Hiya," I said. "I didn't hear you coming. Date end early?"

She fought a yawn. "More like late. It's almost two a.m. I thought I heard you were in the infirmary."

"I broke out. The quiet was getting to me."

"How're you feeling?"

Frustrated. Overwhelmed. Confused. "Oh . . . you know."

"Want to talk about it?"

I did but not with Candy. Not that she wasn't a nice gal, but I needed Jayne to help me pick through this tangled mess. "Not really."

She dumped her bag on the ground and joined me in the sand. "I'm glad you're here, anyway. There's something I've been wanting to do, and since you have experience in the matter, I thought you might help."

"Sure. What's the plan?"

She reached into her bag and pulled out what appeared to be a piece of paper. No, it was a photograph. "I want to say good-bye to Irene, like you did to your friend. Despite everything, she liked it here, and I think she deserves to have a little memorial of the time she spent walking these beaches. Would you help me bury her picture?"

"Sure." I took the photo from her and tried to make out the figure in the dim moonlight. Candy passed her flashlight to me, and I illuminated the image in its warm glow.

In the picture, Irene was walking on a beach with her head

thrown back in a laugh. She wore a makeshift swimsuit fashioned
from her WAC uniform, and her bandeau top threatened to slip
down and show off her ample chest. She reminded me of the women
on war posters—equal parts wholesome and sexy, independent and
alluring. Even in black and white you could see the sun reflecting
off her blond hair. The men must've been nuts over her. "She was
beautiful."

"Wasn't she?"

She wasn't just beautiful; she was familiar. No wonder I had been
so drawn to her when I first saw her floating in the water. Irene was
a dead ringer for Gilda DeVane.

When we arrived at the barracks, we weren't alone: Captain Lambert was just returning from her own late-night sojourn.

"Nuts," said Candy. "If she catches me out, I'm doomed."

I pushed her toward the jungle. "Lie low. I'll distract her."

Candy ducked behind the foliage and receded into the darkness.
I wondered if she was sharing space with Gris and Lefty and, if so,
how they'd take the intrusion. Captain Lambert arrived at the barracks door just as I did. As her eyes landed on me, the loopy grin on
her face dropped into a sneer.

"What's the meaning of this?" she asked.

"I couldn't take the infirmary anymore, so I decided to scram.
What's your excuse?"

She crossed her arms. Her breath smelled of whiskey. "I don't
believe that's any of your business, Miss Winter."

I winked at her and shifted just enough so that in order for her to
keep talking to me, her back would have to face the barracks door.
"I see. You two kissed and made up."

"I beg your pardon."

"You and Late Nate. So what did it take? An apology? A gift?"

She raised her chin. "I have no idea what you're talking about.
The rear admiral and I have a strictly professional relationship."

Candy seized the moment and, with her shoes in hand, tiptoed
out of the jungle and into the hut.

"If only the same could be said of you and his whiskey. So it didn't bother you that he was seeing Gilda?"

Her mouth briefly opened before snapping shut. She attempted to recover from the shock, but as she squared her shoulders, the light in her eyes dimmed. "What the rear admiral does in his personal life is his business."

"Is that so?"

Her voice faltered. "Yes, it is. Now I suggest you get inside the barracks at once, or I'll write you up for curfew violation."

I walked around her and started toward the door. She remained frozen where I'd left her.

"Aren't you coming?" I asked.

She didn't respond. With clenched fists, she marched away from the camp and toward the rear admiral's quarters.

We laid low the next day. After I caught Jayne up to speed on my activities from the night before, she fetched my things from the infirmary. When I got tired of lying around the barracks, I moved out to a hammock on the beach shaded by towering palms. As I passed between sleep and waking, my mind turned back to how much Irene Zinn had looked like Gilda.

What if Irene had never been the intended victim but was merely in the wrong place at the wrong time? Maybe it was Gilda the shooter had intended to kill, and when they realized they'd made a mistake, they followed her all the way to Tulagi to finish the job.

It made as much sense as any of my other loony theories, except for one thing: Why was Irene at the dock the day she was murdered? She wasn't supposed to be going anywhere. In fact, she should've been in LA getting ready to start her career.

"How're you feeling?" Kay joined me, toting along an ice-cold bottle of Coca-Cola. She popped off the top, and I greedily drank down the sweet, chilled liquid.

"Thanks for that. I'm better. Just a little shaky. I should be ready to go back on the road tomorrow." I finished off the Coke and deposited the bottle in the sand. "What's going on between you and Violet? Jayne said you're still at each other's throats."

"I'm getting a little tired of her big mouth."

"You know you're going to have to give me more detail than that."

Kay sighed heavily. "I found out she's the one who squealed to Late Nate about our visit to the POW camp."

"No sir!"

"And I'm pretty sure she's the one who told Lambert I used to be a Wac."

I would've shook my head in disgust if I wasn't feeling so loopy. "She only shot herself in the foot, you know. Thanks to her, Spanky is off to New Georgia tomorrow."

"Tomorrow she'll have my sympathy. Today she gets my wrath."

I shaded my eyes with my hand. "I've been wondering about something, and you might be able to help me figure it out."

Kay sat in the sand Indian-style. "What's that?"

"Why was Irene at the port the day she was murdered?"

She started at the question, clearly unprepared to hear it. "Maybe she was seeing someone off."

"But who?" The only romantic connection she had was Dotty, and by then they were long broken up. Besides, he was already here in the islands.

Kay picked at a scab on one of her knees, reopening the tiny wound. "Me."

"Irene came to see you?"

She nodded, still fixated on drawing her own blood. "It wasn't just me. She called me the night before and told me she was going to be in San Francisco, that there was someone there she was supposed to see. She knew our ship was taking off that day, and so she asked if we could meet up and have a bon voyage lunch."

"Why didn't you say anything?"

"I don't know. At first I thought she stood me up, and then when I heard what happened . . . I was in shock. And the longer I waited to say anything, the worse I thought it would look if I did come forward."

If I ever became wealthy, I was going to buy Kay a backbone. "So who did she come to see?"

"She didn't tell me. She said she would when it was all over, but for now it needed to be a secret. She was excited—whoever it was, their meeting was supposed to be a good thing. I got the feeling it was someone from the studio, or maybe it had something to do with promoting the movie she was in."

"Could she have been seeing someone?"

"Romantically? No. She wasn't ready for that."

"Because of Dotty?"

She hesitated before nodding.

"What happened between them?" I asked.

She looked behind her as though she was worried he was standing right over her shoulder. "They grew up together, and everyone assumed they'd get married. He adored her, but I think he always had a white picket fantasy in his head. He wanted a wife and children, not a movie star. And for a while she convinced herself that that was what she wanted too. But she had this incredible talent. You should've seen her when she stepped onstage. She just lit up from inside. I suppose I'm the one who encouraged her. I knew she had what it took to succeed, and I hated to see her waste it. When I found out MGM had been courting her—"

"So MGM was the studio she signed with?"

"Yes. And when I found out she'd turned them down to join the Wacs, I really let her have it. She wasn't happy here—she was having some sort of problem with one of the higher ups." Late Nate. Knowing he was selling supplies to the enemy must've enraged her. "She was like me. She hated conflict. The more I talked to her about it, the more she started rethinking Hollywood. It drove a wedge between Dotty and her. They grew apart and when she left the WACs and went Stateside . . ."

I knew how this story turned out. "Dotty turned to you."

Again she nodded. "I know it sounds like I engineered the whole thing, but I really wanted what was best for her, and I didn't think it involved staying on this island. I always knew Dotty didn't care about me in the same way. She was so beautiful and I was . . . well, I was . . ." Her voice faded as I filled in the blanks. She wasn't the stunning blonde whose picture I'd helped bury that morning. But that didn't mean she wasn't worthy of affection. "I was so in love with him that I thought it wouldn't matter if he didn't love me as much. I was willing to overlook the fact that he'd rather it be Irene than me."

"And then what happened?"

"He got hurt and shipped home to convalesce. And I—"

"Found out you were pregnant."

The surprise showed in her eyes. "How did you know?"

"Jayne overheard you during your physical. Is that why you left Tulagi?"

She nodded, shaking loose tears that had started to fall. "One of the nurses lied for my discharge papers."

"Ruth?"

Again she nodded.

"You know she really wants to see you. It's obvious she cares about you."

"I'm afraid to see her. She's going to want to know what happened, and I don't think I could bear to tell her."

"She thought you were keeping the baby?"

She wiped at her tears with the hem of her shirt. "That was the only way she would agree to help send me home. And at the time I really thought I would keep the baby. Dotty didn't know I was pregnant, and I had this stupid fantasy in my head that I'd have the baby and then I'd run into him and like one of those sickly sweet movies, I'd announce, 'This is your son,' and he'd realize that I was the one he was meant to be with. But when I got to LA, Irene told me she'd received a letter from Dotty telling her he still loved her. I was heartbroken. I told Irene I was pregnant, but I said the father was some married officer I'd fallen for. She was the one who suggested the abortion."

"Do you think Dotty could've found out you were pregnant?"

"Irene and Ruth were the only ones who knew, and neither of them had any reason to tell him."

But what about Kay? Did she regret what she'd done enough to want to punish Irene? After all, it might secure her and Dotty's future if Irene were gone once and for all.

"I know what you're thinking," she said. "But believe me when I say that what I did, *I* did, not Irene. She was my best friend. She was like a sister to me. I never blamed her for being the one he chose. I love Dotty. I always will. But I already tried to force him to love me once. I'm not stupid enough to try to do it again."

I hoped she was right.

I recounted my conversation with Kay to Jayne over a light lunch in the barracks. She and I spent a rainy afternoon playing checkers and trying to figure out our next move.

"Poor, Kay," said Jayne. "Dotty and she certainly seem cozy now though."

"If it lasts. She seems to believe she's always going to be a substitute for Irene in his eyes."

I felt like something had shocked me.

"You okay?" asked Jayne.

"Where's the copy of *Screen Idol* I had at the infirmary?"

Jayne fished it out, and I rapidly flipped through the pages until I landed on the picture of Joan Wright, MGM's "next big thing." The one the writer had callously described as a "young Gilda DeVane."

A girl who looked a lot like the photo I'd seen of Irene stared back at me from the page.

"Any idea where Kay is?" I asked Jayne.

"Probably with Dotty. Why?"

I didn't answer her. I grabbed my rain gear, and with Jayne fast on my heels, headed outside. We fought the mud and the downpour and made our way to Dotty's tent. Kay wasn't there. He was alone.

"This is a nice surprise," he said as we entered. "Next time you might want to wait until the rain dies down first."

"Thanks for the advice," I said. "But this couldn't wait." I thrust the magazine at him. "Turn to page twenty-nine."

He alternated his gaze between the slick and me. "What's on page twenty-nine?"

"Just look at it." He licked his fingers and opened the magazine. "Is that Irene?" I asked.

He nodded slowly. "I guess that's where they got the picture from."

"Who got the what?" asked Jayne. She squeezed the water from her hair and peered over his shoulder.

"*Stars & Stripes.* The latest issue arrived this morning." He fished a newspaper out from a pile on his desk and passed it to Jayne. On the first page was Gilda's obituary, accompanied by the photo Dotty had taken of her standing by the ersatz sink. He gestured for Jayne to turn the page, and she did so until she saw the photo of Joan. Beside it was a brief article.

Former WAAC Captain Was Newest
Hollywood It Girl

Hollywood police have confirmed that Irene Zinn, the former WAAC captain found murdered in the San Francisco Bay, was also a Hollywood actress reported missing by MGM two weeks ago. Zinn, who performed as Joan Wright, was about to make her celluloid debut in the war comedy *Mr. Hogan's Daughter.* This is the second tragic news facing the studio. Last week former MGM star Gilda DeVane was killed by enemy fire while touring with the USO Camp shows in the South Pacific.

It is not yet known if MGM will open *Mr. Hogan's Daughter* as scheduled.

"I can't believe it took them two weeks to figure out they were the same person," said Dotty. "I guess that's Hollywood for you. They probably didn't even care she was dead until she failed to show up for a rehearsal."

"Why'd they make her change her name?" asked Jayne.

"She said they thought it was too similar to Irene Dunn." He looked at the picture in *Screen Idol* again. "I had no idea they thought she was going to be such a big deal. She always downplayed it, like she was just doing bit parts here and there."

I took the paper from Jayne and reread the article. Irene wasn't just some random actress with a studio contract: she was being marketed as Gilda's replacement just weeks after Gilda had been fired by MGM, the same studio Violet had been employed by before starting to tour. What had Violet said the first day we met her? That someone at the studio used to call her Baby Gilda?

What if Violet was the one behind all of it? She could've planned on killing them both from the get-go. If Gilda and the woman intended to replace her were dead, the studio might be willing to give Violet another chance, especially after she returned from the very same tour Gilda had died on. All those speeches she made about how much Gilda was missed—it all had to be a calculated attempt to drum up good press for when she went home.

"Rosie?" said Jayne. "What's it all mean?"

"I'm not sure yet," I said. "But I'm going to find out.

CHAPTER 28

The Candy Shop

After dinner that night, we joined the boys at the swimming hole for a farewell evening of booze and conversation. While the others tried to distract one another from what was going to occur the next day, I watched Violet like a hawk.

There was a problem with my theory. Although Violet was the most logical suspect, she had a rock solid alibi for the night Gilda and Jayne were shot. There was no way she could've been the one to fire the gun. Could her plan have been more subtle than that? Was Kay right that Violet killed Gilda by discouraging her from taking the Atabrine? Malaria seemed like an awfully undependable weapon, but perhaps Violet knew something I didn't. She could've done something to guarantee that Gilda got sick. Of course, if that were the case, how to explain the gunshots? Coincidence?

Spanky sat with Violet glued to one side, Mac to the other. Every time he got up to get a beer or take a leak, I could see the fear in her face that he might never come back. I caught Kay watching her, too, and I could see her anger starting to melt away.

"Did you hear they're going to change the name of Tokyo harbor?" quipped one of the fellows. "They're thinking of calling it Bombay. Get it?"

The comedian was rewarded with more laughter than the joke deserved. Someone pulled out a harmonica and played the tune to "Anchors Aweigh." Mouths moved to the words, but no one seemed willing to give voice to lyrics that described shipping out the next day.

I leaned back on my elbows and stared up at the cliffs high above the island. A flicker of movement caught my eye. There was a light bouncing around the entrance to one of the caves.

My breath caught in my throat. I almost screamed that there were Japanese hiding up there, but something stopped me. I'd seen the light up there before, and nothing bad had followed. Whoever—or whatever—was there, didn't appear to intend any harm.

What if—?

"Got room for two more?" Billy and Peaches approached the swimming hole. Jayne jumped up at the sound of Billy's voice and leaped onto him, wrapping her legs around his waist. He laughed at the overt affection and spun her around as if she was a child.

Peaches came to my side and offered me his hand. "Good evening, Miss Winter," he said.

"Good evening."

"My companion insisted we crash the party tonight. I hope you don't mind."

I let him pull me to my feet. "Of course not, though you guys really have to come up with a way of forewarning us when you're coming here."

Rain started to fall and the party began to break up. The men bound for New Georgia had a busy day tomorrow. There would be another round of vaccinations, a check of supplies, and one last chance to write home before they found themselves in the thick of battle.

"Want to go for a walk?" asked Peaches.

Violet, Spanky, and Mac were heading off on their own, and Jayne and Billy had already disappeared. I wasn't sure what became of Kay, though it was likely she was off with Dotty, relishing the idea that he was safe from whatever may come to pass. "As long as I'm back by curfew," I said. "I'm on Captain Lambert's list as it is."

He took my hand again, and we followed the trail down to the beach.

"You seem preoccupied," he said.

"I guess I am." I struggled to find something to say to him. "Do you know when you ship out yet?"

"Word is the day after tomorrow, though I wouldn't be surprised if we're delayed."

"You must be excited."

His face crinkled. "Not exactly the word I'd use. Anxious maybe. We got a little too comfortable here, but it's always hard going into the unknown. I got used to being on land. And, of course, I've also grown to appreciate other amenities." He leaned down to kiss me. I didn't pull away, but I didn't exactly respond either. "Don't be sad, Rosie. I'll be fine."

"I'm not sad."

"Then what is it?"

I didn't have to tell him. It was probably better if I didn't. But we started our relationship with a lie, and it didn't seem fair to introduce a new one when things were going so well. "I found out Jack didn't go into the water that night."

He abruptly straightened. "Found out? From who?"

"The guy who made up the story. Jack got away on foot, and his friends decided to cover for him. They found a body in the water half eaten by sharks and claimed it was his."

His hand tightened around mine. "So where is he?"

"I'm not sure."

"Did the guy say he was still alive?"

"He didn't know. No one's heard from him since that night." I lowered my voice. "He could be in the caves, Peaches. If everyone believed he was dead, they wouldn't have searched them."

He matched my lower volume. "Not that night, sure, but what

about the night Gilda was killed? They tore this island apart looking for Japs."

He was right. If Jack were still on Tulagi, they would've found
him then. Unless the men assigned to search the caves were among
those who'd fought to save Jack to begin with.

Peaches squeezed my hand. "Look, I know you want to believe
this is true, but you've got to be realistic here. He was injured that
night. For him to have survived, he would've needed food, antibiotics, clean water. And not just a little bit but enough to sustain him
over two months."

He was right. It was one thing to buy into the fantasy that he'd
survived that night, quite another to believe that he could last living
in the jungle. Perfectly healthy men were felled by jungle rot, beri-
beri, and a score of other infections. A man with two bullet wounds
didn't stand a chance.

And yet he'd made it through the hardest part by surviving that
night. Was it too much to hope for more?

"I need to be sure," I told Peaches. "I couldn't live with myself
otherwise."

Peaches sat in silence in the sand, trying to assemble what to say
to me. He had every right to walk away right then and leave me to
deal with this on my own, but that wasn't his nature. "Let me talk
to some people. Don't do anything until I've had time to think this
through. All right?"

I agreed that I would wait to act on my hunch. We spent a few
chaste minutes in each other's company before Peaches announced
that it was time to get me back to the barracks. He didn't want me
to be late for my curfew. As we walked there my mind was full of
questions. If men in Jack's unit had made up the story about what
happened to him to protect him, why hadn't Peaches been privy to
that tale? And why had he transferred units when he returned to the
South Pacific?

"Who's Charlie Harrington?" I asked.

"What?" Around us the rain began to form pockmarks in the sand.

"The fellow who wrote me when Jack went MIA: Corporal Charlie Harrington."

"I told you: he's the fellow Jack confided in, who the CO claimed committed suicide."

"But corporal isn't a navy rank."

Peaches didn't say anything for a while. I hoped he was as puzzled as I was, but I suspected something else was afoot. "Charlie was a marine."

It couldn't have been more obvious that he was lying if he crossed his fingers and stuck them behind his back.

"Why are you fibbing?" I said. "No one's heard of him, including the guys in Jack's crew. Why is that?"

Peaches stared up at the sky. "Because he didn't exist."

The first letter I received from the imaginary Corporal Harrington had managed to bypass the censor. The second landed on the censor's desk and was taken to the higher-ups once they realized it contained Jack's name.

"We tried to hunt out who had written it," said Peaches. "Eventually we figured out it was one of the men writing on Jack's behalf, filtering news back home just in case his family had been told he was AWOL. The incorrect rank was supposed to be a clue." Pity Jack didn't realize I knew military ranks about as well as I knew German. "They let the second letter go through after censoring it heavily, but then I was told to make sure there was no further contact. By that point, your letter had arrived with the suggested code, and I couldn't stand the idea that you would just suddenly stop receiving letters from Charlie without any explanation. So I wrote to you and told you Charlie had died."

"But why come to see me? I don't understand." And why tell me that Charlie had been murdered? By doing so, he had to know that he'd ignite my desire to find out the truth.

"I felt like you deserved to know what happened to Jack. I wanted you to hear it from someone who was there."

There was more to the story. I could tell, and I think he knew I could tell. If he'd been put to the task of cutting off Jack's contact with people back in the States, if he'd transferred ships, it had to be because he'd somehow been responsible for what happened to Jack to begin with. At some point he questioned what he'd done and decided he needed to set things right. He hadn't just come to New York to tell me what had happened to Jack. He'd made a pilgrimage there seeking forgiveness.

There was no kiss good-night. I think Peaches knew I was start-ing to understand his culpability in all of this and didn't want to run the risk of increasing the distance sprouting between us. He walked away and had almost disappeared into the darkness when he stopped and turned back to me.

"I want you to know something. I might've told some lies, but I care about you. That's always been true."

I didn't respond.

When I entered the barracks, the other girls were already there, preparing themselves for bedtime. I started to do the same when Amelia's voice rang out. "Attention! I want everyone at the end of their cots. Immediately."

We obliged and stood in bare feet while she walked the line in front of us. Raindrops marched across the roof of the Quonset hut. Fortunately, unlike our prior residence, it didn't appear to have any leaks.

"It seems the alcohol I confiscated from Miss Lancaster has gone missing. Does anyone wish to own up to where it might be?"

My eyes immediately went to Violet. Her own peepers were red, no doubt still emotional from her farewell with Spanky. If she'd taken back her booze, there was no evidence of it.

"Very well. If no one is going to confess to the crime, I shall search your footlockers." As we stood at attention, she walked the line and opened each trunk. Violet's was clean. So was Kay's. "Ahem." Captain Lambert stood beside Jayne's trunk. On top of her mess of clothing was a single jar.

"That's not mine," said Jayne.

"You're right," said Captain Lambert. "That's why it's called stealing." She slammed the trunk shut and marched the distance to mine. "Tada!" she said as she lifted the lid. "And here is the remaining contraband."

Violet's other two jars lay end to end on my clothes. One of them had leaked, recently enough that the liquid was still in a puddle.

"I didn't put that there," I said.

"Then who did? Fairies?"

"This isn't fair. Somebody framed us. We're innocent until proven guilty."

Captain Lambert clucked her tongue. "Perhaps that's how it works in the states, Miss Winter, but not in my camp. You and Miss Hamilton are to report to the latrine, where you will be scrubbing the floor until it meets my standards of cleanliness."

"Is this about Late Nate?" I said.

"On second thought, you will also be scrubbing the toilets." She reached back into my trunk and pulled out my toothbrush. "And you will use this to do the scrubbing. Is there anything else you'd like to say? I'd be happy to give you more work."

I kept my lip zipped. Jayne and I grabbed our rain gear and headed toward the latrine.

"Unbelievable," I said. "He's the one who steps out, and we're the ones who get punished."

"How long is she going to make us stay out here?" asked Jayne.

"Until morning at least." I filled a bucket with soap and water and exchanged my toothbrush for a small scrub brush. We worked slowly, neither of us willing to put any effort into the abysmal task. On the wall above us, watching with silent cartoon eyes, was a drawing of a large-nosed man. Graffiti above him told us that Kilroy had been here.

My thoughts alternated between Peaches and Violet. Neither was a particularly pleasant topic. Violet was potentially a murderer, and Peaches was . . . he was . . .

What was he? What Violet did she did for her own selfish reasons. Peaches acted as an officer of the navy following orders from his superiors, not as a man set on destroying another man's life. He must've believed he was doing the right thing. And when he'd come to believe otherwise, he'd try to fix things.

"What are you thinking about?" asked Jayne.

"Violet." I wasn't ready to tell Jayne about Peaches. Yet. "She's the only suspect who makes sense."

"Rosie—"

"I know what you're going to say: How could she have fired the gun when she was backstage?"

Jayne frowned. "No, that's easy. She could've gotten Spanky to do it for her."

I smacked myself on the forehead. How could I have been so dumb? "Of course. And that explains why Mac was in the cliffs. He followed Spanky there."

"But why would Spanky shoot Mac?" asked Jayne.

"Maybe to throw everyone off his track."

Jayne shook her head. "I don't buy that. He loves that dog."

She had a point there. Plus, the dog had been shot with a revolver.

A rustling sounded outside the latrine. We crouched down so that we couldn't be seen through the window.

"What was that?" asked Jayne.

"I think someone's out there." It was probably Gris and Lefty, moving to a better vantage to spy on us. I slowly raised my head until my eyes passed the windowsill. A figure was moving away from the WAC barracks and heading down the road. It was Candy.

I gestured for Jayne to get a slant, and she confirmed what I saw.

"Who is she seeing?" I asked.

"An officer?" said Jayne.

"That's hardly a call for secrecy."

Jayne shrugged. "Maybe it's a taken officer."

Could Candy have fallen under the spell of Late Nate too?

Lightning flashed, illuminating Candy. The bag slung across her waist was so full it looked like she was pregnant.

"I think we just found the missing supplies."

Jayne gasped. "Really?"

"Every time I've seen her at night, it's been when she's heading home and the bag is empty. What else could it be?"

Jayne strained to get a better slant on her. "Do you think Candy's selling things to the Japanese?"

It was possible. Candy knew their language and seemed to have a soft spot for them.

"There's only one way to find out for sure," I told Jayne. "Any chance you're up for a little surveillance?"

Jayne deposited her scrub brush in the bucket. "Anything's better than doing this."

The rain was falling harder, which worked to our advantage. Wrapped in our rain gear, our footsteps masked by the storm, we were able to catch up with Candy just enough to keep sight of her without alerting her to our presence. We ducked behind tents, in foliage, and wherever else we could easily hide ourselves from view. It wasn't a fast trip. Wherever Candy was headed, it looked like it was on the other side of the island.

We arrived in the village and watched Candy enter a small ramshackle hut. We crouched down low and approached the building. Conversation flitted through the air in a strange sort of pidgin English. The inhabitants were thanking her. She was thanking them. I shifted so that I could see through a window. Candy stood in a circle with a native family examining items set on a table. There were syringes, small glass vials of medications, and assorted foods taken from the mess hall. Her bag hung limp and empty across her body. One of the natives produced his own bag and transferred the supplies inside it.

"Well?" asked Jayne.

"She just gave the missing supplies to some natives, but no money's changed hands."

A woman naked from the waist up placed a number of betel-bead necklaces on the table. Candy scrounged around in her pocket and came up with a few bills. In exchange she took the smaller of the necklaces and wrapped it around her neck.

I felt ashamed of myself. Of course Candy was just helping out a native family in need. Why did I have to think the worst of her? Irene must've told her what Blake was up to. When his thievery stopped, Candy decided to take advantage of the situation by taking what she could for people who really needed it.

We started back to camp. We were making good progress when a noise stopped us in our tracks. We ducked into the bushes and froze, waiting for the source of the sound to pass. Someone was out there with us.

"Where'd they go? I'm sure I saw them go this way," said a gruff male voice.

"They couldn't have gone far."

"And yet here we are, still looking for them. What do they want with that other dame anyway?"

"Bet she's sleeping with someone's boyfriend."

Men: they had us all figured out, didn't they?

The bearers of the voices came into view. It was Gris and Lefty.

"If something happens to her again, he's going to kill us," said Lefty.

"There is no again," said Gris. "He doesn't know about the first time, got it?" He peered into the night. I swear my heart was beating so loud it was scaring the birds nesting above us.

"Think we should split up and see if we can find 'em?"

"Naw," said Gris. "I'm heading back. I got a big order that needs to be on that ship."

They turned and headed in the direction of camp.

"What do we do?" asked Jayne.

"I say we follow them. I want to know who's put a tail on us, and I'm not paying to find out." I tried to move out of the bushes, but my rain gear wouldn't budge. I was snagged on something. "A little help, please," I told Jayne.

She searched for what was holding me. "You're stuck," she said.

"So I figured. Unstick me."

She yanked on the rain gear and something ripped. Despite the sound of destruction, I still couldn't move.

"Help me out of this." I struggled to slip out of the poncho.

"But it's pouring."

"Wet I can handle. Their getting away I can't."

We left my rain gear hanging on a tree. As we tried to catch up with the men, I bubbled with excitement. Whoever put them on our tail had a vested interest in our safety and was paying top dollar for the privilege. And clearly our anonymous benefactor didn't want to be found.

All was not lost. I knew there was one person Gris knew who wasn't keen on being seen by anyone these days: Jack.

CHAPTER 29

Shadowed by Three

"Hey!" I yelled in to the night. "Hold up!"

Lefty froze. Gris's hand sank into his pocket and emerged with a piece. The moonlight reflected off the revolver.

"Easy, tiger," I said. "It's Rosie. And Jayne."

Just as quickly as it had emerged, Gris's gun disappeared back into his pocket. "Close your heads," he said.

"Why?"

"Because I said so, that's why."

"That's not good enough," I said. I backed toward the jungle and shielded myself beneath a palm tree. The others followed suit. "See, I've been thinking since last we met. It seems to me we're a lot more dangerous to you than you are to us. After all, we're not operating an illegal distillery, are we, Jayne?"

"Nope," she said.

"And from what I hear tell, that's something the higher-ups wouldn't be too happy about."

"What do you want?" asked Gris.

"A name," I said. "That's all. And then we'll leave you alone to do whatever it is you do that we've completely forgotten about." They didn't respond, so I decided to plunge forward. "Who hired you to shadow us?"

"It's not an 'us,' it's a 'her.'" He pointed his finger at Jayne.

"Lefty said 'us' before."

"He was being polite. Our contact couldn't care less if you live or die."

"Oh." It wasn't the answer I was hoping for. "So who is it?"

Jayne watched our conversation like it was a game she was hoping to learn the rules to so she could join in later on. As Gris did battle with telling us the truth or calling my bluff, she took a step toward him.

"It's Tony, isn't it?"

Relief showed on his face. He wasn't going to have to betray anyone's confidence.

"I'm not saying it is, and I'm not saying it isn't."

"Of all the rotten. . . . Does he knows everything I've been doing here?" she asked.

He showed her his palms. "No. It ain't like a Peeping Tom thing. We just write a letter now and again to let him know you're safe."

"Can't you do that without following us?" I said.

"Again, it's not an 'us,' it's a 'her.' And after the shooting, we decided to step things up, just in case."

I was dumbfounded by Tony's reach. He was hardly the most powerful mobster in Manhattan, and yet here he was with eyes in the South Pacific. "If you were supposed to be tailing Jayne, why were you watching me when Jayne was in the hospital?" I asked.

Gris threw Lefty a look that should've felled him. "'Cause we didn't know she was in the hospital. Somebody"—he elbowed Lefty—"told me it was one of the other girls who got hit."

"So you were there the night Gilda was shot?" I asked.

Lefty nodded and rubbed at the spot where Gris's elbow had made contact with him.

"Did you see anything unusual?" I asked him.

"Sure did. There was a wolf in the cliffs, and it wouldn't let me pass. Big thing with teeth like knives. Thank God I brought my piece with me." He pulled out a revolver that matched Gris's and pantomimed the scene.

I decided it wouldn't help anyone to tell him he hadn't shot a wolf. He'd shot Mac, Spanky's dog.

By the time we finished cleaning the latrine, the sun was coming up. Or at least it was trying to. It was raining so hard by that point that we couldn't be sure if it really was dawn.

I only got about an hour's sleep before the blasted bugle announced that it was time to rise and shine. I groaned and rolled over. Candy was back in her bed, safe and sound. She grinned at me and stretched her arms above her head.

"Good night?" I asked.

"Great night," she said.

The rain pounded a Sousa march on the tent roof. Surely they didn't expect us to get up when the weather was like this? It was cruel to make us do anything but fall asleep to the steady rhythm of the storm. My eyes began to close again, and my body went limp. I was almost totally out when Violet's voice woke me.

"We're traveling today," she announced.

"In the rain?"

"As long as there's no lightning, we can fly. It's another hospital visit. Most of the men are going to be shipped out at the end of the week."

I groaned again. I didn't want to perform. My head still hurt, and I wanted to wallow in self-pity. Slowly I got dressed and packed up my things for our trip. I was about to put on my rain gear when I remembered it was somewhere in the jungle, snagged on a tree limb. "Nuts," I said.

"What's the matter?" asked Kay.

"I lost my rain gear."

She pointed toward the end of her cot. "I've got Gilda's. Help yourself."

She left to use the latrine while I opened her trunk. It was still as pin neat as it had been the day we arrived. I didn't see the rain gear on top, so I blindly reached toward the bottom. My fingers found vinyl fabric. And something else.

I parted the neat stacks of clothes and peered into the bottom of the trunk. Gilda's beat-up leather handbag was there, the one she'd had with her that first day on the boat. I wrapped the bag in the rain gear and hurriedly brought the bundle back to my own cot. As I stashed the purse, Kay returned.

"Find the gear?" she asked.

"Yeah. Thanks again."

"No problem," she said with a grin. "You're welcome to borrow whatever you need."

We took a bumpy, frightening flight to another island, arriving much later than we had planned. We were rushed to the hospital, where a group of men responded to our performance with drug-induced apathy. It was not one of our better shows.

When the performance was done, we went back to the airstrip only to be told that the lightning had finally arrived, grounding us for at least a few hours.

Our hosts took us to a tent to wait out the storm. While the others amused themselves by playing cards, my mind kept turning to the purse. Why had Kay taken it? If she wanted it so badly, she could've asked for it the day we each selected a memento.

Unless she already had it.

But why the thievery? It was contrary to everything (I thought) I knew about Kay. I shook the thought out of my head. Violet was our culprit. She was the only one who made sense.

Violet asked no one in particular, "Do you think the men were able to leave today?"

"Probably," said Kay. "They're used to lightning on the ships."

Violet sighed heavily. "I am so tired of all this rain. I can't wait until we're out of here and back in Hollywood."

"You're not going to do another tour?" asked Jayne.

"Oh no. I'm done with the USO." She collected the cards and shuffled them.

"So what will you do?" I asked.

The cards smacked against each other just as a rumble of thunder sounded outside. "Go back to MGM, I imagine."

"Are you sure they'll want you?" I said.

Violet's lip curled in a warning. "I imagine they'll want me more than ever, now that Gilda's gone."

"That's cold," said Jayne.

Lightning lit up the room. "Maybe so, but it's true. I miss her as much as the rest of you, but she's going to leave a void someone's going to have to fill."

That someone should've been Irene.

"And what about Spanky?" asked Jayne.

Violet cut the deck. "Oh, well, that was lovely while it lasted, but we couldn't be more different if we tried. I just don't think we have a future together."

"It might've been nice if you'd told him that," I said.

She rolled her eyes at me. "He'll meet another girl and forget about me, I guarantee it."

But he wouldn't—because he was in love with Violet. So in love with her that he did the unthinkable at her urging.

"You told him to do it, didn't you?" I said.

"What are you talking about?" asked Violet.

"Gilda. You told Spanky to kill her."

"Are you nuts? Spanky wouldn't hurt a fly." Violet wasn't that good an actress. I could see the lie in her eyes.

"How'd you convince him? Did you tell him Gilda was saying nasty things behind everyone's back? Or did it just take some island-brewed booze to sway his opinion? After all, with the way he drank, he probably wouldn't have remembered what he'd done."

Violet pounded the table with her hand. "If he did anything, I'm not the one who convinced him to do it."

"Then who is?"

"I am," said Kay.

A clap of thunder shook the tent. Jayne and I stared at Kay, our faces frozen in horror. Had she really just said that?

"Be quiet, Kay," hissed Violet.

"No. I'm tired of keeping quiet. They deserve to know what happened to her."

"We made a promise."

"That promise ended the day Gilda died."

Violet pushed against the table with such force that it momentarily stood on two feet. The cards slid to the floor. Kay bent down to retrieve them, but Jayne stopped her with her hand.

"No," said Jayne. "Let me."

Kay put her hands on the table to steady it. "Spanky wasn't supposed to kill her. We just wanted to hurt her, just for a little while. But he was drunk and confused and his aim was off. . . ." Her voice faded away. "She would've been fine if it weren't for the malaria."

"You don't know that," said Violet.

"But why?" I asked. "What on earth could make you want to hurt Gilda?"

Kay took a deep breath, and I noticed for the first time the dark circles marring the skin beneath her eyes. "Because she killed Irene."

Gilda was the one who'd asked Irene to meet her in San Francisco that day. Irene thought she was going to meet her idol. She never could've imagined that Gilda's plan was to get rid of the up-and-comer who was supposed to replace her so that by the time she returned from her heroic USO tour, reinvented as the vivacious, brave ingénue, MGM would have no choice but to hire her back.

Kay realized what had happened the day we arrived at Tulagi when we were unpacking our things. It was the purse that was the giveaway—Irene's purse—a bag she hadn't recognized that first day on the boat. "If I'd known she was dead then, maybe I would've seen it for what it was. At the time I just remember thinking that the bag didn't match Gilda's shoes." After learning of Irene's death, she realized the significance of that beat-up leather handbag and decided she needed to see it again. One afternoon, while the rest of us were gone, she opened Gilda's trunk and started looking for it. Just as her hands landed on the bag, Violet walked in and caught her.

"She thought I was stealing," said Kay. "I was afraid that if Violet told Gilda what I was up to, Gilda might—" She swallowed hard, unable to complete the sentence. "So I told Violet what I knew about the purse, and together we went through it. It was Irene's all right. There was no doubt about it. Her identification was there. Her photograph."

Was it really possible that Gilda was a murderer? We knew she was a liar. And while I didn't want to believe her capable of something like this, I'd seen enough bad behavior over the past year to know that people are rarely what they seem. I'd fallen for a murderer. Jayne had dated one. We had lived side by side with someone who killed for what they thought were all the right reasons. And now we were on an island full of people trained to kill based on a military edict. It didn't take much for someone to do something so terrible, especially when they convinced themselves that they had no other choice. Not that that excused her. Murder during wartime seemed particularly unforgivable. We were losing enough men to the enemy—did we have to slaughter our own kind too?

"Is that why it took you so long to admit you knew Irene?" I asked. "Because you were scared?"

Kay nodded. "On the boat, it was shock that kept me silent. But once I realized what Gilda had done, I didn't want her to think that I could identify her as the killer."

A chill passed through my body. Kay was right. If Gilda was willing to kill for her career once, it wasn't farfetched to assume that she might do it a second time.

"So whose idea was it to shoot her?" Neither responded, but a look passed between them that made it clear: Violet was the one out for justice. Kay was too meek to ever propose anything beyond keeping quiet. I'd been right about one thing: Violet knew that with both Irene and Gilda out of the picture, she might have a shot at real stardom. "And so the two of you convinced Spanky that it was only fitting that Gilda be punished for what she did—only he screwed up."

Kay began to cry. "We wanted to scare her. That's all. We certainly didn't intend to hurt Jayne too.'

"And when that didn't work out, instead of owning up to what you did you blamed it on a Japanese sniper." I shook my head. "Unbelievable. You were going to let that boy take the fall for this. You were going to let him die just to keep your stupid little scheme covered up. Why didn't you go to Late Nate?"

"Are you kidding?" Violet stood up. "She was sleeping with him. Do you honestly think he would've taken our word over hers?"

No, but at least they should've tried.

"Well, we're going to have to tell him now," I said.

Violet leaned toward me. Through the neck of her blouse I could see a cluster of moles and age spots brought out by the island sun. "If you do that, Spanky's the only one who's going to be punished. He fired the gun. There's no evidence that Kay and I had anything to do with it. And you know Blake's not going to believe a word you two say."

She was right. Somehow, with all their screw ups, they'd managed to stumble into committing the perfect crime.

We finished out the hour in stony silence, relieved when we could finally board the plane and lose our thoughts in the roar of the engines. We landed and went off in pairs in opposite directions.

Jayne and I escaped to the rec hall, where the game tables stood vacant. With *The McCawley* gone, the camp was fast becoming a ghost town.

"I can't believe Kay would be involved in something like that." Jayne followed the curve of a Ping-Pong paddle with her finger.

"Can you really blame her?" I asked. "Her best friend had been murdered. Anyone would want vengeance for that. If you were the one Gilda killed, I might've done the exact same thing."

Jayne picked up a Ping-Pong ball and traced its seam. Neither of us was in the mood for any more game playing. "It doesn't seem right that they'll get away with it though."

"The only one who's getting away with anything is Gilda. She left this earth a saint. Kay and Violet have to live with what they did. I can't imagine that's going to be easy for either of them."

CHAPTER 30

Jack's Little Surprise

"Rosie?" Dotty ducked into the recreation hut just as we were heading out. Rivulets of sweat ran down the sides of his face, and his shirt was darkened with more perspiration.

"What's the matter?" I asked.

"I tried to find you before, but they said your flight back was delayed. They found Jack."

My breath caught in my throat.

"He's alive," said Dotty. "But they arrested him."

"Wait a minute—slow down. Who arrested him? Where did they find him?"

"After you left this morning they sent a bunch of men into the caves on a tip. Apparently he's been hiding out there for months."

"But how—" The question died in the air. Only one person besides Jayne, Gris, Lefty, and me knew that Jack might be in the caves. And Gris certainly wasn't going around telling anyone Jack was alive after he'd lied about seeing him go into the water. "How is he?"

"Good, from what I heard. Some of the natives have been sneaking him food and drugs for a while now. I heard the cave was outfitted with just about everything he needed. Even books and booze."

"Can I see him?" I said.

"I doubt it. He's being interrogated. His leg is bad enough that they have him up at the infirmary. Word is they've got the place locked down tight."

As Dotty left, Jayne took my hand in hers. My head was abuzz with all that had just happened. Jack was alive. He was safe.

"I have to see him," I whispered.

"I know. You will. We'll figure something out."

I didn't eat anything at dinner. Instead, I moved my food around the plate to keep away any questions about my diminished appetite. Violet was noticeably absent from the meal. According to the grapevine, she was also in the infirmary, complaining of a sharp pain in her side. They thought it was appendicitis, though I suspected it was more likely desperation. Violet wanted off this island and back to Hollywood, even if it meant she had to be cut to make that happen.

"She must be awfully lonely," said Jayne.

"Good," I said. "She deserves to suffer."

"That's not very nice. We should go see her. Cheer her up."

"Yeah, I'll get to that just as soon as hell freezes over."

Jayne kicked me in my shin. Hard.

"On second thought," I said between clenched teeth, "it would be the Christian thing to do, wouldn't it?"

Kay sat with us in silence. As soon as dinner ended, she attempted to dash out of the high commissioner's house. Before she'd reached the footpath, I called out to her.

"I need a favor," I told her.

"Of course," she said. "Anything."

"I want you to come clean."

Her face dropped.

"Don't worry: this isn't about Gilda." I told her my plan. She wasn't thrilled about what I was asking her do, but I knew she wouldn't refuse me. I probably could've gotten a kidney from her if I wanted it.

As the moon flashed its lopsided grin, Jayne, Kay, and I made our way to the infirmary with our arms filled with the white and yellow flowers of the frangipani tree. There were guards posted outside the hut, but they had no problem letting us in. They didn't care who entered the building; it was who was exiting it that they were concerned with.

Kay lingered near the door while Jayne and I approached Ruth. She was at her desk near the main ward. The copy of *War and Peace* was open in front of her, though to my eyes it didn't look as if she'd made it any further in the book.

"Hiya," I said.

"Miss Winter! I'm so glad to see you. I was quite concerned when you took off in the middle of the night."

"I know. I'm sorry about that. I was getting cabin fever." I tapped my fingers on her desktop. "Do you think we could see Violet? I understand she came in earlier. We thought we'd bring her some flowers to cheer her up."

"Of course," said Ruth. Before she could stand to direct us to where Violet was convalescing, Kay rounded the corner.

"Hello, Ruth."

Ruth's hand went to her mouth just as a smile spread across her face. "Kay. I was wondering if you were ever going to come by."

"I know and I'm sorry. There's something I need to tell you. Do you think we could talk privately?"

Ruth directed her to a room off to the side. I gestured to her that we were heading into the ward, and she waved us on.

Jayne continued toward the cordoned-off bed that Violet was lying in. I took an abrupt turn and began searching for Jack. It didn't take long to find him.

He was in the room Gilda had been laid out in. I heard him before I saw him. Even tired and sick, he still possessed that resonant actor's voice that could carry a whisper across a sea of people. I lingered outside his open door and eavesdropped as I tried to muster my courage. What would I say when I first saw him? I love you? Or would I just fall into his arms and hold on for dear life?

"They think I might lose it," he said to someone.

"They're just saying that to punish you. Don't let them do anything until you're back in the States." His companion was female and familiar.

"How'd you get in here anyway?"

I moved closer to try to catch sight of who was in the room with him. I could see a head full of curly dirty-blond hair.

"I told them I was your fiancée."

I could hear the smile in his voice. "Clever girl."

"Don't worry about the leg. I haven't let anything happen to you so far, have I?"

Jack came into view. Handsome, self-assured Jack. Thin, yes, pale, yes, but still capable of making my heart stop on sight.

He grinned. It was a tired grin but one that I knew too well. "No, you've been a peach. I don't know why you would risk everything for me like that."

She turned in profile. There was no mistaking her identity. "It's because I love you. Surely you've figured that out by now."

"I love you too, Candy," he whispered.

I didn't stick around to watch him kiss her. Instead I ran out of the infirmary and kept running until I was somewhere in the jungle. Peaches had betrayed me. Jack had betrayed me. Was there anyone out there I could trust?

I hoped I was lost, that I would never leave those dark woods again, that my body would rot away like the corpses of the enemy, but eventually I found my way out and saw the camp in the distance. How had this happened? What was I talking about—it wasn't hard to put together. Candy, not me, had rescued him. Candy, not me, had nursed him back to health and kept him alive by bringing him supplies and arranging for the natives to do the same. And in the process they had fallen in love and I was completely forgotten.

But then I was forgotten before then, wasn't I? I'd never meant as much to him as he'd meant to me.

I walked around the camp in a daze, vaguely aware of the loudspeaker humming with activity. I didn't bother to try to make sense of the words. Unless they were announcing Candy's untimely demise, I didn't care. Let the Japs bomb us. Nothing mattered anymore.

I couldn't go back to the WAC camp. Candy would be there soon, her heart-shaped face illuminated with the sweet memory of her time with Jack. Instead, I made my way out to the beach. I should be grateful he was alive, shouldn't I? Wasn't that enough? If you truly loved someone, shouldn't their happiness and safety be more important than your own? And if that wasn't the case for me, maybe I'd never really loved him. Maybe I was too selfish for it. That was why he had left me to begin with, because I was too goddamn selfish to understand why the war mattered to him. Candy knew. I was a silly little actress and she was a soldier. She was everything he wanted, everything I was incapable of being.

I screamed at the night sky as though the moon were somehow responsible for my plight. I wanted to hurt someone, but there was no one there to take my blows. Instead, I struck myself over and over until my thighs were covered with bruises.

I awoke with sand in my mouth and a dull ache in the lower half of my body.

I went in search of Jayne and Kay, expecting to find them at the high commissioner's house, but they weren't there. In fact, no one was. I looked at my watch to see if I'd misread the time. It was still early enough that someone should've been up there eating breakfast. Mystified, I walked around looking for a familiar face to query about the strange lack of activity. At last I spotted Dotty walking hurriedly across the road.

"Hey, Dotty!" I called. "Where is everyone?"

He stopped in his tracks and turned my way. "You didn't hear?" I shook my head. "Things got ugly off New Georgia last night. Two navy planes were shot down and *The McCawley* was hit. They're reporting high casualties. Needless to say, there's a call for immediate retaliation."

"Is that why it's so quiet around here?"

"Yep. I think everyone's frozen solid waiting for word about the recovery." He looked to his left and right before continuing. "I'm hearing that most of the men in Spanky's crew were lost."

"Including Spanky?"

He nodded. So that was how this would all end for Spanky. Just like Gilda, he was going to die a hero.

I thanked Dotty for the news and went on my way. I arrived at our barracks to find everyone still sitting on their cots, trying to make sense of the news. The room was silent except for occasional sobs. Either they knew what had happened and who had been involved, or they were guessing that the outcome wouldn't be good. I looked for Candy but didn't see her. Violet was there though, one arm wrapped around Mac, the other one clutching a handkerchief. Perhaps she did possess some remorse. It couldn't have been comforting to know that the last words you spoke to a man before he went off to his death were a lie.

"Where have you been?" asked Kay.

"It's a long story. Where's Jayne?"

Kay jerked her head toward the right. "She was headed toward the latrine last I saw her."

"Gotcha." I started heading out the door.

"Rosie." Kay's voice stopped me in my tracks. "She's pretty upset."

"Don't worry—I'll take care of it."

I thought the latrine was empty, but I eventually located Jayne's feet beneath one of the stalls. "Jayne? It's me. Sorry I disappeared last night. I just couldn't take coming back here."

She didn't respond. Rather than giving her a chance to lambaste me for my inconsiderateness, I decided to plow ahead. After all: once she heard why I chose to spend the night elsewhere, she was going to feel like one dumb bunny for being mad at me.

"You're not going to believe what happened. I saw Jack all right, only he wasn't alone: his girlfriend was there."

Jayne let out a sound like a hiccup. Was she drunk?

"In case you're confused," I said. "His girlfriend is Candy Abbott. It turns out all those late-night excursions of hers weren't to help out the natives. They were acting as her go between and bringing Jack supplies. I suppose I should be grateful to her—at least someone was helping him. But as awful as it sounds, I felt more heartbroken at the idea that he was in love with someone else than I had when I thought he was dead."

Still she said nothing. Kilroy stared down his long nose at me.

"Come on out of there. Please. I could really use a shoulder right now."

The latrine door swung open. Jayne's face was red and puffy. Wads of toilet paper, stained with mascara and eye shadow, were twisted around her fingers.

"Why are you crying?" I asked.

"It's Billy," she whispered. "His plane was shot down." She paused an agonizing interval as though she needed extra air in her lungs to get through the next sentence. "He's dead."

I went to her and took her in my arms. She collapsed against me and began to shudder with emotion. She was so small. Had she always been so tiny? Or had being here reduced her mass until even her bones seemed to have grown hollow?

"Oh, Jayne. I had no idea. When did you find out?"

She tried to talk, but the words couldn't free themselves. She sighed heavily once, twice, until the sound became a whisper. "A few hours ago."

While I was out on the beach cursing Jack and Candy for being alive and in love, she was in this dingy latrine mourning the loss of the man she thought she was going to share the rest of her life with. But that's always how it was, wasn't it? Everything was about me. Even when she got shot. This whole damn trip had been me, me, me.

I ran my hand through her hair. "I'm so sorry. I should've been here."

She shook her head against my chest. "You're here now. That's all that matters."

———

Spanky and twenty-eight other men were killed when the Japanese torpedoed *The McCawley*. Billy was shot down on his first solo mission when he attempted to take out the Japanese from the air. Peaches was luckier. He made it out safe with two more kills to his credit. I didn't bother to congratulate him. Maybe someday I'll be willing to hear his side of the story about how Jack was found, but I'm not ready yet.

The day after the news hit Tulagi, Yoshihiro disappeared from the POW comp in the middle of the night. Word is he made a clean sneak, though nobody's been able to confirm how that happened.

Kay decided to retire from performing. She's ready to go home and live a normal life, with Dotty by her side.

Violet's mysterious side pain earned her—and Mac—a trip home. If her career has taken off since her return, the trades haven't picked up on it yet.

Jack's leg injury was extensive enough that they decided to send him back to the States to wait out his court-martial hearing. Candy received an emergency discharge to go with him. I didn't see either of them before they left.

As for Jayne and me, we've written to Harriet to see if she can help us get out of here sooner rather than later (sweetening our request with a promise to relay information about a certain supply stealing CO). Jayne wants to go home. She wants to meet Billy's family and be there for his funeral. When she asked me to go with her, I didn't pause before answering. It only seemed fair that if she was willing to accompany me on my journey, I would do the same for her.

ENJOY ALL OF THE
ROSIE WINTER MYSTERIES!

978-0-06-113978-9

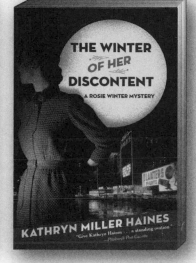

978-0-06-113980-2

978-0-06-157956-1

"[Haines'] real success is her pitch-perfect rendering of the early '40s." *Kirkus Reviews*

"Haines brings home the painful price the 'greatest generation' paid more gallantly than anyone then knew."

—*Publishers Weekly*